stay *for* me

Stay for Me

ISBN—paperback: 978-1-942834-52-6

Cover Design:
Sommer Stein, Perfect Pear Creative

Editing:
Ashley Williams, AW Editing

Proofreading:
Michele Ficht & Julia Griffis

Formatting:
Alyssa Garcia, Uplifting Author Services

Cover photo © Wong Sim

The Arrowood Brothers Series

To my Aunt Donna, thank you for always being the safe place I could turn to. You've held my secrets, my hopes, and always encouraged me. I can only hope every little girl grows up with having a friendship like ours.

stay for me

NEW YORK TIMES BESTSELLING AUTHOR

CORINNE MICHAELS

one

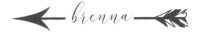

Beep. Beep. Beep.

Ugh.

It can't be six thirty already. I swear, I just fell asleep.

I roll over, check the clock, and sure enough, it's time to get my ass up. My hand slides across the sheets to feel the cold, and I want to cry. Over the last eight months, I've felt like I'm living the same day on repeat. I look for him, ache for him, try to feel the warmth that was once there, but it's gone.

Just like he is.

"Mom!" Melanie's voice screeches at the end. "Get up!"

I sit up in the bed, drape my legs over the side, and close my eyes.

I can do this. I've been doing it this long, and I'm doing the best I can. The kids need better, and I have to be that for them even if the pain is still so intense I want to give up.

Ten days ago, we moved into this new house, which is a simple house in the middle of nowhere, but it's close to my husband's—my now-gone husband's—family and the place he's buried.

I'm struggling to breathe, to find something to hold on to that will let me know that life will be okay again. It will be. I know this, but I'm alone, and it hurts. I don't have Luke or his steady faith to remind me that I'm a warrior and I always find a way. I'm the one having to push myself up and remind myself that this isn't just a deployment. It's forever. He's gone. He's buried in the ground, and I'll never hear his voice again.

When I closed on this place, it should have been a time of joy. Instead, I sat in that cold chair, signing the mortgage papers with just my name. There were no smiles or jokes as we notched another address on our list. It was tears that filled the space as my pen swiped along the final black line.

My head tilts back to the ceiling and the hurt in my heart grows.

"*Mom*! Sebastian won't get out of the bathroom! I have to do my hair!"

I release a deep breath. "I'm coming."

Clenching my teeth so hard they may shatter, I get to my feet, pull a robe on, and shuffle out the door.

Melanie gets one look at me, and her eyes bulge. "Oh my God!"

"I look that good?" I joke. Sure, I haven't slept in a week and was up crying half the night, but I don't think I look *that* bad.

"No, it's . . . your eyes are swollen. If Miss Cybil were here, she'd be screaming."

"It's been a rough few months."

Plus, Cybil wouldn't say shit. When I met her, we were two lonely military wives, stuck in Pensacola without any family or friends, and I was pregnant. Cybil was a sweet Southern girl with a thick accent and a heart of gold. We've been best friends for twelve years.

She's a peach. On the outside, she's soft, sweet, and you think she's easy to bruise. But on the inside, there is a pit. A hard shell that's impenetrable and able to withstand almost anything. She's my rock, and I miss her more than almost anything.

Mel sighs and then looks at the bathroom door. "I know."

And she does. It's been rough on all of us and we wrestled with the idea of coming to Luke's hometown. Not because we don't love it here or want the family close but because it meant another life altering change.

We were a military family. Always close to a base, stopping the car at sunrise and sunset to hear the national anthem, and living in cramped houses that had more issues than we could count, but it was our life.

After having held Sebastian in my arms as he sobbed hearing the jet fly over the house, I knew we had to go. It had gone from being a source of joy, of knowing his father could be in that plane, to an ever-present reminder that Luke is gone and will never fly again.

I left, stayed with my in-laws as we looked for somewhere to live. This house came on the market, and thanks to one of the teachers I met at my new job, I was able to grab it quickly. The only issue is that it's small and the kids don't have their own separate bathrooms.

"He has to get out of there!"

"You will be totally fine, Melanie. I promise that no one will care if your hair isn't perfect."

"You don't know that. What if these girls are mean? What if the boys don't like girls who don't wear makeup? Why can't I get ready in your bathroom? Why won't you let me put eyeliner on?"

The life of a preteen girl is always so dramatic.

"Well, I need to get ready in my bathroom. To answer your other questions . . . you're twelve, your father said he didn't want you to do it, and I'm going to abide by it because he's dead and I'm tired."

Her eyes meet mine, and then she sighs. "I'm sorry, Mom. I shouldn't have said it . . ."

My sweet girl, always the caretaker. She may only be twelve years old, but you'd never know it. She's sometimes more grown up than most of the adults I know, but that's the life of a military child. They grow up too fast, understanding that a family is its own unit and everyone needs to do just a bit more.

Then she lost her father, and her childhood became non-existent. Gone was the girl who spent hours on fashion and beauty. Instead, she has been trying to be an adult and I'm do-ing everything I can to stop that progression.

"Don't be sorry, sweetheart. I am. I shouldn't have snapped. I was wrong."

She waits for me to breathe normally and chews on her lower lip. "I'll get Sebastian and me off to school."

"No, that's not necessary. I just need to get going. It's a first day for all of us."

Luke's favorite saying was that everything happened for a reason. He felt that kismet was real, and that it was the reason we met. I don't know if it's true, but I never argued. I was eigh-teen years old, met a man who was a pilot, and I fell—hard. Within a few months, I was pregnant with Melanie and we were married.

No one thought we'd last—in a way, I guess we hadn't, but it wasn't the ending anyone had in mind.

"Did Grandma make our lunches?"

I really freaking hope so. I was unpacking while she helped

get things ready for today. "She said she did last night."

"Did she make Sebastian's sandwich without the crust?"

"I gave her all the instructions."

She sighs, knowing that, most likely, it didn't happen. "She's as bad as Daddy. He doesn't make the sandwiches right either."

Her body tenses at her slip. She never mentions Luke. She pretends that he's just deployed and that we didn't suffer the most unimaginable pain a family could feel. Melanie has taken it horribly. Luke was her world.

Her hero.

The father that every little girl dreamed of. He may not have always been there because of his job, but neither she nor Sebastian ever felt neglected. His job came first, yes, but kids never felt that. It was only me who got shafted in the time department when it came to Luke's job, and I accepted my role. I was to handle everything at home—the kids, appointments, moves, and shuttling them around. I ensured that our home was a well-oiled machine, and if something broke, I got it fixed.

However, no one told me to plan for me being the broken piece or what happened when the plane went down.

"Everyone is trying," I tell her with a smile, thankful that my mother-in-law has been able to step in and help.

"I'll check on the sandwich while Sebastian is *hogging the bathroom*!" Mel screams the last part so loud I wince. Then she heads downstairs, missing the soft sound of her brother laughing at her.

"Sebastian, you have five minutes, buddy. All you need to do in there is brush your hair and your teeth. Doesn't take more than that."

"Okay, Mom!"

He's eleven and this is really just to irritate his sister. I love my kids, but I really hoped to have today go smoothly.

It's their first day of school in Sugarloaf. They've met a few kids over the years when we visited Sylvia and Dennis, but it's all uncharted for them here. Typically, a new school is no big deal, but this time felt different because we had left military life behind. There was camaraderie between military kids. They understood how hard it was to be the new kid, year in and year out, and tended to be more welcoming.

Now, they're going to a place where these kids have known each other their whole lives.

Not even thirty seconds later, he's standing at my door. "Do I match?"

I look at him, dark brown hair just like his father's and that grin that is impossible to resist. Then I look at his attire and groan. "I thought you and Grandma laid your clothes out last night?"

"We did."

Oh, Jesus. "And that's what you want to wear for your first day?"

"Granny said it had character."

I snort. It has more than that. "Sebastian, sweetheart, that doesn't match. Go put on the pair of new jeans I bought you."

"What about the shirt?"

This is not the hill I want to die on, so I say, "If you like it, I think it's great."

My mother-in-law has a thing for loud colors and animal print. If it has stripes or spots, she owns it and wears it. I am nothing like that, but she and Sebastian bonded over it years ago, prompting her to help him, "Dress to own the world." If he likes the shirt, I am not going to stop him.

A boy named Bruce or Troy or God-only-knows-what with fists the size of watermelons will probably have something to say about it, but Sebastian has long since tried to make people like him. He's a sweet boy who loves to make us smile and constantly entertains us with jokes or music. He writes songs, plays the guitar, and has straight A's. I couldn't be any prouder of him if I tried.

"I wish Dad were here."

"Me too."

"He would've liked the shirt."

I fight back the tears that threaten to form. "He would've bought a matching one."

One thing that Luke didn't have was fashion sense, but he loved trying to give Sebastian the confidence to wear what he wanted. If he—a big bad navy fighter pilot—would wear a zebra shirt, then Sebastian would too.

"Do you think he's in heaven watching me today?"

"I would bet all my dollars."

Sebastian's face falls slightly. "I miss him."

I give him a soft smile, one that is a signature. It says, *I understand, I wish it were different, but I can't fix this.* "I know you do, but it's a good thing that we're in this town with Granny and Pawpaw, right?"

He nods, but I can see the disappointment. "Yeah."

"It's not the same, though," I tack on. There's nothing that will make this better for any of us, and trying to give him false hope is only going to make it worse.

We are alone.

We're no longer the Allens, a family of four. We're just three of us, down a spoke on the wheel that will never be mended.

I lost the man I love and the father of my children because of a mechanical failure. So many apologies. So many nights spent crying, wondering how our life would be if he hadn't reenlisted three months before that.

If only he hadn't let me down.

If only he'd loved me enough not to go to work that day like he promised.

If only . . .

But *only* is a dream that I can never have because reality took him from us, and now, we only have each other.

"No, but I have you."

"Always."

Sebastian rushes forward, arms wide, and I pull him tight. His hugs are the best. They're full of warmth and love.

He lifts up onto his toes, kisses my cheek, and hugs me tighter. "I love you, Mom."

"I love you too."

Melanie comes back up. "Crisis averted."

I laugh. "Thank you, Mel."

She shoulders past Sebastian and darts into the bathroom. "Jerk."

My son rolls his eyes. "Sisters."

As they get themselves ready, I head to my bathroom, dressing in a pantsuit that I hope says hip but still professional. Working as the district counselor will be a huge change of pace from what I'm used to. In California, I was in a rough area. The kids I dealt with needed help in all areas of their lives, from escaping drugs, gangs, and abuse to passing SATs and applying to colleges. My days were never boring, and I loved helping everyone who entered my office.

Mrs. Symonds, the principal here, laughed and told me to prepare for days where I'd be searching for problems to solve.

I'm still excited and ready for any challenge that comes my way.

The kids meet me downstairs, backpacks slung over their shoulders, and I can feel the tension in the air. "You guys ready?"

They nod. Our house has very deep-seated traditions for the first day of school, and I'd like just one damn thing to be the same for them. They file into the room, pushing the other out of the way as they try to win the implied race.

"Move, squirt." Mel's voice is hushed.

"You move! You're stupid."

Oh, siblings. "Both of you stop."

"She hears everything," Sebastian says with wonder.

"Yes, I do. Now, stop being buttheads and let's have our cake."

They come into the kitchen area and grab a plate. This was something Luke and I came up with after our first duty station change. On that first day, we have cake for breakfast. It's a celebration of the wishes we want to make. Even though this isn't a first-first day of school, it's a first for us in Pennsylvania, and we're going to count it. Plus, cake has eggs, and eggs are a breakfast food. Sure, the sugar, oil, and frosting negate anything healthy, but I don't care.

Each slice has a candle, and in order for the wish to be put out in the world, it must be spoken aloud.

"Melanie, you go first."

She lifts the cake, staring at the flame. "I hope this year I get all A's and I finally get a boyfriend."

Sebastian laughs. "Yeah, right. No boys are going to want to go out with you. You don't even wear makeup."

"Sebastian!"

He shrugs.

Oh, I don't have enough strength for this.

She glares at him and then blows her candle out.

"You're next, Mom."

I hope this year I don't fall apart.

They don't need to hear that. Instead, I bring the cake up and wish for something that might actually happen. "I hope this year gives us new friendships, lots of laughter, and we love our new home."

"That's sweet, Mom," Mel remarks softly.

Sebastian's voice is opposite of hers. "And boring."

"Yeah, yeah, you go, Mister Adventure."

He grins and then closes his eyes. "I hope that I can stop missing Dad so much, I meet some cool kids, and I get to see Jacob Arrowood, tell him how amazing he is, get to go on set, and become a famous actor."

Melanie and I share a look because Sebastian might just get a part of that wish.

two

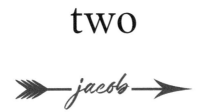

One month later

"**I** am not staying in that thing!" I tell Declan for the tenth time as I stand at his porch with boxes.

"You're not staying here, Jacob. I'm married with a newborn. I love you, brother, but you really don't want to stay here either."

If he thinks that is going to deter me, he's wrong. "Better than staying in that shack."

"It's not a shack. I stayed in it for six months, and Sean managed it as well. Your spoiled ass can handle it too."

He's out of his damn mind. He stayed there voluntarily because he didn't want to stay with Connor. Sean did it because he was trying to win over Devney. I don't have a damn reason to. "I'd rather not attempt it."

"Go to Connor's then."

"He's got two kids. You only have one. When it comes to

chaos, that's better."

Declan huffs. "I swear, we should've tossed you off the mountain as a kid."

"Yeah, but you didn't. Now, let me in."

He shakes his head, arms crossed over his chest. To anyone who didn't know him, he might look intimidating. Not me. I find it hilarious.

I start to make my way up the porch steps but then see the only thing in this house that is scary shove her way past him. All five-foot-two inches of Sydney Arrowood stands there, brow raised and ready for battle. "Jacob Arrowood, you try it, and I'll knee you so hard in the balls that they never come back down."

I wince because I don't doubt that she'll do it. "Syd."

"No."

"I can't stay in that box. I'm claustrophobic."

"You are not! You used to lock yourself in that chest your mother had as a hiding spot and you loved the dried out well down on Mrs. Beackerson's land. Not to mention, you know you have to stay on Arrowood land. That's the agreement."

"Yes, but you merged your land with ours, so really, this *is* Arrowood land." It's a stretch, but I don't care. The damn thing doesn't even have running water. It's a compost toilet. Seriously, I didn't know that was a thing.

She sighs and steps toward me. "I love you, Jacob. I do, but I don't love you that much. You are not moving in for six months. Not when I have a baby and Declan."

"He's worse than the baby, isn't he?"

Syd nods with a grin.

"Nice," Declan adds.

"Glad to see your hearing works, old man."

Declan gives me the middle finger before Syd's hand

touches my arm. "Ellie has the tender heart. You should try her. Devney would let you stay in the main house if you begged enough. But seeing how they're getting married in a few days and will probably be humping like rabbits when they get back from their honeymoon, I'm not sure you could beg enough. Plus, they have Austin, who needs stability, not their homeless uncle . . ."

"Syd, I'm begging. I'm begging you to let me in this house, you won't even know I'm here." I'm the damn charity case in the family.

She rolls her eyes. "No."

"You know I'm a big fucking deal in the real world, right?"

"Yes, but you're in Sugarloaf now, and we really don't care how big of a deal you've become. Here, you're just Jacob, the idiot brother who once starred on that horrible sitcom that I made a meme out of."

"Wait, *you* made the meme?"

She grins. "It doesn't matter who made the meme, the point is that you're not staying here."

I should've known it was her repaying me for putting a rubber snake in her bed or when I convinced her a bear ate Declan. That was a fun one.

It was also when I realized that acting might just be something I was good at.

Right now, all I want is a normal house to sleep in. So, I play nice. "You're seriously going to turn me, your favorite brother-in-law, out?"

Not like I'm really homeless, I just don't want to stay in that tiny house.

Sydney doesn't look apologetic. "I really am, but for the record, you're not my favorite, Sean is."

My mouth drops at that. "Sean? Why the hell is he everyone's favorite?"

"He's the nice one."

Okay, that's true, but who cares about that? Nice is over-rated. "I'm the attractive one," I counter.

"True." Sydney looks back at her husband and shrugs. "But it doesn't change the fact that your ass isn't staying here."

Declan shakes his head. "Wait. You think he's the attractive one? What the hell does that make me?"

Sydney's fingers slide against his face. "The perfect one."

Well, this is a bust and making me nauseated. "It's not a great idea to start a marriage off on lies," I shout as I stalk off to the car.

"And this is another reason you're not staying here," Syd yells back.

"Some welcome home I get!" I say.

"Welcome home, idiot!" Declan calls back.

If I didn't have a box in my arms, he'd get a fist to the face.

I'm clearly going to have to stay in that damn thing or with Connor. The tiny house is a more appealing option. I love my brother, and he's great and all, but we've always been the ones who bicker. It doesn't matter how old we get, when we are around each other, my inner ten-year-old comes out. God only knows what the hell living together would be like.

Also, I love my nieces, but I'm not ready to have that twenty-four seven. Hadley is a handful—a loving, beautiful, adorable handful who never stops talking. I need to study my lines and prepare for my movie that begins shooting as soon as I get back.

"Come for dinner tomorrow, Jacob," Syd says as she wraps her arms around the jackass she married.

"Oh, I will. If I have to sleep in that damn thing, you're all feeding me!"

She laughs while Declan shakes his head. They might think

I'm kidding, but I'm not. I've lived in Hollywood for the last nine years without having to cook. I am a pro at takeout and delivery, but this is Sugarloaf, and there's none of that here.

I'm not sure how I'm going to survive without help. Hopefully, Mrs. Maxwell is still on the welcoming committee and will bring over a casserole or some shit. I make a mental note to stop by and visit with as many neighbors as I can.

Mom was always part of that crew. If someone came by, she fed them. If that's still part of the town's MO, I'm all for it.

I get the box back into the car and stand with the door open, leaning against the frame. "I really expected more from you, Syd. You could've offered the barn at least!"

"Where would I sneak off to have hot, crazy sex with your brother if I did that?"

I gag. "God that mental picture is now burned in my brain."

"You're welcome!"

I get in the car before anyone can say anything else. Now, I'll have nightmares of them as well as what Sean and Devney will be like after they return from their honeymoon. I take the scenic route as I make the drive back to the Arrowood farm.

The corner store where I had my first job is still there. So is the gas station with the old pumps that they won't change out because the new ones are complicated. Then there are the new things like the bakery that Mrs. Symonds's daughter owns, a pizza place, and a dairy barn.

It's the same in so many ways, but it feels different. It was like the first night after my mother died. Everything was there, just as it always had been, and yet, it was as though the house were empty. The most important thing was gone, and that void has remained.

After a few winding turns, I get to the entrance.

It doesn't matter that in the last eighteen months I've been here several times. I still feel the same knot in my stomach as

I get to the gate.

I stare up at the sign that has been there for fifty years and sigh.

"What's one truth about an arrow?" I ask as I look up, wishing it were my mother's voice asking. "Removing half the feather will create the curve and alter its course."

She always made it seem like we needed to stick together, but in the last few months, I've realized that isn't it. How does removing the feathers or creating a curve bond us together? It doesn't. She clearly thought I needed to change directions—I think. Is it because I'm the one who always bends? Is it because I need to remove something in my life? Or that I never follow the right path? She never explained it, she would just smile and tell me that one day I'd understand.

Well, I'd like that day to hurry up and get here because it's pretty lame not to understand what the hell my meaning even means. My brothers had lightning strikes with theirs, and I'm over here, still trying to figure out a riddle that no one has the answer to.

"A little help here, Mom," I say. "I don't think I'm asking for too much after all these years. The other three idiots got easy ones, but you gave me the one that requires an answer key." I feel like an idiot looking up at the sign as though she's going to answer. Still, there's an overwhelming sense of her around me. "What would you think of all of us now? Would you at least be happy with three out of four of us being married? Well, Sean isn't yet, but he will be in, like, four days."

The sun peeks out of the clouds, and I smile. I thought she would be happy.

I get up to the house, and there's a car there.

I park next to it, not knowing who the hell would be at the house since my brother is in the Caribbean.

As I open the door and get out, a woman emerges from the other car. Her long red hair blows softly in the spring breeze, her blue eyes lock on mine, and for a moment, I don't know who I am. Everything escapes me. My name, where I am, the ability to breathe and think is gone.

I've seen beauty before.

I've known women who are every man's desire, but this woman is . . . something else.

"Hi." She waves tentatively as I stand there, staring. "Are you . . ." I watch as awareness strikes her. "Oh. You're Jacob Arrowood. I'm . . . I didn't think . . . I mean, I just . . . yeah, I'm Brenna Allen. I bought the house that Devney owned. It's just down the road a bit. I guess her brother lived there before. I'm sure you know that since you're from here and all, and . . . I'm rambling. But, anyway, I came by to bring this." Brenna lifts a casserole dish. "It's for Ellie, but I'm not sure where her house is since it's a little confusing . . ."

Brenna's voice drops, and she pulls her lower lip between her teeth. I need to say something instead of standing here like a fucking idiot. "Okay."

Okay?

That's the best I can come up with. Jesus, I need to be slapped. I clear my throat and try again. "I mean, thank you, I'm sure she'll appreciate it."

"Is Ellie here?"

"They live a little down the road that way. It's the third driveway."

Brenna closes her eyes and sighs. "I'm sorry. Ellie mentioned it was past the main house, but I don't know which one the main house is."

"This is the main house."

"I see that now." Her cheeks blaze, and she ducks her head. "Well, what about Devney? I'd love to say hi since . . . I'm guessing this is her house?"

"Yeah, that would be great. I'm sure she'd love to see you,

but my brother whisked her away to St. Lucia."

"Oh! Wow. That's one heck of a whisk."

I smile—or, at least, that's what I hope I do. "Yeah, my brother is a romantic at heart. He is surprising her by proposing and then marrying her in a few days."

Brenna tucks her hair behind her ear. "That's sweet."

"Or really stupid if she says no and he's paid for all of us to fly out there to celebrate a wedding that won't happen."

Her deep blue eyes look up, nearly taking my breath away. "Luke always said a man only asked that question when he knew the answer." She laughs. "I would hope that your brother is confident."

I take a step toward her, wanting to ease the look of pain in her eyes, and then stop myself. "I'm sorry to hear about Luke. I didn't know him well. He was a few years ahead of me."

No idea what possessed me to explain that, but at least I'm talking in full sentences.

"Thank you. We miss him a lot. It's always so weird when people say they're sorry." She smiles. "I mean . . . I appreciate your saying it. It's just that we're finding a new normal and doing our best even though we miss him. My son, Sebastian, especially."

I remember that. After Mom died, people were always apologizing, but we were just trying to live without the core of our family. I feel like an ass for bringing it up.

"Ellie mentioned your son is a big fan of *Navigator*."

She nods. "Yes, he loves you. You play a superhero that happens to be a fighter pilot as your day job in the movie, so . . . I'm sure that's a part of it. I don't know why I just explained what you do since you clearly know that. Anyway, he pretty much worships the ground you walk on."

I laugh. "That must be shaky ground then."

Brenna's smile is soft as she takes a step back. "I'm sure

you're worthy of the praise. After all, you're willing to spend time with a kid you've never met. I can't tell you how much I appreciate it."

"I lost my mother at a very young age, and I remember all too well how hard that was. I think her death shaped all of our lives in a lot of ways, so if there is a way for me to help someone through a similar situation, I'm happy to do it."

"You're very sweet to say that, Jacob. Or is it Jake? I never know, and I hate to assume."

"Jacob. Only one person is allowed to call me Jake. She's nine and pretty much owns all of her uncles."

"I understand. Sounds like the little girl is lucky to have you." Brenna's smile is warm but ushers in an awkward pause. "Well, I should go, but I'm going to be late getting back, would you mind giving it to her?" She extends the tray of food toward me, and I grin. I have one meal down.

"I would, but you see, I'm living in this house by myself for a week, and well, I will starve to death if I bring this to Ellie."

Her lips turn up, and the sadness in her eyes disappears. "So, you're telling me that this casserole will save your life if I give it to you instead?"

"That's what I'm saying. I'm a man in need of food, and Ellie is completely capable of cooking for herself."

"In that case, consider it yours."

"You're the hero here, Brenna."

Her smile does something to my heart. "I appreciate you thinking that."

"I appreciate the casserole."

"It's my pleasure."

She starts to walk toward her car, and there's a need so deep to stop her, to exchange even a few more words, or see her deep blue eyes brighten, that I step forward as if to follow her.

"Brenna," I call out, forcing her to stop.

"Yes?"

"I'd like to meet Sebastian whenever you think it would be okay. I leave for Sean and Devney's wedding in two days, but then I'll be back here for six months and will have more free time than I'll know what to do with."

Her smile is stunning, and my throat feels tight. "He'll love it. He's had a rough first month at school. Well, he's had a rough nine months in general if I'm being completely honest. Sebastian is a sweet boy who is trying to fit in somewhere he's not sure that he does."

I planned to make a sarcastic comment about how I'll save him, but the look in her eyes tells me she's past jokes. She's suffering, tired, and overwhelmed by everything on her plate, and this deep urge to make it better fills me.

I need to stop that shit.

She's a widow.

The widow of someone I knew and liked. Also, she shouldn't get involved with a bachelor from Hollywood who has zero intention of ever moving here.

Not because of the past or because I am nothing like my idiot brothers who found farm life more appealing than the city, but because my life doesn't exist here.

There's nothing in the world that could make me stay.

So, I give her my signature grin. "Hopefully, we'll turn it around for him."

"I hope so too."

three

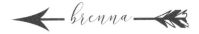

"**S**o, you met him, and you felt *nothing*?" Cybil asks on the screen, pulling her long blonde hair to the side.

I hate that she demands all our calls be video. It's really inconvenient not to be able to hide my face.

"What does that mean?"

She laughs. "I mean, is the man as beautiful in person as he is on television, darling? You can't tell me that you didn't look."

"Sure. I guess. He isn't ugly if that's what you're asking."

I fight back a smile as I think of him. In the handful of minutes I spent with him, he made me feel things I haven't in a while. My cheeks were heating with warmth as though I were sixteen again. I found myself oddly nervous but also giddy because of the way he looked at me—like a woman. A woman who was in front of a man, not the widow who lost her husband in a horrible plane crash.

It was a herculean effort to get in the car and not stay, talk, relish in the attention. Even though there was a wave of guilt so deep that it almost drowned me. It's too soon to think of another man, even if it were just a skin-deep attraction.

I feel as though I'm betraying Luke, which is stupid, but I can't help it.

The tears wouldn't cease that night, looking at photos of Luke and me, scrolling through his Facebook account and seeing the photos of him and his friends smiling. It made me hate that I thought about another man.

The psychologist in me was raging at the feelings I knew were ridiculous. If a client were sitting in front of me, I would've told them that feelings were just that, and sometimes we needed them. That it reminded us that life went on, people moved forward. Yet, I would've wanted to slap myself if I had heard that during my—feelings.

Her laughter gets louder. "Oh, honey, you should see your face. My daddy would've said, 'Sugar, you look like you swallowed a bee.'"

Cybil has no lack of things her daddy would've said, but this one has me stumped. "Swallowed a bee?"

"Yeah, you know, like your face is pinched because you're trying hard to make it look like you didn't just eat a bug."

I have no idea what the hell she means.

"No one knows what the hell your daddy was saying, sweetheart. I don't even think he knew. He made shit up as he went," Reggie says a second before his dark, handsome face comes on the screen. "Hi, Brenna."

"Reggie! My favorite husband."

"You know it," he jokes back. "You look good, getting tan?"

"Tan? Are you crazy? I don't tan—I burn."

"Well, that's a problem I don't have to worry about."

I smile and tilt my head. "And I am envious."

Reggie grabs the phone from Cybil and flops on the bed so I can get a good look at him. His hair is shaved lower than usual, and his deep brown eyes look mischievous. Reggie is one of the most handsome men I've ever met, which isn't something I would tell him since he'd use it later on. He grins. "Look how lucky I am. I have two beautiful women in bed with me right now."

"You're stupid."

"You love me," he counters.

"I do."

I love that he has never treated me with kid gloves. He was Luke's best friend. They were in the same boot camp class, went to flight school together, and then had the same first duty station. Cybil, Reggie, Luke, and I were our own unit, and she and I never had to worry because we knew they had each other's backs.

When he died, Reggie took it as hard as I did. They were brothers even though blood didn't run between them.

Cybil rolls her eyes as she rests her head on his shoulder. "Oh, stop it, you two. You can have your affair once I'm dead."

We both smile, and I roll my eyes. "We aren't going to wait until then, Cyb. We are already in love."

He smirks. "I love both my women." That has her turning and biting his chest. "Damn it, woman."

She raises one brow. "My best friend. You can't have her."

I sigh and lean my head back. "I miss you guys."

"You should come back," Cybil says, not bothering to hide her hatred that I left California.

She knows why I couldn't stay. "The kids are happy here. There's no jet noise."

Reggie clears his throat, the unease clear between the three of us. "We all miss Luke. Each time I get in the cockpit, I feel . . . well, I feel him with me. Don't think it's easy for any of us."

"I know it's not. But moving was the best thing for us. We have family here and it's quiet."

Cybil smiles softly. "I know, buttercup. I just miss you. And, of course, Mel and Seb. They were the closest we were ever getting to kids."

"You're welcome to raise them," I joke.

"No thanks, sugar. We're just fine sending them gifts and loving on them. And don't think I don't know what you are trying to do by keeping Reggie on the phone. Tell us about meeting Jacob Arrowood!"

I knew she wouldn't let this go. I also know that lying to Cybil is a mistake. She sees through it all—hence why it's always video chats. She knows me too damn well.

"He was nice and extremely attractive, but that's it."

Reggie's face changes just slightly. "Do you like him?"

"I met him for about five minutes, so I don't know."

"Did you want to jump his bones?" The animation in Cybil's voice scares me. She's almost too excited over this. However, the only person who can rival Sebastian's love for the Navigator, is my best friend. She's a total superhero movie geek and is who got Sebastian into it.

"Define jump."

"Oh, oh, oh! I knew it. He's hot!" She slaps Reggie's chest and he jumps.

"You're abusive!"

"You can take it, Big Guy." She turns back to me. "Now, tell me on a scale of one to ten . . . what's he in person?"

An eleven. The girl inside me wants to swoon and sigh, and if Reggie weren't watching me with a keen eye, I might have done that. But he is watching, and I don't.

"I really didn't have time to rate him." I shrug. "Not to mention, for all we know, he's just that . . . looks. He could be arrogant and a total asshole."

"Yeah because total arrogant assholes just love spending time with kids," Cybil scoffs.

"I'm just saying that I didn't spend a lot of time with him and during that small amount, I wasn't looking at him like a potential anything. He was a guy. Just a guy."

I'm a liar. A really big one.

Cybil purses her lips and Reggie takes the phone from her and sits up. "Brenna, you know he would've wanted you to move on, right?"

I nod. "I know."

"We talked about this—Luke and I did—because when you're deployed and know there's a chance you won't make it back, it's important you know that someone will watch out for your family," he explains with kind eyes. "You don't have to feel like you're doing something wrong if you like someone. Not saying it should be him, but just that . . . he wanted you to be happy above all else."

Cybil wraps her arm around his shoulders and squeezes him. "We all want you to be happy, Bren."

"I know. I do, I know. It's just that . . . I miss him, and I feel like somedays I don't miss him enough anymore. There are days where I don't think about him as much, and I don't remember the sound of his laugh as clearly anymore. And now, to see a guy and even wonder what it would be like to be kissed by him? It's hard. I'm struggling with it. But since meeting him, that's what's plaguing me. This feeling that I'm doing something wrong by even thinking twice about another man."

"So, you thought about kissing him?" Cybil picks up on the one part of that.

I sigh. "I swear that you're ridiculous."

"Maybe so, but you're a beautiful, young woman who has every right to want it."

"Want what?"

Cybil smiles. "To be wanted."

Every Wednesday is movie night in our house. When Luke and I were newlyweds, we couldn't go out for dates, so we made the dates come to us. We tried to do the same tradition at least once a month if he was around. Since he's gone, the kids have decided Wednesdays are now for family movies. We rotate who chooses, and tonight is Melanie's turn, which means . . . romantic comedy.

This chick flick, however, mirrors life closer than I care to admit. The girl is alone after her husband died . . . and she met a man she can't stop thinking of. Ugh.

I glance over at my kids, and Melanie's eyes are glued to the screen while Sebastian's head is lolled to the side as if he hates that it isn't his week. Not that we don't know what he'd select—*Navigator*. Another night of watching Jacob save the day. He's a fighter pilot by day and flies in some weird suit when he's saving the world. I can only imagine all the comments Luke would've made about the movie and the holes in it.

"How much longer do we have to suffer?" Sebastian groans. "This movie is torture."

He's right about that. "Not sure."

Sebastian huffs. "This is killing me! She loves the guy, why won't she just give in?"

Melanie turns to him with a glare. "Shh. If she did, the movie would be over."

"Yes, that's what I want."

A small laugh escapes my lips.

Then, on the screen, a voice draws my attention to look. A pair of eyes that I've thought about for the last few days are there. I blink a few times, trying to stop my mind from playing tricks on me. But it's him. Jacob is there on the screen, handing the girl her change.

"Hey! That's Jacob!" Sebastian notes.

"No one cares, dummy." Melanie huffs.

My heartbeat accelerates, and once again, the butterflies fill my stomach. He looks so strong and sure. It's a small part, nothing to even notice if it weren't for how popular he is now, but his smile . . . his smile makes it hard to breathe.

"I care," Sebastian says. "Mom looks like she cares. You're the only one who doesn't care, *Mel*."

Melanie's eyes narrow. "Be. Quiet."

He rolls his eyes and groans.

He manages to do that for about four minutes as the female debates again if it's too early. "Seriously, Mom, this chick needs therapy."

Mel pauses the movie and actually growls at him. "You try losing your husband when you're young, and see what happens. She's scared. She's lonely. She's afraid it's too soon to like another guy. God, Sebastian, you're such a stupid boy. She just needs time to realize it's okay to move on! Her heart and her head are at war because . . . she loved her husband and she doesn't know if liking another guy is the right thing. She's a widow, and none of us can know how hard that is."

Everything around me seems to slow as her words sink in.

Sebastian's wide eyes are on me. "Mel . . ."

Her attention whips toward me, and she gives me the same wide-eyed expression my son is still wearing. "Oh, God. Mom, I'm so sorry."

I shake my head, pushing my own thoughts away. "No, it's okay."

"I didn't think . . ."

"Melanie, it's okay. I am a widow. I lost your father, whether you think I'm young or not . . . very young. I'm clearly not trying to date, but you're right, she needs time." The horrified look on her face doesn't budge, so I get up and move to her. "It's all right."

"Sometimes, I forget he's dead," she admits. "It feels like it's just a deployment and he'll be home in no time."

Tears fall down her cheeks, and I pull her close. "I understand."

"I'm sorry, Mom. I didn't mean to hurt you."

Pulling back, I take her face between my palms. "You didn't hurt me. You weren't being mean or spiteful. Sometimes, it feels like he's going to walk in that door at any time." She nods, and I wipe a tear away. "Don't cry. We are all going to forget and end up saying things. It's part of the process. We're learning a new normal, just like the woman in the movie. She's struggling because she probably worries about letting go of the past and what it means." My hands drop, and she sniffles, as do I.

It's almost too much. The talk with Cybil and Reggie the other day and now this. Luke always said that everything happens for a reason. That the universe is often telling us something we may need to hear. Well, I hear you loud and clear, Luke.

Maybe it isn't really him, but I'd like to think so.

"I think Daddy would want you to be happy," Sebastian says softly.

"Yeah?"

He nods. "He wouldn't want you to be alone."

No, he really wouldn't. Just as I would have wanted him to

find love again had it been me who had died.

"I'm not alone, I have you guys."

"But if you wanted to move on, Mom," Melanie's voice is soft and apprehensive, "it would be okay."

I pull both of them into each arm and hold them close. "Maybe someday."

And I hope that someday I'll feel ready, but today isn't that day.

four

"**D**o you take this woman to be your lawfully wed-
ded wife?" the priest asks as tears stream down
my face. I have a pint of ice cream that I'm fin-
ishing off as I watch the season finale of a crappy reality show.

"Yes, I do."

I shovel another spoonful in and sniff. "Good for you. Who
cares that you're setting yourself up for a lifetime of disappointment only to be alone in the end? You're marrying a man
who made out with two other girls just yesterday."

"Umm, Mom?" Melanie asks from the side of the couch.

"Yeah?"

"Are you crying?"

"No, my eyes are leaking."

She rocks on her heels. "Okay then. I see you're handling
things well."

I ignore her and let ice cream smooth my emotions.

"I wanted to ask you if we could get a horse."

I turn my head to her, wondering who the hell this kid is. "What?"

"A horse. I mean, all the kids here have them."

"Right, but that doesn't mean we should. Do I need to remind you about the cat? Or the dog we got after we decided we just might not be cat people? Or the gerbil? We can't even talk about the six hamsters, God rest their souls."

We try, but we are . . . clearly, not meant to have pets.

"The cat was not our fault," Melanie tries to defend.

"It ran away and refused to leave the neighbor's house. Like, left the house, ran over there, and then tried to claw my face off when I forced it to leave only to run back again."

Melanie sighs. "It's because you called it Craphead."

"It was a crap head! It crapped and then rolled its head in it. I thought it was fitting, not derogatory."

She huffs dramatically. "And how was I supposed to know you don't use bleach to clean the hamster cages? I didn't know the fumes would kill them."

I really should've paid more attention that day, but of course, the car broke down, I burned dinner, and Luke called from God only knows where to tell me the death in his unit wasn't him. After that . . . I was done—and so were the hamsters. Greg, Bobby, Peter, Marsha, Jan, and Cindy got buried together to the theme song of *The Brady Bunch* as I lowered the box into the ground.

"Mom, we need something to take care of."

"Start with me."

I'm half kidding on that. I'm okay for the most part. Today is just . . . hard. Maybe it's because yesterday I spent hours with two students who are struggling at home or maybe it's because it feels like the world is crumbling and I have no one to help shoulder the burden. Whatever the reason, I woke up this morning, turned my head to the empty pillow, and cried.

I wanted all of this to be a bad dream, but it's not. So, I let it out and remembered that I have two amazing kids, a great job, a home, and I'm doing okay.

I will politely ignore the fact that I'm eating ice cream for dinner.

"Will you do me the honor of always taking my roses?" The question from the television seems louder than before.

I glance up, seeing him extend it to her.

"Always." Her tears fall as does my heart.

I release a heavy breath and force my emotions back down my throat. I can't cry. I've done enough of that lately and I'm not even sure what the hell I'm crying over. It's been months and I've been fine. After counting down until I think I can speak without tears, I look up at Mel.

"No horse."

She comes around the side and sits. "Why are you crying?"

I shrug. "Life."

I've never hidden real life and feelings from my kids. It's okay for them to know I'm sad, happy, angry, crazy at times, and I can laugh. I want them to see it's healthy to have emotions as long as they process them correctly. So, when Luke died, they saw my tears, they watched me get up each day and do what I had to, and we've supported each other through our grief, which is why I think we're all doing okay.

Most days.

"You miss Dad?"

"Always." I echo the word the girl on television just said.

"Me too." Melanie rests her head on my shoulder.

I lean over, press my lips to the top of her head, and hand her the ice cream. She scoops a spoonful and Sebastian runs in, skidding to a stop and snatching the container from Mel.

"Hey! I want ice cream. Don't eat it all!"

"Too bad, I was here first." Melanie snatches it back.

"Give it here!"

She grins and shoves a scoop—not a spoonful—into her mouth and somehow manages to smile at the same time.

"Mel!" Sebastian whines. "I hate you!"

Her lips are moving, but all I can hear is, "Wha ba ha ooh."

Have kids they say . . .

"Please, can we not fight tonight?" I ask with a huff.

"Sorry," Sebastian says and then crawls up next to me, wrapping his arm around mine. "Can we watch a movie?"

"It's not Wednesday, stupid."

I cut in before this gets out of hand. "No, it's not. It's Friday, but sometimes, you need two movies in a week."

She shrugs and shovels another heap into her mouth.

"So, we can?" Sebastian asks excitedly.

Just the idea of it makes my head ache, but it'll keep them quiet. "What movie?"

He tilts his head as though I'm a total idiot for asking. Of course, he wants to watch the new Jacob Arrowood movie for the ninetieth time.

As much as I don't want to, there's a part of me that wants to see his face again. I wonder if, now that I've met him, the green in his eyes will be as vibrant on screen as it is in person or if his smile is the same.

"Put it on." I find myself saying without really thinking more on why I reply that way.

"Yes!"

"This counts as his Wednesday movie choice!" Melanie says as she gets to her feet. "We aren't watching this again in a few days. It's Mom's choice."

"Fine," Sebastian agrees quickly.

And why wouldn't he? We are watching his movie no matter what.

"Jacob Arrowood is the best Navigator ever. He has that look when he's ready to save everyone that makes it so no one can help but believe him. I bet he's a real-life hero who is nice and does things for people because he can. I bet he can really fly a plane, just like Dad did."

I doubt it, but I'm not about to burst his bubble. He isn't wrong about being a nice guy. Jacob was nothing like I expected. He was kind, ridiculously attractive, and made me feel a little sense of peace. Since meeting him a week ago, I haven't been able to get him out of my mind.

It also doesn't help that Cybil put these thoughts in my head about being wanted.

He's probably complicated, and I have enough of that to last me a lifetime.

The movie cues up, and Sebastian's joy is palpable. I wish I could be like that.

Grief doesn't work on anyone's timeline. Some days are so hard that I feel as though I'm drowning while other days are easy. There are times I can think of Luke without a single ounce of sadness. I imagine him so vividly, smiling at us as we're trying to unload the groceries in one trip, our fingers losing circulation as we load up because multiple trips are unnecessary. I can close my eyes and hear his deep voice telling me he loves me and he'll always return to me.

Oh, how that was a lie.

The opening scene comes on, and Sebastian starts in with all the reasons Jacob is worthy of an Oscar. "He knows all the right turns and angles to make sure he takes down the terrorist who is trying to destroy the city without hurting the civilians."

Melanie huffs and goes to the other couch by the window. "Yeah, he's great."

"Shut up, Melanie. He is great and you're just pissed because we're watching my movie."

"I'm sure that's it."

"You both give me a headache."

They quiet down for a few minutes.

"Mom?" Melanie calls without turning away from the window.

"What?"

"Is Grandma coming over today?"

I close my eyes and count to five. I love my in-laws. They're amazing and generous and truly have helped us more than I can say, but they're killing me. They never call before coming by or ask if it's okay. I've lived most of my life on my own. I got married young and basically grew up while raising a family. I appreciate their help, but stopping by this late on a Friday is a bit much.

"Not sure."

"There's a car in the driveway, and it looks like hers."

I get off the couch, head toward the door, and adjust my messy bun. When I pull the door open, I find it's not her.

No, it's not anyone in our family.

It's a man.

A very, very attractive man. One who happens to be playing on my television at this very moment.

My eyes widen as I stare at Jacob, who is smiling at me.

"Hey."

I push him gently and then close the door behind me. "Hi, are you okay? Is something wrong? I mean, I didn't . . . expect you here now or like . . . at all. Of course, you're not here for me, I'm guessing. Because that would be weird, right? What the hell is wrong with me?" I say the last part under my breath and pray he didn't hear.

"Sorry to swing by, but I was driving home from the airport and saw your lights on. I figured I could meet Sebastian and hopefully set a time to hang out."

"Right." I look at my feet and bite back a groan. Please, kill me now. I'm in my leggings and off-the-shoulder shirt that has a huge stain on it from a popcorn and butter incident, and no bra. I quickly wrap my arms around my chest, to conceal my horrible attire.

"Now isn't a good time, I'm sorry."

"No! That's not it. Please don't be sorry." If Sebastian realizes he's out here and he doesn't meet him, I'll never hear the end of it. "We weren't expecting anyone. We're just watching a . . . something . . . and you surprised me."

He laughs once. "I'm an idiot. I didn't have your number or a way to get in touch with you that wasn't passing notes through my sister-in-law. I jumped the gun."

"I promise, you didn't. I'd love it if you'd like to come inside—as long as you can ignore any mess you see—and meet Sebastian. My daughter is here too, Melanie, and she will also probably freak out a bit."

Jacob shrugs and then runs his fingers through his coffee-colored locks. "I'm ready if you are."

Right. Jacob Arrowood is coming into my house at eight thirty on a Friday night. Not a big deal. I mean . . . it's cool that there are still some boxes in the corner and I look like complete shit. Once he sees me in the light, he'll probably run out the way he came.

Here we go.

I push open the door and hear the intake of air through Sebastian's lips. "Oh my God!"

"Sebastian, this is Jacob Arrowood. He happened to be in Sugarloaf and knew you were a huge . . ."

Before I can finish, Sebastian is on his feet and rushing

toward us. "I'm not a huge fan! I'm your biggest one ever! Wow! You're in my house! Wow! Mom! Look!"

I smile at the sheer joy that is on his face. "I see."

"Did you know that I've seen all your movies? Even the crappy ones."

"*Sebastian!*" I admonish as the heat floods my cheeks. "I'm sorry, he's . . . eleven."

"It's fine," Jacob says with a laugh. "I think they were pretty crappy too."

"I didn't say *he* was crappy, Mom, just the movie. You know, that stupid girl movie that Mel made us watch."

Lord deliver me from boys.

"Can I get you something to drink?" I ask, hoping we can move on from the crappy movie talk.

"No, I'm good, thank you though."

Melanie comes out of the kitchen, her eyes wide and jaw hanging open. "That's my daughter, Melanie. She has also seen your movies as Sebastian pretty much demands them anytime it's his turn to choose, as you can see now." I jerk my head to the movie that's playing, and he grins.

"Whoa." Is all my brilliant daughter says.

"It's nice to meet you, Melanie."

She nods a few times, mouth still gaping.

Jacob crouches in front of Sebastian. "I stopped by because I wanted to ask you a question."

"Really?"

"Yeah, see, part of my job while I'm here is to annoy my brothers, and there's nothing in the world they hate more than me getting to have fun while they're working hard. So, I wanted to know if you would like to go fishing in this awesome creek I have on my land on Sunday?"

"Can I?" Sebastian asks. I nod, knowing my voice will

crack and I'll probably cry. "I love fishing."

This man, who he idolizes, is asking him to just hang out for a few hours. To do something that he and Luke loved to do, no less. Of course, Jacob couldn't have known that, but my heart swells in gratitude.

"Me too." He extends his hand for a fist bump, which Sebastian returns quickly. "Awesome. I'll pick you up around eight in the morning?"

"Sure! I won't sleep at all so don't worry if you want to come earlier or even tomorrow!"

It's completely true. The kid is going to be wired as though he drank four energy drinks.

"All right, well, let's plan for eight on Sunday. I have to get home, unpack, and do some work tomorrow, but Sunday, I'm all yours. It was nice to meet you, Melanie."

Melanie is still standing like a statue, still not speaking. "I'll walk you out," I say, hoping to save her from further embarrassment.

"Sorry to spring this on you," Jacob says as we get to the door.

"It's fine. I appreciate it more than you know. Fishing is . . . something that really matters to Sebastian."

"Really?"

I nod as I hold the door with both hands. "Yeah, he and Luke used to go a lot. I'm sure he's really going to enjoy getting to do something he loves with his idol."

"God," Jacob says with a huff, "I should be the last person a kid idolizes."

"Why is that?"

He smiles, and it's a look I think got him out of a lot of trouble at some point. It makes him even more incredibly handsome, and the charm oozes off him. "Because I've made a lot of mistakes, broke hearts, and my moral compass is a bit off."

"The hearts part I don't doubt."

"Oh? Why is that?" He tosses my question back to me.

I lean my head against the edge of the door. "Well, as a psychologist, I tend to see things in a different way."

"Are you psychoanalyzing me?"

"Would you be scared if I was?"

"Do you always answer a question with another one?"

I laugh a little. "Would it bother you if I did?"

Jacob bursts out laughing and then leans in. "It would."

Is he flirting with me?

No. I'm crazy. He's not flirting, but am I? I don't think so, but it's been thirteen years since I've flirted with anyone. In order to avoid looking like I'm doing that, I stay where I am and soften my voice a bit and take on the psychologist side of me.

"I see. Well, to my point, I don't think your compass is as far off as you think. If it were, you wouldn't have shown up at my house after flying in from St. Lucia to make plans to take an eleven-year-old boy out fishing at eight in the morning on a Sunday."

"Can I ask you something?"

"Of course."

"How old are you?"

The change in direction of the conversation has me stumbling to catch up. "What?"

"It's a question that, once again, you responded to with another."

I shake my head. "No, I wasn't trying to evade, it's just that we were talking about you . . . and then . . . you ask my age."

"I'm trying to figure out how you have two kids, were married, and somehow went to school to be a psychologist. You definitely aren't old enough to have all that."

He's not the first to think this. "Well, I met Luke when I was eighteen, got pregnant almost immediately, got married—immediately." I chuckle at the memory of us telling our families that plan. "Then I started going to school while raising babies, him deploying, and growing up. I'm thirty-one, to answer the question."

Jacob leans in, his voice deep and low. "And this just further proves I'm not worth idolizing, but you are. I'll see you Sunday."

He turns and walks toward his car as I stand here—dumbstruck.

five

I grab the cooler I packed and hop on the ATV. The sun hasn't fully come up over the trees, and I hope when I zoom past Connor's house, I wake them. Serves them right for not letting me stay with them. Hadley wouldn't even offer me the tree house.

Last night was my last night in a house until the end of my sentence here. I was told that I was welcome to stay in the guest room until Sean and Devney got back, which is this afternoon, but then it was out to the tiny shithole with a composting toilet.

I swear if anyone in Hollywood hears about this, I'll never live it down.

I do an extra lap around Connor's house and, not wanting to leave Declan out of the fun, I do a few laps around his house before heading down to the creek.

This is my favorite spot. As kids, we would come here and spend the day fishing or just splashing around before having to head back to the hell that was our home. Whenever I was here, I felt at ease, and that hasn't changed.

The sun is peeking up over the tree line, and the horizon is painted in bright oranges and yellows before it settles to the deep blue of dawn. There's something about this morning's warm hues merging with blue that has me thinking of Brenna. The way the sky mirrors the colors in her deep red hair and the higher sky is the shade of her eyes.

Last night, I was restless thinking about her. How cute she looked in her leggings and that sweatshirt. She was beautiful, even in disarray. I've always been around gorgeous women, but they are never like that around me. Their makeup and hair are always perfect. Brenna doesn't live that way.

However, this is a bad road to go down, and I have to stop thinking of her and focus on her kid, who is struggling. It has absolutely nothing to do with my wanting to see her again. Nope.

Liar.

I check my watch, seeing that I spent an hour out here thinking of the wrong thing, hop on the quad, and head over to Sebastian's house.

I use the trail that we used thousands of times sneaking over to Devney's house. It takes no time to cut through the woods as though it's been days since I last rode this instead of years.

Before I can get to the door, Sebastian is outside and rushing toward me. "You have a quad! That's so cool. I want one, but Mom says they are too dangerous."

I smile. "It took me a long time to get one. When we were kids, we had a tractor or the horse. That was it."

"Melanie wants a horse."

"Good choice. Tractors are slow."

Sebastian laughs. "I have my pole and lures all ready. Do

I just hop on?"

I'm not sure what the protocol is, but I'm pretty sure I need to talk to his mother first. "We'll head out in a few. I just want to let your mom know where we'll be and how to reach me."

He nods once as if this is a good idea, which is encouraging.

When we get to the door, Brenna is making her way toward us. Jesus, there goes my whole bullshit line of thought regarding her. She's even more gorgeous than the last time I saw her. Her auburn hair is down, falling in soft waves past her shoulders, and when she looks at me, I want to fall at her feet. I've seen her three times, each time has been a drastically different side of her, but the feeling when I see her is the same. "Good morning," I say, keeping my voice even.

She's a widow. She's a single mother, and I will not think about dipping my stick where it doesn't belong. Get a goddamn grip, Jacob.

"Good morning, Jacob. I see that Sebastian found you quickly."

I run my hand through my hair, feeling a little off balance. "He did. I wanted to let you know where we were going and give you my number in case you need to get a hold of us."

"Oh, yeah that would be great. I probably should've asked for that, but Sebastian has a phone and . . . I'm rambling—again." She stops herself with a laugh.

"Can I have your phone?"

She hands it over, and I type in my number into a new text thread and then tap out a message. Before I hit send, I need to make sure that she understands how vital it is to never share this. "Now, this number is my *personal* cell phone."

"*Okay,*" Brenna says with confusion.

"I mean that, only ten people in the world have this number. It's very confidential."

Understanding seems to strike her as her eyes widen. "Oh, so this is like top secret."

"Very much."

"I see. Don't worry then."

I send the message so she has it and also now I have hers. That shouldn't make me happy, but it does. I hand the phone back to her. "There, that's my number in case you need anything."

"I appreciate this. I mean, if I sold this to the tabloids, I could probably pay off my mortgage, right?"

I don't say anything as I try to think of the right response. I hadn't pegged her as that type, but I don't know her.

"Jacob, I'm kidding! God, you should see your face. I would never. Not only because I'm not an asshole but also because that would be incredibly horrible after you're taking my kid out, which leads me back to my not being an asshole."

I laugh as though I knew she had been kidding the whole time. "I know. I didn't think you would. I knew you were kidding."

"You didn't, but that's okay. I promise not to share this with anyone, but I do suggest not giving it to Sebastian."

"Why not?" he asks from beside me.

She looks down at him with one brow raised. "Well, let's think back to a few weeks ago when you told everyone at school a secret about your sister that you weren't supposed to?"

Sebastian waves his hand at her. "Please, that was different."

"How so?"

"It's *Melanie*! No one cares about her! She's annoying and stupid and deserved it. I like Jacob, I wouldn't do that to him."

I cough to cover my laugh.

Brenna rolls her eyes. "Right, well, until you prove to be trustworthy no matter the situation, I don't trust you, and neither should anyone else."

My hand clasps his shoulder. "Those are the breaks, kid. All moms are just wired to know the way it goes. It sucks."

"Does your mom know when you're telling the truth?"

"My mom died when I was your age, but when she was alive, she always knew. It's why I thought she was an alien or something because no matter what lie I told, she figured it out. And if I did something wrong, somehow, Mom could always tell."

He leans in, voice quiet so only I can hear. "They're not normal."

"I agree," I whisper back.

"I heard that," Brenna informs us.

"See," Sebastian counters.

I nod. "They're aliens."

"Aliens or whatever, you guys have fun. I'm planning on running Melanie to the store, but I won't be far or gone too long. I assumed you'd be fishing at least an hour?"

"Definitely. We'll probably be much longer than that. Is there anything he needs to be home for?"

She shakes her head. "I have no other plans."

"Great. We'll be off and hopefully we'll bring back something to cook."

Her face goes a little pale. "Sounds . . . great."

Sebastian laughs. "Mom might be an alien, but her weakness is fish guts."

"Good to know. We'll do all the work so she doesn't have to see it," I say with a wink.

We turn to leave, but Brenna clears her throat, causing the two of us to halt. What is it about women and the throat clear?

She looks at her son with her head tilted and puts her coffee mug down. "Are you forgetting something, Sebastian?"

He smiles and heads toward her. His arms wrap around her middle, and they hold each other tight. She ruffles the top of his head before letting him go, and my chest tightens. It's such an innocent gesture, but one that my mother would do each time she hugged me.

"Now, go have fun, be good, and please don't forget your sunscreen." Brenna smiles at me, lifting her hand with a wave.

He huffs the way a boy does when his mother embarrasses him, and I grin. "Do you need a helmet or something to ride?"

Sebastian's eyes fill with horror. "No!"

I laugh. "All right, I just don't know any of this stuff."

"If you asked my mother, I'm sure she'd say we do, but she's a little paranoid about my getting hurt."

"That's a woman thing. My brothers' wives are the same. Let's head out, and we'll hopefully catch something good."

The ride back to the creek isn't long since we cut through Sydney's property to get to mine. The weather is perfect for being out like this. We're at the beginning of where spring and summer meet, so it's cooler in the mornings, but midday is perfect.

We set up, and it doesn't take me long to realize Sebastian is a pro. He feeds his line, ties off the lure, and scopes out a spot. "I think over here the rocks will allow the fish a chance to bite."

I nod in agreement. "Good call."

"My dad and I fished a lot."

"Your mom mentioned that. I remember your dad being out here when we were kids."

Sebastian gives a reluctant smile. "He loved the water. He loved to get me up before anyone else so we could go fish. The week before he deployed, Mom would wake up to find us gone every morning, and . . . it was our thing."

It breaks my heart to hear the pain in his voice, but I understand it. Things my mother did with us that never happened again was not easy to accept. There's nothing that will make it better other than time.

And even then, sometimes, even that won't help. There were days I would do nothing but sit at my mother's grave and talk. I wanted to be close to her. If she could hear me, surely, she'd find a way to come back and help us. We were her heart, and we were breaking, but help never came, at least not in any way that we needed.

"I hope that it's okay we're doing this. I wanted this to be fun for you."

"It is. I swear, it's all good."

"I don't mean that for you to feel guilty, Sebastian. I just don't want to make you sad."

He shakes his head quickly. "You're not. I missed fishing. There's been no one to take me . . ."

"While I'm here, I would be happy to be your fishing partner if you want."

His eyes widen. "You want to hang out with me *again*?"

"Sure, why wouldn't I?"

"Because you're the Navigator! You're *Jacob Arrowood*, that's why!"

I laugh. "I'm just Jacob. The Navigator is a role, one that I love and am honored to play, but here in Sugarloaf, I'm just Jacob, and you're a cool kid who likes to fish."

Sebastian tries to reel in his excitement. "Right. I mean, we're just two cool guys who are hoping to get dinner caught."

"Exactly. So, tell me how it's been since you moved to Sugarloaf."

Sebastian sighs as he casts his line. "I want to like it here.

Melanie does, but . . . the only thing I love to do they just cancelled."

"What's that?"

"They cancelled the play."

"I'm sorry to hear that."

He shrugs, but I can see he isn't so accepting of it. "I was excited because this year they were doing *Grease*."

"And what role did you want to audition for?"

I can totally see him as wanting to play Danny. It's always the role that most want. It wasn't mine, but . . . I was never really a conventional guy. The side characters get to have fun and none of the criticism the main roles get.

He smiles. "Kenickie."

I definitely didn't expect that. "Really?"

"Yeah! He's the coolest, even if he's sort of a jerk."

"It's a good role. It's actually what I played in college."

"Wow. I didn't know that. I don't need to be a main character yet. I want to learn and be good before that."

"Very smart. I did the same thing."

I laugh, remembering how uncomfortable I felt at the time. I was supposed to be studying finance because that was what I thought I should do, but there was this calling to be on stage. I signed up for a few drama classes, thinking I would hate it and realize that it was finance that was my passion.

I was terrified before the first time I stepped on stage in front of a live audience and thought I would pass out, but the minute the lights were on me and I fully enveloped the role, I thrived.

I loved being on stage.

"Did you always want to be an actor?"

I shake my head. "No, it was luck and a lot of being in the

right place at the right time. I thought I'd be like Declan and go into business, but when you feel the lights, hear the clapping . . . I don't know, there are some of us who are just meant for it. It was a really amazing time for me when I found the stage."

"It sounds like it, but it won't happen here. It's another thing that I have to give up."

"Why did they cancel it?" I ask. If I remember Mrs. Finnegan is still the drama school teacher for both the middle and the high school. She's . . . beyond passionate about the theater and was always up our asses about auditioning, but since I was much too cool back in the day, I brushed it off.

"Mrs. Finnegan fell and broke her leg. She needed surgery, and there's no other teacher that will fill in."

"That sucks."

He nods and adjusts his line. "I wish you could help. You're a real-life actor who could probably direct the play better than Mrs. Finnegan or anyone else in the world ever could. It would be so cool, and it would make so many of us 'drama geeks' really happy."

Oh shit. How the hell do I extricate myself from this? I got this pretty awesome kid who loves drama, just lost his dad, and was forced to move, and this would make things better for him. I really don't have a good reason to say no. I'm not doing shit for the next few months anyway.

"Well, how about we see if I can help?"

"Are you for real?" Sebastian asks.

"Absolutely."

six

"I hope it's okay that I stopped by," Devney says from the doorway.

"Of course, it is, but didn't you just get home from your wedding today?"

What is it with this family and stopping by after the airport?

"Yes, but . . . I needed a break from the house. Sean is unpacking while on the phone with his agent. Austin is grumbling about schoolwork he missed, and I wanted to return this." She holds out the casserole dish that I gave Jacob.

"Thank you. Would you like to come in?"

She looks over my shoulder and into the house, and I see the hesitation in her eyes. This was her brother's house, and I suddenly feel guilty for suggesting it. Before I can speak, Devney smiles and nods. "I'd like that very much."

We go inside, and her smile widens. "Wow, you did so

much to it already. It looks amazing."

"It's just a bit of paint."

She turns, her eyes are a little watery. "It's beautiful, and I'm really happy to see it."

I release a heavy sigh. I understand grief so much. "It hasn't been too long since you lost them."

Devney shakes her head. "Some days, it feels like years."

I nod. "And others like it was just yesterday."

She wipes at her tears and laughs a little. "I'm sorry, I'm not normally overly emotional, but . . . I found out while we were on our honeymoon that I'm pregnant, and . . . well, I keep crying."

"Oh! Congratulations!"

"Do you know that you're the first person I've told?" Devney asks with amusement. "I haven't said a word about it to anyone, and here I am, blurting it out. I almost wonder if it's not because I'm . . . because you're in what was my brother and sister-in-law's house." I don't have to be a psychologist to know that her showing up here was about more than a casserole dish.

She smiles ruefully. "Maybe that is why, although, it wasn't a conscious reason."

"Sometimes the unconscious reasons drive us more than we'd like to admit."

"Spoken like a therapist."

"Guilty as charged."

Devney looks around the room. "How are you guys settling into Sugarloaf?"

Such a loaded question. It's one that most people think they want a truthful answer to, but they don't. "We're doing our best," I say, settling onto the couch as Dev takes the seat across from me.

"I guess that's all any of us can do." She eyes the table where Luke's picture sits. "I didn't know him that well. Sean probably knew him the best of everyone, but . . . I'm really sorry."

I release a low breath. "I appreciate that. We're all really doing okay."

Most of the time.

"You don't have to put on a brave face with me. I know you don't know me, but I promise that there's zero judgment here. I went through hell the last few months, and . . . I'll never be the same as before, how can we be?"

"There are days where I'm fine. Others, well, they suck."

"How's today?"

I think about all that happened in the last twenty-four hours and smile. "Today is good."

She eyes me curiously. "I'm glad."

I'm not sure what it is about Devney, but she gives off such warm vibes. A lot like when I met Ellie. We hit it off instantly, and I've been grateful for the friendship. As a military wife, most of my friendships were fleeting because they were there and then someone was moving. But with Devney and Ellie, I know there is potential for long-term friendships.

"I am too," I tell her. "Jacob came by the other night. He's actually out with Sebastian now."

"As in my brother-in-law?"

"Yes."

Her brows raise and she leans back. "Well, I'll be."

"Should I be concerned that he took him fishing?"

"No! No, not like that. I've known these boys my whole life, and Jacob is a great guy. Truly. He's sweet and funny and I wouldn't worry at all. It's just that he's been away from here for so long, and it's nice to see him doing something in this town that he loved—fishing. And the fact that he's with your son is really great. His mother would be really happy."

I was worried that my son was out with some random guy and I was being too naïve, so having her say that eases my apprehension.

It's easy to think that this town is out of some kind of storybook where people are kind beyond reason.

"He mentioned he lost her when he was young," I say.

"They all were. Connor, Ellie's husband, was the youngest and didn't handle it well, but out of all of them, I think Declan took it the hardest. He was the oldest and thought he had to take care of them all. Jacob was . . . different. I don't know, it was as though he lost a part of who he was when she died and replaced it with sarcasm and a grin."

"I worry about my kids feeling like they don't know who they are without their father too."

Devney leans forward and rests her hand on mine. "Your kids have you to love them through it."

I give her hand a squeeze. "Just as yours has you."

"That's a whole other level of drama, but, yes, Austin has me and Sean who love him very much."

Austin is a great kid. I've spent quite a bit of time with him at the school. He talks about his parents and his new parents with a lot of confliction and admiration. He loves Devney and is glad he has her, but he's also struggling a bit with the loss of his parents and what it all means.

"And I think that all we can do is love our kids and help them process their grief."

She watches me, seeming to think a bit before speaking. "Who is helping you, Brenna? I'm not asking to be rude, but I have Sean as my shoulder. Your kids have you. Your mother-in-law has your father-in-law. It's a lot of shoulders, but I worry who will help carry your burden."

The flippant woman in me wants to scoff and pretend Devney is being ridiculous. However, I am alone. I left my friends in California. My family is gone or aren't a part of our lives. I moved here because the only people who could help were Luke's family, but I can't cry to his mother when she's grieving her only son.

"I'm not sure."

"I hope you know that I'm now your friend, and I will always be here to listen."

"You're very sweet."

She laughs softly. "I have my moments, but I also came by to invite you to dinner next weekend with Ellie, Sydney, and me."

"Oh, that's really nice of you, but I couldn't."

"Why not?"

Because I don't know. I can't say that, so I look around, trying to get a good excuse. "I'm . . ."

"You'll be there, great!" She gets to her feet with a smile. "I thought you wouldn't be able to resist. It's at my house, which is where you came with the casserole. It'll be a lot of fun, bring the kids so they can all keep themselves busy while we get to enjoy a bottle—or two—of wine." I open my mouth to say something, but she keeps going. "Any time after six. Most of us come right around that time and let the kids burn off energy running between the farms while we cook." She walks to the door and opens it, still not taking a breath. "Don't worry about bringing anything! See you this weekend!"

The door closes, and I feel as though I just got railroaded, only it doesn't hurt, it feels a bit like a gift.

"Mom!" Sebastian comes running up the steps with the biggest smile. "We had so much fun! It was so awesome."

"That's great, sweetheart."

"I smell like fish."

That's gross. "Then why don't you get yourself in the shower."

"Okay!" He turns back to Jacob, who is walking toward us. His sunglasses are on, hair windblown, and he looks like the Hollywood star that he is. He's unbelievably attractive, and I really would like to stop thinking about that. "Thanks again, Jacob!"

"Anytime, dude." Jacob's deep voice fills my ears.

He stops in front of me, and I smile up at him. "This was really sweet. Thank you."

"It was fun. He's a great kid, and it was nice to spend time with him. I haven't fished in years, so I should be thanking you for letting me take him."

I tuck my hair behind my ear and smile. "It means a lot to him to have a man hang out with him. I like to think I'm cool and all, but you definitely outrank me."

He chuckles. "No one can ever outrank a mom."

I wish that were true. "I can assure you that some of the teenagers I see on a daily basis wouldn't agree."

"Teenagers are nature's way of preparing adults for what hell looks like."

I giggle. Jesus. I just giggled. I pull myself back together and attempt not to act like a girl with her first crush. "I imagine that's exactly what hell is like."

"I guess I'm about to find out myself."

"Oh? Are you suddenly getting a teenager or planning to go to hell?" I ask with a mischievous grin.

"God no. Sebastian mentioned that Mrs. Finnegan hurt

herself."

I nod. "So sad, and he's crushed that the play won't happen. He really loves acting, and it's been a great outlet for him."

Jacob runs his hands through his hair. "I called Mrs. Symonds, and she's going to let me direct the play. She's willing to make an exception as long as I do some paperwork to be a substitute or something and if I can find a current member of the school system to make sure I don't corrupt the children of Sugarloaf."

I'm stunned. "You're going to direct the play?"

"I'm going to have to get a teacher first, which I'm sure I can sucker Ellie to do it. Hopefully."

My heart, which was already swollen with admiration and gratitude, gets even bigger.

He came, met Sebastian, and took him out for a day. That alone probably made my son's year. He doesn't have to do anything more, but he is. He's going to direct the middle school play, and . . . I don't know that I can hold back the emotions.

"I'll do it! I'll supervise," I say quickly and then want to clap my hand over my mouth.

"You will?"

I guess I just declared that and have to now. "Yeah, of course. I work for the school, so I can help, and it would be great to spend time with Sebastian."

It also means I get to look at you a bit.

Jacob's smile makes my insides melt. I really need to get over this. I do not crush on men who are famous. I don't crush on any man because I'm a widow who is still grieving. This is stupid and reckless. But then I look into his green eyes and logic and rationale cease to exist.

"That makes things easier. Ellie has the baby, and I wasn't sure I could really get her to do it."

"No, I'm happy to. I'll let Ellie know she's off the hook this weekend."

He laughs. "Yeah, Devney texted me that she stopped by and mentioned you might be coming to the family dinner this weekend."

Did he just say *family* dinner? "You'll be there?"

He smiles and shrugs. "Well, I am part of the family."

Oh, how in the world did I get forced into this? I should've said no. If it were just the girls, I could handle it, but being around the whole family is too much.

"Of course. She just made it sound like a girls' night not a family dinner."

"Don't worry, the guys normally get thrown out of the house after a few minutes. Then it becomes more of a girls' night than a family dinner. Not that they ever allow me to stay anywhere."

We start to walk toward the house. "Do your sisters-in-law throw you out of a lot of places?"

"No, but I like to give them shit." Jacob leans in, his voice conspiratorially low. "I'm still a little pissed that they're not impressed with who I am. They're making me sleep in a trailer that has a composting toilet."

I laugh. "Are you serious?"

"Yup."

"That seems more like hell than teenagers."

"I'll let you know tomorrow since tonight is my first night in it. But with the way Declan and Sean complained about it, it's going to be a long five-ish months."

"I'm sure it's not that bad."

"It's a tiny house that has a generator, propane, and no hot water unless you go outside the night before and turn on the pump. And remember what I said about the toilet? I promise that it's horrible."

I smile, trying to imagine whatever this trailer thing looks like. "I'll take your word for it." We're now at the top of the stairs, and I'm not sure what to do. "Well, I guess I'll see you later?"

Jacob nods slowly. He reaches out, touching my wrist for just a second. One touch is all it takes to light a fire inside my heart that has been cold and filled with ash.

I stare down at where his hand was, wondering if I imagined it.

"I look forward to it." He flashes a grin and then heads back down to where the quad is.

Jacob looks totally unfazed while I'm desperately pushing aside my thoughts about the touch. He's a great guy. He's funny, easy to be around, and did something incredibly sweet for Sebastian. The touch was innocent, and I'm making it into something that it wasn't.

Jacob waves, and I lift my hand, returning the gesture as he drives off, wishing I didn't look forward to seeing him again as much as I do.

Mrs. Symonds, the school principal, enters my office with a warm smile. "Hello, Mrs. Allen, you look lovely today."

I rise out of my chair and come around the desk. "Thank you. You do as well."

"I wanted to see how you were settling in."

"I'm doing great. Sugarloaf is very welcoming, and even though we came after school had already begun, the kids are doing well."

She nods. "I'm happy that's the case. This town is filled with wonderful people, but sometimes, we're a bit hard on newcomers."

"Maybe it hasn't been that way because I'm an Allen."

"Luke was very loved here, but I'm sure that's only part of it. The other part is because you're just a very warm person as well."

I smile. "I appreciate that."

"Listen, there is something I wanted to talk to you about."

"Okay." I scramble to try to think of something I could have done wrong or forgotten, but I come up empty.

"I received a call from Jacob Arrowood the other day, and I wanted to verify that you agreed to help him."

"Is it about the middle school play?"

"Yes. He said that you volunteered to supervise him."

"I did. I probably should've asked you before saying something though. I'm sorry if I overstepped."

She waves her hand dismissively. "No, it's not that. I'm actually really grateful that it's you. It will give you a chance to bond with some of the students."

"I see."

"Jacob has grown up to be a great man. I thought it was incredibly sweet of him to offer to help with our play."

I nod. "Yes, I agree."

"He's such a big star, and even though he's busy preparing for his new role, he said he wanted to pay back the community that helped him reach where he is now. We are so fortunate to have someone like him around when we needed it most."

The warm feeling I had is back again. He is being selfless in a world that is anything but that. He's giving something to kids that was taken when it's inconvenient for him.

Jacob is nothing like I assumed.

I thought he'd be arrogant, rich, and entitled. I thought he would be a playboy to the hilt because that's what we see and believe actors are. Then he showed up at my door, basically proving me wrong on every front.

I release a deep sigh. "I'm happy to help if all he needs is a school-approved supervisor."

She clasps her hands together. "He's coming in early next week to fill out the paperwork so that we're covered for all liabilities. Oh, the kids will be so excited, and I'm sure we'll sell out all the seats if people think they'll get a chance to meet Jacob. We'll raise so much money for the drama club."

"Yes. It sure will."

She gets to her feet, and I do the same. "Let me know if you have any problems."

"Of course."

The only problem I have is that I keep thinking of him, and I really don't want to.

seven

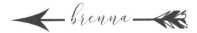

I'm sitting on the bed, staring at the fifteen outfits I've laid out to go to a backyard barbeque. I don't know what to wear. Nothing feels right. Everything looks like I'm trying too hard, which I am, or like I'm a slob, which I'm not. What do you wear when you want to impress a guy but you don't actually want to look like you're trying to impress him?

It's official, I've lost my mind.

Melanie walks in, looks at the piles, and raises a brow. "Did you see a mouse or something?"

I sigh. "No. Why?"

She points at the mess on the bed. "Are you finally updating your wardrobe?"

I bristle at that. "What's wrong with my clothes?"

"Nothing if you're from the last millennium."

"You're grounded."

Melanie seems uncaring. "Sure I am. What are you worried about?"

"The barbeque tomorrow."

"Because?"

"It's people that I don't really know. I want to make a good impression."

She sits beside me. "They'll love you, Mom. You already know Devney and Ellie, right?"

I nod.

"See, and you know Jacob."

"I do."

I can still feel the way his hand felt on my skin. How hot and intense that stupid touch was. I haven't done anything but wonder about what being with him could be like, which is very dangerous territory.

Melanie starts to pull out items from the pile. "Why are you nervous if you know all of them?"

"I don't know."

"I don't either because Jacob has already seen you . . . not impressive."

I laugh. "This is true."

Melanie shifts a bit. "Do you like him?"

"Who?"

"Jacob."

That pride about being honest I was feeling now is completely void. "I don't know him enough to like him that way, if that's what you're asking."

Melanie keeps pulling clothes out, not looking at me. "I know you guys are going to work on the play together."

"Yes, we are."

"And?"

I wait for her to stop fidgeting with the items in front of her and look at me. After a few beats, she does. "What are you asking me, Mel?"

"I don't know. Do you like him? Do you want to date him or anyone else? I'm not judging you, Mom."

I know my daughter, and I know where this is going. "Why are you asking this?"

"Because I want to know."

Luke and I used to joke all the time about how each of our children was exactly like one of us. Melanie has my red hair and keen eye. She notices things, observes people, and always wants to help. It's also a bit scary because, if she is like me, she also knows what the hell I'm thinking and not saying.

"I think he's extremely kind and generous. He made Sebastian very happy, and now he's going to help with the play." I give a very non-answer, answer. "I think that Jacob is everything that Hollywood says he's not."

"Maybe, but he is really hot."

I burst out laughing. "There's that too."

"So, you like him?"

"Sure. He's nice and is doing something for your brother."

"Okay, but like, do you like him, like him?"

"Melanie . . ."

The thing is, I do like him. I like him a lot more than I ever thought possible. I have a million reasons why I shouldn't think about him that way, but my heart doesn't seem to care. I also don't lie to my daughter, which means I have to evade this.

"I like him, but no different from how I like Aunt Cybil."

She laughs. "I don't believe you."

Good. I don't believe myself either.

Her hand covers mine and Melanie looks up at me. "I know

I'm just a kid and don't know much about this stuff, but I think about that movie we watched and how she was so afraid."

"She was. It's really scary when all of a sudden you don't have a husband anymore. The feelings for or attraction to anyone else isn't a betrayal. All of that is terrifying."

That's the part of myself that I keep trying to convince, the one that doesn't quite believe I am single. Regardless of the ring that's on my hand, that man is gone. He will never return to me, and I am not sure how to get my mind around it.

Melanie wraps her arms around her middle. "Well, I know that Aunt Cybil is your best friend, but I love you, Mom. If you're scared, I can help."

I have the best kids in the world. "You are a very sweet girl."

"You're young and very pretty."

"Well, thank you."

"You're welcome, but your clothes suck."

I laugh. "I'm sure Aunt Cybil agrees."

She nods. "Oh, she does. She thinks you dress like an old lady. Although, if you ever start wearing clothes like Grandma, I'm having you committed."

"If I ever wear anything that looks like it should be skinned, you have my permission to."

"It's a deal. Anyway, I think you should wear something cute. Even if you don't *like* Jacob, you should still look hot."

I'm afraid to ask, but I can't seem to stop myself. "Why should I look hot?"

Her head tilts to the side and shrugs. "It just sounded like something Aunt Cybil would say."

At that, I laugh. "Yeah it really did." I pull her close and kiss the top of her head. "Now, help me find something to wear that doesn't make you cringe."

She looks down at the pile. "That might not happen."

eight

Dinner with my siblings reminds me of the saying about a box of chocolates . . . we never know what the hell we're about to bite into.

Tonight, I'm hoping it's not one of those jelly-filled ones that leaves a bad taste in my mouth. I'd prefer a mint chocolate that is smooth and warm.

I walk up to where my three brothers are standing on the porch. "Did we get kicked out already?"

Declan sighs and jabs his thumb toward Connor. "This one made a comment about his wife's cooking abilities."

I wince. "Bad move."

"Thanks, genius."

"Happy to help," I quip back and look at Sean. "You're out here too? What, did you agree?"

"Devney said something about my smirk."

I laugh. "What was it I said at your wedding about you all

being a bunch of fools? Notice that I didn't get kicked out."

Connor snorts. "Only because you haven't been inside yet."

"Or because I'm smart and won't let a woman hold me by the balls."

"If you had balls, we'd worry for you," Sean replies.

"Says the man who got traded for the woman he loves. Balls. Gone."

Sean rolls his eyes and takes a drink. "At least I have a woman who wants to touch my balls, how long is your dry spell, brother? A year? Two?"

I flip him off. I'm not having a dry spell. I'm focusing on my career and trying not to end up in a tabloid for boinking some chick who wanted to film it. After I got the role as the Navigator, my publicist, Catherine, and I had a long—and I mean ridiculously long—conversation about the women who will suddenly want anything they can get from me. I thought I had it all figured out, and then the release happened. She wasn't wrong.

Which, of course, I won't ever tell her.

Since then, I've had a strict no-dating policy until I'm at least through this role. So, like, ten years . . . yeah, I need to rethink that.

Not a snowball's chance in hell I'm telling these fuckers that. "It's a choice."

Declan laughs. "Whatever you say."

I turn to him with a smirk. "Didn't your wife say I was the hot one?"

"She was joking."

"Was she?" I tilt my head to the side. "Didn't really sound like it to me."

"Wait," Sean breaks in, "Syd said that you're the hot one?

What the hell?"

Declan raises his cup while shaking his head. "Exactly my thoughts."

"No, I mean I'm clearly the hot one out of you idiots."

Connor laughs. "Yeah. Right."

"You think you are, Duckie?" I ask with a chuckle as I call Connor by his hated nickname.

"Fuck off," he replies.

"I'm even called Stud."

Oh, here we go. I roll my eyes. "No one fucking calls you that except you. No one. Not a single freaking person because it doesn't mean you're a stud, it means you're as dumb as a wood pole."

He grins. "Say what you will."

Declan breaks in. "Can we all agree that Jacob is not the hot one and leave it there?"

"Tell that to the thousands of women who formed a club in honor of my hotness."

All three of them burst out laughing, and then Sean hands me a beer. "The fact that you think delusional people make sense is enough for us to worry."

Just then, my favorite sister-in-law of the day exits. "Bean, will you set these dumbasses straight as to who is the sexiest of the four of us?"

Sydney sighs dramatically. "Jacob, but not by much."

"See."

"Seriously, wife?" Declan growls.

"Oh, calm down. I said not by much."

"But you did say I was the hottest one, so who cares where the rest fall in," I say smugly.

"If you did have to rate us, who would be next?" Connor's

voice rings with mischief. He's clearly enjoying Declan's irritation.

Sydney doesn't hesitate. "Jacob, Declan, Sean, and then you."

I burst out laughing, hand slapping against my chest as I see Connor's crestfallen face.

"Really, Bean?"

"It's the fear of ducks thing. It makes you look like a pansy."

"I'm a fucking SEAL!"

She gives me a shit-eating grin before turning back to him. "Former. But you're . . . not a very scary one."

My brothers and I lose it.

She leaves, and the four of us take our seats on the porch, still chuckling as Connor mutters all sorts of angry nonsense under his breath.

The laughter dies down and Sean speaks first. "Is it normal for things to be weird once your honeymoon is over?"

I look over, knowing this wasn't easy for him to ask. Declan speaks first. "Weird how?"

"Just . . . weird."

Declan and Connor share a look. I'm definitely not one to speak on this shit. I'm not dating or married.

"Again, I'm going to ask how?" Declan tries again.

"She's exhausted for one. Second, it seems as if something is bothering her."

"You guys have been back for a week," I say, unable to be quiet because I'm not sure I know how.

"I know that."

"Do you? Because aren't girls supposed to be depressed after their wedding? I swear Ellie said some shit about a post-wedding depression one time on the phone." That was an hour-long call I can never get back. I still don't know if she was drunk when she called me, but then she started to get upset, so I just listened.

Sure, it was my birthday, which was why I answered, but then she was going on and on about being bored and not knowing what to do with herself because the wedding was over. I kept looking down at the phone, wondering what the hell was going on or if she thought maybe I was Syd.

Connor grins, clearly knowing what call I'm referencing because, of course, I called him to let him know his wife might need psychiatric help. He laughed and said that was what we missed out on not having a sister.

He's a real helpful bastard.

Sean shrugs. "Maybe, but she didn't have to plan a wedding."

"Yeah, you took that from her."

Declan laughs. "Who knew Jacob was the authority on women?"

"Oh, you are? Please, you three don't know your asses from your elbows. Yeah, yeah," I cut them off before their stupid retorts can fly from their mouths, "I know you're married, I'm not. All that shit is great, but you fools don't know a damn thing. You"—I point to Connor—"were going to fuck it all up until Declan and Sean booted you in the ass and gave you advice you needed." I turn to Declan. "Don't even get me started on you. You're the royal fuckup in relationships, and if the three of us didn't know how to handle you, you wouldn't have handled anything." Then my gaze goes to Sean. "And you were going to let Devney go until *I* reminded you that there are baseball teams in Pennsylvania." I feel proud at this little tirade. "None of you should give any advice."

"That doesn't change the fact that it feels different," Sean says with a shake of his head.

"Maybe because it *is* different, you jackass. You're like a goddamn freight train. You went from being her best friend to her husband in like seven months. Plus, she's now a mom? Give the girl a break and maybe take some advice from the master of women."

I don't think I'm a genius, but it doesn't take one to see what's going on.

Sean rolls his eyes. "If you're a master of women, why the hell are you alone?"

"Because I choose to be."

"You say that," Connor's voice is low. "I just wonder if it's really a choice or a safety thing."

"My life is filled with paparazzi, rumors, scandal, and drama, and that's before I spend countless hours prepping and filming. Bringing a woman into that isn't fair. Not to mention, I'm never going to find women like you have. Ever. That shit doesn't exist in the land of plastic."

I don't want an actress or a model. I've been there, done that, and got a lot of autographs. What my brothers have, that's real. Each of them has a woman who my mother would be proud to call a daughter.

A woman like Brenna.

Stop it, Jacob.

"You're here for five more months," Connor says with a smirk. "There's time."

I'm about to respond with how I have no intention of dating or ever finding love here when a car pulls up, causing all three of their heads to turn in that direction.

The white sedan stops, and a smile forms on my lips because I'm a fucking fool.

Why am I smiling? Why does the idea of seeing her make my heart beat just a little faster?

Because I'm a fucking idiot, that's why. She is sweet, funny, and each time she blushes, I have to force my hands not to touch her. She doesn't ask me stupid questions or try to get some inside information, and it makes me want to talk to her for hours.

I stop myself from going there, willing my head and heart to prove that, when I actually get my eyes on her, it will be different. It's all just some stupid infatuation that isn't real. That, when I see her today, she won't affect me and that gut check, want-to-weep-and-fall-at-her-feet bullshit won't be there. Once it happens, I can prove that it was just in my head or because I was taken off guard or she's not really all I remember at night when I'm alone.

"Who is that?" Declan asks.

"Brenna," I reply, not moving my eyes from her car. I should look away, appear as if I don't care, but the pull to see her emerge is too strong.

"Oh," Declan says. "I didn't know she was coming."

Sean gets to his feet, and I do the same. "Devney invited her."

"That was nice," Connor says from behind me.

The doors open and Sebastian is out first. He waves enthusiastically, and I lift my hand as well.

"Sebastian is the kid, he's awesome and happens to adore me."

"Oh, great, just what we need." Connor laughs. "Another person to inflate your ego."

And then she gets out. Her deep red hair flows down her back, moving softly like waves, and my fucking chest aches.

Damn it.

"Well . . . wow." Declan's voice trails off.

"Told you she was beautiful. She's . . ." I can't finish the thought before a set of groans from my brothers causes me to face them.

"Jacob, don't do it," Sean warns quietly. He told me at his wedding that it was a bad idea.

"I'm not doing anything."

He snorts. "Well, right now you look like you're ready to fall at her feet, so don't tell us you're not doing anything. Not to mention, we all heard about your fishing day and new venture."

I glare at him. "It's not because of her."

"Explain that to my wife when she hounds you about it later. Don't fuck around with a girl you plan to leave."

I am not looking for a relationship, especially not one that would be complicated. "I'm not an asshole," I tell him.

"I know that. You're far from an asshole, Jacob, which is why I worry."

I turn to him. "I would never do anything like that. I'm just . . ."

"You're fucked, that's what you are," Connor says. "I felt the same about Ellie, and well, we all know how that went. It's like she steals the air from the earth and you're left only able to breathe when you see her. I get it, we all do. Just be careful, Jacob. Getting involved, even if it's just one-sided, with a single mom is a minefield, and those kids don't need to be hit by shrapnel."

I want to reply with something smartassed and biting at the same time. I'm not getting involved. I'm just lusting after her, and I need to get laid so it'll stop. A girl who can work off this dry spell energy so I can behave like a normal person around Brenna and not want to hump her leg.

"Hi." Brenna's voice is right behind me, forcing me to shut it down and behave.

I turn and slip into the role of a friend who has zero interest in the girl before him. "Hey, you made it."

"Sorry I'm late," she says and looks around at my brothers.

"You're not, we just came early to annoy Sean."

He steps forward with his arm extended. "I'm Sean, Devney's husband."

"Yes, of course, I recognize you." Brenna's cheeks redden a bit, and I shove my hands into my pockets to keep from reaching out to her. "My husband was a big fan of yours."

Sean grins. "I liked Luke very much, and he was a great player too."

I step in and save her from having to talk about Luke. "This is Connor, he's married to Ellie."

He extends his hand as well. "We met briefly at the school."

"I remember. It's so great to see you again."

She turns to Declan. "And you must be Declan?"

The same motion of greeting is repeated. "I am. I'll repeat what these guys said, it's great to meet you. I've heard all good things. Have you met my wife Sydney?"

"No, I haven't yet. But Ellie and Devney have both spoken about her so much I feel like we're already friends. Everyone tells me how wonderful she is."

"Don't believe any of it," I say quickly. "She's the devil. Truly and inherently evil. We only keep her around because we're worried that a demon might escape if we killed her."

Brenna shakes her head with a laugh. "I'll do my best to remember that."

Sean scoffs. "Please, she just likes to give Jacob the most shit, which is why we love her."

"She sounds like my kind of people. These are my kids, Melanie and Sebastian."

Melanie gives a little wave, clearly feeling out of place, and Sebastian is practically bouncing out of his skin. "Sebastian is who I was telling you guys about. We fished, and he caught three more fish than I did."

"Five," Sebastian corrects.

Declan laughs. "That's impressive. Jacob is one of the best fishermen I've ever met."

"Well, Sebastian is clearly better." This kid beams, and Brenna's eyes lighten.

God, she's really freaking breathtaking.

Sean clears his throat, causing me to look away. Fucking observant bastard. "It's great to meet you all, and welcome to our home. Devney is really excited you agreed to come."

The girls come out as if they heard us mention their names.

"Brenna! You made it! I'm so glad," Devney fusses over her. "And this must be Melanie and Sebastian?"

"It is." Brenna hands Devney a plate of something. "I know you said not to bring anything, but . . ."

Devney laughs. "I understand. I'm the same way. Please, come in and have some wine. We were just bitching about the men in our lives and how dumb they are."

I look over at my brothers' faces and chuckle.

She tucks her hair behind her ear and smiles. "Thank you."

Sean steps forward. "If you want, the kids are all out playing by the tree house—or, mansion if we want to be technical . . ."

"I'll take them," I offer.

Devney's eyes meet mine, and I can see the questions swirling. Damn these women and their ability to make something out of nothing. "That's sweet of you, Jacob."

"I'm a sweet guy."

"You most definitely are." She winks, and I wonder if she knows why I offered. "Come on, Brenna, let's head inside."

With that, I head out, away from Brenna and my thoughts about how much I want her. It's safer at the tree house.

nine

The Arrowood family is amazing. That's all I keep thinking. Today has been so much fun. We ate, laughed, had
some wine, and are now around the fire as they all
make fun of each other. The kids are chasing fireflies, all getting along and playing nice.

When I pulled up, my heart was in my throat. I was so
worried about what they'd think of me, if it would be constant
talk about Luke, or how weird it would be to hang around with
two famous people. Not to mention, I was terrified to see Jacob
again.

But, instead of being weird, it's been the most relaxing day
I've had in far too long.

These people are a family. One that is filled with bickering
and trying to embarrass someone else before they are the tar-
get. It's everything I wanted growing up, and they welcomed
me into their fold with open arms.

"I bet I could throw this farther with my left hand than you can throw it with your right," Sean challenges Declan after they were arguing. I lost track of what the disagreement was this time.

Declan scoffs. "You're on. You think you're some hotshot, you're not, pretty boy."

"I believe the name is Stud."

I giggle and finish my wine in one gulp.

"Brenna, you'll have to forgive the boys for their bad behavior. I can promise you, their mother raised them better than this," Sydney says as she slaps her husband's chest.

"I love it."

"You love their constant shit talking?" Devney asks with a raised brow.

I shrug. "I was an only child, so our house was very . . . quiet. We didn't have constant laughter and our family dinners were just the three of us. This is so much fun."

Jacob laughs. "I think the four of us would've traded places with you when we were kids."

"That's because you didn't know what solitary childhood was like."

He raises his hands. "Easy, Doc."

I roll my eyes. "That wasn't me as a psychologist, it was me as a person."

Sean nudges Jacob. "Be careful, you might end up as her next test patient."

"Me?"

"You're the most in need of therapy," Declan says with a chuckle.

Sydney snorts. "That's debatable."

Jacob glares at him. "I've already illuminated you jackasses on how superior I am in my thinking."

"Really?" I say, unable to help myself.

The three brothers laugh.

"Here we go," Sean says while rubbing his hands together.

Jacob turns back to me. "Do you think I need help?"

"We all need help, but I'm wondering if you might need it more."

Connor walks around and fills all the girls' cups again—except for Devney's as she shakes her head. "He needs it more than anyone. I'd bet my house on it."

Jacob flips him off. "Says the douche canoe who is afraid of ducks. And I'll take your bet if that means you're in the tiny house."

"I was six when I was afraid of the duck." He ignores my second comment about the house.

Sydney clears her throat. "Six*teen*."

"You're a liar, Sydney Arrowood," Connor says with a huff.

"There's a story here," I say, curious as to where this is going.

Connor shakes his head. "We can get to me later, let's stay on the topic, Doc. My brother Jacob here has some issues. Deep-seated issues. Things that . . . I don't know if anyone can actually help the poor bastard get through them."

"The only issue is that I'd like to beat all three of my brothers until they cry," Jacob says through his teeth.

The brothers all laugh. "Anger management might be a good place to start."

"I've known them since they were all small, trust me, there's no shortage of issues here," Devney informs the group. "However, Jacob has the most hope between all these boys."

"Why is that?" I ask.

Devney smiles. "He loves the deepest and has the biggest

heart."

My eyes move to him, and his gaze is cast toward the fire, unwilling to look at anyone. Jacob has shown that his heart is definitely big. Offering to work with teenagers when you're a Hollywood superstar shows it.

"I can see that," I say, and his eyes cut to me but his head doesn't turn. "I mean, he spent time with an eleven-year-old boy he had never met and is now going to direct their play."

Beer flies toward the fire and Sydney pats her husband's back. "You okay there?"

Declan nods. "I'm sorry, did you say that Jacob is directing a play?"

"For the middle and high school kids."

He turns to Jacob. "Well, when we said to make sure you do something while you were here for the next five months, I didn't expect this."

"Sebastian mentioned it, and . . . well, I couldn't tell the kid no. I have other reasons too."

He looks to me, and there's something in his eyes. Something I don't know how to interpret. It's a sense of longing mixed with apprehension. The butterflies in my stomach take flight, causing a nervous rush to go through me.

What is it about this man? Why am I so pulled to him when every instinct I have is telling me that I shouldn't feel this?

It's been so long since I've felt this way about anyone other than my husband, but Jacob Arrowood makes me feel like a woman. Someone to be desired, cherished, and cared for. My chest rises and falls a little harder as this realization dawns on me.

Ellie smiles and reaches her hand toward him, breaking my and his moment. "I think it's wonderful, Jacob," she says. "Mrs. Finnegan was so upset that she had to cancel. This makes me proud to be an Arrowood. You're not only the hot one but you're also the kind one now too."

"Let's not go that far," Sydney says with a laugh.

Connor clears his throat. "It's great that you're doing it. You were worried about being bored."

"I wasn't worried about being bored. I have a movie to prepare for."

"Well," Declan speaks up, "I think it's a good use of your time."

Jacob rolls his eyes. "I'm so glad I have all of your approval on how I'm spending my time."

"No one has issues with what you're doing, Jacob. In fact, we're proud of you." Sean reaches over and punches his arm. "You have a talent you're going to share with kids. If their coach broke his leg, I would offer to help out if I could. I'd just hate to see you mixed up in something you can't get out of when you leave."

I can sense the tension around here, and I feel like there's another conversation happening that I don't know about. I look down at my phone and internally groan. It's late, and I have to be up stupid early tomorrow. "I really need to get home. Tomorrow my mother-in-law wants to ride out early to go to breakfast."

"Oh, that's too bad," Devney says as she gets to her feet.

When I rise, the wine or . . . something, hits me. I stumble a little, but Jacob reaches out quickly to grab me.

His hands are around my waist as I plaster to his chest. The smell of smoke and cologne fills my nose, and the sense of security wraps around me.

"Sorry," I say softly.

"Are you okay?"

I nod. "I'm fine."

Although, I'm not.

He releases me and drawing breath is just a little difficult. I feel slightly dizzy, but I'm not sure if it's what caused me to wobble or if it's the fact that I didn't want him to let go.

Devney is at my side a second later.

"Oh my God, I thought you were going to fall."

I rub my cheek and try to smile. "I guess I had a few too many glasses."

The truth is, I haven't drunk more than a glass of wine in a very long time. Before the fire, Ellie, Sydney, and I finished off two bottles.

"I'll drive you home. Sean can follow in my car," Devney offers.

"That's not necessary," I say quickly.

Jacob's voice cuts in. "I'll drive them. I stopped drinking before Sean."

"Well, I'm totally sober," Devney says.

"As am I, and I don't have any kids to worry about getting to bed."

Devney's eyes dart to me, and I shake my head. "No, please. I can call my in-laws." I don't want any of them to go out of their way for me.

"I insist." Jacob leaves no room for argument.

Devney jerks her head toward the car, and Jacob heads that way. "Brenna, it's late, and there are more than enough people here, please, don't fight us on this. Plus, the women in this family may not have been born Arrowoods, but we're just as stubborn. Jacob can drive you home and that's that."

I would rather call Dennis than ride with Jacob while I'm slightly tipsy.

"I know I'm arguing for nothing."

She loops her arm around mine and starts to lead me away.

"The boys are very passionate about not drinking and driving. They suffered from having a severely alcoholic father who didn't much care for the welfare of others."

"I wasn't saying I should drive."

"Oh, I know," she says quickly. "I just mean that they take the fact that you were drinking at our home as their responsibility. That's all. Please, let Jacob drive you, it'll set his mind at ease."

"Okay. I just . . . I feel like an ass."

"Why?"

"I drank too much, I guess."

She smiles. "You were relaxing among friends. I'm hoping you had fun?"

"I had a blast. You have no idea how much I needed this."

"Good."

Ellie and Sydney come up from behind us. "We're all packing it in too."

Ellie sighs. "BethAnne is teething, which means I'm getting almost no sleep, and Hadley has riding lessons in the morning."

"Deacon is in the same phase. It really sucks," Syd says.

Devney looks away and grips each of their arms. "I have to tell you. I haven't told Sean yet, but I'm pregnant." Both of them go to yell, but she cuts in and whisper yells. "*Be quiet!*"

"Right. Sorry. Oh, Dev, this is amazing," Syd whispers. "I'm so happy."

"When are you going to tell him?" Ellie asks.

"Soon. I want to see the doctor and make sure it's good first. You know how Sean is, and I don't want to watch his head explode over it. Plus, I want to give myself a little time—" She turns to me. "Because I don't want you to be in the dark, Austin is my biological son. I gave him to my brother when he was born. I was young, and it was the most difficult thing

I've ever done. I didn't plan to get pregnant so fast, and I know Sean didn't either. We . . . well, it'll be a shock, and I worry that Austin will struggle too."

"I was adopted, and I think there's something beautiful about someone who gives a better life to their child and yet still loves them. I'm sure that Austin will be okay with it. He may need a bit of time, but he'll come around. He's a great kid."

"I know there's been a lot of family drama unearthed here in a few hours, but I promise that we're all fairly normal. Well, maybe not, but we try."

"I think normal is overrated."

"Mom! Mom!" Sebastian comes flying up beside me.

"What?"

"Jacob is going to drive us home. Which is cool."

I laugh a little. "I know."

"I'm really glad we moved here."

I look over to see Jacob walking toward us. His dark brown hair looks tousled just the perfect amount, and his green eyes seem a bit guarded.

"Ready?"

I smile over at the girls, and they each pull me in for a hug before I head off to the car, feeling nervous all over again.

The ride isn't far, and thankfully, Sebastian and Jacob talk the entire time. Melanie interjects herself a few times, but those two go on and on about the movies.

"No way! You're not going to walk away from a role like that."

Jacob nods. "That's what I told my agent."

"I mean, the Navigator is the best superhero."

"He is."

"The way he knows how to fly the plane and then at night he's able to save the world without anyone realizing he's the same guy. It just shows how superior he is." Sebastian's animation grows.

I lean my head back, looking out the window as they keep going. I've missed not having to drive when we needed to go somewhere. It's funny how many things change in an instant and you suddenly start missing things you never paid a second's thought to before.

While I was used to doing things on my own, this was all so different. It felt lonely the entire time.

We pull into the drive, and the kids are out of the car, racing to be the first one to make it to the door. "Thank you for driving us home," I say as Jacob comes around to my door, opening it like a true gentleman.

"Of course."

We stand outside the car, looking up at the door and I feel horrible that he went out of his way. "How will you get back now?"

He laughs once. "I'll walk. Trust me, I appreciate the exercise as much as I appreciate not being stuck in that tiny house."

"Sebastian thinks it's the coolest thing ever."

"It's a shithole. Not really since it's probably worth a ton of money, but it's not ideal."

I can't imagine. "Well, I really appreciate it. Everything really. Your family is so sweet, and you're very lucky to have them."

"It wasn't always this way for us," he says and then looks away.

"What do you mean?"

Devney told me about his father, but I'm not sure he would be comfortable with my knowing that.

"Just that my father was a drunk abusive asshole, so once

we left home, my brothers and I only saw each other randomly. It's only really been in the last nineteen months that we've spent time like this together."

"That's kind of sad."

He shrugs as we walk. "It is, but now that everyone has families, I think it'll be different. However, drinking and driving is one thing that we'll never allow, I hope you understand."

I reach out, placing my hand on his arm. "Of course. I would've never driven drunk."

"It's something I can't ever let someone do around me. Even if someone says they're fine, I just won't risk it."

Sounds like something more than just protectiveness.

"Oh?"

He nods. "My father, well, he killed two people in a drunk driving accident."

My lips part, and a soft gasp escapes. "Oh, Jacob."

"It was terrible, and my brothers and I have only just really dealt with it the last two years. The people he killed were Ellie's parents, and . . . well, it's been a lot of unearthing our past."

I move my thumb against his forearm. "I can imagine. I'm sorry if you thought I would be reckless."

"I didn't. I just wanted to make sure you were safe, Brenna."

I don't know if it's the wine, but the air is so thick around us. He lifts his hand and brushes the pads of his fingers gently down my cheek. "Why?"

"Why, what?"

Why do I feel this way?

Why does your touch feel so damn right?

Why am I not stopping this?

"I don't know," I confess.

Jacob's green eyes are soft in the moonlight. My breathing is heavy as his thumb traces along my jaw. "Are you going to be okay?"

I want to tell him no because this, right here, is making my head spin. He's dragging me back to a place I don't know if I'm ready to be.

I take a step back, needing to get control before I do something stupid like kiss him. I give him a soft smile, hoping that it lessens the awkwardness. "I'll be fine. Thank you for bringing us home."

"You're good?"

"I'm good."

And I am. I think I'm getting there, at least. While there are things that feel unsettled in my heart, I know that this is all part of the process.

Like the girl in the movie who is finding her legs, I might not be able to run yet, but I'm not crawling any longer.

ten

"**B**renna?" A deep voice calls from behind me as I'm on my way to my car. I don't have to think hard on who it is. I hear his voice pretty much once a week on my television. And I can't lie . . . I am a little excited to see him since it's been almost a week.

I take a deep breath and mask the slight joy racing through me as I turn. "Jacob, hi."

"Hey." He smiles, and I swear my heart sputters. "I was just finalizing some paperwork with Mrs. Symonds, and I thought that it was you."

"Yeah, it's me," I say, feeling shy. "I was just heading to lunch and then I have a break before I have to get the kids from school."

He nods. "A break?"

"Yup. It's a luxury I do not squander. I have this glorious two-hour break once a week."

"I don't blame you. I was heading to grab a bite too."

"Oh?"

There's only one restaurant in this town that serves anything edible. I'm not sure what the hell to say. Right now, it's sort of awkward.

"What if we eat lunch together?" Jacob suggests.

"Together? Us?"

"Is that a bad thing?"

"No, of course not!" I say quickly and then clear my throat. "I just . . . I was going to read over something, and I was a little . . . anyway, I just . . . I haven't had a lunch date in forever."

"Are we going on a date?"

"No! I didn't mean to imply that we were going on a date-date." Please let there be a meteor or something that comes down and saves me from myself.

Jacob smiles but then covers it quickly. "Would dating me be so bad?"

"I'm sure you're a great dater," I say and then shake my head. "I mean, I'm just going to run myself over with a car now."

He laughs louder, and my belly dips. "I'm kidding. I wanted to talk about the plan for the play. Mrs. Symonds said it'll take another few days to process the paperwork and since you're my assistant—"

My eyes widen. "Assistant?"

"Did you want to be a co-director instead?"

"I want to be the silent teacher who is just sitting there making sure you don't turn *Grease* into some crazy movie with space aliens."

"Now that would be interesting." He grips his chin and stares off.

Oh lord, nothing good comes from that look. "Let's go get

lunch and discuss your evil plans."

"Sounds like a date."

I laugh, and then Jacob goes around the front of my car and opens the passenger side. "What are you doing?"

"Getting in the car . . ."

"My car?"

"Did you want me to drive for our date?"

"No, it's not a date, remember?"

"Of course." His voice dances with mischief. "We both have to come back here anyway, and it's easier than taking two cars."

As a matter of principle, I want to argue, but he made a good point. "All right, then."

We drive in silence the whole six minutes over to the café and grab a seat.

"Well, well, if it isn't the Navigator in all his glory."

He smiles up at the waitress. There stands a girl with huge breasts that are barely contained by her top and very large—like 1980's size—blonde hair. I wonder if she's single-hand-edly keeping Aqua Net in business. "Magnolia Knightingale, you are the same specimen as you were when we were kids."

She rolls her eyes. "And you haven't changed a bit. You've been back in this town a month now and haven't come to see me? For shame, Jacob Arrowood."

"I apologize, I've been working on some projects. This is Brenna Allen, not sure if you know each other."

Instead of smiling and doing what most would, she plops down in the seat next to me and grabs my hand. "Oh, you poor thing. Your mother-in-law is one of my favorite people. She comes in here once a week, and she was just heartbroken when he died. We all were, especially me. I don't know if you knew this," Magnolia's voice is quiet and sad, "but Luke and I dated in high school. We were in love at one point."

"Well . . ." I look to Jacob for some help, but he just grins. "That's . . . nice."

"So many thought we'd make it, but it wasn't in the cards. He was in such a hurry to get out of this town, and I was never going to leave." She sighs dramatically. "And now he's gone. He's gone, and we're left picking up the pieces of our broken hearts."

I grab a napkin from the table and hand it to her. "It's all right."

Magnolia dabs her eyes, and I want to laugh. I've never heard of her. At all. Not once in all the years I was with him did he talk about an ex-girlfriend from home. But Magnolia seems pretty torn up over it.

"Thank you, honey. I was so sad to hear about his death. The town mourned for him. I think I'll always have a part of me that feels sad about what could've been. I was going to stop by when you all moved in, but I thought it would be awkward."

Jacob coughs to cover a laugh. I glance at him and fight back my own burst of laughter. This is the oddest and funniest thing that has happened since his death. I've cried, held friends crying, and dealt with a lot, but this is nuts.

Finally, Jacob gets control and takes pity on me. "Magnolia, why don't you get us both some lemonade and buttered rolls."

She shakes her head and rises. "Of course. Anything for Luke's widow."

Once she leaves, I cover my mouth with my hand and chuckle.

"Oh, that was priceless."

My hand drops. "That was crazy."

"*That* was Magnolia. She's a piece of work. I think she and

Luke might have dated for a whole day before he realized her nickname Hell-no-lia was earned because that's what you said when she asked you out . . . hell no."

I stifle another laugh. "That was mean, I shouldn't laugh."

"That could've been his baby mama if he hadn't been smarter. Magnolia would've gotten knocked up just to keep that man in her clutches."

I can't picture Luke with her, but then again, no one ever imagined he and I together either.

I glance over at Magnolia and smile a little. "Well, then I'm glad he saw the possible error of his ways."

Jacob leans back with a sly grin. "Is that your professional opinion?"

"Maybe or maybe it's just that, in the end, I won. I got the guy, the kids, the life and . . . well, I got the folded flag."

As soon as I say it, I want to take it back.

"Brenna . . ."

I lift my hand to stop him. "It's not what I meant. I didn't say that for a reaction, and I'm sorry."

"No, it's all of us who are sorry."

"You know, I never understood why people apologize for my loss. It's not their fault. No one went in and broke a part on Luke's plane just to see what would happen. It was a mechanical failure, and no one is really to blame. Why do we say we're sorry?"

Jacob moves so his arms are resting on the table in front of us. "Because we're sorry that someone we like or care about is hurting. We're sorry that families suffer because someone they love is gone. I hated when people said it after my mother died, but as an adult, I get why they were sorry and where the apology comes from."

I take my lower lip between my teeth and slide it back and forth. "And when you lost her, how was it for your father?"

He releases a heavy puff of air. "Let's say that you're handling it the polar opposite of him."

"That good, huh?"

"It wasn't easy for any of us, and that's putting it mildly."

This topic is definitely not what I had thought we'd venture onto, and honestly, I don't want to talk about Luke right now. I know this isn't a real date or anything, but it's the first time I've been out with a guy who wasn't Luke since I was eighteen.

Jacob won't ever be anything other than a famous actor who was nice to my kid, but maybe this could be a sort of practice for whenever I am ready.

I'm attracted to him, and sometimes I get the feeling he's flirting with me or, at least, he could think I'm pretty.

Magnolia brings the glasses of lemonade and then takes our order. I try not to seek out glimpses of him over my menu, but I fail. I want just one more look at him. His dark brown hair is pushed to the side, slightly curling at the ends, but his eyes? God, they're magnificent. The green is so light in the middle and darkens as it goes out to a thick black band that keeps the shape.

Jacob looks up, and I feel the heat rise in my cheeks. Damn it. He caught me.

I clear my throat and give Magnolia my order. "I'll have the grilled cheese and a pickle, please."

"Our grilled cheese is one of the best."

I smile. "It's my favorite."

Jacob's eyes don't leave me. "I'll have the same." He hands the menu over to her.

"I'll get that right out. I have to say, I am so glad we met," she informs me. "If you ever want to know about Luke as a teenager, I'd be happy to share stories."

I break our stare, not wanting to be rude to Magnolia while

also needing to calm my racing heart. "That's really nice of you."

"It's nothing really. I never knew that it was redheads he was attracted to. I would've dyed my hair if that were common knowledge."

If I were drinking something, I would've choked.

Jacob smoothly steps in. "Magnolia, we're on a time crunch here so if you could get our meals out that would be great."

"Sure thing, *Navigator*." It comes out like a growl.

I hold in a laugh and cover my face with my menu that she didn't take from me.

"Not funny."

I lower it slightly. "It is, though. You might have your own baby mama if you're not careful."

"She's a fucking mess. Half the people in this town are, but being out of here for nine years has been a gift."

"Why did you never return?"

"There aren't many movie career opportunities here. Plus, this town holds a lot of memories I have tried to forget."

I understand that all too well. "It seems you have great brothers."

He takes a sip of his drink. "We're a close group and have been through a lot together."

"I always wanted a big family. I wished for it."

"It has its benefits, but then again, so does being an only child."

I nod while playing with the straw. "I always knew that I wanted to have at least two kids."

"You had them young."

"It wasn't part of my plan," I admit. "I was *really* young

and not prepared, but it worked out. Luke was the best mistake I ever made, that's what I used to tell him."

He smiles. "It sounds sweet in a weird way."

"We were weird. I was this gangly redhead who was desperate for a night of fun after my first year of college. I had never really had a boyfriend, but I wanted to just let loose."

"That's how you guys met? At a party?"

I nod, remembering it. "It was total luck that we bumped into each other. My roommate dressed me in one of her outfits that made it look like I had boobs. She did my hair and makeup. We were both standing there, started talking, and then we were making out."

"Ahh, and one thing led to another?"

I chuckle. "I am the walking billboard for hooking up and getting pregnant. We were together maybe three times before I was pregnant with Melanie. Luke and I just clicked, though, so he asked me to marry him right away."

"And you said yes," Jacob muses.

"I did. Luke was the only guy to ever tell me I was pretty. That night, my roommate did more than magic. God knows it was the only time I ever thought I was even mildly attractive."

He blinks a few times. "You didn't think you were pretty? You're kidding, right?"

"I'm not pretty. I'm passable."

Jacob's green eyes lock on mine. "You're more than passable, Brenna. I promise that you are so much more than passable."

My heart begins to beat a little harder. Again, I wonder if he's flirting. It's not always outright, but it's the way he says things and then he looks at me, stares really. Jacob is over-the-top gorgeous, which is why I know I have to be losing my mind. He could have any woman in the world, and there's no way he's interested in a single mom living in Pennsylvania.

"You don't have to—"

"I am telling you that I am surrounded by women who think they're pretty, who work way too hard to be passable, and you outshine every single one of them. You aren't passable, you're gorgeous. I'm not just saying that either. The moment I met you, I thought . . . holy shit, that woman is breathtaking."

I don't know what to say. Every ugly duckling part of me is screaming out that he's crazy and lying, but the way he's looking at me tells me he's not. He really thinks I'm beautiful.

I swallow once and tuck my hair behind my ear, wanting to hide the blush that I'm sure is on my cheeks. "Thank you."

"Did Luke never say this to you?"

I look up. "He did. He always told me how pretty I was, but . . . I don't know . . ."

"You didn't believe it."

How does this man know my thoughts so easily? "I didn't."

"Then believe me, you're beautiful, and if any man says different, he's a fucking idiot."

A nervous laugh escapes me. "You're making me blush."

"Good."

"Good?"

He shrugs. "It means the words are affecting you."

Oh, he's definitely affecting me. My heart, my breathing, the intense tingling that's running through my body. It's all being affected.

"I appreciate you saying it."

"I mean it."

"I believe you," I say.

"You should believe it too, Brenna. There is nothing wrong with knowing that you're beautiful and that guys are looking."

Now that causes me to jerk back a bit. "Guys are looking

at me?"

He chuckles. "There are at least two men in here who keep trying to pretend they're not, but they can't keep their eyes off you."

My head whips around as I try to find who he's talking about. There are only about fifteen people in the whole place.

He leans forward, voice dropping. "One is with his wife over to the right."

"The other?" I ask.

"Me."

And now I know he's definitely flirting, and I like it. I like it a lot.

I drop my gaze for a moment. "Well . . . that's . . . something."

He laughs and then grabs his drink.

I watch his Adam's apple bob as he swallows. That single movement is unbelievably sexy. Everything he does is. It's a little ridiculous.

When he puts the glass down, I can almost feel the shift in him. As though the cool liquid also helped calm him.

"So," Jacob says, "I figured if we get to know each other, it'll make co-directing easier."

"We are not co-directing."

He shrugs. "Semantics."

"You don't have to do this, you know?"

"Do what?"

"This, be my friend if you don't want."

"Is that what we're becoming?" Jacob asks.

"Isn't it?"

"You're doing it again."

"Doing what?"

He laughs, and I squint, wondering if he's lost his mind. "Answering a question with a question."

Shit. I am. "I don't even realize that I'm doing it."

"I'll answer one of those questions . . . yes, I do know that I don't have to do this. The thing is, Brenna, I want to. Being back in this town was my version of hell on Earth, and since meeting you . . . err . . . Sebastian, things have become bearable. He's funny and getting to hang out with him was a lot of fun."

I smile, loving that he sees my son that way. "He enjoyed it too. I appreciate you doing any of this."

"So, since we're going to spend a lot more time around each other, let's get to the important things, okay?"

"Okay."

"I'll ask the questions. Favorite genre of music?"

"These are the important questions?"

He tilts his head to the side with his brows raised. "Now, that was a question again."

"Damn it. Okay. Music. I like a little of everything. I grew up listening to Elvis thanks to my mother, and then my father loved hard rock. My best friend, Cybil, likes rap music, which, if you ever met her, you'd never believe, but that girl can rap lyrics like it was her calling."

"That's great, but all of those are everyone else's choices, what's yours?"

"I guess, I would say that I really love pop. I like silly, light, and sweet songs where everyone can be happy, smile, and dance around like fools. What about you?"

He grins. "I'm more of a classic rock man."

"I can see that."

Just then Magnolia returns, places a plate of complimentary fries down, and then is gone.

"All right, favorite movie?"

That one is easy. "*Sweet Home Alabama*."

He rolls his eyes. "The one where she goes back home because she's married to one dude while the other gives her a ring from Tiffany's?"

"That's the one."

"Are all girls nuts?"

I laugh and grab a fry. "Maybe. What's yours?"

Jacob leans back. "You guess."

My first instinct is to go with one of his movies, but that seems a bit stupid and too easy. Not to mention, most creative people don't like their own work. They scrutinize it, finding flaws where there aren't any. No one has to tell them they suck because they tell themselves enough.

"Jurassic Park?"

He laughs. "No, but you're at least not going with anything of mine. I would never choose any of those."

"And why not?"

"Because they're shit."

I roll my eyes at his self-deprecation. "I know a lot of people who would beg to differ."

Jacob shrugs, letting the comment roll off as though it's nothing. "Back to the pick."

There's no surprise in what Luke's was . . . *Top Gun*, but I don't see that being Jacob's. I don't really know him, so I'm not sure if he's more serious or if he likes something more like *Fast Times at Ridgemont High*.

"You have to give me some hints. I need to at least know the mood of it."

"Okay, it's a classic."

"Like *Casablanca*?"

Jacob's brow rises as his head lowers. "Does any man who still has possession of his man card like *Casablanca*?"

"No idea since I'm not a man."

"The answer is no."

"Okay, so when you say classic, do you mean like Fred Astaire or classic man movie like *Fast and the Furious*?"

He shakes his head.

"What?" I ask with a hint of laughter. "I am trying here, and you're no help."

"You're supposed to be the psychoanalyst here."

"No, in fact, you are," I remind him.

"That's right. All right, it's a classic guy movie."

I wrack my brain, trying to think of the movie that would fit Jacob. Something that he might have watched that defined a change in his life and brought him toward acting. "*The Godfather*?"

"Very close."

"*Scarface*?"

Finally, he takes pity on me. "*Goodfellas*."

I nod, seeing that. "All the greats."

Jacob takes another fry from the basket. "It's truly one of the best movies made. I remember watching it with Declan and thinking . . . I need to be this one day."

"A mobster?" I joke.

He laughs. "No, the movie is definitely not inspirational. It was more that a movie could do something for someone. That it could make a difference in a kid's life. I wanted to be that. I wanted to make someone inspired by art."

I lean forward, my hand meets his, and I squeeze. "And that's what you're doing, Jacob. You being here, helping these kids, giving them a play from an actor they adore . . . you're making a difference. You've already done it for Sebastian."

His thumb glides against the back of my hand, and everything around us seems to disappear. Jacob and I are sitting here, holding hands as though it were the most natural thing in the world. The beating of my heart is so loud that I can barely hear Magnolia approach with our lunch. Quickly, I pull my hand back, placing them both in my lap, and work to get my heart rate under control.

"Thank you for that, Brenna," Jacob says after Magnolia takes her leave.

A few breaths pass, and I plaster on a fake smile as though something crazy didn't just happen between us. "Of course."

And then I force myself to eat and pretend everything is fine.

eleven

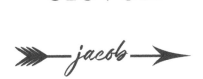

Mrs. Finnegan is everything I remember and more—a maniac. That's the only word I can manage to come up with. She's fucking nuts.

Anyone who agrees to work with these kids has to be certifiable.

Which is now what I am.

"Okay, everyone, listen, I will not be signing any autographs, taking photos, or doing anything along those lines until after the play is done." I see the one kid with his phone up and point to him. "Stop posting on your Snapchat and all that. If it gets out that I'm in this town, I'll go to ground, which means no play." I go back to looking at students who are here for the auditions, most of whom probably aren't the least bit interested in the school play. "I am here as a teacher and to make sure the school play happens. If you're not here to audition, then please leave, but be sure to buy your tickets to the play, which I will happily sign as a souvenir as well as do an after party where we can do photos."

I watch as at least half the students get up and head out the auditorium doors.

My eyes find Brenna's, which are dancing with laughter before she goes back to looking at the papers on her lap. At least she's enjoying my discomfort.

"All right, now that we've got that out of the way. I'm Jacob Arrowood, and I'm going to be the director of *Grease* this year. Mrs. Finnegan has given me about six years' worth of papers to read on each of you, and we don't have that time. So, this is going to happen pretty fast because the play is in three months, which . . . you know, is insane, but it's what we got. Auditions will be in a week. Any questions?"

Hands go up within a half a second. "I do, I do!"

"Yes, person with the blue shirt."

She stands. "Is it true that you got fired from *Navigator*?"

My head jerks back a little. "What?"

"My mom said that you probably got in trouble doing drugs or whatever and this is your community service."

The bratty kid sits, and I want to say that her mom probably hasn't had sex in the last decade and that's why she is pissy. That would probably make Mrs. Symonds fly off the handle and get me in trouble. Not to mention, I know someone is recording this crap.

Brenna stands. "Clarissa, we all know that's not true, and it's not polite to relay gossip. Mr. Arrowood is a famous actor who has volunteered his time to help us not miss out on our yearly play. We need to be kind." She sits back down as if she didn't just verbally spank the kid.

I make a mental note that, no matter what the hell this girl's talent is, she's in the chorus or an understudy.

Another hand goes up. "Yes."

"Mr. Arrowood, I heard that you were really bad in the

play you did and not really a good actor, do you even know how to be a director?"

I swear, I'm going to kill someone. I go to speak but again, Brenna is on her feet before I can open my mouth.

"Mr. Yates, I know that you weren't just insulting the director, correct?"

He shakes his head. "No, Mrs. Allen. I was just asking a question."

She sighs. "Let me be clear, I will not tolerate any disrespect. Anyone who forgets that will face the consequences of Saturday detention or worse. Now, if anyone has questions pertaining to the play, you're welcome to ask, otherwise, we will not be rude or anything less than grateful, understood?"

I fight back the smirk that I want to give the little girl and the other kid. I know I'm not mature, and I don't feel bad about that. They just got verbally whacked by Brenna, and I feel victorious.

However, I'm not fifteen, and I channel my inner Noah Frazier. He would never let this shit fly and neither will I.

"I can handle this." I wink and then turn back to the kids. "Unless any of you are more knowledgeable on set design, costumes, casting, tone, musicality, or putting a scene together, I suggest you not question me. I've worked on numerous types of movies and plays. It shouldn't be you questioning my ability, it's me evaluating yours. Worry about yourselves, your roles, and impressing me before asking anything else. To be clear, I'm not here for any other reason than because I want to do something to help the community who made me who I am. I will push you hard to be better actors and actresses. I want this to be the best play this town has ever seen. If you're not up for it, don't try out. I will cast you for the roles that fit best, even if it's not the one you signed up to audition for. You have four days to study the lines from the section based on who you're trying to be casted as. I suggest you take that time and work hard. I'll see you at four o'clock."

I grab my packet and head out of the room. There's nothing like a dramatic exit in show business.

The only issue is, I have no fucking clue where I am. Since I went to school here, they've combined the middle school and the high school into one building and built a huge wing. I'm lost, and I would be wasting the dramatic flair I was going for if I have to pass the kids again.

So, I slip into an office on the right and hope to God it's not some restricted area or a student lounge. Not that we had anything like that when I was a kid, but it seems this generation gets all kinds of crap.

After a few minutes, I figure the coast should be clear and reach for the doorknob, only to freeze when someone on the other side turns it.

Shit.

I step back, and Brenna enters. Her breath hitches as she sees me there. "Jacob." Her hand flies to her chest. "What are you doing in my office?"

"I'm sorry. I ducked in here to . . ." Saying that I came here to hide makes me sound like a pussy, so I am not admitting that.

"I understand. I was irate on your behalf. I don't know what is wrong with some of these kids lately. I think they just want to look cool."

Good, she thinks I was mad. I should've gone with that. "It's fine. I would've done the same shit at their age."

She tucks her hair behind her ear. "I would've been hiding under the seat."

"Because?"

"I would've been far too embarrassed. Well, I probably wouldn't have been in the auditorium in the first place."

I try to imagine what group she would've been with then. If she doesn't like attention, it wasn't sports or drama. I wonder if she was a loner or more like Devney, who was pretty but not exactly popular. She much preferred to sit and watch Sean than try to fit in with any group.

Brenna, though, she has me stumped.

"Were you in the band?"

She shakes her head. "I can't sing or play an instrument."

"Hmm, so no chorus. Sports?" I ask because my assumption could be wrong.

"I did cross country."

Goes back to the thing about being alone. I could never have done it. Running for miles doesn't sound like fun, but more than that, it's fucking isolating. Just me and my thoughts for however long, no thanks.

"So, no to the music cliques, cross country isn't really a jock thing, so that leaves us with what?"

"You're trying to group me?" she asks with a raised brow. Her voice is playful, and I smirk.

"Kids run in packs."

"Not all of them."

"So, you were a lone wolf?"

Brenna grins and then leans her butt against the desk. "I'm going to let you do the psychoanalyzing again."

She looks relaxed, and her smile is easy. It's so alluring that I have to fight back the urge to put my arms on both sides of the desk, trapping her there and leaning in to see if her lips would be easy against mine. I've imagined kissing her since our lunch together.

Last night, while I was in that shithole of a box reading my next script, I pictured her as the woman my character could be in love with, even if he doesn't have one. I saw her deep blue eyes and long red hair before me as I spoke my lines aloud.

After I slapped myself, I threw the script across the room,

which was about four feet, and mentally beat myself up because my character is single—as am I.

She's not in the plan. She's not a woman I need to think about like this. Brenna is a single mom who definitely doesn't need some asshole from Hollywood coming around to fuck things up for her. Stability is not what I will provide.

I slip into myself, using every skill I've honed over the years to keep from making a mistake or letting my dick do the thinking. "I see. I think you were an academic. You liked studying, reading, but did a sport to keep yourself from seeming like a nerd. Maybe even top of your class?"

"Definitely not, but you're somewhat close." Her head tilts to the side, and her gaze fixes on mine.

"Hmmm." I purse my lips. "Which part?"

"The academic part."

"I figured. No one wants to go to school to be a psychologist if they don't like learning."

She laughs softly, cheeks reddening in the most adorable way. "Not while raising two kids and being married to a man who is never home."

It's crazy. I don't think she understands how amazing that accomplishment is. "I didn't even finish college."

Brenna pushes off the desk and moves toward me. "And look at all you've done, Jacob."

"I make movies and play pretend all day." I need to sound like it doesn't matter. I need it not to matter what she thinks.

That was one of the last things my father ever said to me. On top of telling me I was worthless and stupid, he said that if I dropped out of school to pursue acting, then I was a disgrace to my mother.

I've never forgotten that. I've heard those words over and over again. I've worn them like a tattoo in my heart, reminding me that she would've thought I was a fool.

However, Brenna's voice is soft and comforting. "You make little kids believe that there's more in life than all the crap hands they've been dealt. That means something. It's . . . well, it's heroic."

"I'm not a hero, Brenna."

"Maybe not." She shrugs. "But to them, you are."

"My character is."

I am no one's hero. I'm a fuckup from Sugarloaf. I've done nothing other than land a role of a lifetime. I haven't been a good brother, uncle, or friend, and I damn sure was a piece-of-shit son. I'm smoke and mirrors, and glass always breaks. I'm a guy who is fighting so hard against the urge to pull this gorgeous woman into his arms and show her just how destructive he can be to the people around him.

"If you think that your being here today wasn't epic to every kid in that auditorium, then I don't know what is."

I do. I run my hand through my hair and turn my back on her. "Luke was a hero. He fought and died for this country. I give nothing. Trust me, that story about my father? That was only a fraction of it."

"We all have pasts, Jacob. Every one of us have made mistakes, but it's what we do now that matters. Luke wasn't a Saint. Believe me."

Luke was a good guy. He wasn't a man who would lust after a widow who lost everything.

"Maybe so, but he sure as fuck wasn't from the pits of hell."

"Sure, maybe Luke was a hero, in his own way. He fought for this country, and he died on a routine flight. A mechanical failure that cost him everything. It's easy for us to think what we do doesn't matter, but it does."

"I thought he died overseas?" I question.

"No, I've heard that a few times since being here. He was

home. He was supposed to be home that day and went into work. There was nothing heroic about it. Look at me, I'm a school psychologist. What the hell makes me special? Nothing. Except, to that kid who comes into my office when he's at his lowest and I give him something to hold on to, I might be everything. Heroes don't wear capes or save the world, they do the right thing. Heroes don't get to define their moments, the people they save do."

I feel her behind me, she's close, her words reaching inside me, pulling the broken man I've buried back up. I can't turn back until I can push the words from my head.

But then . . . I feel her hand.

Her soft touch is on my back, moving up to my shoulder. I lock my muscles, not allowing the sensations to elicit a reaction.

"Jacob," her soft voice beckons me to turn, "what you're doing . . ."

I can't help myself. I face her. Her eyes are soft, long lashes framing the bluest eyes I've ever seen. Neither of us speak.

Neither of us move.

We just stand as if we were acting out a scene that has been scripted.

And God do I have urges.

Her lips part, small breaths of air escaping them, and I can feel the tension. I could kiss her. In her eyes, I see the desire swimming. Brenna's chest rises and falls and then she swallows deep.

I don't know that I have ever wanted anything as much as I want her right now, but I can't just act. I hear my brother's warnings in my head as clearly as I can see her hesitation.

I remember her pulling back from me the other night, the apprehension that lingered when I willed her to do it with everything in me.

"I want to kiss you," I confess, wanting her to know she's not misreading anything.

Her breathing accelerates.

"I want to press my lips to yours so fucking much."

"I want . . ."

"What do you want, Brenna?"

She shifts a bit closer. I can feel her breasts just grazing my chest. "I want you to kiss me, but . . ."

The desperate part of me wants to reach out, grab her, and kiss her senseless, but I know that would be wrong.

Slowly, I bring my hand up, lightly curling my fingers around her wrist. Her pulse is quick, and I fight back a smile. I graze the skin on her arm, moving at a pace that should nominate me for sainthood. When I reach her neck, my thumb brushes her cheek, and she leans into my touch.

"But what?"

She doesn't answer, so I slide my other arm along her back, and her hands rest on my chest.

She's not ready. She can't do this. She's lost too much, and I'm being a selfish asshole.

"Do you feel that?" I ask as her palm settles over my heart-beat.

She nods.

"You make me feel this way. Just being near you . . . you're so damn beautiful. So smart. So brave. I know I'm a bastard for even thinking of kissing you, but I would be lying if I said I don't."

Her chin dips a bit, and I take a chance and gently press my lips to her forehead. "And you make me feel a lot more than I'm ready to feel. I can't . . ."

I lean back and use my hand to tilt her chin up to look at me. Once her lashes lift and those blue eyes meet mine, I know this isn't the right time. "I shouldn't push you."

"You're not."

I am.

My hands drop because if I keep touching her like this, I'm going to kiss her, and that would be so fucking wrong.

She takes a step back at the same time as I do. "I should go."

Brenna's hand is on her throat, and her head bobs. "Okay."

"I'll be back next week for auditions."

And I walk out of the room before I do something really fucking stupid.

twelve

"**B**ecause I'm a fucking idiot!" I reply back to Cybil when she asks *again* why I didn't kiss him.

"Let me get this straight, you like him, he tells you how gorgeous you are, he *tells* you that he wants to *kiss* you, and you say . . ."

"I want to, but I can't."

She rolls her eyes and groans. "You, my friend, are an idiot."

"Yeah, I know."

"Do you?"

I glare at her. "Yes, Cyb, I know."

"Because Jacob Arrowood is the hottest guy in the world. I'm sorry, even being married, I'd have kissed him before he could realize his mistake."

It must be nice to be Cybil. "Yeah? Even if Reggie were gone? Even if your entire life suddenly dropped out from beneath your feet? Because I can tell you that all that self-assured bullshit wouldn't be there anymore."

That's the thing, if Luke were alive and I never had to actually worry about it being a possibility, I would say the same shit.

Cybil's tone softens but still has that toughness. "Maybe not, but are you going to live your life this way? Are you always going to be afraid to put yourself out there? This is honestly the perfect first relationship or whatever after Luke."

My eyes go large and jaw drops open.

"No, listen to me," Cybil says quickly. "He's there for what? Four and a half more months. That's it. It's a good small window to get your feet wet. You know he's leaving. You know that he has no intention of staying there, and you're sure as hell not moving again. So, it's perfect."

I release a heavy sigh. "And then what?"

"He leaves and all that good sex and fun allows you to make way for the right guy. Look, you are going to want to date at some point, but that little town is not brimming with men, right?"

"Right, and I don't know that I would ever want to date someone from here."

Cybil smiles. "Exactly! So, this solves your problems. You can get back on that horse, get ridden well, and then find a new mount. It's like Daddy always says, you can learn to try or die trying."

I roll my eyes. "What the hell? That one makes no damn sense!"

She shrugs. "I'm not sure about that one either, but my point is that this scenario might just be perfect."

Perfect is not the word I'd use. "Cybil, I got married at eighteen because I got pregnant. I have never dated and don't know how casual even looks. I don't know that I can go from the love of my life to a guy who is leaving in four and a half months."

"You just said it. You don't know how to do casual, and this wouldn't have any other option than being that."

Maybe she's right or maybe she's insane. "All he said was that he wanted to kiss me. He didn't say anything else. Let's just . . . not get ahead of ourselves."

She laughs. "Yeah, Adonis wants to kiss you but nothing else, sure, we'll go with that."

"Who is Adonis?" Sebastian's voice sounds from the doorway.

Shit. I have no idea how much he heard.

"He's just a guy from Greek stories," I answer.

"And he wants to kiss you?"

I smile and shake my head. "No, your aunt is a mess and likes to be stupid."

He looks over at the phone, lips in a wide grin as he rushes to the bed. "Aunt Cybil!"

"Sebastian!"

The two of them chat, and I nibble on my thumbnail, pondering all that she said. Could I even do anything like that? I can't see it as a possibility. There is nothing about me that doesn't scream permanent. Not to mention, what the hell do I tell my kids? I'd be going on dates and being around Jacob when it wouldn't make sense. Sure, they have already expressed that they want me to be happy, but it's different for kids when it's reality.

Then I'm a therapist in a small town, and that has a certain level of respectability. Whether or not my personal life is any of their business, people tend to insert themselves where they want.

And they love to talk about Jacob and the Arrowood brothers.

"Mom! Aunt Cybil wants to come visit."

Oh, no. No way. I know her, and I know exactly why she wants to come. "I wish we could, but you have a lot to do if you get cast for the play."

"But I want to see Aunt Cybil. She would be great to practice with if I get a good part."

Cybil smiles, completely unrepentant for shamelessly using my son's love for her against me. "I would, honey. I sure would. I can be an excellent Sandy."

At that, I snort. "Yes, you're very pure."

"Daddy always said that purity is a rarity."

"Wow," I cut in quickly, "a daddy-ism that we can actually understand."

"Hush your mouth," Cybil snips back. "Listen, I have off work and Reggie is working on getting more flight hours so . . . I'm free as a bird. I would love to come see your little town and meet *all* your new friends!"

Even if I say no, Cybil will get on a plane and show up. She's insane and intrusive, and I love her more than I can say. Sometimes, when you're a military wife, your friends become like spouses. They're there for the good and bad times, hold you together when you're falling apart, and that's been Cybil for me. Maybe her coming here would be a good thing.

And then I remember what is probably prompting this visit.

"If I say no, would it matter?"

She shakes her head with a grin. "Not even a little, darling."

"Well, I guess I'll see you next week."

Sebastian runs out of the room, calling Mel's name to give her the news.

"I swear, Cyb, if you do anything . . ."

"I'm not going to do a damn thing, but this gives you several days to come up with a good excuse." She hangs up, and I know I'm in a world of trouble.

Ellie Arrowood is the luckiest woman to ever exist. That's all I can think as I sit in her beautiful home as her husband is washing the dishes.

Yup, he's washing the freaking dishes. *Without* being asked.

"You know you got the deluxe model on husbands, right?"

She looks behind her, smiles, and nods. "That I do. He also does the laundry."

"Well, that's just unfair."

"Maybe so, but it's a burden I'm willing to carry."

I laugh softly. Melanie is watching the baby while Hadley helps Sebastian with the play. It is really cute, and I love that even though they're not the same age, they seem to get along.

We chat a bit, and then Connor kisses her cheek. "I'm going out to work on a project."

"You mean on the tree house?"

"No, I mean to work in my office."

She laughs. "Okay. I love you."

"I love you," he replies as he leaves the room.

"Sorry about that," Ellie says to me once he's gone. "He's been working so hard on his new company and doing things with the girls."

I remember those days. "I get it. It's hard to juggle it all."

She nods. "But it's what we all must do, right?"

"Right. So, about the child you want to discuss . . ."

"Yes, thank you for reminding me." She grabs the paper from her stack and hands it to me. "I asked them to write a fictional story based on some part of themselves. I wanted them to blur the lines between fiction and non-fiction, forcing the reader to decipher where the author's truth blends with their imagination. This one, I don't know, it just . . ." She takes a pause. "I feel that there is very little fiction."

I start to read and can see why Ellie is worried. Here is a story about a girl whose father touches her, makes her feel uncomfortable, but she doesn't know what to do. I read, feeling the knot in my stomach tightening the farther I get.

"I think you were right to bring this to me," I tell her.

"The thing is, writing wise, this is brilliant. I can't tell if it's a call for help or she's an amazing writer who has an ability to make me believe the fiction. Do you know what I mean?"

I nod. "It was the assignment."

"Yes, and her set up is that she lives in a small dairy town, which she does. She has the same hair color, build, and some personality traits. That would be enough non-fiction for the assignment. I don't know, Brenna, it just made me uncomfortable, and I wanted to bring it to you and see what you thought. Also, I'm going to see Mrs. Symonds tomorrow to report it. I don't have much to go on, but I'd like you there as well."

"When girls write about things like this, it's often a call for help. I want to at least pick up the phone. You're doing the right thing."

Ellie breathes a long sigh. "What do we do now?"

"Well, I'm going to talk to a few of her teachers to see if there is anything else I should be aware of. If she's had anything in the past, it'll be in her file, and then Mrs. Symonds and I will talk to her as well as filing a report based on what she tells us."

"If you land on the last one, please tell me. I'd like to help her as well, plus, Sydney knows everyone in the judicial system here and can help us if we need it."

We may need all the help we can get. In a large city, dealing with child abuse is difficult, but I imagine that in a town where everyone knows everyone, it's even harder. Working in the district I did before, I only had one abuse case that we couldn't prove, and it about broke me.

Sebastian comes running in the room. "Can we go to Hadley's tree house?"

"If it's okay with Mrs. Arrowood."

Ellie smiles warmly. "Of course, Hadley, be careful and don't be bossy."

The little girl with beautiful green eyes bats her long lashes. "I'm not bossy."

A loud scoff comes from behind her. "That's a lie if I've ever heard one."

"Uncle Jake!" Hadley rushes toward him, wrapping her arms around his middle.

"Hi, my sweet little Hadleybutt."

"We're going out to the tree house!" Hadley exclaims.

"That's great. Listen, Sebastian, don't let this girl have an inch or she'll take a mile. Trust me, this goes for all women."

I roll my eyes. "That's not true, don't listen to him."

He squats in front of the two of them. "Are you practicing your lines?"

Sebastian nods. "Every day."

"Good. You ready for tomorrow?"

"I really hope I get the part."

Jacob doesn't give him false hope. He doesn't lie or offer promises. "Whoever does the best will be cast. I know you want the part, and no matter what part you get, I know that you'll try your best, right?"

"You mean if it's not what I audition for?"

"Not every actor is meant for the role they want. Sometimes, we have to do whatever we're asked in order to improve and grow. Like the role I took in that crappy movie you watched."

Sebastian's eyes grow wide. "You did that to learn? I thought maybe you were just broke."

Jacob laughs once. "I was that too, but I learned a lot about disappointment because I auditioned for the lead and didn't get it. I could've been angry and said screw it, but I didn't, and guess what?"

"What?" Hadley asks, as interested as Sebastian.

"The director of that crappy movie was Noah Frazier."

Sebastian's eyes widen. "You mean the same Noah Frazier who made *Navigator*?"

"The same one, and do you know why I probably got that part?"

He shakes his head.

Jacob grins. "Because I didn't complain once. I worked harder than any actor on set. I was there, even when it wasn't my day to shoot, so I could learn more, and Noah noticed. Never underestimate the value in working hard when no one is looking."

Hadley sighs heavily. "Come on, Sebastian, Uncle Jake isn't making sense. No one wants to work when no one is looking."

Ellie groans and looks heavenward. "You guys go and work on Sebastian's lines while I pretend you didn't say that."

What he just said makes me want to weep. He taught Sebastian a lesson that I hope he takes with him. I know he's only eleven, but that advice is gold no matter how old you are. My son may never be an actor, but he'll have to work at anything he wants to do in life.

The two kids rush off, the screen door slamming behind them.

I hear the scrape of the chair as Ellie stands so she can kiss his cheek. "I didn't know you were coming today."

"It's your night to feed me."

"You need to learn to cook."

"I have no running water, and you want me to cook in that thing?"

I let out a little giggle at the sound of exasperation in his voice.

Jacob's gaze finds mine, and that tingly feeling rushes over me. My breathing grows a bit labored as I wonder what it would be like to kiss him, to give into the want that is growing each time I see him. I imagine the way his hands would feel on my body, those soulful green eyes watching me touch him.

I swear he can see it all. It's as though he can read every thought, desire, and need that is racing through my head.

I blame Cybil for these thoughts.

"Jacob, you're going to have to figure it out because we aren't feeding you for the next four and a half months," Ellie says as she walks toward the cabinet.

Jacob raises one of his brows and turns to his sister-in-law. "I'm on a rotation, that was the deal for having to sleep in that damn thing."

"I said you could stay here a few nights," Ellie says with her brow raised.

"But if I did that, I'd have nothing to complain about or hold over your head. I prefer to eat and run."

"Well, next weekend you can go into town to the festival to get your own food."

He groans. "The hell I can. I'm not going to the festival."

"We're all going as a family, and that means you too, Jacob. This is all the time we have with you, and Hadley will be devastated if you don't go," she informs him and then turns to me. "Brenna, you and the kids are going, right? Do you want to come with us?"

"We are, but I'm pretty sure Sylvia and Dennis will want to come with us. They mentioned something about taking the kids for the weekend."

"Then we can all meet there and they can take them back to their place when we leave. It would be great for the kids. Melanie and Sebastian can hang out with Hadley and Austin. Plus, I'm sure you'd like time with people other than your in-laws."

Ellie knows all too well how crazy Sylvia is driving me. When she mentioned—demanded—we attend the fair, I was livid. I'm not a child, and I know she's needing to mother someone, but I can't handle it.

I'm trying, but my patience is wearing thin.

This morning, she came over before school to drop off clothing that was more "suitable" for Melanie. She let me know that I was giving her a bit too much freedom in her attire, and she found some things that were a little more modest.

I wanted to scream, but I smiled, took the clothes, and threw them in the basement still in the bags.

She can say that again, but then I look at Jacob. "I'm not sure . . ."

"Jacob, you will need to just go over there and pick them up, then they can't refuse us."

"Me?"

She nods. "Of course, you. Sebastian won't be able to resist."

"Ellie, that's not really necessary."

"No, but if the kids know this is the plan, neither of you can bail on us, so I'll be sure to make sure that part is covered.

You and Jacob can meet us since he knows the town better. It also gives you the perfect excuse to get time around people your age."

"I don't know . . ."

Jacob moves a bit closer. "I don't mind."

I look over, shocked. "What?"

"I'll get you guys on my way over. We can be outcasts together."

"You're *not* an outcast here."

He's like the second coming of Christ.

He laughs. "I assure you that, among my brothers, I am."

Ellie scoffs. "You are out of your mind. This town loves you all."

"They loved when we left."

"That might be true, but they're welcoming you all back with open arms." Ellie turns and goes back to the cooking. "I mean, you've been here a month and a half and there's still no press. It shows that they're either not impressed by you or they're willing to help you."

Jacob rolls his eyes. "Anyway, I'll get Brenna and the kids, and we'll meet everyone at the festival."

"I'm glad I have a say in this," I say under my breath.

He smirks and then leans closer, whispering, "If you're afraid to be alone with me . . ."

"I'm not scared at all." I'm fucking terrified.

"Good. It's a date."

thirteen

My phone is blaring for the tenth time, and I know if I ignore it again, my publicist will just keep calling. I love Catherine Cole. She's amazing at her job, but she's a pain in my ass.

"Hello, Cat."

"Oh, well, look who answered his phone. Hello, Jacob. I was starting to worry that once again, you ran out of the country again like when you disappeared for your brother's wedding without telling me."

"And face your wrath again? Never."

She laughs once. "Funny. Now, you have fifteen minutes to prepare yourself."

I glance out the wall of windows in my tiny shithole, wondering if she's going to appear out of thin air.

Catherine sighs in exasperation. "I'm not there, dummy. You have a conference call with Noah about scheduling the scenes he wants to reshoot, which you'd know about already if you had answered any calls, texts, or emails."

"Fuck."

"Yes, fuck. Fuck is a good word because you would have been fucked if I hadn't covered your ass for not returning emails."

"I forget about email."

"Yes, well, we'll talk about that when we have more time."

If one were to meet Catherine, they'd think she was a sweet, kind woman with dark brown eyes that seem almost like melted chocolate. What most never realize is that she has fangs, and she bites.

It's lucky for her that her husband, Jackson, also scares the fuck out of me, so I try not to piss her off. It keeps her fangs tucked away so I won't get bit . . . and then probably shot.

"It's why I pay you the big bucks. To keep me on my toes."

"Yes, I remind myself of that daily. It shouldn't be a long call, but he had a few concerns for the sequel. It might be nothing, but since *Navigator* did so well, we need *Flight Plan* to do better, and the trailer is rolling out soon."

The story of having a success. In this movie, I go up against my nemesis, who happens to be my brother, only I don't know that. Of course, we leave this movie off on an epic cliffhanger that will leave them panting to find out what comes next.

We are supposed to start shooting the third movie as soon as I'm back.

"Have you read the new script?" Catherine asks.

"I did. Did you?"

She clears her throat. "I am . . . trying, but it's . . . well . . . horrible."

"Oh, thank fucking God. I hate it."

"Me too!"

The two of us launch into a conversation about what a shit job this new writing team did with the third script, *Forced Landing*.

"I'm going to bring it up to Noah," I tell her. "If I can't get through it, there's a problem."

"Are you sure you want to do that?"

It's a risk, but Noah most likely has concerns as well. The one thing that sets him apart is his ability to see a script and just know. Now, we're all sort of contractually bound to this series of movies, but that doesn't mean he can't send a script back to the writing room.

"I think it's the right thing."

"I agree." Catherine takes a pause. "How are things in Sugarloaf?"

"Fine."

"Fine?"

I know better than to hide things from her. Not to mention, if she doesn't know about the dumb things I'm thinking, she can't protect me from them. It's a lesson she drills into all her clients.

"I met someone. Someone who I really shouldn't like, but I can't seem to stop myself. She has two kids, and I like them too—so much so that I'm directing the middle school play."

There's a silence, and I look down at the phone to see if she's still there.

"Hello?"

"I'm here," she says softly. "What's she like?"

Brenna's face comes into my mind, so perfect, so clear that I'd swear she was in front of me. Her long red hair falls around her shoulders, just grazing the tops of her breasts. Those blue eyes with flecks of yellow staring back at me, begging me to kiss her and yet not at the same time. I can see her smile, the way her face bunches up when she's truly happy.

Fuck. I'm in so much trouble.

"She's beautiful. She has the most gorgeous red hair, freckles so light on her face you have to really be close to see them, and her eyes are ones you get lost in. But that's not even the best parts of her. She's funny, smart as hell, and has been through a lot of shit but isn't jaded."

"Well, that was descriptive. I meant more like . . . is she crazy?"

I laugh. "No, she's not crazy. She's actually a therapist."

"Please tell me not yours."

"Fuck off."

"I'm just asking. Anyway, what about your timeline?"

"What about it?" I ask.

"Just . . . you know that you can't get involved with anyone, Jacob. I'm not saying that to be mean, but you know the way these things go. You're the hottest new actor in Hollywood, and the only reason you're getting this respite is because they think you're off the grid in Canada to prepare for *Forced Landing*. If they find out you're in the States and seeing someone? The press will hound her and the kids."

"I know."

"I know you do, but this is reality."

"And what about my life, Cat? Am I not allowed anything anymore?"

"Of course, you're allowed a life." She sighs. "I just don't want to see you hurt. My job is to protect you. That said, it sounds like you really like her."

It's not a question. Catherine has known me long enough to hear it. "I do."

"Then, who cares what I say? Go for it. You only get one life, Jacob. I'll be here to mitigate whatever the fallout is."

"I don't care about *my* fallout. I care about hers. She's a widow. She has two kids, and I'm not moving back here. Ever. I have four and a half months before I leave Sugarloaf, and I'm not going to end up like my brothers and put roots down in this godforsaken town. She'll be the one broken, so there's no going for anything."

"Famous last words."

I roll my eyes. "Look, I don't even know why I'm arguing because it doesn't matter. I'm going to focus on my career and not get involved anyway."

"You did say that."

"Why do I feel like you're mocking me?"

Catherine laughs. "Because I am. You know, in the last few years, you've never talked about a woman like this. Yeah, sure, you had those random hookups, and that one actress—whatever her name is—that you sort of liked, but I can hear a difference."

If she were in front of me, I'd flip her off. "We're friends, I like her kids, and we're working on the play together."

"Okay. Whatever you say." I think she's going to drop it, but then she says, "If it weren't something you were thinking about, you wouldn't have brought it up."

"Nothing is going to happen."

"I know. I believe you, Jacob. Truly. I mean, I don't at all, but—"

"But you're a pain in my ass."

She snorts. "Yes, and you're a walk in the park. Anyway, enough of this, I just got the email that Noah is on the line. I'll start the video call."

A few seconds later, Noah Frazier and Catherine's faces are on the screen.

"Jacob, it's great to see you again."

"Noah, same."

He smiles warmly. "How are things?"

"Good. You?"

A little girl's head pops up from behind him, smiling mischievously. He turns. "Aubrey! I am on a call, shut the door." His voice is firm, but she looks totally unfazed.

She walks in and does what he says. "You promised no work today and that you'd take me to the store."

"And I will, but you need to give me some time."

She tilts her head and then her eyes see the screen. "Is that Catherine?"

"Hey, sweetheart," Cat says. "Where is your mom?"

"She's out with Aunt Nicole. Noah promised he'd take me to the store so that I could get something Mom said I couldn't." Aubrey rests her elbows on the desk and then props her head on her fists so she takes up the whole screen.

Catherine chuckles. "How happy I'm sure she'll be."

She shrugs.

My phone pings with a text.

Catherine: Noah's girlfriend is my cousin-in-law. That's how Aubrey knows me. I used to represent Noah, but when they started dating, he went to another publicist.

Me: So, Noah left your company for another one, and now you have to work with him again because you represent me? How is that working for you?

Catherine: It happened years ago, so calm down. Besides, I would have broken the contract with him either way because of conflict of interest.

Aubrey speaks again. "Wait! You're the Navigator, aren't you?"

I smile. "I am."

"That's cool." She turns to Noah. "Can we please go before Mom gets back?"

"I'm sorry about this, guys," Noah says and then mutes the call as he talks to her.

Catherine laughs. "Kids."

"I have a niece about Aubrey's age, I get it." Hadley would be the same way if Connor were gone a lot. She adores him, needs him, and is attached to his hip when she can be.

Noah unmutes as Aubrey sits in the chair behind him with her arms crossed. "I'm back. I forgot that you're back home now. How's that going?"

Catherine answers for me. "He's directing the town's school play."

Noah's eyebrows shoot up, and he lets out a chuckle. "Really? Well. Wow. Good for you. How's that going?"

I'm not sure if being annoying is grounds for termination. "It's fine. We have auditions later today."

"The fun part . . . said no director ever."

"Any tips?" I might as well get advice where I can.

"Just follow your gut. Cast someone who will work hard if they're the lead. Talent is great, but hard work is better." Aubrey shifts and whispers in his ear. Noah sighs and then returns to the topic of the call. "Listen, I would love to shoot the shit, but that's not going to happen. I want us to go over some options of reshoots and talk about prep for the next movie. I know you're spending time in Pennsylvania, so coming out to the studio would be a pain in the ass, and honestly, I need to be home for a bit. What about if we work out a schedule sometime next month?"

I nod. "That's fine."

"Good. I appreciate it. I also wanted to see if you had questions about the script for *Forced Landing*."

"I do. I actually . . . I have issues."

"Yeah?"

"Noah, we've always been straight with each other. I respect you and your work not just as a director but also as an actor."

"I appreciate that," Noah says earnestly.

"But this script . . ."

"It's total shit?" he finishes.

I breathe a huge sigh of relief. "Yes, thank you."

"Don't thank me. I've spent the last three weeks making the writers redo it to where I'm happy with it. They should be done this week and then we'll send it out. We will not have a delay, so you'll have to work hard to get the new one down. As soon as we're sure it all ties in I'll need you to be ready to head to L.A. for any reshoots for *Flight Plan* when I call."

For a new script, one that's better, I'll do whatever it takes. "Of course."

"Good."

"Noah? Can we go shopping *now*?" Aubrey asks.

"One minute, sweetheart." He placates her and then turns back. "I have to go, but the biggest change to the series is that you're going to have a love interest. One that isn't fleeting and she'll carry through the rest of the movies."

"Really?" That was one of the big things that Noah wanted to leave out when the first movie was written.

"Yeah, the more I think about it, the more I want it. Once you get the script, you'll see. We're adding a redhead superhero female who is going to knock you on your ass. I gotta run. Talk to you soon and send me an email once you read it over."

He disconnects, and I'm left feeling as if my fictional life and real life are mirroring each other just a little too much.

fourteen

"**A**ll right, everyone." I clap my hands as all the kids settle down. "I was very impressed with the work you guys did today. There are some very talented people in this group, and I look forward to announcing the cast tomorrow."

They all look around with huge smiles.

A hand goes up. "Yes, Clarissa?"

"Can you tell us now if you know who will play the leads?"

"I can," I say and then pause. Again, the kids fidget in their seats. "But I won't."

A groan goes through the auditorium, and I fight back the urge to laugh. Now I see why Noah started acting less and directing more. This is fucking fun.

"Now, everyone head home and go over the script if you want, it'll help you prepare in case you're selected for another role than the one you auditioned for. Remember, there are only so many lead roles. It's not an insult if you're selected for something else. Every role, no matter how small, is important. After all, without the supporting cast, a play would be boring."

After the talk with Sebastian about taking roles you don't always want, I was taken back to the earlier parts of my career. When things were always bleak. In Hollywood, actors are a dime a dozen. I was unprepared for that reality. I got there, thinking I was hot shit and would get any role I wanted.

I was an idiot.

The kids get up, grab their stuff, and shuffle out, except for one.

"Hey, Jacob?"

"Sebastian, you did well today. I was impressed."

"You were?"

I nod. He has talent oozing out of him. I was worried that his passion for the theater meant he wouldn't be good, but thankfully, that wasn't the case. I could see the amount of work he put into the role, and I'd be a fool not to cast him.

"I was. Good job. How do you feel you did?"

He sighs and looks over at his mother, who is doing her best to ignore me and failing. "I think I did okay. I had fun, which Mom says is the most important thing."

"Your mother is very smart."

He smiles. "Don't tell her that."

I laugh. "Did you want to ask me something?"

He shifts his weight, and I can tell that whatever is on his mind, he doesn't want to really ask. "It's not a question."

"Okay."

"It's more . . . I heard something around school."

I lean against the stage. "Whatever you have on your mind, you can say it."

"All right. Here it is. I heard that you went on a date with my mom."

Okay, that definitely wasn't what I was expecting. "It wasn't a date, we had lunch to discuss the play."

"Everyone is saying you're dating her."

I let out a heavy breath. "I'm sorry they're giving you a hard time. We're not dating."

He shakes his head. "I heard her talking too."

Now my interest in piqued. "Yeah?"

"She was telling Aunt Cybil that she wanted to kiss you."

I could fucking do a jig right now, but I keep it together. "A lot of women want to kiss me," I say as a joke.

"You should ask her out."

"Sebastian . . ."

"No, I'm serious. She didn't smile a lot before. She was always sad and never wore makeup or did her hair. She does now. I think she likes you."

I smile, thinking of how hard this probably is for him. "I like your mom too."

"You have my permission to ask her out."

"I appreciate that."

He extends his hand. "Thanks for the talk."

I put my hand in his and shake. "I appreciate that we were able to settle this like gentlemen."

"If you hurt her . . ."

"I'll hurt myself," I promise. "Now, Saturday we're all going to the festival in town, and I'm picking the three of you up. How about we go fishing before it?"

Sebastian beams. "I'd like that."

"Me too, and thanks for the talk."

Sounding much too old for his eleven years, Sebastian smiles. "Any time."

I'm nervous.

I'm never nervous.

And, yet, here I am, standing outside Brenna's door, feeling like a sixteen-year-old kid about to pick up the girl who is way too pretty for him. Only I'm not going on a date. I'm not sixteen. And there will be no kiss at the end of tonight.

Not that I wouldn't give my left nut to have that be untrue.

I thank God for the years of acting classes and the roles where I had to be someone else because tonight will be the show of a lifetime.

Brenna and I will never be, so I have to pretend that what I told her in that classroom was a lie and that I'm completely uninterested in her in that way. It's just a night at a festival with a lot of freaking people.

I lift my hand to knock, but the door flies open. Melanie is there with a big smile. "Hey, Jacob."

"Hey, Mel."

She opens the door wider, waving her hand to come in. "Mom and Sebastian should be down soon. He was on the phone for hours telling all his friends in California that he got the part."

"He was the right Kenickie."

And he really was.

"He's really excited."

"As am I."

"So," Melanie says as she plops down on the couch, "what is this festival like?"

I'm really glad this was the question she asked. God only knows how I would have handled it if it were something about her mother.

"It's small, there will be a band, food, and rides. At least, that's what it was like when we were kids. Oh, and of course, they'll have the tractor pull."

She purses her lips. "A what?"

"Tractor pull. It's where tractors are suped up and try to pull a heavy sled as far as they can."

"That sounds . . ."

"Country?" I finish for her.

She laughs. "Just not something I've ever heard of."

"Really? Your dad did it."

Melanie's jaw falls slack. "He did?"

"Yeah, he was great at mechanics, and he put a ton of work into his tractor. I'm surprised he didn't talk about it."

"Dad didn't talk much about Sugarloaf. He was gone a lot, and when he was home, we were really his focus."

"It sounds like how it should've been," I say.

Melanie shrugs. "I guess."

"You don't sound so sure."

"I just, I feel like all these stories about him from when he was younger don't really make sense. It's nothing like the guy I knew. He was a pilot, disciplined, and super boring. He loved me and Sebastian, but he loved to fly the most. When he wasn't flying, he was preparing for it. I don't know . . ."

"You feel like you didn't know him that well?" I guess.

She pulls her red hair to the side and starts to braid it. "I knew what he wanted me to know."

"Is it like that with your mom?"

Melanie laughs softly. "No, definitely not. Mom is an open book. She tells us about when she was a kid and what it was like growing up in Minnesota."

I wonder why Luke didn't talk about his childhood. It's not like he grew up the way I did. His parents were more than loving, and from what I remember, he didn't want for much. Sure, he most likely had to help around the farm, but most of us did.

"Well, if there is anything you want to know, I'll do my best to fill you in, but you might just want to talk to your grandparents about him," I suggest.

"I bet they'd like that."

I smile. "I bet they would. I know when my mom died, my brothers and I would sit around and tell stories about her. It helped us feel like she wasn't really gone."

A few seconds later, Sebastian rushes in. We talk about the play, and he's going a mile a minute about how excited and grateful he is that I gave him the part he wanted.

"I promise I won't let you down," he promises.

"I know you won't."

The few kids who got the major roles all earned it. They clearly took this seriously and worked really hard to impress me. I followed Noah's advice to trust my gut, and I knew within the first two minutes of each audition which character the kid would be best as.

"I'm ready," Brenna announces as she enters the room, and my mouth goes dry.

Holy fucking shit.

She's wearing a white top and a jean skirt. It's simple. It's nothing that is even remotely trying to be sexy, but on her . . . it's like a million-dollar dress. The fabric clings to her in all the right places. Her hair, which is pulled to the side, is slightly curled at the bottoms, and her eyes—Jesus, they're like sapphires shining in the light.

"Great," I croak out and get to my feet.

She smiles softly. "Hey."

"Hey."

"Sorry I kept you waiting."

I shake my head. "You didn't. I just got here."

I would've waited an hour just to get to see her. I can't stop looking at her. I know we're in her living room with her kids, but no matter how much I tell myself to stop staring, my eyes won't obey.

Brenna looks down, her lower lip between her teeth.

Did she dress like this because she knew we'd be together? I know she feels the pull that I do. I can sense it when we're together, and it's getting harder to deny. I wonder if tonight feels as much like a date to her as it does for me.

Melanie clears her throat. "You look beautiful, Mom."

"Thanks." She still doesn't look up.

I feel like an ass for not saying that first.

"Come on, Sebastian, let's get our bags in the car so we're ready for Grandma and Grandpa."

I hear the door click closed and wait for her eyes to meet mine. When they do, I see the apprehension swimming in them. All the promises I made about staying away from her are gone. I can't do it. I want her more than a thirsty man needs water. "You look more than beautiful," I tell her.

"You look very handsome."

I smile and make my way toward her. Grabbing her hand, I pull it up to my lips and place a soft kiss against her knuckles. My voice is low and filled with desire. "I don't know how much longer I'm going to be able to resist kissing you, Brenna. Each time I see you, my fucking chest is tight and I want to pull you in my arms and make the ache ease."

"Jacob . . ."

"I love the sound of my name on your lips. Makes me want to know how they taste." Her breath hitches, and I know I've pushed as much as I can. I release her hand and step back. "I just wanted you to know that. Come on, let's go to the festival."

Her eyes are wide, and she blinks a few times. "Right. Festival." Brenna takes a step toward the stairs.

"Brenna?"

"Huh?"

"Where are you going?"

She looks around and then touches her lips. "I'm not sure."

I chuckle. "Come on, the door is that way."

I lead her out and hope I can manage to keep my hands to myself all night.

fifteen

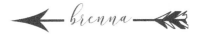

Now that my brain has returned from the scrambled state Jacob left it in, I'm having a great time. The kids are having a blast, running around, riding the rides, and seeing their friends.

This is the happiest I think I've seen them since we lived in Florida.

California was a rough time for them. Luke was deployed within two days of us arriving, and they never felt like they truly fit in. I don't know if it was the private school or if it was because they missed Pensacola, but it was hard for them.

And then Luke died.

Here, they have wide-open spaces, friends, and they fit in. It's nice to see.

Melanie rushes over and grips my arm. "Can I go watch the tractor pull?"

"Umm . . ."

"Please, Mom! Chrissy and Carrie Ann's brother is pulling in a few, and we want to go see if he wins."

I have no clue what she's talking about, but she seems really eager. "I guess, just make sure you have your phone on you."

She rolls her eyes. "Of course, Mom!"

Jacob leans in, his warm breath against my ear. "She'll be fine. They almost never end in a wreck where someone gets hurt."

I turn to him. "What?"

He laughs. "I'm kidding. I'm seriously surprised you know nothing of this. Luke was a champion one year."

"Oh, I've heard about it. He told me all about that year and how much the girls in this town helped him celebrate."

Jacob grins. "The girls are always the best part."

"Well, that's great, but *my* girl isn't going to be the best part."

"Point taken. Still, I'm sure she'll be fine."

I relax a little and nod. Melanie is a smart girl, and I was boy crazy at her age, so I can't really be surprised that she is too. Jacob and I walk through the carnival section, looking for Sebastian and Austin.

We spot them on one of the many spin-until-you-puke rides, both of them grinning and laughing as it whips them around and around.

"Declan used to make the four of us ride until we threw up."

"And you thought that was fun?"

"It was a rite of passage. Whoever hurled first had to do all the chores in the morning. We would eat until we were so full that we thought we couldn't make it to the ride, and then . . . then we manned up."

"I don't know what the hell is wrong with the Y chromosome."

He playfully nudges me. "We're not all that bad. We do have our advantages."

"Name one."

"We can open the jars you can't."

"I guess that's one. Give me five then," I challenge him.

"The jars count as one. We can reach things up on the shelf, carry heavy things—"

"I can carry heavy things."

He sighs. "Okay, fine, we can carry *very* heavy things. That's three. Hmm . . ." Jacob stares off to the side. "Orgasms."

I burst out laughing. "I assure you that we women can handle that on our own too."

"Oh, can you? Please enlighten me."

I smile and look away. "Next."

"Babies."

I'll give him that one—kind of. "You know, thanks to modern medicine, we don't really need you for that either. However, we do need the sperm, so I guess we kind of need you."

Jacob turns against the fence, facing the crowd, while I look at the ride. "You're making me feel rather insignificant."

"Has that ever happened before?"

"Nope."

"Welcome to the club of mortal men."

"I'm not sure I wanted to join this club."

I smile. "I bet not."

"Mom! Jacob! That was the best ride ever!" Sebastian grips the metal fence, breaking the playful conversation we were having.

"I'm glad."

"Can we go again?"

"Do you have enough tickets?" I ask.

Austin holds up a book. "Sean got us each a book so we could ride until we puked."

Jacob laughs. "That's the Arrowood way. We ride until we drop. Glad to see my brother is teaching the future how you do these small-town festivals."

The boys beam. "Can we keep going?"

"Sure. Just . . . try not to puke, Sebastian."

He elbows Austin. "I bet you I last longer than you."

Austin snorts. "You're on."

And a lifelong friendship has been born. Boys.

The two of them dash off to get back on the ride, and Jacob's hand grazes my arm. "The kids are going to ride again, how about we have some fun?"

My stomach dips as I wonder what his idea of fun is. "I don't know if we should go too far . . ."

"Come on, Brenna. Your in-laws went home already, you're out with a very handsome movie star. Don't think, just let yourself go for a minute." His hand is extended, waiting for me to decide. There's a part of me that knows this is a tipping point.

He's told me clear as day he wants to kiss me, but he hasn't, and each time he pulls away to protect me, I want it a bit more.

I thought I was going to melt to the floor today when he talked about his name on my lips.

If I go with him, I'm showing him that my heart is saying to let him lead.

Maybe Cybil is right. I could let myself feel again, knowing it'll never be anything serious. I could let the attraction be what it is and get my feet wet without letting my heart get tangled. Jacob wants me, and I want him. We're both adults, and . . .

And before I can talk myself into or out of it, my hand is in his.

He leads me to the Ferris wheel and hands the man a book of tickets. "We want to go until we don't have any more tickets and keep two cars in front and behind me empty, okay?"

The guy stares at Jacob. "Of course, Mr. Arrowood. I'm a huge fan. I loved your last movie. I can't wait for the new one."

Jacob is gracious and offers to sign the book of tickets. "Will that do?"

The operator nods. "Yeah, you can ride all night."

Jacob's warm hand engulfs mine as he helps me onto the ride. We get seated and start the climb. "What would you have done if I were afraid of heights?" I ask as we inch higher.

"I figured you might have mentioned that before we got in line."

"Fair point."

"You know that the rumors are going to fly about us now." Jacob leans back, his arm going behind me.

"They already are."

"The perks of a small town."

I grip the bar in front of me to keep from nestling myself against him. I want to. Oh, how much I want it, but I need to know what this is before we go down any road.

"What are we doing, Jacob?"

"Riding the Ferris wheel."

I laugh softly. "You know that's not what I'm asking."

"I'm not sure," he admits and then leans up, taking my hands in his before locking his gaze with mine. "I promised myself that I wouldn't feel this way. I have talked to my brothers and my publicist about how I know that my feelings for you are unfair. I'm leaving in a few months. I have a contract and a ridiculous filming schedule. The press. Crazy fans who are delusional about the amount of say they have in my life. None of that is fair to you. I'm able to live a very quiet existence in Sugarloaf because this town isn't impressed with me. The rest of the world thinks I'm hiding away in Canada. When I step back into the life I have, all the fucked-up shit comes with it. So, I'm not sure what we're doing, but I like you. I want to kiss you, touch you, be around you, and hear your voice. I wanted to direct a play just to make you and your kid happy. Whatever we're doing is up to you."

With my heart pounding so hard it might leave my chest, I lean forward and press my lips to his.

sixteen

The second her lips touch mine, it's like I become someone else. My hand cups her face, tilting it so I can get
a better angle. I kiss her like I'm a man who has gone
without seeing the sun and is getting his first glimpse of the
light. Her hands rest on my chest, and she lets out a breathy
moan. I feel us move up a little higher, and I hope the view of
us is obstructed enough that the entire town can't see me kissing her.

I'm not sure I would care if they could, though, since I
never want this kiss to stop.

As we glide around, I feel us starting to descend and pull
back. "Brenna."

Her lips are a little swollen, and her chest is heaving. "I'm
. . ."

"Don't say sorry. I'm only sorry we're on a ride and about
to go back down where too many people might see. Including
your kids."

That causes her to move farther back, hand on those lips I just kissed. "Oh my God."

I look around, seeing we're still not that close to the bottom. No one seems to be staring, which is either very good or they're trying not to appear like they saw. We go back around again, the wheel moving swiftly past the loading and unloading ramp since I bought five seats on the ride.

I watch the people and see the kids below, waving frantically. I lift my hand back to them and smile.

"I think we're fine," I tell her.

"I kissed you."

I raise a brow. "That you did, beautiful."

"I-I kissed you. Like, I just . . . kissed you."

"Brenna . . ."

She sits back, her eyes wide as she looks straight ahead. "I don't know what to say."

"This is the first time I've ever had someone react this way," I admit. "I'm not sure if I should be flattered my kiss left you a mess or worried."

"It was a good kiss," she admits.

"Yes, it was."

"I am just shocked that I did that."

I lean close, so she can feel the honesty in my words. "I liked it, and I'd very much like to kiss you again."

Hell, I'd like to kiss her everywhere. I'd like to do a lot more than that too. Maybe I can work this out of my system. She takes up so many of my thoughts that it's pathetic, but the reality is so much better.

Brenna runs her hands down her face. "I like you, Jacob. I like you, and that scares me because I haven't liked anyone other than my husband in a very long time. It's been over thirteen years since I kissed another man. The thing is, I liked kissing you too . . ."

"Don't say anything else," I stop her. "You don't have to. I get it." She isn't the kind of girl who is going to enter into some kind of weird relationship or whatever this is. I knew it, and I was still a fucking idiot. I don't want her to feel guilty or apologize. "Just know that I liked it."

"I have to say something, though. I liked it too, and you have no idea how much I want to do it again. But what does this mean?"

"I'm not really sure what you're asking."

"I mean, we become, what? Make-out buddies? Do we hook up and then just pretend nothing happened? I'm not sure I can be that girl. I have two kids, one who adores you and one who is a young woman who sees way too much. How do I explain whatever we're going to do to my kids when I don't understand it myself?"

And here is what Connor was talking about. "I'm not asking for anything."

She turns to me, taking my hands in hers. "I know you're not. It's me. Doing what I do for a living causes me to look at the entire thing. I analyze and overanalyze and then talk myself in circles. I'm asking though. What would this be?"

As much as I'd love nothing more than to tell her what I know will get her to agree, I won't do that. I won't ever be a man who uses women to get what he wants.

"I can't stay here, Brenna. So, whatever it is we do will have an end date."

She tries to smile, but it doesn't reach her eyes. "I figured."

"I will never lie to you. I won't make you think there's more if there's not. I want you. I have never wanted another woman like this. You consume my thoughts, but I can't promise you more than whatever we share while I'm living here."

"And I appreciate that. I just have to think about it. I don't know if I can do . . . that."

"I understand, but it's all I can offer."

Brenna and I lean back, going around another time.

After a few more turns, she speaks softly. "Every time I look at a Ferris wheel, I'm always going to remember this night and you."

"That's something. I wish it could be more."

She takes my hand and squeezes. "Don't say that. It's everything, Jacob. It's everything."

seventeen

I roll over for the hundredth time. I can't sleep. I can't stop thinking about Jacob. I feel his lips, taste the minty remnants from his tongue, and deep earthy scent of his cologne. It's too much. I'm too hot.

I sit up, toss the blanket off my legs, and sigh. "What am I going to do?"

My life has been a series of serious decisions. I've never been young and carefree. The night I met Luke changed the trajectory of the path I was on. There aren't any regrets, but what if it could be just a little different?

I could allow myself a chance to enjoy something that doesn't have to define my life. Dating—or whatever it is we'd call it—Jacob wouldn't give me roots, but it might allow me wings for a bit.

I look at the clock, seeing it's five in the morning. There's not a chance I'm going back to sleep, so I decide to take a walk. The kids are at my in-laws for the night and won't be home until later, which means the house is too quiet.

It's early summer, and I haven't gotten to see a sunrise in a long time. Devney said that there's a spot in the back of the property that has some of the best views of Sugarloaf Mountain. I might as well go see it instead of sitting around here and dwelling.

After making sure my sweater is wrapped tightly around me, I grab a blanket as well, and head out.

As I walk, the sky starts to brighten, and I just breathe.

My mind wanders as I make my way toward the creek that Devney said runs through the property. In the time that we've lived here, I've only ventured out this way twice. It's probably not my smartest idea to do it when no one is home to notice if I never make it back, but it's too late now.

Each step has my mind taking apart another moment of last night.

I kissed Jacob.

I didn't hesitate, I just leaned in and did it. It was my first, first kiss in thirteen years.

"I want you. I have never wanted another woman like this. You consume my thoughts, but I can't promise you more than whatever we share while I'm living here."

He wants me.

He wants me, and I want him, and we're both single adults.

The thing I keep going back to is that I only have one life. I've seen death take someone early. I'm sure Luke had regrets. There were things he wanted to do, we wanted to do, but we put them off. Each year that want slipped away as something else took precedence.

I don't want to ever look back on my life and wish I had chosen courage over fear.

Taking a chance with Jacob is the risk that might have the biggest reward.

The sounds of the creek start to become clearer, and then I freeze when I hear something.

"Damn it!"

My heart starts to race. I have no idea who would be out here this early, and on my land no less. Or at least, I think I'm on my land.

I really should've thought this through.

I start to turn, not wanting whoever it is to see me.

"Brenna?"

That voice. Jesus, please tell me that my mind conjured it because it's five in the morning, I didn't brush my hair, and I am wearing ratty old sweatpants and a US Navy shirt.

I hear squishing footsteps making their way toward me.

Don't turn around. Don't do it. Walk away.

"What are you doing out here?" Jacob's voice is not a hallucination, and he's right behind me. Great.

I turn, plastering a smile on my face. "Oh, you know, just . . . taking my morning stroll."

"You're out here every day?" he asks with a hint of skepticism.

"Sure! I love to get some fresh air before the world wakes up. Plus, the view of the mountain here is really spectacular first thing in the morning."

He nods slowly. "It is."

"What are you doing?" I volley back, hoping he doesn't hear the slight tinge of panic in my voice.

"Well, *every* morning, I come out here and fish."

And I would like to please throw myself off that mountain. "Every day?"

He smiles. "Every. Day."

Of course, he does. "We must just miss each other."

"Yes, that must be it. Don't worry, I'll adjust my plans to make sure we don't miss again."

"Right. You should . . . because I'm out here all the time. Like you are."

Jacob waits two seconds before he calls me out. "You're a terrible liar, Brenna. Don't go into acting."

I release a long sigh. "Fine. I couldn't sleep. Devney mentioned the sunrise over the mountain, and I—wait, am I on your land?"

He laughs. "You're on Arrowood land, yes, but not mine. It's a section where Sydney and Declan's butts up to yours. It has the best fishing, so I just use it without asking."

"How nice of you."

"It's the least they can do since I'm sleeping in that damn glorified trailer."

"Instead of?"

He shrugs. "Anywhere that's not mobile."

"It could be worse."

Jacob gives me a side glance. "You have no idea. Do you fish at all?"

I shake my head quickly. "Do you remember the whole fish guts aversion? I would be horrible at it."

"I bet you wouldn't. I bet that you could fish better than you think. Unless you're scared, of course."

There's a playful edge in his tone, one that instantly puts me at ease. This is what I like the most about being around him. He makes me smile and forget that my bedraggled attire isn't what I hoped he'd see me in the next time we crossed paths. I can either make the best of it or run away with my tail between my legs and pretend this never happened.

Since I'm not the run-away kind of girl, I go for the first.

"Are you challenging me?"

"Are you accepting?"

I smile because he's doing it to me now. "You're answering a question with a question."

"I wonder where I might have picked up that annoying habit."

Laughter escapes my lips, and I shake my head. "She must be a smart person, whoever she is."

"What makes you think it's a she?"

"All women are good at being evasive."

"Don't I know it," Jacob replies. "And here you are proving your point. Are you up for a little early morning fishing?"

I nod once. "Sure. I have no idea what I'm doing, but I might as well learn."

We walk side by side over to the area where he has a few blankets, a tackle box, a thermos, and a book.

"What are you reading?" I ask.

"It's a book on how to be a director."

"Really?" I ask.

"I've never done it, and I really don't want to let the kids down."

Could he be any sweeter? I don't think so.

"That's really amazing of you."

"What is?"

"That you care."

Jacob shrugs and then leans down to grab his pole. "Here, come cast the line."

"You only have one pole?"

"I wasn't exactly planning to have company at five in the morning."

Yeah, that makes sense. I wasn't planning to see anyone

either. Thank God I brushed my teeth.

"Of course. I just didn't want to ruin your morning."

"Brenna, you showing up here is the exact opposite of ruining my morning."

The breath escapes my lips in a rush, and I'm sure my cheeks match my hair. Not knowing what to say, I take the pole and mimic what I think I'm supposed to do.

"What are you doing?" Jacob asks with a laugh.

"I'm going to fish."

"Not like that you're not." He steps up behind me, covering my hand with his. The heat from his touch warms me everywhere. "Here, you hold it with your right hand like this. Loop your pointer finger on the line right here." He places it where he wants it. "Good. Don't let go of that or you can lose all your line."

I'm losing something.

"Now, with your other hand, you flip the bail."

"Flip the what?"

His warm chuckle vibrates against my neck, and his fingers wrap around my wrist, bringing it up to the place he's trying to get me to flip. "This is the bail."

What I wouldn't give to have someone bail me out of this right now. I'm swimming up shit's creek without a paddle. His arms are wrapped around me, holding me against his chest, and it feels too good.

"If you say so," I manage to sound halfway normal.

"I do. Okay, we are going to pull the rod back, and when we rock back forward, you're going to ease up on the line and let it go, okay?"

I nod and pray I can hold on to the rod, line, and my self-control.

When he does the motion, my back is flat against his chest,

and I want to close my eyes and sink into him. He's so warm, smells so good, and looks so unbelievably handsome that I'm not sure I will be able to keep from mounting him if he doesn't stop touching me soon.

Once we're stretched back, Jacob brings our arms forward, and I watch the hook go flying forward into the creek.

"I did it!"

When he speaks, his voice is low and filled with heat. "You did." I feel his lips graze the shell of my ear and then move toward my neck.

"Jacob," I say his name and shiver.

"Hmm?"

"You're kissing my neck."

The deep rumble sounds like a yes, and he keeps moving, his lips touching the skin there while his arms hold me to him.

He lifts his mouth just long enough. "Tell me to stop, Brenna."

I should. God, I know I should, but I just don't want to.

"I can't."

Jacob's nose moves against my skin back up to my ear. "Can't or don't want me to?"

I lean back, warmth flooding my veins. "Does it matter?"

"Yes. It matters."

My head is swimming, and I pull my wrist free, sliding it up behind me to wrap around his neck. "I don't want you to stop."

He brings his hand up my back, holding me while I hold him. "I couldn't sleep," he confesses. "I couldn't think of anything other than that kiss." Breathing is so hard right now. I can't think with his lips touching the sensitive skin behind my ear. "I want to kiss you."

"Me too."

He takes the pole from my other hand and throws it to the ground. Before I can register what he's doing, I'm turned around and in his arms.

Jacob takes a beat. I see the reluctance in his eyes. This time, it won't be a surprise or a spur-of-the-moment thing. This kiss will be purposeful, and I am ready for it.

"Kiss me, Jacob."

His hands cup my cheeks, and he moves slowly. Each second that passes has the anticipation growing. There's something inside me that knows this kiss will change me forever. We are crossing a line, changing the definitions of our relationship, and I'm giving up any pretenses that I don't want him.

I want everything of his.

My eyes flutter closed, and then the pressure is there. It isn't rough or eager, it's a slow and sweet kiss. One that shows he's considerate of more than just his want.

He tilts our heads, deepening the kiss, and my arms slide around his middle and then up his back. I hold tight, not wanting any distance between us. His tongue slides against mine in a dance that I didn't think I could learn the steps to, but Jacob leads me.

The worries I had about feeling guilt aren't here. Instead, it's acceptance and peace that settles around me.

This thing between us will never be more than a small sliver of time.

We'll never love, and we'll never have a future, but we can have now.

I can have him.

For whatever time we're allowed, I can let myself become whoever I want, and I'll figure the rest out later.

He pulls back, kissing me softly once more. "And that should've been our first kiss."

"What's the saying? First is the worst, second is the best?"

I tease.

"And what about the third?"

I lift up on my toes. "Third is where we kiss like grown-ups who are out without anyone in the world knowing."

"What does that mean?"

I gather every bit of courage I possess and lay it all out there. "It means I want more, Jacob. I want whatever we have. No promises. No questions."

His green eyes stare into mine, searching for something. "I respect you too much to use you."

"Is it using if I'm asking?"

"You understand what you're asking for?"

I nod.

"I need you to say it, Brenna. I need to know that you're going to be okay when I have to leave. I care about you and the kids. I don't want anyone . . ."

I bring my mouth to his, silencing whatever crap he was going to say. I'm very aware of what this will and won't be. There're just zero fucks left in me to care. The rational woman inside me knows that I'll end up crushed in a few months, but I've listened to her for too long.

He kisses me deeper, the passion between us is a hundred times stronger than it had been last night. This is all-consuming, and I'm on fire.

It's incredible kissing him. As though, if his lips were to break from mine, I might not survive it. I shove back the feelings that threaten to destroy the serenity I'm enjoying. Moving on isn't easy, but it sure feels good. It's new and my heart isn't separating in two, it's just growing to make room for this—for him.

He breaks the kiss but moves his lips down my neck and then back up to my ear. "I want you."

"You have no idea how much I want you."

"Take what you want, Brenna."

I move my hands down lower, seizing the control he's giving me. My hands grip the hem of his shirt, and I pull it up, revealing his chest.

Oh. My. Holy. Lord.

This man can't be real. And if he is, he sure as hell can't be attracted to me. But then I see his eyes. The way the thick black around the green is intensifying. There's no denying that he wants me, and I'm so out of my league.

I've been with one man. One. My whole life.

I met Luke, lost my virginity to him. My life wasn't about being seductive and alluring. I was lucky that I could put mascara on for my wedding. That's how inept I was.

It was over the last thirteen years that I learned how to really be a woman.

But right now, looking into his eyes, I feel breathtaking.

"Tell me what you're thinking," he coaxes.

"That this isn't real."

He presses his lips to mine. "Does that feel real?"

"Yes."

"What else?"

I'm torn on how honest to be, but at this point, I'm not sure I could stop the words. "That I won't be . . ."

"Be what?" he asks after a few seconds of silence.

"Be what you're expecting."

eighteen

Is she out of her mind? She's everything I want and don't deserve. Brenna is beyond beautiful, kind, and trusting. Every ounce of me knows that I'm a fucking bastard for doing this, but I want her more than my conscience wants me to stop.

I take her face in my hands, waiting until those blue eyes lock on to mine. "I don't know what you think I expect, but all I want is you."

Her hands move to my chest, resting over my heart. "I've only been with one man. I'm . . . I'm not sure that I'm very good at any of this."

I want to laugh, but I'm not stupid enough to do that. "Brenna, it's been a really long time since I've been with anyone. So, if you want to talk about expectations, you have no clue what I'm worried about being with you. I worry that you think I'm some fantasy and you're going to be disappointed when you realize I'm just a fucking man."

She lifts on to her toes, lips just brushing against mine. "I guess it's a good thing I prefer reality and real men."

I grin. "Me too."

And then I kiss her. I tilt her head, giving myself the best angle, and she melts against my chest. I move us back and then pull her down to the blanket. She breaks the kiss and smiles. "I'm glad you had a blanket."

"I am too."

"Did you plan this?"

I laugh. "No, but I'm happy I was prepared."

Brenna's smile grows. "This feels like a dream. You and I out walking in the sunrise and finding each other."

She's sitting up on her knees as I lean on my elbow. "I like it when you smile."

"You make me smile a lot."

"Good. I'd like to make you do other things."

"Oh? Like what?"

I lean up so we're face to face. "I'd like to make you moan."

"I'm sure I'd like that."

"Oh, I know I would. Let's see how long it takes me."

I press my lips to the hollow of her neck with the intent of slowly making my way toward her ear, which is what made her moan last time. I kiss her. "One." I kiss her again, just a bit higher. "Two." I move up again. "Three." Her breath is coming faster now as I move my hands down her shoulders to her chest. The soft moan she makes when my hands graze her nipples spurs me on. "Four," I say against her ear. "I bet I can do better."

"Jacob . . ."

"What? Tell me what you need."

The low grumble in her voice would've brought me to the

ground if I weren't already there. "You. Please . . ."

Jesus Christ. I'm so fucked it's not even funny. I know that what I'm doing is stupid. I'm leaving here, come hell or high water, and she's already pierced some part of my heart. I think of her constantly and search for ways to spend time with her.

She makes me smile. She gives me hope that maybe I'm not destined to live my life alone like my father did. Brenna sees me as the man I want to be instead of the man I forced myself to become.

She may need me, but the woman *owns* me.

"You have me, Brenna. Fucking hell, you have me," I confess before the need to touch her skin and get lost in her is too great. "Tell me if you want me to stop," I say, praying that she doesn't do it.

"Don't."

"Thank God." I climb higher and touch the silky, warm skin that had been hidden under the shirt. "I want to see you." Brenna's eyes meet mine, the heat flames higher between us, and then her dark lashes fall. My lips slide along the column of her neck. "I want to touch you and kiss you everywhere."

"Jacob . . ." Her voice is soft, alluring, and I want to drown in it.

Her fingers slide into my hair as my mouth gets to the shell of her ear. "Tell me, Brenna, what do you want?"

I feel the way she tenses before her hands slide up my chest. "This. Us. You."

"Oh, beautiful, you have me at your mercy."

And she does. In this moment, I'm hers, and I don't know that I'll ever get all of myself back.

My fingers grip the hem of her shirt, lifting unhurriedly, our eyes find each other as I start to bring it higher. She nods, giving me the go ahead.

Slowly, I reveal the most perfect pair of tits I've ever seen.

I toss the shirt over to where mine is. "You're so beautiful. So fucking perfect. Tell me what you want, sweet girl."

I need her to keep giving me permission.

"Touch me."

I move my hands back to her breasts, watching her face as I tweak her nipple between my thumb and forefinger.

"Yes." She breathes the word as her head falls to my shoulder.

I guide her to the ground, knowing that, to really explore her, I need to be free to move when and where I want. The sun isn't fully up yet, but the light it casts around us makes her look ethereal. Her dark red hair shines, and I swear, if I could paint, this is what I would immortalize on my wall.

I lean down, wanting to kiss her, wishing I never had to stop. My hand moves down her body, kneading her breasts, and then I slide down, my lips trailing a path to where my hands are. I lick around her nipple as her fingers glide through my hair.

She tastes like heaven and sunshine. I'll never fucking forget this. No matter what or who comes into my life, Brenna Allen has cemented herself in my head. This is why men write songs and poetry. It's shit like this. The girls who we shouldn't touch but who allow us in for a minute. The women who remind us what it's like to have a heart.

"You're going to ruin me," I tell her.

"Believe me, you're going to destroy me."

"I don't know that I care if I destroy you for another man."

I need more of her. I need all of her.

"Then do your worst," she challenges.

She should've never said that because my worst is going to wreck us both.

I lean back just far enough to pull her pants and underwear

down. After I get them off, I pull her knees apart, seeing her arousal clearly. My fingers move to the inside of her legs, and her trembling makes me grin.

Our eyes meet, my heart falters as I say words that I know will change everything. "I'm going to make you mine, sweet girl."

My lips move to the inside of her knee, trailing wet kisses along her skin. I go higher, my tongue sliding up her thigh, going higher until I get to right where I want to be. Her fingers grip the blanket as her breathing becomes more labored. "Please, Jacob. Please don't make me wait."

She gasps and moans as I lick her clit. She's so responsive that it makes me want to learn every bit of her and drive her to the brink, bring her back down, and do it again. I feast on her, loving her taste and the way her hips move as I find a new spot or motion that makes her feel good.

Her muscles tighten, and I move my tongue faster, sliding against her clit harder, adding pressure as she whispers my name. I don't know if I've ever felt so fucking turned on before. Just the idea of being inside her after I make her come is almost enough to make me blow my load. I'm so fucking hard.

"Oh, God. Jacob. I—I! Oh!" I flick her clit faster, moving my tongue and varying the pressure, needing her to come before I embarrass myself. "Yes!" she screams, and I keep going, loving the incoherent sounds that are coming from her lips.

Once her legs fall limp, I move, climbing up to her, and I can't resist licking her nipple again. "Well, I'm two for two."

Her chest heaves as she tries to calm her breathing. "This is a game I'm definitely willing to let you win."

I don't know how much longer I can wait to be inside her. "Brenna," I say softly. "I need . . . I need to know if you want to stop."

Her hand reaches up to my cheek, brushing the stubble from yesterday that has grown in. "No, I don't want you to stop." She moves her hand between us and rubs my cock. "I know what this is. I'm not going into it with my eyes closed, Jacob. I want this . . . whatever it is for however long we have."

Now it's my lungs that draw to get air. "I won't ever lie."

"I know."

"And we can't tell people."

The smile is a mix of understanding and disappointment. "I know that too."

"It's because . . ."

"I understand. You make me feel beautiful, and you make everything not hurt. I told you, I'm not blind to what we are and what the rules are. Now, the sun is coming up, and I would really like it if you would make love to me."

I am the luckiest son of a bitch who ever lived. I lean down, kissing her lips, and she pushes my pants down. I kick them off and when I feel her damp heat against my cock, I have to mentally sing a nursery rhyme to stop myself from losing it.

Then it hits me. I don't fucking have a condom. "Brenna, I don't have protection."

Her lips part, and she groans in frustration. "Are you clean?"

I nod. "I get tested every six months, but I haven't been with anyone in a few years."

"I've only ever been with Luke, and I had an IUD put in about four years ago."

There's a level of trust that's passed between us. One that I'm not sure I'm ready to process. "Are you okay with this?"

She nods. "I think, if you don't take me in about thirty seconds, I'm going to explode."

"Thank fucking God," I say as I push forward.

And then, when I'm inside her, I realize that heaven is real, and I'm definitely going to hell when I lose her.

nineteen

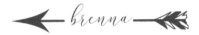

His fingers are making patterns along my spine as we lie on the blanket by the water with the sun just now peeking over the trees. My head is on his chest, and his sweatshirt is draped over us. A myriad of feelings swirl together inside me, each passing as quickly as it appears.

I had really great sex—with Jacob.

Just that brings a hundred feelings that I can't name.

I was so worried, but he soothed all that away, telling me how beautiful I was, kissing the stretch marks on my stomach, and saying how they only made me more breathtaking to him.

Jacob could have any woman in the world, and yet, he chose me.

I snuggle in a little tighter, loving how I fit against him while also knowing I need to distance myself.

"I should get back," I say, but he pulls me tighter.

"Just a few more minutes."

I smile and sigh. "I want to stay a lot longer, but the kids will be coming home soon, and I need to shower."

Jacob kisses the top of my head. "All right, that's a good reason."

Forcing myself up, I pull the shirt, clutching it to my chest. Then I grab my clothes and throw them back on. Jacob lies on the ground, hand behind his head, fully naked.

He is so damn beautiful it should be a sin.

"Like what you see?" he asks in a taunting tone.

"Maybe."

He chuckles. "Anytime you want to meet up, you let me know."

I grin and then crawl toward him. "I will."

"You will what? Want me or let me know?"

I give him a lusty kiss and then pull back. "I guess you'll have to wait to find out."

Jacob grabs me to him and then rolls us so he's on top. "I could always take you again now. Make sure that this wasn't just once."

I would like that very much, but my kids will freak out if I'm not there when they're dropped off. Plus, there will be questions, lots of them, and I don't want to lie—because I suck at it. "I wish I could, but I really do need to get back."

He sighs, kisses me again, and then helps me up. Once I'm standing, he grabs his pants and pulls them on. "Come on, I'll walk you back."

"You don't have to do that . . ."

"Do you know which direction the house is?"

I purse my lips. "Not really."

"Then I think it's a good idea. Plus, I want to."

That's sweet. I smile and nod as he gets himself presentable. Not that him fully naked is not damn near perfect, just not for walking me back. Heaven knows my in-laws like to surprise me with breakfast randomly, and that would be quite a sight at the house.

Once he's dressed, he throws one arm around my shoulders, tucking me safely against his chest. I really missed this. The feeling of being cherished and held. I hadn't realized just how much the loss of something so simple would affect me.

It was a turning point in my grief, one I didn't even think I needed. The entire time, I was in the moment with him. I could only think, see, and feel Jacob. Yes, the sex was beyond amazing, but so was the way he cared for me.

Not once did I feel uncomfortable or unsure. He took his time to ensure that I was completely okay with what we were doing. It means a lot to me that he was so wonderful.

As we stroll, I look up at him. "Thank you, Jacob."

His brows knit together, and we stop. "For what?"

"Just making this all easy for me. I don't have to guess or wonder with you, and whether or not you believe me—it matters. The last eleven months haven't been easy for us. I've struggled with if or when I'd be willing to do this. Well, any of it. If I could ever let another man in without thinking of Luke."

He clears his throat. "Right. I . . . I'm not really sure what to say."

"I didn't, if that's what you're wondering. All I thought about was you and me and how perfect this was. I know it means nothing more than what it was—sex, but still you made everything great."

"Brenna . . ."

"No, please. You don't have to say anything. In fact, I'd rather you don't. Let this be what it was, and . . . like I said, no promises."

If he says something to agree with me, then it will probably bother me. If he says something that contradicts what I'm telling myself, then that will be a disaster. I'll skip both options and stay in a safe place.

"Can I ask when I can see you again?" He pulls me into his arms and smiles.

"I'll see you tomorrow at rehearsals."

He nods. "That you will."

"Where we will pretend we haven't spent a morning naked in the woods."

Jacob laughs. "I'm very good at pretending."

"I'll need to remember that."

We start to walk again, and when I can just make out the outline of the house, I stop, knowing I need to say goodbye to him and wanting nothing other than to bring him inside. I step closer to the house, but he grabs my wrist, and I press myself closer to him.

"I know you don't want me to say anything, but I need to say that what we shared today wasn't just some casual sex. I care about you, and I care about your kids. I'm not saying that we can have more, but you're not just some nameless girl, okay?"

There are so many questions I want to ask, but I can't let my heart get tangled in this web. It's not good for anyone, especially me.

"Okay."

"I mean it."

And I believe him, but I'm on dangerous ground here. "I know you do, but I have to go."

His eyes fill with heat again as he keeps me there, hands firm against my back as he kisses me. "I'll see you tomorrow."

I smile, and my stomach does a little flip. "I'll see you tomorrow."

And then I turn and walk away, refusing to look back. I have to always keep my eyes forward, even when I want nothing more than to look back.

"Sugar, I have returned to you!" Cybil's voice echoes from the other room, and I drop my hairbrush and rush out.

"Cyb? What? How? You're here!"

She looks like she just walked off a magazine shoot and is grinning her wide grin. "I took the red-eye so I could be here right away! I can only stay two nights, but I came!"

Two nights with my best friend. Two nights I need desperately.

"You sure did! And you didn't call!" I say as I rush forward to hug her.

As soon as her arms are around me, the tears form. So much has happened in the last three hours. This is just too much. I start to cry, unrelenting and ugly tears as Cybil holds me to her. "Oh Lord, honey, I knew you'd be happy to see me, but not crying like this."

"Cyb." I hiccup. "I'm so stupid."

She pushes my shoulders back and then guides me to the couch. "It's a good thing I came out. I know stupid and how to fix it. Tell me . . ." I look up, and she gasps. "You had sex!"

"What?"

"You had sex with Jacob! I can see it in your eyes."

I release a loud huff and then wipe my tears back. "You can't see sex in someone's eyes."

"Maybe not, but I sure as hell know it's true."

"I did."

Cybil squeaks. "When? How? Where? Most important, was he hung? I mean, are we talking like a horse or more like a small dog? I'm hoping for the horse because it would be a shame if he was sporting a small pecker. Remember that model that we liked? We all saw a full frontal, and he was *small*. So disappointing. If I were him, I would've had that thing photoshopped to be much bigger. CGI that shit or something. Oh, and was he good? Did you at least have an orgasm or did you have to fake it?"

There is so much to unpack in that little tirade. "Today, literally two hours ago. In the woods after he taught me how to fish—kind of—and as for the rest of your questions . . . shut up."

She blinks rapidly. "So, it's new. Okay. No wonder you're a bit raw—in more ways than one." Cybil grins.

"Really?"

"I'm sorry, I'm a little shocked, which is what I'm thinking has you all twisted like a pancake."

"Pretzel," I correct.

"Same shit. Listen, you had sex so, of course, you're going to need to cry a bit. It's okay. You answered all the stupid questions . . . what about the peen?"

I groan, head falling back against the couch. "*Cybil.*"

"It was small. So sad."

"He was not small," I correct her.

"Oh, so he was hung?"

"He was amazing. He was perfect, and I'm an idiot."

She sits beside me, watching me. "You're not an idiot, Bren. You're a woman who has had a shit ass year. Besides, I'm here now, and Daddy always said that a friend in need needs to have a friend with deeds or was it . . . a friend in deed? I can't remember."

"I can't keep up with you."

"It's irrelevant. I'm here, and I will save you from yourself."

"I have no hope."

She waves her hand in front of me. "Please, you may be able to fix others, but you're a damn mess when it comes to your own issues."

"You're the one who told me to do this with him! And look at me."

"Yes, look at you!" Cybil gets to her feet. "You're alive. You're glowing. You had an orgasm! What a shit friend I am."

"You're missing what's wrong."

Cybil lifts both brows. "Which is?"

I open my mouth to speak, but the words die on my tongue. What is the problem? I'm not sure. I'm confused and worried that this will end badly, but then I know how it will end. He's already told me, and I'm well aware of it. I'm the one who offered myself up on a platter. I said no promises, so what exactly am I worried about?

"You know, I don't know."

"I'll tell you what. It's that you are too damn self-aware. You know all the complications in every situation, and your mind can't ever just be. You're looking for problems because you always have to fix something or someone or your damn self."

I stare at her, wishing I could deny it.

"Exactly!" Cybil says with glee. "You can't tell me I'm wrong. You had sex with Jacob, relish in it! Enjoy your life, Brenna. Have some damn fun before you find the next Mr. Perfect and you're hating that you didn't do this."

The breath leaves my lungs in a loud explosion. "And what if I fall in love with him?"

"Could you?"

"Yes."

She sits back beside me, taking my hand in hers. "Then you do whatever you can to avoid it, and if it does happen, be prepared for me to come out here, hold you as you cry, and tell you it'll be okay because, Brenna?"

I look up at her. "Yes?"

"It will be okay. It always works out in the end."

I really hope she's right.

twenty

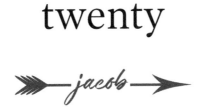

After a few deep breaths, I knock on the door of Brenna's house. When it flies open, it's not her standing there or one of her kids, but a gorgeous blonde with a big smile.

"Well, hello there."

"Hello?"

"You're looking for Brenna, I assume? You are a lucky man, Jacob Arrowood. If I weren't married to the most gorgeous man in the world, I might just want to fight her for you."

I have no idea who this person is, but she definitely knows who I am.

"I'm sorry, but you are?"

She laughs. "I'm Cybil, her very nosey best friend who is very much on your side, but we'll keep that last part between us, all right?"

"Sure."

Sebastian comes running to the door. "You're coming too?"

"You guys are going out?"

Cybil rubs the top of his head. "You go let your mama know that someone is at the door and she should come." She drops down and whispers. "But don't tell her who it is. Let's let it be a surprise!"

He runs off, and she opens the door wider. "Come on in. We were just heading out for some fun since I leave first thing in the morning to head back to California."

I nod. "Where do you live in California?"

I really hope it's not Hollywood. If so, I'm in deep shit and my entire existence here is about to be screwed. Not that I'm not walking a tightrope daily as it is. It's been a few weeks, and thankfully, I haven't been outed, but who knows how much longer that's going to last.

"We're stationed at Lemoore. You see, Luke and my husband, Reggie, were best friends and basically spent their entire careers alongside one another."

There's a slight bit of relief. "I see."

Cybil sits on the couch and smiles. "So, tell me, how hard is it being out here instead of Hollywood?"

"It's an adjustment."

She laughs. "I'd say. I suggested we order food, and Brenna just laughed at me because there was nothing that delivers."

That part definitely sucks. "It's nice for privacy."

"Yes, lots of woods and such. Probably a stream or a creek near too?"

The hair on the back of my neck prickles. She knows. Of course, she knows, she's her best friend.

"Yes, there are lots of woods and a creek."

Cybil nods. "Do you guys have lots of fishing?"

I laugh once. "Yes, fishing is something a lot of people around here do."

"I bet they often catch a really beautiful fish then. I hope you aren't the kind that tosses the good ones back."

One would have to be stupid not to hear the meaning in her words. "I think there's often an understanding between the fish and the fisherman, don't you?"

Cybil's lips turn up. "You're right, and Daddy always said that there's no business in the business of others."

What? I look at her, trying to take apart the statement so I can respond, but thankfully, Brenna rushes in. She's wearing a pair of yoga pants and tank top. Half her hair wet and piled up on the top of her head, and the other part down and dry. "Who is it? Oh. Jacob." She pulls the clip free, letting it all fall down. "I was . . . I wasn't expecting you."

I get to my feet and smile. "Sorry to barge in."

"No, it's totally fine. I was getting ready and didn't know it was you." She glares at Cybil.

"I was driving by and wanted to ask if I could take Sebastian out, but I see you guys are busy."

Brenna tucks her hair behind her ear. "That's sweet, but Cybil leaves tomorrow, so we were going to that new drive-in a few towns over to see a movie. Maybe you guys can do something later this week?"

"Sure. That would be great."

Cybil's eyes move back and forth between us, and then she clears her throat. "Bren, honey, I'm really thinking this jet lag is too much."

"What?"

"Yeah, you know, I'm tired as all hell, and I don't know that I can handle a movie. I'd much rather just stay home with the kids."

Brenna blinks a few times. "Of course. It's fine if we stay

here."

She walks toward me and places her hand on my arm. "Jacob, would you mind taking Brenna to see the movie? She was so excited about it, and it would break my heart if she missed out. The kids didn't really want to see it, but I was using the guilt trip that I'm infamous for." She laughs. "Brenna, you don't mind if I get a little quality time with my niece and nephew alone, do you?"

Her jaw is clenched so tight I can hear her teeth grinding, but there is a smile on her lips. "Cybil . . ."

She clasps her hands in front of her. "Oh, sugar, you're the best. You can go with Jacob, see that movie you were talking about, and the kids and I will hang here and talk about you." I want to say something, but before I can, Cybil grabs a large basket and shoves it in my arms. "Here's all the food, and the tickets cost me a fortune so you have to go and not waste this chance. You don't mind taking Brenna, do you?"

"No, but I'm not sure—"

"Well, I am." Cybil walks over to Brenna, pushing her toward me. "You guys go. The kids and I will be just fine."

Brenna looks like she's ready to kill her friend. "I'm not even ready!"

"Jacob, can you wait a few minutes?"

This was not at all what I showed up here for, but there's a part of me that's sort of glad this is how it's ending up. This morning, when I was at the creek, I waited for her. I kept thinking that maybe she'd show and we could spend a little more time together.

Which then led to me spending all day coming up with some fucking reason to see her and talk about what happened.

Brenna turns to me. "I'm so sorry. You don't have to do any of this."

"What if I want to?"

Her head jerks back. "You want to take me to a movie? Tonight?"

I think about the talk I had with Sebastian and how he thought it would be good if I asked his mother out. "Yes. I'd like that. It wasn't exactly what either of us expected, but if you want to see the movie, I'd like to take you."

She gives her best friend a dirty look, and then her eyes turn back to me. "You're sure? God, I feel like you just got bullied into going out with me."

I want to feel her skin beneath my fingers, kiss her lips to show her that I'm very sure, and soak up every possible minute I have with her. Our time is limited, and I don't want to waste any of it.

"I'm sure, Brenna. Go get ready, I'll wait."

She releases a deep sigh and then smiles. "All right."

I wink. "Go, we don't want to be late. The previews are the best part."

The drive-in is about an hour away, and the ride is quiet, but it isn't uncomfortably so. We listen to the radio, talk a little about the weather, and that's it.

When we get there, the sun is just fully setting and we have probably another ten minutes before the movie starts. I give the tickets to the attendant, who thankfully doesn't recognize me with my hoodie up. Once we're in, I find a spot way in the back where we have total seclusion.

"Do you have binoculars in the glovebox?" Brenna asks, looking around.

"What? Of course not."

"We're going to need them to see the movie from back here."

I smile, but it isn't the relaxed one I normally wear. "We're not close to Sugarloaf. If I'm spotted . . ."

"Right."

"As soon as the movie starts, we can pull up closer."

I can feel the disappointment rolling off her. There's another option. I reach behind the seat and grab Sean's baseball hat and my sunglasses. I pull my hood up over the hat and slip the glasses on.

Brenna bursts out laughing. "You think that's less conspicuous?"

"We can move up now."

"And have every person here wondering what idiot is wearing sunglasses when there is no sun?"

"I'm trying here."

She shakes her head. "It's fine, Jacob. We can stay back here or you could put the top up so we won't be seen easily at all."

Yeah, that was probably a better option. "But a drive-in movie is always better in a convertible."

Brenna turns her head while resting it on the back of the seat. "I'll have to take your word for it."

The spotlights around the parking lot go off, and the screen glows white. Fuck this. If she wants to see the movie, then that's what will happen. I move the car, keeping the lights off and hoping it won't draw attention to the car, and grab the best spot open I can find.

Brenna's hand finds mine, and she squeezes. "You didn't have to do that."

"Yeah I did."

She rests her head on my shoulder, and my heart thumps

loudly. This feeling that she stirs inside me is growing stronger each day. Brenna is the girl who could make it all so easy to give it up.

The previews start, and there is my face.

Her head lifts, and I watch her watching the screen. I know this scene by heart because it's where everything shifts for my character. I could close my eyes and see it all. We must've reshot this one part a hundred times from different angles. I'm proud of this part. I dug deep, remembered all the fear of being a small boy and wishing there was someone to save me. Seeing it through Brenna's eyes has me on the edge of my seat.

There's a slight lift to her lips as my voice comes through the car speakers.

"I won't let you die!" I yell as I'm unable to get the wings on my suit to work. *"You hear me, kid? I won't let anything happen. Do you trust me?"*

The boy nods.

"Give me your hand, and I'll pull you up."

He tries to let go but slips. *"I can't!"* I try once more to get the button to initiate the suit, but it fails again.

"You can. You have to believe that you're strong enough. You have to remember that no one other than yourself is capable of telling you that you can't. I'm here, and I won't let you fall, but you have to reach for me."

I hear Brenna's breath catch as she watches.

"You promise?"

"I promise."

The boy steels himself at the same time as I do. I'm on the side of the building, reaching my hand out to him. *"Trust me."*

He extends his hand once more and when our fingers touch, I lose him.

"No!" Brenna gasps quietly.

It's a crushing scene, one that shifts the entire plot of the movie. The rest of the preview is only a few seconds, showing a small casket and Navigator watching the funeral from the side, unable to show his face. I feel her eyes on me.

"He dies?"

"Fictionally."

"How horrible."

"It is. He doesn't take it well."

"Who?" she asks.

"My character."

Brenna nods. "I would think not. You just promised him that he'd be okay and then watched him fall to his death. Gosh, you had to be crushed. I'm so sorry."

I laugh at how emotional she's getting. "You know it's a movie and *Flight Plan* is only the start of the Navigator's storyline?"

"Of course, I'm just saying."

I lean over, pulling her face closer. "I like it when you feel for my character."

Her fingers rise, touching my cheek. "I guess my heart doesn't like to see even you fake being hurt."

"You could kiss it and make it better."

She laughs a little. "I could."

"I wouldn't mind."

Brenna leans closer until her lips are a breath away from mine. "What if someone sees?"

I don't give a flying fuck. Let everyone see. Let people make whatever assumptions they want. I've gone hours without this woman, and it's been hell. I'm losing my mind, and the only thing that will help is her. Then I remember that it's not just me who risks losing something if people do see.

So, I pull my hoodie up, and feel her warmth near my mouth. "Better?"

"I don't know that anything could make this better," she murmurs, and then I lean in and give her a sweet kiss.

twenty-one

Jacob's fingers are tangled in mine, and I'm leaning against his shoulder. We've moved into the backseat, which makes me feel like a teenager who is getting ready for a night in a make-out location. However, it is by far better for cuddling.

And Jacob is a great cuddler.

I have no idea what the hell the movie is about other than it's super sappy. Mostly, I can't focus because he comments on every cheesy line.

"No dude says that," Jacob clarifies.

"You know, for an actor, you're the worst person to watch a movie with. I figured you'd at least be quiet and observant."

He snorts. "This isn't acting, beautiful. This is crap. Lots and lots of crap. The sad part is that, before *Navigator*, I would've given my right or left nut for any part, including this."

"It's a good thing you didn't lose a nut then."

"You like my nuts?"

I roll my eyes. "All men are the same."

"That we are."

"Now, shh so I can watch the movie."

He pulls me tighter to his chest and does that. I start to get into it a bit more, but then cars start to leave.

Jacob looks around, noticing it too. "See, others think this isn't worth staying for either."

"We drove an hour out here, paid to see the movie, and we still haven't had the cake."

He lifts my chin so he can look me in the eyes. "I didn't say we were leaving. I have a few hours with you, and I intend to enjoy every minute of them."

I really wish he weren't so sweet. The fears I have about falling for him become more real each time I'm around him. If he were a jerk, it would be easy to just have great sex and call it a day, but he's not.

He's directing a freaking play to make my son happy.

"Good. I like that."

"Now, it seems we have fewer people to worry about seeing us." Jacob's hand moves down my back, bringing me tighter to his chest.

"And what would they see us doing?"

He grins, his hand moving to my leg. "For starters, they might see me trying to get my hand under your skirt."

His thumb grazes the top of my thigh.

"That would be embarrassing if someone saw."

"We wouldn't want them to see when I went completely under though."

I shake my head, agreeing as he does just that. "Jacob," I gasp as I feel him graze my underwear.

Thankfully, I adjusted my wardrobe when Cybil basically shoved us into this date.

My breathing grows shallower as he moves it to the side and starts to play with my clit. "You like this? You like the idea of someone seeing me do this to you?"

It's not exactly a fantasy I had, but there's an element of danger to it that thrills me. Mostly, though, it's him. It's that Jacob wants me badly enough to risk us being caught.

"I like you doing this because it's you."

The sound that comes from his mouth tells me he likes that answer. "You're the only woman I want to do this with." Jacob looks around and grins. "We're one of only two cars left. Come here." He pulls me so that I'm sitting between his legs. "Watch the movie." I start to turn, and then I feel his mouth on my neck. He kisses it, running his lips down, and then his hand cups my breast. "Tell me what you see."

Oh, God. I can't talk through this. "What?"

"Tell me what's happening on the screen."

Who the fuck cares? The only thing I can focus on is what Jacob is doing to my body. He has one hand on my breast, the other one moving up my leg. I'm going to combust if he keeps this up.

"I . . . I don't . . ."

He stops moving. "Are you struggling to pay attention, beautiful?"

"Yes," I admit.

His low chuckle vibrates against my back. "Do you want me to stop?"

I should say yes. I am a mother, doctor, woman who is raising a pre-teen who I would kill if she was doing this, but here I am, in the middle of a drive-in, getting it on with my non-committed guy who I slept with the other day. If I was in therapy, we'd fill a whole session on the issues here.

"No," I tell him.

He turns my head so that he can kiss me, and the hand on my leg starts to go up again. We kiss, no longer giving a shit about the movie or anything else. Kissing Jacob is unlike anything I've ever felt. We fit together so perfectly.

We kiss until a drop of water splashes against my forehead and I break away, turning my eyes to the sky.

He glances up too, asking, "Is that rain?"

As though God himself answers the question, the sky opens up, and it's not rain that hits us, it's a monsoon.

"Shit!" Jacob yells and grabs the blanket that was in the back, tossing it over me.

A convertible at a drive-in is pretty cool, unless you're stuck in a storm.

He jumps over into the front as water fills the car, drenching everything. I try to push the water off the seats, all to no avail. I can't keep up with the torrential rain. He tries to start the car to get the top up, but he's struggling with the keys.

"Is there another way to get the top up?" I ask.

He groans, and as soon as he gets the car started, he slams a button on the dash. The top starts to rise, slower than I swear it went down.

He shakes his head. "Come on!"

I start to laugh as the rain seems to come down harder. I'm soaked all the way through. There's not a part of me that's dry. The blanket was no help, and there's water everywhere inside.

Finally, the top goes up and he locks it on both sides. Jacob turns to me, drenched as well, and then bursts out laughing.

The two of us are in hysterics as we look around the completely saturated car and at each other.

"Are you okay?" he asks.

"It's just rain."

"This wasn't what I had in mind for our first date. I know that it didn't go as planned, but maybe we can make the best of it," he suggests.

"How?"

He turns the radio on in the car and then hops out, coming around to my side to open my door before offering me a hand.

"Will you dance with me?"

I look up at him, wondering if he's lost his mind. "It's pouring."

He smiles so wide it knocks the wind out of me. "Are you afraid of getting wet? Come on, Brenna, every woman should get to dance in the rain at least once in her life."

I put my hand in his and step out into the downpour. He tugs me to his chest and while there's music playing in the background and rain drumming on every surface, I don't hear anything but the sound of his heart. In the middle of a crazy storm, Jacob dances with me, and I feel the brick wall I had erected start to crumble.

twenty-two

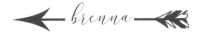

This week has been a shit show. One thing after another has gone wrong. The girl that Ellie brought to my attention had been in tears. She said she wrote it as fiction, and it wasn't anything like that. Every red flag was being thrown and danger light was flashing. There was something too practiced about her answers, as though they were part of a routine that had been engrained in her.

We filed the reports, but without her cooperation, I don't know that she'll get the help she needs.

Then Cybil found out that Reggie was deploying again.

My son is driving me absolutely insane because he's rehearsing his lines all day long. I swear, by the time this play is over, I'll be able to be his understudy.

The worst, though, is that I haven't really seen Jacob since that magical night in the rain. We've barely talked at rehearsals. He's so busy trying to corral these kids and making the play a success, and all I do is make sure no one is posting things on social media. We have a phone bucket, and we use it. Jacob explained to the kids that if this got out, and he was outed, the play wouldn't go on. All of them are passionate and excited to work with him, so they agreed to keep it offline.

Well, we all know it's coming, but hopefully, it'll be after the play at least.

My phone pings, and I smile when I see the name.

Speak of the devil.

Jacob: Is it too late to cancel the play?

Me: I would say yes.

Jacob: These kids are nuts. Half of them have already quit because they realized I was really not going to be fun.

Me: Well, you're not supposed to be fun. You're the director.

Jacob: I blame you for this.

Me: Me? You're the one who volunteered!

His response comes immediately.

Jacob: You're the one who gave birth to Sebastian.

Me: Yes, and that means you had to direct a small-town middle/high school play?

Jacob: It means that you owe me dinner.

That makes zero sense, but then this seems to be Jacob's big issue—food.

Me: None of your sisters-in-law will feed you?

Jacob: Nope. So, you're next on the list.

Me: I'd hate to wonder who is after me.

Jacob: Let's not ever have to go there.

I chew on my thumbnail, not sure of what to do. I could

invite him here. Let him spend time with Sebastian, and make sure he eats. Not that it's my problem, but we're friends. Friends who happen to have slept with each other. Still, Jacob has never done anything I didn't want.

And I was just upset because I haven't seen him. This would sort of kill three birds with one stone. Sebastian would be happy. I would be happy. And Jacob would eat something. Okay, four, if I want to be ambitious and think that maybe Jacob wants to see me too, but I won't officially put that on the list. Then maybe we can also make a plan for this weekend since Sebastian is sleeping at Austin's house and Melanie is going to stay at a friend's house.

Ugh. I really need to give myself therapy.

The best advice I give is to trust yourself. I'm a smart woman. I know what I want to do—what my gut is telling me to do, and that's to do what makes me happy.

Me: Then come over and let's make sure we don't see you go down to the next rung.

Jacob: I'm on my way.

I look around, my house coming together bit by bit, but the mess is ever-growing. I call for the kids. Melanie and Sebastian are at the bottom of the stairs a few seconds later.

"Jacob is coming for dinner. Not as your director, but as our friend," I say, cutting off any questions from Sebastian. "We need to clean up before he gets here in, like, ten minutes, so, it's all hands on deck . . . go!"

The three of us scatter, picking up anything lying around and shoving it in places it doesn't belong but won't be seen. This is what we would do before my mother would come to visit before she died. She liked to just stop by because it wasn't as if she lived three hours away and stopping by wasn't really stopping by, but that was her thing.

Growing up, my house was a museum. Everything had a place and that place was never altered. I've never prescribed to that thinking. Our home was always clean, but not immaculate. We lived in our homes. Messes are part of living because life isn't meant to be tidy.

That's not to say that I want Jacob to see it this way for a prolonged amount of time.

There's a knock at the door, and like prairie dogs hearing a sound, our heads snap up in unison.

"Shit. Okay, Mel, you do what you can about the dishes, and Seb, you go make sure the bathroom is good. I'll stall."

Sebastian gives me a salute, and Melanie rushes into the kitchen to do her part. I smooth my hair back just as another knock comes from the door.

I release a cleansing breath and open the door with a wide grin. "Hey."

"Hey." He extends a handful of wildflowers. "Thank you for taking pity on me."

"These are beautiful. Thank you, and there's no pity, we are happy to have you."

He leans in. "My next rung was Magnolia."

I burst out laughing. "Well then, if I'm only one above Magnolia, it seems you owe me much more than flowers."

"You name it, and it's yours."

"I'll think about this and get back to you."

He smirks. "Good. And I'm happy to pay in the early morning."

I blush and let that comment go.

Jacob enters the house, and a split second later, Sebastian barrels around the corner. "Jacob!"

"Hey, dude."

"Mom said you're eating with us. You're going to love her lasagna."

Thank the Lord that the one day I actually planned a dinner was tonight. Movie night was last night, which is always pizza, and then I try to make up for the fact that I don't cook nearly as much as my kids deserve and make a grand meal the next night.

Lasagna is a fan favorite in this house. It was a recipe that my Italian neighbor gave me, and it's amazing.

"I can't wait to try it," Jacob says.

"How do you think rehearsals went?"

I lift my hand. "No, sir. You're not talking about the play. Jacob isn't here for that, he's our friend, and we're going to treat him as such."

Sebastian lets out a long breath through his nose. "Didn't you say that we ask our friends about their day?"

"Nice try, son."

"I'm being considerate," Sebastian tries again.

"You're being a nudge, and I don't like it. The play is off the list of approved topics."

Jacob doesn't need more pressure than I know he currently feels.

"Fine," Sebastian grumbles. "How was your day *other* than the play?"

He chuckles. "It was good." Jacob drops into a low whisper. "The play part was awesome too, but don't tell your mom."

I roll my eyes. "Deliver me from all the boys in my life."

Sebastian and Jacob high five, and then Sebastian heads off to his room to finish his game before dinner.

"He is probably on with his friends from California," I explain.

"Hey, I get it. As cool as I am, I'm still old."

I laugh. "I assure you that you outrank all of us."

He looks around and then grabs my hips, pulling me close to him. I gasp and then his lips are on mine. It's not a long kiss, but it still makes my toes curl. "I missed you."

My hands are on his chest, and I sigh like those girls in the movies. "I saw you today."

"But I couldn't kiss you."

"No, you couldn't."

"And I really wanted to."

I want to all the damn time. "I'm glad you did."

He leans in again, giving me another kiss that is less frantic and a little sweeter. I swear that he's able to bring me to my knees far too easily. My kids could walk in at any moment, but all I care about is the way his lips feel on mine.

There's a noise from the kitchen, and Jacob releases me. I take a step back and try to return my heart rate to normal.

Melanie exits, says hello to Jacob, and then heads to her room.

Jacob walks around, taking everything in. "The house looks great, Brenna."

"Thanks. I've tried to keep with the integrity of it, especially since it used to belong to Devney's brother."

"Jasper was a good man. It was a shame that he and Hazel died."

"Yeah, and with Austin and Sebastian being friends, I just want to be careful not to hurt him in the process."

"I'm sure that they all appreciate it," Jacob says as he continues to look around.

"Were you friends with Jasper?"

"Not really. He was older than me, and I didn't know him much more than being Devney's older brother."

It's crazy to me how many degrees of separation we actually all share in this world. "Did you know Luke?" I ask, wondering why I'm bringing him up. "I only ask because he didn't talk much about his childhood or Sugarloaf."

"I can relate to that," Jacob admits. "I try to avoid thinking about this place and avoid coming back whenever possible. But I knew Luke in a casual way. We weren't friends, and I didn't run in that circle—the baseball guys. I hung out with my brothers, and that was it. I didn't want to bring people around my home."

"Well, hopefully being back this time is better."

Jacob grins, his eyes flaring with heat. "Oh, this time there is something in this town that makes it infinitely better."

"Really?"

A small dimple that only comes out when he makes a particular smile appears. "Absolutely."

"And is it something or someone?"

He stands in front of me, brushes the hair back from my forehead. "It's you, Brenna. You make being back here better."

I bite my lower lip as the heat floods my cheeks. "You're making it really hard to behave."

His fingers grip my hair, gently sliding down the strands. "You're telling me."

I take a step back, knowing one of us has to do it and I'm the one with the most to lose if someone walks in. I clear my throat and then Jacob walks around the room again.

He stops in front of the small memorial my mother-in-law asked us to put together. I didn't want to. In fact, it was probably the first fight that Sylvia and I ever had. In the end, I agreed to have it out for one year, after that, we weren't going to have a shrine to Luke in our living room.

The folded flag from his funeral is in a wooden box on the small table. There are a few photos of him, his parents, and then the photo that Jacob seems to be staring at. "That was his last homecoming."

"Was he gone a lot?"

"Yes."

The photo is of the four of us, and we all have varying degrees of emotions on our faces. Luke is smiling, holding Melanie tight against his side. I'm on the other side of him while Sebastian stands in front of us. There's a sense of relief that is evident on my face, but I can see the strain in my smile. Sebastian is staring up at Luke as though he can't really believe he's there in the flesh again. Melanie is her normal sweet self, just happy her daddy is home. What's the most striking is the way that Luke is staring at me. I know he loved me—that was never a question—but there's a mix of awe and so much love in his expression as he gazes at me while I stare forward, not able to look at him.

"You don't look happy," Jacob remarks as his thumb grazes my cheek.

I lift the frame, remembering that day. "It was the longest deployment we had ever done. I remember getting dressed to go and not caring about anything other than being *done*."

"What do you mean?"

I hated this deployment. I hated everything. "Homecomings are a mix of emotions. There is so much uncertainty, frustration, relief, and anxiety."

"I figured they were a big party. That's what it was like when Connor returned."

I shake my head and give him a small smile. "For single guys, they are. For the married guys, so much changes while they are gone that it's an adjustment for everyone once the joy wears off. He was so ready to come home and have everything be normal again, and I just couldn't muster the energy to be happy about that. Every time Luke left, we all had to learn to deal. Our daily routines were thrown off, and we had to find a way to make it through. We'd settle into it, get our home running, and then he'd come back, once again, throwing it off. This deployment was supposed to be six months, but then he got stop-lossed twice because of issues with other squadrons, and it ended up being eighteen months. As the kids were bouncing in their seats to see their dad, I was dreading it."

His hand finds mine, and we lace our fingers together. A simple gesture that offers the support I need to get through this. The emotions of that day were ones that I struggled with admitting to myself. With Jacob, I don't feel guilty. It's as if I know he won't judge me and maybe he'll even understand it.

"Because you were tired."

I look up, his piercing green eyes with yellow flecks stare back at me. "Yes."

"And you felt guilty about it?"

"More than you know."

"Why else?" he pushes, and I hate that he knows me well enough to know I'm holding back.

"Because I didn't want to go through it again. I just wished he'd stay gone or come back and stop leaving. I was so lonely and tired of being lonely, you know? I wanted my husband. My kids deserved a father who was there. And I knew all of this was unfair to Luke. It was just how I felt, and I hated myself for it."

Jacob's gaze doesn't move and that pull that's constantly between us grows. "Any man would understand how you felt, Brenna. He would've seen the sacrifices you made. I can't ever imagine what it was like, but Connor talked about the hardship of marriage and the military. I'm sure that, no matter what you think, if he had known how you felt, he would have understood too."

I fight back the urge to cry. He has no idea how much I needed to hear something like that. All these years, I've held on to it. I never told Luke how I felt, and it felt like a betrayal. There he was, fighting for our family, dealing with his own stress, and I was being petulant.

I release my hold on his hand and step back. "I hope so, and I'm also pretty sure there was a time or two he felt the same."

"Then why are you holding on to the guilt?"

Tears well in my eyes, blurring Jacob's face. "Because now he's gone and will never come back. There won't be another homecoming for us."

"No, and I'm sorry that you're alone again."

A tear falls, and I wipe it away. "I'm being ridiculous. It's been almost a year, and I have tried to move forward, but it's hard. We fought the day before he died. I think that's what still weighs so heavy on me."

It's as though a dam has been opened and the truth of my heart is spilling out. Unfortunately, Jacob is in the path of it all.

"What did you fight about?"

Another tear falls. "He was supposed to watch the kids the next day. He promised me that he would be home and cleared it with his command. I had a court case for a child abuse charge that I needed to be at. Then, at nine, right after we got the kids to bed, he got a call that he had to fly. He was an hour short, and he had to be in the air before noon, which meant he had to work."

I don't remember the things I said. I know I was angry and so was he. I'd always grappled with why his career was more important than mine. It was the way it always was, and most of the time, I accepted it. I made the sacrifices for him because that was what society told me I should do. There was a part of me that was resentful that it didn't matter that I worked just as hard to get where I was. I was a mother, and regardless of whatever income I made or how important my job was, I would always be a mother and a wife who just happened to work.

So, I unloaded.

"Listen, I get guilt. Trust me, I've practically drowned in

it over the years, but Ellie helped show us that forgiving ourselves is the best way to help move past it."

"I just always wondered how he could walk out that day
and dismiss me so easily. It was as if our marriage shifted the
second that door closed."

He places his finger under my chin, lifting until we're staring at each other. "He knew how you felt. Trust me, no man
would let you go without a fight."

My breathing starts to increase, and I step back, needing to
put some distance between us. I'm too raw, too vulnerable, too
emotional, and too lost in the past. My mind isn't working, and
I need some space. "I have to check on dinner."

Jacob seems to understand and nods. But he leans in and
gives me another soft kiss. "Of course. I'll just go check on
Sebastian."

"Perfect. He's the second door on the right."

I enter the kitchen and lean against the counter. I'm falling
in love with him, and I don't have a chance in hell of stopping
it.

twenty-three

"You were right," Jacob says as he wipes his mouth. "This lasagna is the best I've ever had."

"You don't have to lie."

"I'm not! It was great."

Sebastian agrees. "It was your best ever, Mom."

"It really was, Mom," Melanie adds on.

I smile at my sweet kids. "Thank you. Now, can you guys clean up, and I'll be in to do the dishes in a bit."

Melanie rises first, grabbing the plates before Sebastian takes the rest.

"Thanks again for this," Jacob says. "I swear I will move you up the rung now."

"Oh? Who will I overtake?"

"Sydney. God love the woman, but she cooks like shit."

I burst out laughing. "I'm sure she'd appreciate you saying

that."

He raises his hands. "Hey, I'm starting to feel bad for Declan."

He's a mess. "Would you ever say that to her face?"

"Not a chance." Jacob leans back in the seat, arms stretched out and grin wide. When he sits back upright, he sighs deeply. "I envy this."

I look around to see what he's looking at. "The mess?"

"The fact that you sit around with the kids and eat dinner. When my mom was alive, dinner was sacred. The four of us hated it, of course, but looking back . . . I wish we had more of them."

"You were close with your mom?"

He nods, seeming to be drifting to a faraway time. "I was probably closest to her. Connor would like to think it was Sean, but Mom and I just understood each other. I could be sitting across the room, look over, and I swear she could read my mind." He looks back to me. "Which wasn't always a good thing."

We both laugh. "But she was the glue . . ."

"Yeah, and when she died, it was like everything came undone. My father, our family, the life we had, but my brothers and I, we became impenetrable."

I've seen it happen before. The four of them had to be what their mother was in some way. "I'm not at all glad that you had to endure any of it, but it's a good thing that you had each other to weather the storm."

Jacob tries to smile, but I know it's fake. "We made each other a lot of promises, and one was that we'd never be like our father. For eight years, we lived without ever allowing ourselves the opportunity to break that vow."

"What do you mean?"

"After the accident, my brothers and I promised to never

risk becoming him. No kids, no marriage, control our anger . . . all that."

"That sounds very noble."

He laughs. "It was stupid. It also was lonely as hell."

"Well, I just told you that marriage doesn't always equal not being lonely."

"True. This was just . . . punishment."

I'm fighting back the urge to tell him what I would tell a patient. Jacob doesn't need that. So, I reach out and take his hand. "Your brothers have all married and are having kids now."

"They are."

"But you won't?"

His eyes meet mine, and I shiver when his thumb rubs the top of my hand. "I can't. I want to. I would for the right girl, but what I've seen Hollywood do to couples? I can't do that to someone. Not willingly."

I knew what his answer would be but it doesn't make it any less thoughtful or brave. He is willing to put aside his own wants and needs to protect others instead of just jumping in and throwing another person to the tabloid wolves. It's sweet, kind, and I hate it. Being with Jacob has made all of his reasons seem like utter shit to me. Who cares about the tabloids? Who cares what Hollywood, the media, or the world think about us? I don't. I want him. I am falling in love with him, and that means accepting that life—for him. I'll take it all if it means I get him too.

That's just one slice of our problem though because Jacob won't stay. I won't leave. There was a part of me that hoped for at least a maybe. A chance that, if I did get my heart entangled, it wouldn't end in heartbreak. I was being a stupid woman.

"I see."

Jacob leans forward, extending his other hand. Without

pause, I place mine in his. "I would give anything to have met you earlier."

"You don't have to say that."

"I know I don't. I'm saying it because I wish it could be different. I wish I could come over, have dinner, and watch a movie before getting to spend time with you after the kids went to bed. It would be you if I could choose someone."

I clear my throat. "You could choose differently, Jacob. You could try."

He shakes his head. "To what end? I have to leave."

"And I have to stay, so I guess being honest is the right thing."

He looks away. "I don't think it's the right thing. It's just the only option. Being out there, seeing marriages fail more than they succeed, seeing how couples are torn apart by the media . . . how would that be fair to you or your kids? How could I live with myself knowing that I harmed a family? I'd be no better than *him*."

He's doing everything he can not to be like his father, which means keeping his heart free. The sad part is that he's failing. If he were truly trying to do that, he wouldn't be here with me tonight or directing Sebastian's play. Jacob's arguments are all invalid. Hollywood isn't destroying marriages—it's the people in them. I want to tell him all the ways that it could be different for us if he wanted it to be, but I'd be fighting for what? Jacob and I made an agreement. No promises and no questions.

Sure, he makes it hard for me to sleep at night. Yeah, when I'm around him, I want to run into his arms and soak up the strength and comfort he offers. And who cares if, every time I see him, I find yet another thing about him that makes him perfect for me? No matter how much we both want things to be different, they are what they are.

So, I keep my mouth shut.

Sebastian exits the kitchen, and Jacob and I lean away from each other quickly. He looks over with a smirk. "We did the dishes for you."

My eyes widen, and I plaster a grin on my face, hoping he didn't see us holding hands. "You did?"

"Yup."

When Melanie joins us, her shirt is drenched. "I did the dishes. Sebastian flung water."

"Well, thank you both. The floors probably needed to be mopped."

"Do you think we could *please* hang my new mirror after Jacob leaves?" Mel asks.

She's been asking for a week, but I haven't had a minute to think. "Of course."

Sebastian, not willing to squander this chance, jumps in. "Oh! Can we fix the shelf that Papa hung? The books slide off the end."

"I'll do my best."

My father-in-law has started to do things wrong in an effort to get us to stop asking—at least, that's my theory.

"I can help," Jacob offers.

"What?"

"I can hang a mirror and fix the shelf."

"Jacob, that's sweet, but—"

He lifts his hand. "My handyman skills are limited, but I can do this. You cooked me dinner, so consider it a thank you."

Melanie looks like she's about to squeal because, for all the things I can do, hanging pictures is not one. I try, but at some point, whatever I put up, always comes down.

She jumps in. "That would be great. Seriously, I have been asking my gramps, but he's been hanging everything else because Mom—"

"Mom has been busy," I try to offer an explanation.

He purses his lips. "I'm sensing a story here."

"No story."

Mel laughs. "Nope, not a story, just broken glass."

"Melanie!" I hiss.

"My mother is amazing at fixing things, but not hanging them."

I groan. "Children were put on this earth to annoy adults."

"Dad used to make fun of her because sometimes, in the middle of the night, something would just . . . fall. It was always something she hung."

"And just for that, now I am going to hang the mirror."

Jacob chuckles. "So, there's something you're not great at?"

"I'm not great at a lot of things."

He leans in close. "Thankfully, cooking isn't one of the things you suck at."

I roll my eyes. "Keep it up and Magnolia will go a rung higher than you in the friendship category."

"You wound me." His hands cover his heart as he says it.

"And now I'm doubting your acting skills."

Melanie grabs my arm. "Mom, please let Jacob hang it for me. I promise I won't make fun of your clothes or your hanging ability again."

That's a lie. Just today she made a comment about my shoes and asked if I borrowed them from my mother-in-law. She said they were frumpy and I should try to wear heels more because they made my legs look leaner. I didn't realize my legs looked fat. Thanks to my daughter, I stood in front of the mirror for ten minutes raising up on my toes.

"If Jacob really wants to do it."

He puffs his chest out. "Of course, I want a chance to show off my manly skills."

"You're hanging a mirror," I deadpan.

"Which is something you apparently can't do."

Mel giggles. "Come on, Jacob, I'll show you where the tools Grandpa keeps here are."

The two of them head off, and I go into the kitchen to inspect what my kids actually did to the dishes. As I suspected, they put the four plates and forks into the dishwasher. That's it.

There are still various bowls and cookware on the counter and stove, and there is a dusting of flour all around the room. I love making this dish, but I absolutely hate cleaning up after it.

I make my sauce two days before I plan to make the lasagna, and the day before, I make my own noodles, which is a process. Then assembly happens, and it's chaos in the kitchen.

As I'm walking around, I hear my phone buzz, and there is Cybil's face on the screen. I could ignore her, which is what I want to do, but she'll just call again. If I don't pick up, she'll call Melanie or Sebastian. The fact that I would send her to voice mail is enough to make her think I'm hiding something. So, it's time to be quick.

"Hey, Cyb."

"Hey, you. What are you up to?" She pulls her blonde hair to the side as she takes a sip of her wine.

"Nothing. Just getting ready to clean up from dinner."

"Daddy always said having kids means less mess for adults."

Normally, I'd point out that, once again, that makes no sense because having kids definitely doesn't mean less mess of any kind . . . ever, but it will launch into something much longer than I care for.

"I only have a few minutes, what's up?"

"Why the rush, sugar?"

Because I have Jacob Arrowood in my house, and I don't want you to know.

"I have a busy day tomorrow. I want to spend a little time with Sebastian and Melanie before they're gone over the weekend."

Her smile is wide as she nods. "Kids are gone for the weekend? Hold on." She puts the phone down. "Reggie! Can you bring the laptop in here, please?" A pause, and she huffs. "I didn't ask where it was. I know it's in the kitchen. I'm asking you to bring it to me." She looks back into the camera. "I swear. I love the man more than any woman ever could, but he's maddening some days."

"And you're a walk in the park."

She nods. "Exactly. I'm damn near angelic."

"As much as I'd love to debate this, I have to go."

"Brenna Allen, you do not rush my calls. We have a lot to discuss. I know you had your date in the rain, but since then, have you seen him? Have you guys . . . you know . . . done it again?"

"Cybil Daniels, I love you, but I'm hanging up now."

Her jaw falls slack, and she stares at me. "Are you kidding?"

"Not even a little. I am going to clean my kitchen and then go be with my kids." And pray that no one tells you that a man is here.

"Fine. I'll call you tomorrow, and we can discuss—"

Jacob's deep voice cuts off Cybil, and my plan to hide him being here is gone. "Brenna? I found your drill, but you're missing some pieces."

Shit. Shit. Shit.

"Not a problem, I'll just get off this call and be right there."

"Great."

I smile at him, hoping to God that he doesn't hear whatever is next to come out of Cybil's mouth.

"Holy lying bitch! You weren't trying to clean your kitchen, you were trying to hide the fact that Jacob is there!" Her voice is so loud that it wouldn't matter if I had her on mute, he'd hear.

"I'm not lying. Yes, Jacob is here. All of us had dinner—as friends. He's helping Melanie out by hanging a mirror in her room."

"I'm sure he's helping with a lot more than that in your bedroom."

I hush her and walk to the other side of the kitchen. "Cybil, stop it. Whatever happens is not something I'm going to discuss."

She raises one thin brow. "Fine, then tell me that you feel nothing other than lust for him."

Once again, I hate my aversion to lying. I tiptoe over to the door and don't see any shadows under the crack at the bottom. "I can't say that."

She's giving me her version of a whisper. "I knew it! I called it, Reggie."

He grumbles something as the laptop bounces on the bed. "Please, I'll pay you to come back here and take her."

I smile. "Hell no, she's all yours."

Cybil gives us both a look. "I'm going to pretend this is you both fighting to keep me."

"I love you, but you need to butt out. Whatever it is that's happening here, it's not your business."

"No, it's not, but you are starting to have feelings for him. I can see it in your eyes. Now he's over for dinner and hanging mirrors? You need to be honest with yourself or you're going to end up hurt. You are falling for him."

I bite my nail and sigh. "Maybe, but men like Jacob Arrowood don't fall in love with girls like me."

And that's the reality I need to remember.

twenty-four

"**W**hat is your issue?" Sydney asks as she sits next to me at the table.

"Huh?"

"You're not yourself tonight."

I push the food around on my plate, thinking about Brenna. After the weekend her kids were away, we've barely found time for each other. Two nights ago, we met out by the creek again. She didn't have a lot of time, so we just sat around talking, laughing, and fooling around.

I'm aching with need for her. It's not normal, and I'm starting to freak the fuck out about how I feel.

But when I walked her back, it was like something was different. The excuses for why we can't work started to slip away. I saw a chance that I didn't think I would ever have, and it has me fucked in the head.

I only have three months left here, and I don't know that I

can keep my heart from her.

"I have a lot on my mind."

She leans forward and hums. "I see. So, you're thinking about a redhead with a killer smile."

"I sometimes wonder if I didn't do Declan dirty by telling him to get back with you."

Her smile is devilish. "If he's suffering, he deserves it."

I can't argue with her there. "It's fine, Syd. Everything is fine. I'm just tired, trying to do right by these kids, and I have a call with Noah tonight."

Sydney reaches out, placing her hand on my arm. "Jacob, you know that I'm not blind and that this town has the ability to hold a secret as well as a bird keep its feet on the ground. People are talking. You've been back three months, and you've spent most of that with Brenna."

"Of course, they are! Brenna and I are . . ."

"Are what?"

"We're friends."

She nods slowly, watching me. "I've known you my whole life, Jacob."

"I'm aware of this."

"Right, but I *know* you. Maybe not the way I know Declan, but I'd like to think out of all your brothers, I was closest in friendship to you. Sean has always been the kindhearted one. Declan was the protector, and Connor was the baby. But you, you were a different kind of protector. Where Declan was trying to navigate how to be the responsible one, you were the sheepdog, making sure the flock was safe. You'd take the hit if it meant that they didn't have to."

I lean back, not wanting a trip down memory lane but also not stupid enough to stop Sydney. She scares me slightly. "Where are you going with this?"

"It's still who you are at the very core of you. You're doing it now without even knowing it. You're keeping everyone safe, even if it means you're miserable."

I glare at her. "Syd, I love you, but you're so far off base here."

"Am I? I don't think so. You've never had serious relationships, and not just because of the accident either. And now, you're lying about your feelings and what you want most in your life to protect Brenna and yourself."

"I'm not lying. In fact, I'm being so fucking honest it's ridiculous."

Not once have I lied to Brenna. I've told her how it is even when I wanted to lie to myself and believe it could be more. The dinner at her house changed the dynamic between us. We weren't talking about movies and stupid shit. She opened up in a way that was far more than I ever expected. We went from being two people hooking up to something more. Whether we meant it to happen or not.

"Maybe you think that. Maybe you don't really love Brenna. Maybe you do. I see the way you look at her when you don't think anyone is watching. I know that the two of you are in a world of trouble because I'm pretty sure she loves you too."

I open my mouth to rebuke her statement, but she puts her hand up.

"Don't argue with me. I know women, and I know when someone is lying. You know it as surely as you know that she's not just this random hookup you're trying to pretend she is. No matter what, I worry about you, Jacob."

I give Syd that smile that's worked for me for years. "The only thing to worry about is when you'll finally be able to make some money off the portion of my land."

She sighs, looks over at the kitchen door, and then turns back to me. "You're still going to sell your part?"

Oh, not her too. "Why wouldn't I?"

"Because your mother wouldn't want you to."

The blow comes like a fist to the gut. Sydney has never been one to hold back, but that was low, even for her. My mother is the only thing that would stop me from selling, and I think she knows that.

"My mother is gone, as you so clearly pointed out."

"Yes, she is." Her hand grips my wrist. "She's gone, but the land and the farm lives on. I know that you four all think of it as your father's farm, but maybe that's where it all went wrong. It was your mother's farm. Her heart and soul went into this place. She raised her four wonderful sons here. Sure, your dad tarnished it as much as he could, but she's still here, Jacob. You know, I always thought your mother was the most brilliant woman in the world. She gave you all this key to living."

"What are you talking about?"

Sydney sighs. "The truth about an arrow. Sure, you all bitched when she forced you to say it, but look at how absolutely incredible your sayings were. You were kids when she saw your flaws and gave you all the words and advice you needed to survive life."

"I don't even know what the fuck mine means!"

She leans back in her chair and takes a beat. "Removing half the feather creates the curve. The answer is right there, Jacob."

"Women make this shit complicated. What curve? What feathers? Remove what? It was my mother's way of torturing her boys and then making it seem like wisdom. You know what curve I got? A right hook or an upper cut from the man she married. Or maybe it was when she died and left us in the hands of a man who would rather we had died instead of her."

"I didn't mean to upset you." Sydney's lip trembles, and I feel like an ass.

"No, please don't apologize. It's me who needs to say it to you. I'm just pissed off, and you don't deserve my being a dick. There's a lot on my mind, and . . . I need to go for a walk."

Her smile is soft and understanding. "I figured you might."

I lean down and kiss her cheek. "I'm sorry, Syd. You know I love you."

She gets to her feet and winks. "I know. I love you too. Go see your mom."

On the walk out to the gravesite, I think through what Sydney said. Would my mother feel this way? Would she want me to stay here or keep the land even if I never come back to it? I'd like to think her heart would want whatever made me happy, but what the hell do I know? I was a kid when I lost her. I've spent more of my life without her than with.

When I get to the small fence that surrounds her headstone, I see my brother get to his feet.

"Hey, Jacob," Sean says as he walks toward me.

"I didn't know you were out here."

He looks back at the flowers lying on the ground. "I come every now and then. Usually when there's something on my mind."

"What brought you out today?"

Sean claps me on the shoulder with a smile. "Devney's pregnant."

My sour mood evaporates and I grin. "Really? That's amazing."

"Yeah. It is, but I'm scared as fuck."

I laugh and roll my eyes. "You're already a great father to Austin. Plus, if any of us should have kids, it's you."

"It's different. Like, this is half of me."

"That's sort of the way it works. How far along is she?"

"She was pregnant at the wedding."

"I thought she was glowing," I comment.

Sean sighs and then looks back. "I can't help but wonder what Mom would think of all this. Three of us having kids, settling down, and living on the farm."

"Did you and Sydney talk before this?"

"What?" The confusion on his face lets me know they didn't.

"Nothing. Forget I said anything."

"Okay, I usually do that anyway."

I shove him, and he chuckles. "I'm just saying that I came out here to tell her, and then . . . I don't know. I can't help but think about her."

"I know what you mean. Syd said some stuff about how Mom would want me to keep my land."

His brows raise. "Really. And?"

"And what?"

"Are you thinking of keeping it?"

The thing is, until she said it, I had no intention of it. I don't want to live here, but suddenly, I see myself doing just that. I know actors who have multiple homes and get to live a life away from the hustle of Hollywood, but I don't know if I'm there yet.

I'm still learning and growing my career. There are more roles, different ones, that I want to take. If I can't get to auditions, I'm not sure how that would work.

I huff and look toward the gravesite. "No. If I need to feel close to her, I can come visit you fuckers."

He nods. "Yeah, but it's not yours. Don't you want a piece of it? It's not like you need the money from the sale."

That's not why I want to get rid of it. It's because I don't need a connection to this place. Sugarloaf holds no future for me.

"I don't need the headache."

"I'm prepared to buy you out, Jacob."

I figured that was going to be how this went. Sean owns the house, and the last portion of land makes sense for him to buy. Connor took a great piece in the back that has the tree house he built, and Declan bought the land that butts up to Sydney's, which made it huge. When Declan's friend Milo was out here, he did some research and found out my portion would perk, meaning they can build on it, making it more valuable.

However, I'm not taking money from my brothers. "I don't want that."

"You'd rather sell it to someone who would build a house?"

I shake my head. "No, I'd rather split my portion and gift it to you all. You're right, I don't need the money."

"Do me a favor, don't mention this to anyone else. Give it time, see where the rest of your six-month stint leaves you."

"It's going to leave with me getting on a plane," I tell him.

"Okay, and if that's the case, then we'll discuss buying you out or you signing it over. Whatever you want."

I release a heavy sigh. "I figure it's the least I can do for my nieces and nephews. I went from having no chance of being an uncle to being one to many."

Sean laughs. "Yeah, I didn't see this being our lives."

"Maybe not, but I'm happy for everyone, especially you. You and Devney are going to be great parents."

"You would be a great dad too, Jacob."

I don't want to think about that. "I left that behind me a long time ago."

"We all thought that." My brother smiles and jerks his head. "Thanks. Go talk to Mom. I'm going to go tell Connor and Declan before the barbeque tonight."

He heads out, and I turn toward the grave. I squat and press my palm to the top of the headstone. "Hey, Mom." Each time I come here and talk, I feel ridiculous in the beginning. Rationally, I know she's not here. This place really doesn't hold her, but seeing her name makes it feel like she might be.

"It seems that you're having a busy day here with your needy sons. I wish I was here to tell you good news, but nothing like a baby or a marriage from me. Instead, I'm not sure what I really came out here for. Maybe I just needed to talk and have no one give me their advice."

That's most likely the real reason. "I met a girl. She's everything you would want for me, Mom. Plus, she has these two kids who are great too." I release a heavy sigh, hearing the shift in my voice as I think of Brenna. "My feelings don't matter because I can't bring her into my world. I can't give her the kind of life she needs. There's no stability, privacy, or chance at real happiness like she would want. She wants to live a life that someone like Connor could give her. Where the man she loves is reliable and around."

Brenna telling me that she felt alone even though she was married was that nail in the coffin. When I'm shooting a movie, I'm gone for months. There are no big breaks in the movie schedule I'm currently signed on for either.

"The thing is, even though I know all of this, I want to be around her," I admit. "I keep telling myself that whatever I'm feeling will go away, but then I see her, and I want to kiss her, pull her into my arms, and . . ." I look back down at the name and remember that my mother probably isn't the right person to confess that last part to. "I like her. I like her a lot. Mom, I could love her, and wouldn't that be the fucking biggest joke?"

I try to imagine what my mother would say. I have no idea if her infinite wisdom would've extended into adulthood. Maybe she only had the right words for us as kids or we glorified the way she always knew what to say. I don't think that last part is true because she really did. If we were sad, she could make us happy. If we were lost, she was the compass to show us where to go.

"I could really use your help because I'm afraid that I'm going to mess up, tell her how I feel, and not be able to fix it. How do I make myself not fall in love with her? Or how do I pretend I'm not already there?"

I may be an actor, but I can't fool myself.

twenty-five

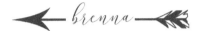

brenna

The kids are staying at their friends' houses, and I'm sitting in the living room, drinking a glass of wine, and eating chips. It's not a glamorous evening, but it's exactly what I need. The last few days have been difficult. My feelings for Jacob are growing, and as much as I tell myself to stop, I find it impossible.

I am in love with Jacob. Head-over-heels, want-to-write-his-name-on-my-notebook-a-hundred-times, carve-our-initials-in-a-tree kind of love.

So, I have to start preparing for a cataclysmic heartbreak. I lied to myself when I said I could do just sex with anyone. I'm a commitment girl, and apparently, I have a heart that doesn't care about what I tell it.

When he leaves, I'll break, and it'll suck, but as Cybil says—I'll survive. In the meantime, I need to protect myself as much as I can.

So, while what I want to do is call him and tell him to leave his door open for me, what I'm going to do is watch crappy television and not think about anything.

Only, as soon as my ass is nice and comfortable in the chair, there's a knock at the door. I groan as I get up, wondering who is disturbing my night of rest, and see someone who I am not at all unhappy to have here.

"Jacob."

So much for that plan.

"Sebastian texted me," he says with a grin.

"Oh?"

"He said that he and Mel were out at their friends' houses, so he couldn't play a video game tonight."

I lean against the door, smiling that my son gave Jacob the idea to come over. Also hating that I'm smiling because this is against the plan I just put in place. "So, you thought, hmm, that would be a perfect time to go seduce his mother?"

He steps forward, pulling me into his arms. "Can she be seduced?"

I feel like Renee Zellweger in *Jerry Maguire*. He had me at the knock on the door. I didn't stand a chance. "Oh, I'm sure she can."

He leans down, pressing his lips to mine. "Then I better get to work."

We both move at the same time, and I kick the door closed with my foot, not wanting to break away from him. He tastes like sin and pleasure all wrapped up in a neat little package.

Who needs to stay away when I only have a few more months of Jacob?

His tongue slides against mine, and I moan. This man does something to me, and I can't explain it. It's as though he reaches into me, takes the broken parts, and mends them. My heart will be decimated when he leaves Sugarloaf, but I don't want to stop this.

His hands are in my hair, pulling it free from the ponytail, before they move down my back, holding me tighter to his body.

"Jacob," I say softly.

"Bed or the couch, beautiful?"

"Both."

He chuckles softly, and then lifts me into his arms, carrying me to the couch. When he sits, I'm straddling his lap, kissing him as fiercely as I can.

I move my lips to his throat, and I can feel his erection as I rock back and forth. "God, I missed you today."

"Yeah?"

He nods. "I thought about you all day, wishing I could make some kind of rehearsal on a Saturday just to see you."

It would be so easy to read into his words, to think he's saying that because his feelings are deeper than just sex for me. In some ways, I think they are, but Jacob has been clear that we are just this.

"You're seeing me now." My voice is low and husky.

He pushes me so that he can really get a good look. "Not enough of you. I want to see all of you. I want you naked."

I pull my shirt over my head and watch his eyes flare with lust. "You have the most beautiful body, Brenna."

"I think you win in that category."

"Not even close." He comes closer, his tongue darting out and licking my nipple. "You're gorgeous." His tongue makes the same movement on the other side. "You make me so fucking hard." To make his point, he moves his hips up, letting me feel it. "I swear . . . when you walked in yesterday in that skirt, all I could think about was how I wanted to get you in a dark corner and see if you could keep quiet while I fucked you."

The image of my hands on the wall in my office or a closet

somewhere, Jacob pulling my skirt up and slamming into me as I bit down to keep from yelling causes heat to pool.

"Now, that would've been interesting."

He sucks my nipple into his mouth, moving his tongue in a circle. "Interesting? I think it would've been something much more than that."

My fingers tangle in his hair as he continues to lick and suck. He moves his hips again, his hard length gliding along where I want him most. Then his hand is between us, pushing the thin cotton shorts over so his finger can graze my clit.

I have never been like this. It wasn't that sex was ever bad, but I was never this consumed.

I want him. I need him to make the ache that's in my chest ease.

Everything is so intense, and I know that this time with him will be the same.

"Jacob . . ." I'm asking, pleading, and maybe begging for more.

"What, beautiful?"

"Please, I need . . ."

"Tell me."

I look down at him, and his green eyes are filled with so much desire that I could drown in it. "I need you inside me."

His head falls back, and he easily lifts me up. "This time, I won't deny you," he says as he pulls his pants down. "It's been too long, Brenna. I've craved you too much."

I stand and strip, watching as he gets naked.

It's as though the two of us are speaking the same language. It's been a week since we were together this way. Seven days of nothing but replaying the memories, imagining his hands on my skin as I showered. Seven mornings of debating going for a walk just to happen upon him.

My dreams have been filled with fantasies of the two of us.

Seeing him at rehearsals and having to keep my focus away from him was torture. It was as though, if I allowed myself to look at him, I might just do something stupid.

When we're both naked and panting, something shifts in the confines of the room, and he moves toward me at the same time that I go to him. We clash, and I swear thunder rumbles when we do.

Our mouths fuse together in the most frantic and desperate kiss. I can't get deep enough, feel him strong enough, and I want all of him. There's emotion thick and filling every nook of this living room.

I'm on my back, Jacob braced over me. Two seconds ago, we were standing, and I have no idea how we ended up on the couch while we were kissing, but the heat of his body burns me everywhere.

"I want you," he tells me. "I need you and . . . fuck . . . I just need you, Brenna. All the fucking time."

I feel the same, but I won't confess it. "This is crazy."

He kisses my neck, grabbing a handful of my hair and pulling it back to expose more of my throat. "You do this to me. You and no one else."

I want to let myself trip and fall into the idea that he means that, but I know he just feels that way because we are both clearly desperate for what we shared again. It's not feelings—it's lust.

My legs fall open even wider, needing him inside me. "Please, Jacob. Please."

He moves, shifting forward. When he enters me, I scream out in pleasure. It feels so good. It's as though all the pieces that were floating have settled, and I'm whole again.

Of all the men in the world to make me feel this way, I wish it weren't him. Not because he's wrong but because he's right. In a few weeks, Jacob has shown me that I'm ready to move on. Too bad it can't be with him.

"Rock, paper, scissors for it," Jacob says as he holds the very last spoonful of mint chocolate chip ice cream.

"It's my ice cream!"

"It's my spoon."

I roll my eyes. "I own the spoon."

"Yes, but isn't possession nine-tenths of the law or some shit?" he counters. "I'm clearly in possession."

We're sitting at the kitchen table, completely naked, and he's feeding me ice cream. I never thought this would ever be my life. Not just because he's Jacob but because this is fun. I'm smiling, happy, completely sated, and comfortable, which is odd because I'm freaking naked in the kitchen.

"Okay, fine, but this is totally unfair."

"It wouldn't be unfair if you won."

I grin. "This is true."

"Okay, well, let's settle this fair and square. Winner takes all."

Both of us put our fist out. "You're going down, Arrowood."

"Don't be so sure, Allen."

I try to think about this and be strategic. Jacob is a pretty solid man. He knows what he wants and doesn't budge. When I think about what he'd choose, I think it's a rock. I'm totally going to win. If I pick paper, I'll cover rock and win, get my ice cream and then maybe Jacob can be my cherry on top.

I give him an alluring smile. "Ready?"

"Always."

We both pound our hand. "Rock, paper, scissors, shoot."

I lay out paper, and then Jacob shocks me with scissors. His wide grin and the twinkle in his eyes are his only reaction to his win. "Well, it seems you've been beat." He takes the spoon, bringing it toward his lips.

"Wait!"

"What?"

"Don't you want to share?" I ask. "It is sort of both of ours."

"Yes, but I won it, and . . . I don't know . . . I mean, how much is it worth to you?"

I lean back, giving him a view of my breasts as I play with my hair. "I'm not sure."

Jacob grins, his eyes moving up and down. "How about just one lick to start with?" He moves closer, lifting the spoon until it just brushes my bottom lip. "Can you do that?"

"Are you asking if I can resist?"

"Can you?"

"Depends what I'm being told I have to hold out against."

"Is there something else you'd rather?" Jacob asks, pulling the spoon back.

"I wonder . . ." I move a bit closer, my lips nearing his. "If I were to taste a bit of the ice cream somewhere else." Jacob's eyes flare, and my mouth is right there. I could kiss him so easily.

"Where else?"

I fight back the smile when I hear the hitch in his voice.

And then I close my lips around the spoon and take the whole thing.

Jacob lunges forward, grabbing me around my waist. "You little sneak!"

I laugh as I swallow the ice cream and we fall to the cold ground. "Hey!"

"Hey, yourself! You stole my ice cream." Jacob lies on top of me as he tickles my side.

"What was that about possession?"

"Ice cream thief!"

I giggle and squirm from both his assault and the cold tile beneath me. "Jacob! Stop! I'm sorry!"

His big arms cage me in, and he pushes up a little. "Are you?"

"Maybe."

One brow raises as he stares at me. "Maybe?"

"Well, I mean, I wanted that ice cream."

"Did you?"

I nod and press my hands to his strong chest before moving them up to his shoulders. "I did."

"And what about what I want? That ice cream was on my spoon. You owe me something for taking it from me."

His words stir the heat inside my core, and I'm awfully glad we're still naked because it will make round two of tonight much easier.

"I do?"

"Yup."

I grin, moving my fingers along his jaw. "What do you want?"

His deep voice is low and warm. "Lately, there's only one thing I want."

"Yeah?"

He nods. "Yeah, I want you."

twenty-six

I roll over, breathing in that warm apple scent that is all Brenna. She shifts in her sleep, snuggling deeper into my arms, and I nuzzle her hair.

Waking up like this is everything I swore I'd never want. I was a liar and an idiot. I don't know how I'm going to give this up.

She moves a bit more, rolling over a little to look up. "Hi, there."

"Hi."

She smiles softly. "How did you sleep?"

It was one of the best nights I've had since I've been back. There was no wind causing branches to hit the windows or a generator kicking off because it ran out of gas, causing me to wake up in a sticky sweat.

"Good. You?"

She reaches back and runs her nails lightly through the

scruff on my cheek. "I slept great, even with your chin scratching me."

I lean in, rubbing my face against her back, and she laughs as she moves away. "Like that?"

"Yes, knock it off!" She slaps at my shoulder playfully.

"You know, this is the first time I've gotten to see you wake up in the morning."

She rubs her finger against my jaw. "I like it."

"Me too."

There is a warmth in her eyes that I never want to forget. When she looks at me, it's as though I can move mountains. And for her, I want to.

"Last night was really great," Brenna murmurs.

"How often can you get the kids to sleep out?"

"Not often enough."

I want to tell her about my revelations regarding us and my feelings. I think she feels the same, but I'm not sure. Her deep blue eyes watch me, assessing me, and I wonder if she can read my thoughts. After a few seconds of silence and just staring at each other, her stomach growls.

"Hungry?"

She nods, and the connection we shared just moments ago snaps away. "I wake up early every morning absolutely famished. I'm sorry."

I look over at the clock. "This is early?"

"Well, I guess to some it is. Seven isn't overly early, but for the weekend it is."

I laugh and grab my phone. "It's ten thirty."

Brenna sits up quickly, pulling the sheet with her. "What? It's ten thirty?" She damn near screams. "I never sleep past seven! Get up!"

"What's wrong?" I ask as I hear the panic in her voice.

"You have to go!"

"What? Go where?"

Brenna is out of bed, throwing a robe on and putting her hair in a pony tail. "The kids will be home any minute! You have to get dressed! Quickly!"

Since she's clearly on the verge of a breakdown, I don't argue. I look around, grabbing the clothing we tossed in the room as I carried her over my shoulder last night, slapping her ass for taking my ice cream.

"Oh my God. We can't let them find us like this. And then there's my in-laws! I'm never going to live this down. It's the end of my quiet existence. I'm going to have to listen to lectures about unmarried sex again. They did that when I got pregnant with Melanie. Oh God, oh God, oh God, I can't believe this!"

"Relax," I tell her. "I'm already mostly dressed, and worst case, I'll hide in the closet."

She pumps her hands up and down as though she's doing a push-up and blows a few breaths out. "Okay. Relax. I'm not doing anything wrong. I'm just having sex with a man. I'm an adult, and I can do that. Right?"

"I would like to say yes considering I'm who you had sex with." I walk over and pull her into my arms.

"Don't be charming. Be dressed and be gone before they show up."

Her pep talk didn't exactly calm her. I laugh once, kiss the top of her head, and throw my shirt on. "I'm all dressed now. Maybe you should do the same."

Brenna looks down. "Shit! I have no clothes on. What am I thinking? I'm not. I'm in some sort of post-amazing-night-of-sex haze."

She's fucking adorable.

After another second of her deep breathing, she grabs a dress from the closet and slips it on. "You look beautiful," I tell her.

"I look frazzled and like I just woke up in the arms of my lover. Maybe they'll know. Maybe they can sense the sex on me. Do I smell like it?"

I lean in and sniff. "You smell like apples. I'd bite you."

Brenna doesn't seem as amused by my joke as I am. "Jacob, what we're doing, it's just for us, and I really don't want my kids or anyone else getting the wrong idea about what we are. We're just fucking around, and while I'm enjoying it, my kids, well, they won't understand it. Sebastian loves you. Melanie thinks you're wonderful, and they'll want even the slightest chance that we could be something more than . . ." She points to the bed.

I nod, trying to pretend that I get it and that I haven't thought of nothing else other than wanting to be with her. "We are more than that."

Instantly, I regret saying it because there is a glimmer of hope in her eyes. "What are we then?"

If I were any other man, I'd say: *We're everything I want, and I'm falling in love with you. I want you to come with me because I don't know that I'll be able to walk away.*

But I'm not that man. I'm leaving in three months, and I won't do anything to break her heart. "We're friends."

I'm not a guy who Brenna should want to build a life with. I'm not noble or anything like the man she was married to before. I'm a mess with commitment issues and a Peter Pan complex. No woman would want a life with me.

She nods. "Right. Of course, we are." There's a sting in her response. "My point is that they're not stupid and neither is anyone else in this town. I want to keep doing this, but we can't be reckless."

It's as if I can hear Catherine agreeing with her in my head.

I want to protect Brenna and her kids just as much as she does. If someone in the press catches wind of this, Brenna's nice, quiet, country life will be gone. She'll be starring in every headline, and I won't be able to do a damn thing about it.

I grab my shoes before walking over and kissing her forehead. "You're right. We'll be more careful."

When she looks up, her eyes are soft and she looks so beautiful. "Thank you. Now, go."

I laugh and fight back the desire to tumble her back to the bed and really give her something to thank me for. "I'll see you tomorrow."

"Tomorrow."

Then I step back, feeling her loss everywhere and wishing more than anything I could stay as I walk away.

Sebastian pulls on the line, reeling as fast as he can. This kid has already caught four fish, and I haven't had so much as a bite. I'm starting to think he's jinxing me.

"Slowly," I encourage as he struggles with the fish.

He eases up, allowing the fish to think he's free, and then pulls up fast, moving his hands quickly. The line comes up, showing a huge bass at the end of it.

"Look, Jacob!"

I clap him on the back and help pull it onto the bank. "This is a gorgeous fish."

"He sure is. Mom is going to cry when she sees it."

"Cry?"

He grins. "Or puke."

I laugh because either is just as likely to happen. "You ready to head back?"

He nods, and we pack up.

As we're walking, he seems very in his own head. "Today's practice sucked," Sebastian says as he adjusts his gear.

"Yeah, it did."

Rehearsals were brutal. The kids were getting stuck on this same song over and over again, and I think by the sixteenth run-through, we were all ready to scream. No one wanted to run through it another time, but we did, and it still wasn't right.

"Why is that song so hard?"

Because you're all a bunch of kids with a dipshit as a director.

"It's a tough number with a lot of characters moving around. We'll get it. You guys are working hard." And they are. They suck, but they're trying.

"Yeah, but the play is in three weeks."

If this play and my involvement ever gets out, I'll be a laughing stock. There's very little chance we're going to improve these kids that much by opening night, but even if it's the worst play in the world, I've had fun doing it. I get to see Brenna almost daily. Sebastian has been a lot of fun to work with, and it's great to see people so excited.

"We'll be fine."

"I sure hope so."

He sounds like a little old man. "You know, even the worst performances have something good come from them."

Sebastian looks at me with a smile. "I think that's the same with bad things."

"Like what?"

"Like my dad dying."

My stomach drops, and I clear my throat. "What good

came from that?"

I can't imagine that any of us could've found something positive about losing our mother. We were stuck with an abusive father and hated that no one ever helped us.

Not that we were openly talking about the hell we lived. Declan and Sean always made sure we knew the rules. If we talked, we could be split up, and that was a reality none of us would ever accept.

"I met you."

I stop walking, feeling off balance and unsure of what to say. "I'm glad I met you too."

"It's like the only good thing that came from it all. Mom says we have to find the good, and that's really all I got."

"Maybe, but . . ."

Sebastian continues on. "And then my mom wouldn't have met you, and she wouldn't be smiling so much."

Shit. This isn't really ground I want to be on. "Sebastian."

His smile is sad. "I like that she's happy again. She doesn't cry in the bathroom anymore or walk around like she doesn't know where to go. I think she really likes you."

"I really like her."

"Then you should ask her out again."

The simplicity of his cause and effect makes my chest ache, and there is no way he would understand why I can't stay and always make Brenna happy. "You know I have to leave Sugarloaf soon, right?"

"I know. It's going to suck, and I wish you could stay."

I sink down so we're eye to eye. Saying this part aloud could be the mistake of a lifetime, but it's also the most truth I will ever voice. "If there were ever a reason that I would want to, it would be for your mom, you, and Melanie."

"Jacob?"

"Yeah?"

"Then why can't you?"

I sigh. "Because my job and my life are in California. I'd be gone a lot, and that wouldn't be fair to any of you."

"I get it."

I'm glad he does because it's the biggest load of bullshit. "I wish it were different."

"Me too. You'd be a great stepdad."

My throat is tight from emotion. "Let's get you home, man."

We start to walk again, and my mind is spinning in circles. I want to say more, to rebuke the lie I told and tell him it's because I'm fucking terrified of loving someone else and them leaving me because they'll see the life I can give isn't one that's stable. I want to run to Brenna's house, pull her into my arms and tell her the real reasons and that I'll battle them if she'll let me.

Brenna has dealt with a man who was gone, and my fear is that she won't ever do it again. She has had enough disappointment. How many birthdays did Luke miss? Anniversaries that weren't shared? How many times did she have to endure a night where she wanted him to hold her but his career came first?

Life would be the same with me.

If I need to be on set, I'm contractually obligated to do that.

But then I think of Brenna. I imagine waking up next to her, having meals together, watching movies on Wednesdays, and going to the fair together. I can see meeting her for lunches at the diner once a week and sneaking off to the creek where we can make love under the stars.

And then, as though my mother or God or someone somewhere were listening, I know what the curve I need to make is.

twenty-seven

"**A**nd what about the rumor going around town about you and Jacob?" Sylvia asks.

It's been a week since the last time she dropped in without calling first, and I thought that maybe we turned a corner. Clearly, that wasn't the case. Even if the visits are getting less frequent, the intrusiveness hasn't ebbed.

"There's nothing to it."

"Magnolia said you had lunch together again."

"Sylvia, we have lunch together once a week to discuss the play." Where we end up holding hands under the table or he's doing other things—naughty things.

She goes back to drying the dishes in the rack. "I'm just saying that Luke would've been very disappointed if you were to find someone like him for his replacement."

Anger simmers in my blood because she has no right to dictate anything in my life, let alone try to make me feel shame for who I choose to date in the future.

Two months ago, I would've let this slide, but not now. Not only because she has no right but also because, if there is anyone that I want in my life, it's Jacob. I won't allow her to disparage him.

"First of all, no one will ever replace Luke. That's not how it works. Luke will always be Melanie and Sebastian's father. He will always be a man I loved and raised a family with. Whatever man I choose to love going forward will not be a placeholder for the husband I lost. Secondly, Jacob is a good man. He's been wonderful to the kids and me. How many Hollywood stars would volunteer to direct a play for a bunch of kids? None, so I'm not sure what you think Luke would've been disappointed over."

Her hand flies to her throat, and she huffs. "It's too soon!"

"That's not for you to say."

"It's barely a year, Brenna! How can you be over the loss of him?"

The angry woman inside me wants to lash out so badly, to cut her down and tell her it isn't her place to tell me how to live, but that's not who I am. She's angry at me because she's in pain still. I know this, and while it would be easy to go back at her, to argue and fight, it wouldn't be right. Still, her not being ready to let him go isn't my cross to carry.

I sit on the bed and wait a few seconds. When I speak, it's soft and understanding. "I'll never be over losing Luke."

She tosses down the shirt, anger still radiating from her. "Yet, you're carrying on, doing God knows what with that man, in the town where my *son* is from."

"Do you want me to be alone for the rest of my life?"

That question seems to shock her. "Of course not! But why so soon?"

"It wouldn't matter if it was six months from now," I tell

her. "It wouldn't matter when or who or what town we lived in, it would feel this way."

"I don't need therapy."

I smile. "Maybe not, but we're still grieving regardless if we're talking about it. We're growing, healing, and learning each day. Loss and grief are terrible, and the stages are what they are regardless of if you're in therapy or not. I loved Luke. I will always love Luke. He was a wonderful husband and father. He's gone, though, and I'm not. I want to love again. I want to have someone to share my life with."

She takes my hand in hers. "I don't want you to be alone, Brenna. I'm just . . ."

"You're not ready for me to be ready yet."

The long breath she releases sounds a bit like a balloon deflating. She's no longer angry or filled with rage. Now it's sadness that's speaking. "No, I'm not."

"Jacob and I aren't . . . well, we're just friends."

"You don't have to lie to me, sweetheart. I see what's going on just as clearly as the rest of the town does."

"I promise that there is nothing more than what it is here."

Her soft, wrinkly hand palms my cheek. "That may be what you're telling yourselves, but, as you pointed out, what man directs a play for kids?"

"It was for Sebastian."

Sylvia rolls her eyes with a chuckle. "You're a fool, my sweet girl."

"I've been called that before."

She sits beside me, hand resting on my arm. "I may be an old lady and you may be a fancy head doctor, but let me give you a little piece of advice. Men don't do all that for a little kid. Sure, maybe in the beginning it was that, but I see the truth. He took you to the carnival, that barbeque at their house, and then I heard all about your movie night in the rain. You may be friends, but your heart wants more."

"Where have you heard all that?"

Her hand waves as she laughs. "It wasn't from my grand-kids, if that's what you're wondering. Those two have been tight-lipped and are the best secret keepers I've ever met."

I realize that we've been really bad with keeping this under wraps. If Sylvia heard all this from anyone other than the kids, everyone must know.

And from what Sylvia is saying, she sees the truth of my feelings too.

"Great. So, everyone knows the town psychologist is an idiot."

"Why are you an idiot?" I look up, knowing the truth is written all over my face. "Ahh, I see. I was right about your heart."

"And I was right about being an idiot."

"Most women are when it comes to men."

That's the damn truth. "I'm sorry that you've had to hear all this from other people."

She taps my thigh and then stands. "I knew that one day you'd find someone else, I just hoped I'd be dead by then."

"Sylvia!" I say with a laugh.

"I'm kidding. If Jacob is who makes you happy and he's good to my grandbabies, then don't let a little old lady's issues stand in your way." Her eyes go to the photo of Luke that sits on my dresser.

We only have one life, and I know more than anyone how short it really is.

Jacob and Sebastian are walking toward the house, and I stop, staring at the sight of them. Sebastian looks so happy, and I swear what could be my life flashes before me.

It would be so easy to have a life with Jacob. To love, argue, be happy and also struggle. It wouldn't be rainbows all the time, but the trials and tribulations would make us stronger. It's the tough times that prove the strength we have to overcome. At this point, I should be Hercules.

Lord knows it's going to take a herculean effort not to chase after this man.

My talk with Sylvia still lingers in my head, and I wonder if he could ever let himself build a life with me. If he could see how wonderful he is or how much love he has to give because Jacob is one of the best men I've ever known. I could tell him all this, beg him to stay and love me, to try to give us a chance, but I know more than anyone that the desire to change has to come from within. He has to want for things to be different. My telling him isn't going to do anything but drive a wedge between us.

I promised him that I wouldn't demand more. I have to keep my word.

Jacob's eyes never leave mine as they make their way over. My heart is racing, and I wish I could walk to him and kiss him senseless and negate the statement I just made.

"Hey, Mom!"

I break our hold and smile at my son. "Hey, dude."

"I got a huge fish."

I shudder. "Great."

"I'm going to clean up now." He turns to Jacob. "Thanks for going fishing with me again."

"Anytime."

He gives him a hug and then sighs. "I'll miss you when you leave."

Jacob clasps his shoulder. "We're going to be friends for a long time, Sebastian."

Sebastian runs off, leaving me alone with Jacob. We were planning to sneak away later tonight once the kids were asleep, but now I'm not so sure that's smart. Today has been a day full of truths I wasn't prepared for. My mother-in-law telling me that I've been pretty stupid was a lot, and it spiraled from there. I found an old shirt of Luke's, put it on, and sat at the edge of my bed, wondering what I was doing.

Not just why I was wearing the shirt, but why I was doing everything else.

Then I thought about Jacob and how much I care for him. I took the shirt off, looked at it, and wondered if Luke would approve of what I was doing.

I want to think he would, but do I believe that because it's what I want to believe or because it is the truth?

All of it was weighing so heavily, making it hard to breathe, but then I saw Jacob, and it lifted.

Like the world doesn't feel so heavy when I'm standing in front of him.

"Hi," I say a little breathless and uneasy because I'm not sure what to say.

Jacob looks behind me, and then, when he speaks, the weight increases. "I don't want to do this anymore."

My eyes widen, and I feel as though this is going to be what does me in. I'm going to be crushed in a few minutes. "Do what?"

He sighs. "This. What we're doing with each other. I can't do it anymore."

For a moment, I'm stunned. What the hell happened out there? When we talked this morning, it was him grabbing me and pulling me out of sight so he could kiss me while Sebastian went to get his gear. He was excited about us sneaking off, and now he suddenly can't do this?

"I don't understand."

He rubs his face and starts to pace. "We're both lying to each other, Brenna."

"I have never lied to you."

Jacob's green eyes are a myriad of emotions that are moving so fast I can't determine any of them. "No?"

"No."

"Tell me you don't feel more than just casual about whatever it is we're doing. Tell me that your feelings for me are nothing more than friendship."

I take a step back, and my stomach drops. That would be a lie. I feel so much more. I feel alive and happy, and I want him so much that tears threaten to form. It's not just want though. It's more than that. It's a need that's bone deep.

My breath comes out in short bursts. "I can't do that."

"Neither can I." Jacob advances on me and settles his hands on my hips.

What I thought was being stunned before pales in comparison to this. "What are you saying?"

"I'm saying I can't do this anymore, this casual thing where I pretend that I'm not completely falling for you."

I close my eyes, trying to keep my breathing normal. Here I am, trained and certified to help people get through situations, and I am lost on this one. Everything that we've said from the beginning and all I've been trying to deny is right in my face.

"Why? You're going to leave."

His finger glides down, tracing my jaw. "Ask me to stay for you."

I shake my head. "I won't do that."

"Why not?"

"Because it's one thing to know that someone is leaving and accept the reality of the situation. It's another to think they'll stay and then have them leave. That's why I survived losing Luke." Jacob's silence tells me he doesn't understand what I'm saying. "As a military wife, you form this understanding with God and your spouse that, one day, they might not walk back through that door. Hell, you spend months before a deployment planning for that loss. In some part of my heart, I always believed that my time with Luke was finite. What I got was a gift because, at any moment, it could be gone."

"I'm an actor, not a pilot."

"I know that. My point is that we had a defined time, Jacob. We had months to be whatever it was we wanted to be. I did my best to accept that. I have been trying to mentally prepare for you to leave. I'm falling for you—no, I've already fallen for you, but that was okay for me because you were leaving."

He releases a sigh. "So, you don't want to ask me to stay?"

"No, I don't because if you leave, then what?"

I'm also not stupid enough to ask a question I don't want the answer to.

"The answer might surprise you."

It also might not.

My hands rest on his shoulders, and I move to cup his face. "Then surprise me in a few months. Don't make me ask. If your feelings for me are strong enough, then . . . then stay for me."

He gives me a kiss, it's soft and sweet and filled with a sense of new beginnings. "I'm going to be really bad at this," he warns me.

"What?"

"Being more. I've never had a relationship that wasn't built on the fact that it would never be anything else."

As much as I hate to admit this, I remember Sebastian talking about an actress Jacob dated early in his career. "What about that one actress?"

"I was twenty. That wasn't a relationship. It wasn't real either. I don't know how to be more, Brenna, but I really want you to show me."

twenty-eight

O kay. I'm fine. This is not a big deal. Jacob has had dinner at the house and has been with the kids a bunch of times. I'm not freaking out.

I'm totally freaking out.

Jacob is coming for dinner tonight, and we're planning to tell the kids we're officially dating. Yeah, I'm a damn mess.

I'm standing in the kitchen, stirring the sauce, and trying to go over possible scenarios. This is the advice I would give, so I'm going to take it myself.

They could freak out like Sylvia did, but I don't think that is the likely outcome. I think they're going to be happy and excited, which if this relationship falls apart, would be a loss for my kids too.

And that's the crux of my fear.

"Mom!" Melanie yells, causing me to drop the wooden spoon into the pot.

"Shit."

She laughs. "I called you like five times."

"Sorry, my mind is elsewhere." I grab the very end of the spoon and toss it into the sink. When I turn to her, she's staring at me. "What? Do I have something on my face?"

Melanie chews on her lower lip. "You're nervous." I don't reply. "The only time I've seen you like this was when you had to tell us about Dad."

"It's nothing like that, Mel."

"I didn't think it was. I'm sure it's that you plan to tell us about you and Jacob, as though we didn't already know."

"How could you know something that didn't happen?" I counter.

"Please, Mom. Jennifer's mom told her how she saw you guys kissing at the carnival. Then your lipstick was gone after you went out to the barn a few weeks ago."

My cheeks burn, and I turn away. "That's enough."

Her voice goes a little higher, and she pokes my side. "You're dating Jacob, and you're afraid to tell us."

I let out a deep breath and then face her. "Yes. I'm dating Jacob. Officially. Now. And, of course, I was nervous about telling you."

Mel smiles. "We like him, and we sort of figured this was coming."

"And that's what makes me nervous, babe. He's, like, a big star and this uber famous man. If we break up, who do you think this town and the people in it will turn on?"

My daughter, who is far too wise for her age, just shrugs. "Then they're not people we want in our lives."

"How did you get to be so smart?"

"Dad."

I burst out laughing and pull her in for a hug. "I love you,

Mel."

"I love you too, Mom."

There's a knock at the door, and we break apart, both smiling. "Come on, let me go introduce you to my . . . boyfriend."

We walk hand in hand to the door where Jacob stands with a bouquet of flowers in front of him.

"These are for you." My heart flutters, and I go to grab them, but he takes them back. "Not you." He then extends them to Melanie. "But you."

Melanie takes the flowers, her smile wide as she giggles. "Thank you, Jacob. These are beautiful."

He winks at me and then focuses on Melanie. "It's my pleasure."

Melanie leans in and kisses his cheek. "I'm glad you're dating my mother."

Jacob's eyes widen, and his gaze darts to me. "You told her?"

"She guessed."

"The whole town knows," Mel says with exasperation.

"Apparently, everyone knew before we did."

Jacob shakes his head with a laugh. "And this is reason four hundred and thirty-three as to why I hate small towns."

"What's number four hundred and thirty-two?" I ask with bemusement.

"Cows."

Melanie snorts, and I roll my eyes. "Come on in, you ridiculous man. We still have one more kid to talk to."

Sebastian took it exactly as I expected. He was overjoyed. Jacob won my son's heart the day he showed up at the door, so the mere idea of getting to be a part of his life is beyond Sebastian's wildest dreams.

The paranoid and overanalytical part of me is screaming to proceed with caution. It won't just be one broken heart in this house if things don't work out. The other part of me is saying to stop assuming it will end in failure and just enjoy the journey.

Not sure which side is going to win out.

However, the kids are in their rooms since they have to be up early for school, and Jacob and I are on the couch with a movie on that neither of us is really watching. Instead, I'm just enjoying this. The normal little bubble we have where I'm allowed to rest in the arms of the man I am falling in love with.

"So, how do you think we did?" he asks.

"I think it was good."

"Me too. It'll make it easier for me to be here more often now that they know."

I smile at that sentiment. "I'm going to like you being around more."

He kisses the top of my head. "Remember you said that after you find out I ate all your ice cream."

I think I'll say that always, ice cream or not. Here, it's just Brenna and Jacob. There're no fears of people finding out about us or wondering if what we're doing is right or wrong. We're us. We're content. We've had a good meal, laughter, and we're winding down together.

"Are you hiding some flaw that will make me immune to your charm?"

"Don't you wish you knew?"

"Are you going to answer the question?"

Jacob chuckles. "Are we playing the who answers the

question with a question game again?"

I tilt my head so I can look at him. "I don't know, are we?"

We both laugh softly, and he adjusts us so I'm now lying on his leg. "It's just that we went from casually hooking up with no expectations to dating in a world where there are cameras and intrusive people. The fact that I haven't had a girlfriend in over ten years is going to be a big deal. Add in that you're a single mom in a small town, and it's going to be an even bigger story."

"Did you talk to your publicist?"

Jacob nods and brushes my hair back. "I did. Catherine is going to work up a press release so that we control the narrative. She wants to release a statement and photos of us together in town after the play."

"What photos?"

He clears his throat. "I probably should've mentioned it first. She wants us to have a photographer she trusts come and do a very informal shoot."

I'm not sure how I feel about someone doing a photo shoot because we're dating.

"I know it's uncomfortable," he says quickly. "I hate that it's this way for me, but if we can make the story less like we were hiding it, it should be better, and *maybe* they'll give me some space. Catherine knows how I feel about it. She knows most of your story, and agrees that the kids should be shielded as much as possible. She's a mom, too, and understands that the kids come first."

I'm touched that he feels this way. Also, I know nothing about this world. If I want a life or even a chance at one with Jacob, then I have to be willing to take the bad along with the good. "Okay, we'll do what she says is best."

Catherine knows the world of paparazzi, journalists, and media. I do not. I can get through other situations, but I'm lost here, so I will defer to the professional.

"I have to warn you"—Jacob's voice is low—"it's still going to be bad, Brenna. The press will want to find a story, true or not doesn't really matter to them, and I won't be able to protect you. I wish I could, and the fact that it will be out of my control is going to fucking kill me."

I sit up, crossing my legs and facing him. "Part of the deal when we decided to go forward was knowing there'd be challenges."

"Yeah, but this isn't just a challenge, it's almost like a new life. The things we've enjoyed here, they're not like that there." He runs his hand through his hair.

"I'm not naïve, Jacob. I'm aware that this isn't going to be easy, but you're worth it."

The way his eyes flash makes me wonder if that's the first time he's ever heard anything like that. He looks slightly scared and more than a little stunned.

"You say that now."

"Are you afraid I'm going to think otherwise later?"

Jacob looks away and when he turns back, that crooked grin is there, masking whatever he's really feeling. "Maybe. Do you change your mind often?"

I want to call him out, tell him that I'm not blind, and remind him that he's dating a shrink who knows all the tricks and signs of deflection. In the back of my head, I hear Luke, and I remember how much he hated it.

So many times, we'd be fighting, and I would turn it into therapy. He would yell louder, get angrier than he was before and tell me how tiring it was being married to someone who couldn't let him work it out for himself. I always had to fix things—fix him—and he hated it.

I don't want to do that with Jacob. He's not my patient. He's my boyfriend. One I'd like very much to continue seeing. Therefore it's in my best interests to just be honest.

"No, I don't change my mind. That's what I'm saying to you. I'm here. I'm in this with you, and I'm ready for whatever obstacles we have to face. As long as you're in it with me, I'm here."

The words do what I hoped they would, and the playful smile that was there falls into a look of seriousness. The tight lines around his eyes sharpen. "And if it gets to be too much?"

I lean in, my fingers tracing those lines until they soften. "Then we talk, and we work it out. This isn't something I'm willing to give up on. *You're* not someone I'm willing to give up on."

"Why?"

Because I'm in love with you.

"Because you make me happy."

His eyes close, and he grips my hand, holding it to his face. "I'm going to be a handful."

"I never had any doubts that you would be."

"My career is demanding. I fought against this because of that. You dealt with a lot because Luke was away all the time for work, and now you're jumping back in again."

"It's different this time. Luke never had a choice. You can turn roles down, can't you?"

He nods. "As long as I'm not under contract. Like I said, I don't want to put you through the hell you endured before. You came here wanting simple, and I'm far from that. I don't want to disappoint you or the kids, Brenna. I want to be the hero in your story."

"Just you saying that makes you one." A part of me knew his career would be difficult to handle. When I left California, I wanted to find a guy from a small town who wouldn't be darting off all the time. I thought that, if I found normal, I could finally settle down and be happy. "You know, Cybil asked me if I really would be happy with someone mundane or simple. The thing is, I don't think I would. I would be bored, and you, Jacob Arrowood, are not boring. You're a good man with a big heart and you make me happy. I've dealt with separations before, and we'll find a way through it when it comes to that. If anything, I think this shows how good we can be."

"You do?" he asks dubiously.

"Of course. I like having space a bit here and there."

He comes in close and gives me a kiss. "You're really perfect, you know?"

"Now you're delusional."

"Maybe so, but I'm very happy in this fantasy—with you."

I smile and move in. "Me too."

"Good."

"Now, let's make out on the couch before I have to sneak you out of here."

twenty-nine

"Hey, Declan, what brings you here?" I ask as I step out of this tiny house that still smells like apples from Brenna's hair products.

Tonight, we have a big date. I've gone all out. I want to make her feel special, and it's taken a lot of ingenuity to come up with something when I can't really go anywhere. Those plans require me to get my ass on the road.

"I just wanted to talk to you."

"About?" I ask as I walk toward the car.

"Where are you going?"

"To the moon. Now, seriously, what's up?"

Declan rubs the back of his neck. "I just came by to look at the tiny house. My lease is up on this bad boy a few days after your time is up, and I have to send the owner pictures so he can see what work it needs."

My chest tightens, and I stare at him, not saying anything.

The idea of leaving here in a few months suddenly makes me nauseated. I don't want to leave, and I'm not expecting to move in with Brenna. I need a place, so I might as well keep this damn thing.

"I'll buy it."

His head jerks back. "And do what with it?"

"Own it."

"Yeah, I get that," Declan says with a huff. "I'm asking why the hell you want it? You leave soon and absolutely hate it."

"And now I like it."

That's overstating it a bit, but it has very small perks. Like that sneaking a very sexy redhead in and out undetected is much easier than my sneaking in her window. And the fact that when she's lying in my arms and we look out the floor-to-ceiling windows on the side, it reminds me of our date at the movies—before the torrential downpour.

Declan scratches the back of his head. "Okay, then. I'm not going to ask because I'm sure it has to do with Brenna."

"Why do you say that?"

"Because you have that goofy grin on your face."

"What goofy grin?"

He points. "That one. You're all smiles, and you get that stupid look like you've been hit by Cupid's arrow or maybe it's another arrow who shot her with something else."

I roll my eyes. "Watch it, Dec."

"You're serious about her, aren't you?"

Older brothers are good for very little besides annoying the fuck out of you. My brother is exceptional at that. "What do you think? I just offered to buy this shack on wheels."

Of course, I am serious. Hell, I think I'm in love with her, for fuck's sake.

He smiles. "I'm happy for you. I know the girls are all over the moon about it. They love Brenna and would welcome her into the family."

The visions of us living in her house and being domestic fill me and then evaporate like mist. I can't let myself go that far ahead. We still have a lot of shit to deal with. Our photo shoot is coming up, and we need to prepare for our happy little world to become chaos. I have to pace myself or we'll both end up crushed.

"Well, as happy as I am that the three of them are on board, we're not taking things that quickly."

"I understand. You're scared."

I let out a long sigh. "I'm not scared, Declan. I'm being smart. I'm not going to rush into something that has the potential to hurt her and the kids. Once this story is out next week, we won't be able to live in the bubble that is Sugarloaf. There will be press, photos, stories that aren't true about me and God only knows who else I'm filming with. There's more to think about than my own shit."

Declan chuckles, but it's more of an apprehensive sound. "I don't envy you there, brother. I just want you to also be honest about it. I know what you're feeling. I've literally been there. All three of us have. We grew up and spent most of our adult lives believing we were unworthy and unlovable. It's still hard for me some days. I wait for Syd to wake up and be like, nah, he isn't worth it."

My brother has always tried to be this statue-like figure in my life. I knew he wasn't that way. I've seen him cry when he thought no one was looking. I also know how much losing Sydney broke him to his core. Even during all of that pain, he never voiced it. Talking was not his strong suit. He liked to pretend that being strong meant he *was* strong. It was his way of accepting his reality.

Hearing him admit anything to the contrary is a bit unsettling.

"And you think she will?"

"No, but it's easy to wonder sometimes. For years, we were told what pieces of shit we were. How we didn't do anything right. We were his literal punching bag both physically and emotionally. The only reason we survived was because we had each other and the girls."

Devney and Sydney saved the four of us more than they ever knew because, no matter what, they gave us slivers of joy. Going to Sydney's pond and swimming or riding and caring for the stray animals at Devney's farm, gave us a reprieve from the pain.

"I don't know, Dec. I really don't because, on one hand, I'm pretty sure I'm already fucked. She's everything I want. She's perfect for me in every way. The other hand tells me that I'm not good enough for her. I'll taint her and break her."

My brother's hand grips my shoulder. "That is not *your* hand talking, Jacob. That's *his,* and you can't listen to it. You won't break her. You won't taint her. She's chosen you, but you have to choose her and yourself."

I already have chosen her. I choose her in every way, but it feels too simple, and that scares me. Loving her shouldn't be this easy. It should be a struggle, and it's not. It's . . . effortless. It's like drawing a breath without having to tell yourself to do so. It just happens.

"How did you manage feeling this way for Sydney and not fucking lose your mind?"

He laughs. "What makes you think I haven't? I love that girl beyond reason and all portions of sanity. I would do anything, give up everything, and fight until my last breath for her. It just took me a really long time to understand that meant fighting for her, not against."

"You're a lucky man."

He looks back toward his property and sighs. "I am. And if you let yourself, you'd see that you are too. Now, I'll get the papers drawn up so you can be the happy owner of this tiny house. Wonder what land you might set it on."

"As much as I'd love to kick your ass, Dec, I have a hot date tonight and don't want to mess up my outfit."

He rolls his eyes and laughs. "You could try, Hollywood, but you'd fail."

"Yeah, yeah, we'll see about it."

Declan laughs. "Yeah, when you're not trying to win over your girl."

I look down at my watch, wondering if I can squeeze in a quick ass kicking, and think better of it. Date night is way more important.

thirty

"**W**here are we going?" Brenna asks for the fifth time as we enter the clearing in the woods.

Everything is set up, and I'm nervous for her to see it. I hope I got it right, but this is a first for me. I've never been a romantic guy, that was always Sean. I was more straightforward and sort of prescribed to the idea that it was what it was.

"Just go with it."

She told me how much she hates surprises, but I'm sort of liking this. Brenna is always in control, and I want her to know she doesn't have to be all the time. She can let go and let someone else help her.

"I'd like to see you be blindfolded and not let your mind wander and worry you're being led into the woods to your own death."

"You watch way too many crime shows. If I wanted to kill you, I wouldn't let anyone know we were going on a date."

She turns her head. "Maybe that's part of your plan."

"Yes, my big evil plan to make you happy is to bring you into the woods to kill you after letting everyone know you would be with me."

"It could happen."

I laugh at her ridiculousness. "I guess it could." We take a few more steps before I stop her. "Ready?"

"As I'll ever be."

"I really hope you like this as the place I might kill you."

Brenna leans back into my chest and sighs. "Let's see it."

I untie the blindfold and then wrap my arms around her waist, resting my chin on her shoulder.

Her breath hitches, and I try to see the space through her eyes. There are thousands of candles lit all over. Dozens of illuminated Mason jars hang from the branches, making it look both soft but bright. There are blankets all over the ground and in the center sits a table with flowers and more candles.

"Jacob, this is . . . this is . . ."

"A good place for me to kill you?"

She laughs and then turns in my arms to look at me. "This is incredible and beautiful, so if you want to kill me here, I'm okay with it."

"It's you who is killing me, Brenna. Every time I'm around you, I feel a part of the old me die to make room for something new."

Her fingers lift to my cheek, and she smiles. "From the ashes always comes life. You and I are both burning the past so we can start something new and beautiful."

"When I came here, I swore I would leave without a single hesitation," I confess.

"I swore I'd never risk my heart to be broken."

I move her hair back off her face, needing to touch her and

make sure she's real. "What a pair we are."

"I think we're pretty great."

"You also thought I was bringing you here to kill you," I tease.

Brenna pushes onto her toes and kisses me. "It would be a great way to go."

"How about we not die and just have dinner?"

"Sounds good."

I lead her over to the table where there are two covered dishes. I went out on a limb here because, according to Sebastian, her favorite food is Twizzlers. While that would have been great if we were eleven, it didn't quite work for what I wanted. I tried to have Ellie do a little digging, but she came up empty.

I remembered how she mentioned one food a few times, and since we're somewhat close to New York, I called in some favors.

Once she's seated, I make a very dramatic show of removing the dome to reveal a very fancy version of grilled cheese.

"Oh! Is that from Murray's?"

I nod. "It sure is."

"Jacob! You got me a sandwich from Murray's! This is only the single best grilled cheese I've ever had in my life. And it was once. And I . . . you remembered?"

Thank God I pay attention. "You said it was the best, so I had some brought out."

"You had my favorite food ever delivered to a dinner in the woods. I don't know what to say."

"How about we eat it before it's totally ruined."

Every now and then it's nice to be me, and this was one of those times. I called the owner who sent his chef here to make the grilled cheese so it was fresh. She will never know how much I just ended up paying for a sandwich, but it doesn't matter, Brenna is happy.

She shakes her head and gets up, making her way to me. "I don't care about the sandwich right now. I need to kiss you." I pull her onto my lap, and her fingers are against my scruff. "This is the sweetest, most thoughtful thing that anyone has ever done for me. I love your surprise. I love . . ." She stops, leaving me to wonder how that statement was going to end. If it ends the way I expect it to, what will I say? Do I tell her that I'm falling in love with her and it scares the shit out of me? Instead of saying it, she smiles. "I love everything about this, and you're making it really hard not to feel more for you."

"What if I don't want you to feel less?"

Brenna's blue eyes are searching mine. "What do you want me to feel?"

"Special. Cherished. Desired. I want to make you smile and give you the world. This is our last weekend before we tell everyone and I want you to know what that means."

I should tell her, but I don't want to scare her. Fucking hell, dating is not fun.

"It means everything to me, and every time I'm with you, I feel that way. Thank you."

"You never have to thank me for wanting to show you how I feel."

A second later, her lips touch mine, and I never want this kiss to stop.

"I think they need to be a little closer in the shot," Catherine instructs as she looks at the back of the camera.

I groan. "Cat, seriously. We've been at this for an hour."

She glares at me and then gives Brenna a soft smile. "I'm sorry, but we need the image to say more than the story will."

Needless to say, I was surprised to wake up to a short brunette with a bag of bagels banging on the door. Catherine had flown in to make sure I didn't "fuck it up" with the photographer. She wants the photos to have a very specific feel to them. After a lot of arguing, we settled on which magazine will break the story. She wanted more of a newspaper, but after we talked, we both agreed on a celebrity magazine that focuses on the story and won't sensationalize things.

And here we are, in the field with the mountains behind us and the slightest hint of sunlight on the horizon.

Brenna's hand rests on my chest. "It's fine. She's thorough, if nothing else. Besides, it's beautiful out here, and I'm getting to kiss and touch you a lot."

I kiss the side of her head and sigh. "I guess that is the silver lining here. But we have rehearsal in fifteen minutes and opening night is in two days. Without the dictator here, the photos would have been fast."

She leans back and looks up at me. "It'll be fine. No matter what happens with the play, you being there is all that matters. Besides, this reminds me of our date night last weekend. Too bad you didn't plan a bed then."

Sometimes she says the exact perfect thing to make me smile and let it go. I've been worried sick over the play for the last week. The kids are getting better, but I'm terrified that it's going to look like a joke. We sold out all three shows in under twenty minutes.

It lets you know what the hell they're really coming for.

"And if I had?"

"We would've used it, of course."

"I think we were quite inventive with the pit stop at my

place."

Brenna blushes a deep red and then buries her head in my chest.

I love how open she is. Every reaction is pure. I never have to worry about what she feels because it's plain as day on her face. It's refreshing, and I hope we never grow tired of this.

After another minute, she looks up at me. "Why are you so nervous, Jacob? You're doing wonderful things with the kids. You're putting so much effort into it, and it's coming along great."

I release a deep sigh. All of that is true, but there's a world that Brenna doesn't see, and it's not a kind one. "I'm just worried that the press will get wind of the play and people will see I'm a laughing stock."

"Of a children's musical. Keep the perspective, babe. This was never going to earn you an Oscar nomination. Besides, don't you think the press will be more excited to talk about how selfless you are? You're a superhero who is living out his part. I'm sure that Catherine and your team is prepared for whatever press the play gets."

She's right, but I don't care about that right now. The only perspective I'm seeing right now is how I feel about her. Her happiness is what matters.

"You look beautiful," I say as I push the hair back behind her ear, no longer caring about the play. "You always do, and I don't tell you enough."

"You're very charming."

"Only for you."

She grins. "Four months ago, if someone had told me that I'd be in the woods with you because we were going to announce our relationship, I'd have laughed."

"And if anyone told me I'd be in a relationship with someone from Sugarloaf, I would have had them committed."

"And, yet, here we are."

I look into those blue eyes and get lost. "Here we are."

She presses onto her toes to brush her lips to mine. When she goes back to the ground, I cup her face and say words I never thought I'd say. "I love you, Brenna."

"Jacob . . ."

"I know it's soon. I know we haven't been together for long, but I love you, and I didn't want to wait to say it any longer. I wanted to say it on our date, but I wasn't sure you were ready to hear it."

Tears well in her eyes, and she ducks her head into my chest. After a few seconds, she looks back up. "I love you too. I'm not just saying it because you did either. I can't explain it, but—"

I break off whatever she was going to say by kissing her. We stand here, uncaring of anyone or anything else around us. I love her, and I don't know how the hell we're going to make this work, but there's no other option than to do everything I can to figure it out. Even if it means staying in Sugarloaf.

thirty-one

"**A**re you going to find out what you're having?" I ask Devney.

The older Arrowood kids are all watching a movie inside the house and the babies are asleep while the adults are relaxing outside around a bonfire.

My two kids are with their grandparents for the night since they haven't had a lot of time with them the last few weeks. Rehearsals, school, and they've been busy with their friends has caused a bit of pulling back, which I'm not complaining about.

She looks to Sean and smiles. He rolls his eyes and then answers, "I don't want to know."

Declan rolls his eyes. "You? Mr. Impatient. You don't want to know?"

Sean shakes his head. "Nope. I don't want to."

"I would want it to be a surprise too," Jacob adds on.

"Really?" I ask, my voice going a bit higher.

He nods. "There aren't many things in life that surprise us, I think part of the fun is the doctor holding up the baby and telling you."

I never pictured him as the type of guy who would want to be surprised. "Interesting."

"Well, I for one couldn't wait to find out," Syd says. "Of course, my gender appointment was much more dramatic than any of us cared for."

Everyone laughs, except for Declan, whose eyes look haunted as he watches his wife. "It was hell, Bean. Absolute hell."

She brushes her fingers along his cheek and smiles. "I know, but it brought us to heaven."

Jacob leans in. "Sydney almost died. They found some issues, and it was . . . well, it was the scariest thing I've ever watched my brother go through."

It's clear that Declan still struggles with it. "I'm glad you're all here and safe now."

"Me too," Sydney says. "However, Jacob, you're stupid, and until you actually have a baby on the way, you can't possibly know what you would do."

"Ellie, did you find out?" I ask.

"Nope. Connor and I wanted to be surprised."

"They're also stupid, but I love them," Syd notes. "I needed to plan. I had clothes to buy, and I couldn't handle not knowing."

I laugh. "I was the same. As soon as I could find out, I needed to know. I don't do well with surprises."

Sydney gives me a beer-bottle salute and then leans back in her chair.

All of us laugh and Devney clears her throat. "Sean may

not want to know, but I plan to find out the sex of the baby."

"Wait, you're going to find out?" Jacob asks in disbelief.

"Yes, Sean doesn't have to know, but there's not a chance in hell I'm not."

Sydney nods. "That's right."

"Stay out of it, Bean," Declan warns and then turns to his brother. "I give it three days after Devney finds out before you're begging for her to tell you."

Sean flips him off. "Wanna bet on it?"

Connor laughs. "I got twenty on Sean begging too. He'll never last."

"Knock it off," Syd chides. "I have faith in Sean. Devney is going to hide all the baby stuff she buys at our house and I'll make sure Sean can't get access."

"Like you could stop me from getting in?" Declan challenges.

"Wanna bet on that, pumpkin?"

He groans, and his head falls back. "Why do I even try?"

"I'm not really sure."

Ellie grips Sydney's hand. "This is going to be great, we'll all know and be able to buy stuff, but Sean won't."

This family takes way too much joy in bickering with each other, and it's entirely too entertaining to watch.

"I love our bonfire nights." Sydney sinks into the chair, taking a long pull on her beer before tipping the neck toward the flames.

"Why is that?" Connor asks.

Syd looks around with a smile. "Because I never thought this would be our lives. I hoped, of course, that maybe we'd all be happy, but I didn't think it would be together like this. All four Arrowood brothers here and in love with the best women in the world. I feel like Mama A would be so happy."

Jacob's hand engulfs mine. "She would be happy with who we chose."

I tangle my fingers in his. "I'm glad she would."

He lifts our hands to his lips and kisses my knuckles.

"God, who is pathetic now?" Sean asks with a laugh.

"Fuck off."

"Dude, you were at my wedding not five months ago, talking about how stupid I was and how you were going to never be like us. Now look at you—whipped."

Jacob shrugs as though he couldn't care less. "I'm not whipped, brother. I've just found what you all have, and I'm happy."

"Awww," all the girls say at the same time.

"That's so sweet," Ellie adds on.

Devney slaps Sean's chest. "You shouldn't talk."

"I never said I wasn't whipped. I'm very happy to be in your clutches, sweetheart. There's not another woman alive I'd rather be with."

That seems to mollify her. "Good."

"But I'm saying that Jacob was talking about having him committed if he was like us, and look . . . all it took was Brenna to show up with a casserole, and he was gone."

Again, Jacob doesn't seem fazed. "I'm not going to deny it." He turns to me. "When I saw you, everything changed. I tried to deny it, but things that I thought made sense before—didn't anymore. The dreams I thought were dead all came back."

I brush my thumb along his lips. "You're going to make me love you even more."

"My goal is to make you love me so much that you can't imagine a world without me."

Little does he know I'm already there. I wake up thinking

of him. I fall asleep wishing his arms were wrapped around me. During the day, I wonder where he is and if he's thinking of me the way that I am about him.

I can't remember the last conversation I had that didn't include his name. And then there was earlier today.

When we stood in the woods, staring at each other and confessing how we felt. It was the most beautiful moment I've shared with a man.

Yes, my wedding was something, but it was two kids who weren't sure if what they were doing was right. Luke proposed to me on my driveway three days after we found out we were pregnant. There was no beautiful or elaborate plan.

I can't remember the first time we said we loved each other or if we meant it.

But there isn't a doubt in my mind that I will never forget today.

I love him, and he loves me.

"Were we this gross?" Connor asks, breaking the moment.

Ellie sighs. "We sure were."

"You still are!" Declan offers. "While the rest of us are just as ridiculously in love, we don't go around, unable to keep our hands to ourselves."

Sean chuckles. "Says the man who created the smolder."

"The what?" Declan asks.

"The smolder. You get all broody and stare at Syd like she's wood and you're about to light her on fire."

Declan turns to her. "Do I do that?"

"I mean, you definitely think I'm hot. But . . . I don't know, look at me now like you want me to burn," she teases.

He glares at her, and she looks away. "Didn't work."

Jacob stands. "I'd like to say we had a good time, but that would be overstating the time I'm forced to be around you people. Brenna, how about we head off?" He extends his hand to mine.

"We all know where you're heading off to," Connor says with a snigger.

I feel the heat flood my cheeks and stand, allowing Jacob to cocoon me. "Be jealous."

Unable to look at them, I lift my hand as a goodbye and allow Jacob to escort me away.

As soon as we're out of view, he starts to laugh, and I look at him as if he's crazy. "What?"

"Just that I'm fucking happy, Brenna. I'm truly and sincerely happy. It's . . . funny because I never expected to be happy again."

I understand exactly what he means. I'd been so sure that loving someone and being happy was a dream. Something that was possible but ultimately unobtainable. Jacob has given me the hope that I might get to be happy again. When I lost Luke, I thought that maybe I would like a man, maybe love him in some capacity, but never like this.

Never did I think I'd meet and love with my whole world.

Jacob has given me more in the few months we've been together than I had in all those years.

I push up on my toes, wanting to kiss him so much that I can't stop myself. His hands move to my hair, tightening around the strands as the kiss grows deeper and more urgent.

We start to move, Jacob walking backward, guiding us to the tiny house he's staying in. It's become where we meet, make love, and part ways before the sun rises.

Tonight, I don't plan to leave. I want to roll over in his strong arms and feel safe in his embrace.

He smiles against my lips when he can't get the door open, and when he does, he scoops me up, my legs wrapping around him as we both laugh softly.

"Impatient much?" I ask.

"For you? Always."

He moves into the very small space, dropping me onto the bed before standing back and letting his eyes roam over me.

"What?"

"I keep waiting to be told this isn't real."

I lift up onto my elbows. "Why do you think that?"

"Because when I look at you, I see light and beauty."

"And are you going to drag me into the darkness?" I say with a grin.

"Is that what you want?"

I squirm under his gaze. "I want you in the light or the dark. I like you at dawn and dusk. It doesn't matter when or where so long as you're with me."

His hands move down my neck, pulling the straps of my dress down as he reaches my shoulders. Jacob's lips touch the sensitive skin right below my ear. "You could tempt a man to promise anything."

My eyes shut as his deep voice vibrates through me. "Says the man who every woman fantasizes about."

"And what do you dream about, beautiful?"

"You," I say without hesitation. "I dream about your eyes watching me. Your lips touching me. Your hands on my skin and how I can't . . ." His finger moves to my breast, making a slow circle around my nipple.

"You can't what?"

"I can't think."

And I can't. My brain is total mush every time he touches me. Jacob continues the motion before going to the other breast. "Want to know what I think about, Brenna?" he asks as his head moves down to where his hand is. "I think about your skin on my lips. I dream about how you look at me as though

I'm worthy of you. I think about how I want to wake up next to you and feel your warmth and be able to see your smile."

I'm a puddle of mush. "Jacob." I sigh his name.

He leans down as he slips the dress lower, exposing me to his gaze. "I'm going to make love to you, Brenna. I'm going to show you how I feel, and even then, I don't know that you'll feel just how much I care about you."

I know it. In every bone in my body I feel it. There's nothing he needs to do to show me because it's in his everyday actions. How he shows up, makes me laugh, shows me how much he cares. Jacob is strong and protective. Each day I find something else about him that endears him to me. I want a life with him. I want it all.

I run my hand through his thick brown hair, loving how the strands slide through my fingers and his eyes close at my touch. "Show me."

His hands hook under my thighs, and he pulls me quickly, causing me to lie on the bed in one swift move.

There is a look of smug satisfaction on his face. "Your wish is my command."

His shirt goes flying to the floor and then his shorts. God, he's glorious naked. His body is lean and toned in all the right places. My mouth waters as I travel down his body to where his erection juts out. I can't seem to resist the urge to touch him, so I don't. I wrap my hand around his cock and move up and down.

"Fuck, Brenna." I love that he says my name as though it's a sob. After a few more seconds, he groans and pushes my hand away. "Not yet, baby. I need you more."

He finishes tugging off my dress and tosses it to the heap of our clothing. I groan as his fingers slide against my opening. He teases me, toying with my clit, not quite pressing but exerting enough pressure that I feel it.

"Please," I beg.

"Please what?"

My breathing starts to grow more frantic as he increases the friction. The pressure inside me is building, and his lips on mine are consuming me. The deep strokes of his tongue match what his hands are doing. He inserts a finger deep as his thumb circles my clit.

I'm rocking against his hand, desperate for the edge of the cliff. My nails dig into his back, and that spurs him to go deeper, harder, fucking me with his fingers all while kissing me so I can't make any noise.

I attempt to turn my head, needing to cry out as the pleasure starts to become too much, but he moves with me. I can't stop it. It's too late. I scream into his mouth as he pulls every ounce of my orgasm that he can.

Then he's pushing into me, and what I thought was pleasure before pales in comparison.

Jacob thrusts forward, his eyes finding mine. "I love you."

My fingers graze the stubble on his face. "I love you."

There's no need for words as our bodies say everything else.

thirty-two

The play is tomorrow, and I'm freaking the hell out. These kids have worked so hard, and I'm not sure that we all won't end up completely embarrassed, but I don't quite care tonight. After seeing them earlier, it was clear that none of that mattered. For them, it's truly the love of acting, and I can only hope to have that level of joy the next time I get onto a set.

I grab my phone when it buzzes with a text.

Catherine: *Hey, I wanted to show you the photo that we're going with. It's seriously amazing.*

It comes through the screen, and I can't stop the grin from forming. I had no idea they were taking photos when Brenna and I weren't paying attention, but there it is. It was the moment right after I told her I loved her. Her eyes are on my face, her hands are resting on my chest, and she's looking at me as though I gave her the most amazing gift. Her hair has glints of orange from the sun, and she's radiant. Of course, it's nothing like how she looked last night. That was beyond the capability of any camera to capture.

Me: Wow.

Catherine: Right! I'm so glad the photographer and I were paying attention when you both weren't. This photo will speak volumes as to the depths of your feelings for each other. I think this will be good, Jacob.

Me: I really hope so. I don't want her caught up in some media shitshow.

Catherine: All of the media is a shitshow, I just need to control what shit we throw at them. Can you hop on a call? I have something we need to discuss and Noah wants a conference call as well.

Instead of replying, I just call her.

"Well, that was efficient."

I laugh. "I figured this was easier."

"It is. Listen, I just want to say this . . . I've worked with a lot of actors, and them entering a new relationship isn't something I haven't handled. Noah and Kristin met a few years ago when he was in the middle of a huge scandal. There was a lot of drama, and we dealt with it. No one bothered Kristin. We made sure that she was protected. While I don't make this a policy, I'm always going to do my best to protect the people you love, Jacob. Part of my job as your publicist is to keep your life out of the tabloids, but the other part is to make sure you're happy because, if you're happy, you work better. Brenna makes you happy, I could see that clear as day when I saw you with her."

I appreciate her saying that. "She and the kids are my top priority. I can handle the media, but she didn't choose this."

Catherine is silent for a minute. "Maybe not, but she chose you."

"She did, but I'll still do whatever I can to keep her life

normal. The way that Noah was able to do that for Kristin."

"I understand. Speaking of Noah, he sent an email asking for an emergency call in about five minutes. Can you swing that?"

"Do I have a choice?"

"Not really," Catherine says.

I didn't think so. We talk a bit more about the photo shoot and the article. Catherine decided it was best not to do an interview and to just have her and her team release a statement. I tend to say stupid things when I'm on the record. For the first foot out the gate, we're going to avoid any chance of that.

"He's beeping in now, I'll conference it," Catherine explains.

After a few seconds, they're both on the call. "Jacob, glad you could make it on. Sorry about the short notice. I got a call just a little while ago, and it seems we have a problem."

There's an almost regretful tone to his voice. "What's wrong?"

"We had an issue with one of our servers that housed a scene we need for the third version of the trailer for *Flight Plan*."

"What kind of issue?" I ask.

"One that requires you on a plane tonight to reshoot a major scene."

My stomach drops. "Tonight?"

"I'm sorry, but yes, tonight. I need you in the studio tomorrow."

No, I can't. I can't go to California tonight. I have the play tomorrow. "Noah, I wish I could, but I have a commitment tomorrow that I can't miss."

"I swear, I'm not trying to be a dick, but there's really not a choice here. We have to reshoot tomorrow all day. Believe me,

I do not want to be here either. Aubrey has her birthday party this weekend, Kristin is on a deadline, and I had to get on a plane the minute I found out. You're contractually obligated to be available for reshoots."

I let out a long sigh that's filled with disappointment. "It's opening night for the school play."

"The one you're directing?" Noah asks.

"Yes."

Noah goes quiet, and I can barely make out the sound of papers shuffling in the background. "Listen, I can't make any promises, but we'll do everything we possibly can to get done before lunch and get you on a plane so you're back in time. It would cut it close, but maybe you won't have to miss it. I'll move the reshoots to first thing in the morning so that maybe neither one of us gets our balls cut off for this."

I close my eyes, already knowing that this is going to go badly. I'm going to disappoint them and . . . Brenna.

Catherine cuts in. "I'll make sure to have Jackson's private plane on standby. We'll move heaven and earth to get you home, Jacob."

This is one of those moments where no matter what I do, I'm fucked. If I say no and refuse to go, I'll lose my contract and will probably get sued. I could be blacklisted by every producer and director in Hollywood. If I do go, there is a chance I won't make it back in time for the play and let down people I genuinely care about.

If it weren't this movie. This director. This role . . . I would say fuck it, but I can't. Noah, Catherine, and I know it. I answer the only way I can. "I'll be on a plane in a few hours. I need you to make sure I get back in time."

There is a giant rock sitting in my stomach, it moves and turns, making me nauseated. I'm standing at Brenna's door, knowing I have to tell them and figure out a way to make them understand.

Which, at eleven years old, I sure as hell wouldn't.

Time is running out, so I gather whatever courage I have and knock.

A few seconds go by, and I clench and unclench my fist a few times, taking deep breaths. As time moves, the nerves grow.

Sebastian answers the door. "Jacob!"

"Hey, Sebastian."

"Come on in," he says before turning and yelling, "Jacob is here!"

I'm not really sure what the protocol is for breaking a kid's heart. Do I tell his mother first or do we talk man to man?

Before I have to make that choice, Brenna is there, her smile wide as she walks over to me. I kiss her briefly, and she steps back. "I didn't know you were coming over."

"It wasn't part of the plan. None of this was, but I have to talk to you, and I don't have a lot of time."

"Okay," she says, studying me. "What's wrong?"

There isn't a gentle way of saying this, and I decide to talk to Sebastian first. I can't endure seeing her upset, but he's who I promised to do this for. He's who I owe an explanation to.

I crouch and do my damnedest to look him in the eyes. "I have to tell you something, and I want you to know that, before I say anything else, I am so sorry. The last thing in the world I want is this, and I promise that I'm going to do everything I can to make it right, okay?"

Sebastian looks up to Brenna before returning his gaze to me. Her hands rest on his shoulders. "Okay."

Here it goes. "I got a call from my boss about thirty minutes ago. There was a big issue with *Flight Plan*."

"Oh no. Are you going to be okay? Is the movie happening? Will you still be Navigator?"

Even as I'm about to disappoint him, he's worried for me. "I'll be fine, but Noah is forcing the cast to come back to reshoot a scene."

He shrugs. "That's not so bad."

I shake my head. "I have to leave tonight. We have to shoot the scene tomorrow."

And then it dawns on him, and I want to fucking break something when I see the sadness in his eyes. "Tomorrow?"

"They are forcing us all back, but I told them about the play, and I told them I have to leave by a certain time, no matter what. I might miss just a little in the beginning, but I swear that I'll do everything I can to make it back in time."

Sebastian's head drops, and I hear him sniff. "Don't worry about it, Jacob. Work always comes first."

I don't know that I've ever felt this low. "That's not the case for me. I care about this play, and I am so proud of you. I will be on that plane as early as I can so that I'm here."

Brenna clears her throat, and Sebastian looks up at her. "Why don't you go to your room and let me and Jacob talk," Brenna suggests.

My heart is breaking, and I hate myself for hurting him. The kid has been through so much, and now I'm letting him down.

I get back up, running my hand over my face and pacing. "Brenna—"

She shakes her head, hand going up to silence me. "Not here." Then she turns and heads outside. I do the only thing I can, which is to follow her.

Well, this is going to be even worse. The anger in her eyes

is clear, and the tension in her body is palpable.

As soon as we step onto the porch, she closes the door and releases a breath through her nose. "I can't believe you didn't talk to me before telling him."

"I owed him an explanation."

She shakes her head. "He's eleven, Jacob. He doesn't get told before I do. I'm his mother. I should've at least been aware so that he didn't see my own disappointment. I stood there, reeling from the news the same way he was. How did you think that was okay?"

"I told you I'm new at this."

Brenna's face twists a little, and she runs her fingers through her hair. "I get that, but you have nieces and nephews. Would you have just gone in there and told them? Did you think about how hurt Sebastian would be? How *I* would feel learning this?"

Anger fills me—not toward her, but toward myself. I feel stupid. I did what I thought was right. Clearly, it wasn't, but I'm trying to be fair. "I'm on limited time before my flight. I wanted to treat Sebastian like a man."

She scoffs. "He's not a man. He's a boy. A kid who thinks you walk on water, and you blindsided me."

"So, how much of this is about Sebastian and how much is this about you?"

Brenna's breath catches as she stares at me with her lips parted. "Excuse me?"

"You heard me. You're not upset about Sebastian learning before you. You're pissed that I'm leaving."

"Of course, I'm pissed that you're leaving! It's the night before the play. You . . . you promised them!"

"I don't want to go. It's not like I asked for this."

"Then don't go."

"I don't have a choice, Brenna. I'm under a contract. If I don't get on that plane, I'll owe tons of money and my name will be destroyed in this industry. I'm going to do what I can to make it back, like I said."

"And if you don't?"

Then I'll have to live with the damn guilt. "Then you'll have to direct the play."

She looks away, and I see the disappointment. "I thought . . . I knew this . . ."

"Knew what?"

When her gaze meets mine again, I sink even fucking lower into my self-loathing. "This would be what happens again. You told me, but for some stupid reason, I made myself think this would be different."

There's no anger in her voice, just hurt. "What would be different?"

"That maybe this time I wouldn't have fallen for someone whose job is more important than the people in his life. Here I am again, right? You have to leave, and I have to accept it. That little boy, all the kids in that play, they love you. They need you, and you're going to show them that they mean nothing to you compared to your career."

The blow comes, knocking the wind out of me, but when I take another breath, anger refills my chest. "I'm not Luke. I'm not choosing this, and I'm doing every single thing to make sure that I'm back in time. You think I want this? I debated walking away from my thirteen-title movie deal that is worth millions just to make you and Sebastian happy. Knowing that it would be the end of me, but I made a commitment when I signed that contract. I did the best I could. I'm fucking trying."

Brenna doesn't raise her voice or even react. She's eerily calm. "It's fine, Jacob. I understand your position, and I'll pick up the pieces and the show will go on. I'll handle it because that's my role in this life."

I move toward her, trying to keep my voice down. "I was never supposed to be directing a play."

"Well, now you don't have to worry about it, do you?"

The way she's acting, the robotic and distanced reactions, has me on edge. "I was doing it for you. For Sebastian." She takes a step back, a fire seeming to light inside her. I see the anger now, and I stoke it. "You're acting like it doesn't matter, but I know it does. Get angry and we'll find a way."

She laughs while shaking her head. "You want me to be angry, why? So, I can tell you that this is hurting me? That you're letting me down when you promised to be here? You want me angry, Jacob? Fine. I'm angry. I'm pissed off because, once again, I'm going to be the one who has to sacrifice. Once again, my wants don't matter, but this is my lot in life. History repeating itself over and over. I'm allowed to feel this way even if I knew this was possible."

"Is that really what you think? That I'm him? Am I the same as Luke, Brenna? You're acting as though this is me choosing. You're acting as if you didn't know exactly what you were signing up for when you agreed to be with me. That I never explained to you that, when I'm under contract, which I am and have been since long before I met you, I have no choice but to go when they need me!"

"I need you." Brenna looks away, silent.

"Look," I say, trying to temper the anger boiling inside me. "I'm going to do whatever I can to be here. I'm not willingly choosing my job over you."

I'm struggling because I get it to some extent. She asked him to be there for her and he wasn't. But my being called into set on an emergency isn't the norm. I'm just stuck right now.

"It's just the way it is."

I move toward her, wanting to soothe her before I leave. "I told you this was possible."

She turns away, wiping at her face. "That you did, and I

think that's the worst part. I willingly accepted this—or, at least, I thought I did. I thought that I was going to be okay with it all, and now that I'm faced with it—it just hurts."

When my hand touches her back, she flinches. "Brenna, please don't."

"Don't what?"

"Don't punish me for Luke's crimes."

The tears fall down her face. "I'm not. You have to leave, and I have to figure out how to direct a play."

I take a step back, hating that this is where we're at. "So, it doesn't matter at all that I really have no choice or that I'm going to do everything I can, pull every string and call in every favor, to get back here in time? That doesn't count for anything?"

Again with the silence.

"That's it then?"

"It's reality, right? It's the way it is. I'm going to move forward like I always have."

I nod slowly, tongue to the back of my teeth, completely floored by how easy that was for her. I'm over here, agonizing over having to do this, and she's just . . . done.

"I see. You're moving forward . . . right."

Tears fall down her cheeks. "You were supposed to be different. *We* were supposed to be different."

I laugh once. "You're punishing me because of him. You're acting as though this is what I'm always going to do, and you're going to throw away what we have because of it."

"I'm not throwing anything away, Jacob. I'm not leaving. I'm dealing with the situation, and while you go to work, like you have to, I'll be keeping my kids and myself from feeling the disappointment."

"I was fucking wrecked at the idea of coming here and telling you that this *might* happen. Not because I thought you'd compare me to Luke but because the mere idea of disappointing you and Sebastian was too much. But I see it now, Brenna. It doesn't matter what I say or how hard I try, I will always live in his shadow."

She doesn't love me. If she did, maybe she'd see that I'm doing the best I can. That I have made every effort to do right by her.

Brenna lets out a long breath, and a new wave of tears fall. "That's not fair. You show up here, drop this on me, and want me to be all, sure, honey, go to work, I'll handle it all. Knowing everything you know about my past, about the day Luke died, did you think this wouldn't hurt?"

"Believe me, I knew this would hurt you and I was in agony over it. What I didn't expect is this. You to compare me to him. I told you this was my reality, and you said we'd work it out, that as long as we talked, we could get through anything. And here we are, my first fucking misstep and you shut me out. That's what hurts."

I wait for her to tell me that we can. That she loves me. That we'll find a way once I get back, but instead, her lower lip trembles and she straightens her back. "You should go, you have a flight to catch."

She turns her back and walks to the door. I hate myself for standing here. Of all the things that just happened, this is what I know I'll regret most—watching her walk away.

When she gets to the door, she pauses. "I'll never regret loving you."

That single statement angers me more than any other word we've said to each other in the last five minutes. I make my way up to where she is, hurt and frustration rolling through me. "You'll regret all of this when I'm back here tomorrow and you see that you could've been understanding instead of destroying us."

Then I leave because there's nothing to stay for anymore.

thirty-three

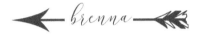

I lean against the door, fighting every urge to run back out there and tell him I was stupid. I did exactly what he said, I'm using my past issues with Luke against him, and it's not fair.

But his taillights are long gone and there's something deep inside me that tells me not to ignore what I'm feeling.

Melanie comes in the room. "Are you crying? Is everything okay?"

I shake my head and attempt to smile. "It's fine. Jacob has to leave for California, and it just . . . took me by surprise."

"Is he going to miss tomorrow?"

I shrug. "He's going to try to make it back."

She walks over and gives me a big hug. "Oh, Mom. I'm so sorry."

"I messed up, Mel. I made him feel worse because I . . . I just couldn't stop myself from going in the past."

Her hand rubs up and down my back. "You were upset. Go talk to him."

I release her, inhaling deeply and trying to keep the tears back. "I think we both need a little time to cool down."

"Is that what you'd tell one of your patients if this were them?"

"No."

"Then why are you doing it?"

Because it's much easier to give advice than take it. Because I'm terrified of what the follow up will be. He was so hurt, and I did it to him. I hurt the man who is selfless to a fault, who has given up his own time to make others happy, and who taught me to love again. I pushed him away because I was scared.

Because I *am* scared.

"Sometimes, even when we know what we should do, we choose wrong because of fear. In my heart, I know that letting him go like that is the wrong thing, but I'm afraid. If we get too much deeper and he chooses something or someone else over me, it'll be too hard."

Melanie shrugs, and I can see that she's unhappy. "I think that doing the right thing, even when it's scary, is always the best choice."

I feel like a failure as a mother and as a professional in this. If I were my patient, I would've said the same. I would have told myself that I was letting fear run my life and that it's unfair to use my issues against the man I love.

And yet I did it.

I was back in time listening to Luke say he had to work instead of in the present listening to Jacob tell me he was trying.

"You're right. I need to fix this."

Melanie nods vigorously. Her phone goes off, and she smiles. "I'll talk to Jennifer while you make things right."

I grab my phone and call him, but it goes right to voice mail. "Jacob, it's me, please call me. We need to talk."

Now I just have to hope he forgives me.

"He'll call, Brenna," Cybil says as she tosses some popcorn into her mouth.

"It's been almost fifteen hours."

"Not that you're counting or anything."

I narrow my eyes. "Really? You're not helping."

"Look, I'm sorry that you and your insanely hot boyfriend got in a fight and you decided to act irrationally, for the first time in your life. Honestly, what the hell were you thinking?"

I sigh. "I wasn't."

"Clearly. That was so unlike you. Even when Luke upset you, you didn't act that way. You were overly understanding."

"And that's probably why I couldn't do it with Jacob."

"Or you're comfortable with him in a way that you never were with Luke."

I think about that and what it means. "I'm not going to be comfortable if he doesn't call me."

"Maybe he needs time to figure out how to handle your crazy ass. Daddy always said—"

"Not today, Cyb. Please. I can't handle any wisdom from your father."

She flops back and shakes her head. "You, my friend, could use all the wisdom in the world right now. For being an expert on how people work, you sure fucked this one up."

And to think, I called her because I needed support.

All night, I waited for a call or a text from Jacob. I battled with calling again, but then I didn't want to come off as desperate, which I was and still am. I was wrong and stupid, and I hope that he gives me the chance to apologize.

"I'm aware of this."

Cybil sits back up, her face grows serious. "I know you're hurting, but he said he was shooting all day, maybe he turned his phone off and didn't turn it back on so he could focus. I'm not sure that actors don't have weird rituals, and maybe it's his."

"Or maybe he heard it but decided I was an asshole and needed to sit in my own self-hate."

"Sugar, you don't know shit about what he's thinking. Neither of us do."

I sigh. "How did I mess this up so bad?"

"Because Luke, for all his great qualities, didn't place you and the kids above his job. Even when he had the choice, and you asked him to get out of the navy, he didn't. You asked him not to volunteer for the deployment, and he did. You begged him to take leave when you were sick and he wouldn't. Yes, all those times there was something imperative to his career, but that's just it. Being a pilot was all he wanted and he didn't really care what he had to give up to keep that. Reggie and I would talk about it a lot because it never made sense—and because I threatened to leave his ass if he tried the same shit. But you complained about it all the time and it wasn't enough for him to change."

She has always been very aware of how I felt about his career. Nothing was more important than flying. It didn't matter that he married me, in reality, he was committed to his job.

I always felt that.

There was always this part of me that wondered what would have happened if Melanie had never surprised us.

"So, you think that's what I was doing to Jacob?"

Cybil smiles softly. "I think that you did what any irrational and emotional woman would do. In fact, I'm sort of proud of you in many ways."

"What the hell does that mean?"

"It means you weren't perfect, Bren. You didn't go deep in your head and explain why your feelings were either right or wrong before you reacted. Jacob makes you lose yourself. He made you forget that people don't always respond the right way and it's the errors that teach us the lessons."

"Another Daddy tip?" I ask with mock sarcasm.

"That one came from you."

"Me?"

She laughs. "Yes, you idiot. You said it once, and it stuck. I tend to like phrases like that."

"Cyb," I say, feeling sad again. "I love him."

"I know, sugar. He loves you too. He'll come around. You'll see."

I sure hope so because I don't want to experience losing him.

thirty-four

I'm fucking over it all. We've reshot this scene four times, and it still isn't right. I'm tired, angry, and can't stop thinking about Brenna and how we left things.

Her message replays in my head, but I'm still not ready to talk to her. For all I know, she called to tell me she really feels the way she said and we're done. I needed my head in the game in order to get through today, which it's clearly not.

"Cut!" Noah yells and then walks toward me. "Jacob, I know you have somewhere else you'd rather be, but I need you to focus so we can get through this scene. Can you give me one good, full scene? We have enough to splice some, but I'd like the sequence to feel like we got through it once."

"Yeah. Of course. I just need two minutes."

Noah nods and waves his finger in the air twice. "Let's start it over from the top. I have a good feeling, people, let's all be on our A-game so we're done before nine."

I open my phone, hovering over Brenna's number, and decide not to do it. If I can make it through this scene one more time, then I'll call.

"You all right?" Eli Walsh asks as he claps me on the back.

"I'm fine."

Eli is my nemesis in this scene. He'll be in only this one movie because, inevitably, I'll kill him toward the end. "You seem out of it."

I shrug. "I have a lot on my mind." That doesn't seem to give him the clue that I don't want to talk about it because he just keeps looking at me. "There's a school play I was directing. It was a big deal because the kid's father died."

He nods. "I see, and you had to let him down to be here."

"Yup."

"Then stop dicking around and shoot the scene. Use your anger and frustration and channel it the right way. There are so many times when I'm not in the right headspace for filming, but in the end, it's our job to fake it. You know all that."

I do, but hearing it from him seems to be what I needed. "I guess I forgot."

He chuckles. "Being out of Hollywood for a while will do that. It's why I really never wanted to do movies, but Noah and I go way back, so . . . here I am."

I didn't realize that Noah knew him outside this movie. "How so?"

Eli glances over at him. "We're married to best friends, and we both starred on *A Thin Blue Line*."

Jesus. I totally forgot that. "Did he handpick his entire cast?"

"Basically. He wanted to work with quality actors," he says as he raises one brow.

And I'm definitely not living up to that.

Noah's voice comes over the megaphone. "Ready?"

"The sooner we nail this, the sooner we're all heading home. Remember that." Eli walks away, and I send a quick text to Brenna.

Me: Filming. We'll talk when I get back.

I shut my phone off and go to work so I can get back to Sugarloaf before the play.

My legs are bouncing as anxious energy courses through me. Making it back to Pennsylvania before the show is going to be close—so insanely close that I might just be tempting fate. We shot the scene in one fluid take. Noah replayed it, but I was already grabbing my shit to go. I knew the second he yelled cut that it was perfect. Every one of us was on point.

He gave me one solid head nod, and I was running to the car that was waiting. I didn't tell anyone back home that I was on my way because traffic in L.A. is always an issue, and with my luck, I wouldn't make it to the airport in time to catch my flight back to the East Coast. Thanks to Catherine's planning, the plane was ready to go the second I got on board. Within minutes, we were airborne.

"The pilot is making great time, the winds are on our side, Mr. Arrowood," the flight attendant says as she hands me a drink.

I'm sitting on the couch across from the captain chair on the small private plane, and I can't even enjoy myself. "Great. Thanks." I accept the glass and then place it on the table beside me. I don't care much about eating or drinking, I just want to get there.

She smiles. "Do you need anything else?"

"Nope, just . . . watching the clock."

"I understand, he's doing his best. I'll be back in a few minutes, just ring for me if you need anything before then." She heads to the front of the plane into the little area where the supplies are.

The only thing I need is for this plane to go faster, but that's not really possible. It's been fewer than forty minutes, but it feels like forty years. I should've at least sent Brenna a text, but I was laser focused on getting in the air.

I pull my phone out of my pocket, looking at the last text.

Brenna: I hoped you'd call. I just want to talk.

I do too, but the conversation she and I need to have is better done in person. We fought and said shit that we probably shouldn't have, but it made me realize that there's no one else I want to fight with. I love her, and if that means that we fight until we fix it, then that's how it has to be.

Me: And we will when we're in the same state.

A few minutes go by, the little dots appear on the text, letting me know she's typing. They start, stop, and start again.

Brenna: Okay.

That was a lot of time for one word, but I imagine that was difficult for her. I send a text to Sebastian.

Me: Break a leg, Kenickie. If I don't make it back, know that I'm proud of you.

Sebastian: Do you think you'll make it?

I don't want to give him false hope.

Me: I'm doing my best.

Sebastian: Okay. We're heading to the school to check on the stage crew. Mom is trying to remember all the things you asked them to do.

Me: I'm sure she'll be great.

Sebastian: I hope you and my mom can fix things. She's

been crying a lot.

My fucking heart breaks. I hate that she's crying. I never knew that heartache didn't come from my own pain, it came from watching the woman I love hurt. That was the worst thing of all.

Me: Don't worry about things. Just focus on your role and your lines.

Sebastian: Thanks, Jacob.

Me: We'll talk soon.

Hopefully we'll see each other sooner.

I toss my phone over on the side table, needing to stop watching the clock and wondering if the stage crew moved the light or if Danny shaved his head in protest of his mother making him eat spinach like he threatened to do.

The pilot rings the phone that's next to my seat. "Hello?"

"Hello, Mr. Arrowood, this is Captain Elliot Lucas, we're expecting a bit of turbulence in a few minutes. Please fasten your seatbelt and stay seated."

Captain Lucas. Like Luke. My stomach does an odd flip, and I can't tell if it's a good thing he's flying or an omen. "Okay. Thank you."

"No problem, we should get through it pretty quickly. Just stay in your seat."

I switch from the couch to the captain chair across the small walkway and pull my seatbelt tight.

The plane bobs once, and I grip the seat. I've never been afraid to fly, but I'm not a fan of turbulence either.

We climb back up, and it feels almost as if we're going over a bumpy country road. I close my eyes, imagining that's exactly what we're doing. I hold on, trying to smile as we go over another big pot hole.

Only it feels like a sink hole. We plunge down before right-ing again.

Up and down the plane goes. There's a loud explosion that comes from outside, and all at once, everything changes.

The lights go out, and the plane isn't bouncing anymore . . . it's just going down.

There is a pinging noise, and the flight attendant is stumbling her way toward me.

"What the hell is going on?" I yell.

"There is an engine failure. We are going to make an emergency landing. I need you to get into a bracing position and try to stay calm."

"Where are you going?" I ask.

"I'm going to be in my jump seat right across from you. I need you to know how to get out of the plane if something happens to me. This is the door. You need to pull the lever up and then you're going to push. If I'm incapacitated, I need you to unbuckle me and take me out of this aircraft with you if you're able to."

"We're going to crash?"

"We're going to make an emergency landing."

Is there a fucking difference?

Jesus. I'm going to die.

I think about my brothers and how I didn't talk to them before I left. I didn't hug Hadley, BethAnne, Austin, or Deacon. I didn't get to teach them all the things to do to their fathers to drive them crazy. I'll never meet Sean and Devney's baby.

Heartbreak takes over as a gorgeous woman with red hair and blue eyes fills my thoughts.

Brenna.

I'm going to die without Brenna knowing I still love her. She won't hear me tell her that I forgive her. I won't get to tell her about the life I want with her and the kids. I didn't make things right with her, and now she's going to have to go through this—again.

"Jacob?" the flight attendant calls out. "Do you remember what I said about the door?"

I nod because, if I open my mouth, I might throw up. We're going down fast. I can hear the pilots going back and forth at one another.

"Stay calm and just follow my directions," she instructs.

My heart is pounding, and I am trying to focus, but I can't fucking breathe. "What's your name?"

"Jessica."

"Okay, Jessica, it's great meeting you, and we're about to go down in a plane crash together, so that means we'll be life-long friends if we survive."

She tries to smile, but it looks mangled. "Get in your position, Jacob."

I nod. "If I don't make it, I need you to tell Brenna I loved her and I was thinking of her."

"Don't think that way."

"My family. I need them all to know that I love them."

"Focus, Jacob. Remember, getting off the aircraft is imperative."

"Will you tell them?"

Jessica doesn't say anything and then I see treetops. This is it. This is the end. I'm going to die on this plane and never see the people I love again. They'll never know how much I care about them and the regrets I have.

I close my eyes, bringing the woman I love to the forefront.

I love you, Brenna.

"Jacob." Jessica's voice is strong and forceful.

"I'm ready."

We are both bent forward, arms crossed over our chests, but her wide eyes are on me the whole time. "Brace! Brace! Brace!"

And the world goes black.

thirty-five

The kids are being really great considering their director isn't here. We have about an hour before curtain is up—or is it curtain call? I don't know nor do I give a damn at this point. I slept like shit last night, well, that's a lie. In order to sleep like shit I would have had to actually sleep, which I did not.

All day, I kept waiting and waiting and waiting for him to call, but I only got a text, and I'm still not sure what any of it means. The subsequent texts were no help either. I haven't heard from him since, and I have no idea if he's on a plane or not.

"All right, guys, I'm winging it here, but I think we're supposed to have the first set up."

The stage director, a junior in high school, smiles and waves. "We've got it handled, Mrs. A!"

"Glad someone does," I say back.

The kids are all milling around, rehearsing lines, and getting their makeup and hair done. The local beauty shop offered their services after Jacob asked them to give back to the kids.

I swear he could sell a penguin snow.

I sit in the seat and look up at the stage, feeling proud of myself for being able to step in for Jacob and sad that he's not here with me.

A hand touches my shoulder, and I look up, hoping it's Jacob, only to see it's one of the moms. "Are you okay?"

Did they seriously hear about the fight we had already? "I am."

"I just figured that you'd be a wreck right now."

"I'm . . . fine. I'm just focusing on making sure the play goes well."

She nods quickly. "Right. It's good to keep your focus on that. I'm sure it'll be okay."

I blink a few times, wondering why she's offering me this bit of advice when we've never spoken before. "Thanks." I get to my feet and start to move when Melanie comes rushing down the aisle.

"Mom! Mom!"

"What's wrong?"

Her hands are shaking and there are tears in her eyes. "Look!"

She shoves the phone into my hands, and I look at the headline: "Breaking News: Jacob Arrowood Plane Crash, Survivors Unknown."

Everything inside me revolts. My vision tunnels until even the screen is a blur, my throat goes dry, and my entire body starts to tremble.

No, no, no. This has to be fake. The press is wrong. Jacob can't be in a plane crash.

"Mom?" Melanie's voice breaks as tears run down her

face. "There are more saying they can't find the plane."

I grab my phone and call his number.

It rings.

And rings.

Each time I hear that noise I want to scream: *answer*.

But he doesn't.

His voice mail picks up. "Jacob. Jacob it's me. Please . . . I need to know you're okay. Please."

"Mom."

I look to her, tears filling her eyes as I feel them trickle down my face. "It's not true. I'm sure . . . there has to be . . . we have to be calm because he's fine."

She nods. "I'm sure." She looks down at her phone again and sniffs. "They're saying where the plane went down it's unlikely there are survivors."

I rush out of the room as my stomach heaves. I can't stop myself from curling over into the garbage can as sickness overtakes me.

This can't be happening.

I can't lose someone else I love like this. Not after all the things I said. Not him, and not now. We didn't have time. We were supposed to have time.

Melanie is there, her hand on my back, her voice trembling as she says, "Please. Say something."

I start to cry, tears that fall silently because I'm too broken to say the fear that's choking me aloud. He's not supposed to leave me.

I push her away, feeling lightheaded. "I can't—"

"I know."

I sink to the floor, barely registering the cold tiles hitting my legs. "This can't be. Please tell me it's not real and I'm dreaming."

Melanie takes my hand in hers. "They don't know. It doesn't mean that he's gone, right? They think, but they can't know."

She needs me to tell her this, but I can't. I've been down this road, bargaining with God and everyone else before, and it didn't turn out okay. I lied to myself and everyone around me, and it broke me.

My lip quivers and so does hers, and then I see Devney and Sean running toward us. "Brenna!"

Tears are falling down her face as she reaches me. "God, you heard." I nod, my body starts to tremble harder as fear overtakes me. Devney sinks down beside me, her hand takes mine and she grabs Melanie's with her other hand. "Have faith. We have to have faith."

I swallow my terror and try to focus on the people around me. "Do you know anything?" I ask.

She shakes her head as a sob escapes her lips. "Sean got a call from Catherine. All we know is what they're reporting. The pilots called in their location when the plane was going down, and they're searching now."

A sound leaves my mouth that is a half cry, half scream. Her arms wrap around me, and I let her hold me together. If they don't find him alive, I'll never be whole again.

"Not another plane crash," I whimper. "Not again. Please, not again."

Sean pulls me from Devney's hold and hugs me to his chest, rubbing my back. "Jacob is too stubborn to die. We have to be strong until we know something."

I already know how this story ends. I'm reliving it, just with a different main character. I should've seen it all before he left. The fight, the flight, the crash. Instead, I didn't say what I wanted. I should've demanded that we speak before he left California. Now, I'll never get to tell him how sorry I am.

How much I love him, and how it wasn't over.

So many unspoken things between us.

"I need to go." I pull back and get to my feet. "I need to take the kids home and—Sebastian."

"Mom?"

The look of fear in her eyes is enough to sober me. I didn't fall apart like this when Luke died, and I can't do it now. My kids need me to be their strength because, while they've only known Jacob a short time, they love and care about him too.

He's been there for Sebastian, filling a hole that his father left behind.

My head lifts as I try to force the tears back and take a few deep breaths. Once I'm a little more under control, I cup Melanie's face in my palm and give her a sad smile. "Until we know more, we have to be strong."

She nods. "Sebastian . . ."

My phone rings, and it's Cybil. I can't talk to her. If I do, I'll never be strong for Sebastian because I'll be too busy breaking down.

Right now, he's oblivious. I don't lie to my kids, but at the same time, I can't let him find out the way I just did. "What do I do?" I ask Devney.

She reaches her hand out, holding my other one. "The news is going to break even wider. There's no way to shield him from it. Austin, Hadley, and the babies are all at Connor's. It might be the best place to go. Let him be with people who understand what he's feeling."

"I'm not family."

Sean speaks first. "You're our family, Brenna. You love Jacob, and he is more in love with you than you know. You should be around us, let us all lean on each other until we hear something."

Devney squeezes my hand. "We came here because you

were our first concern. We came to get you so that you weren't alone."

The tears I fought to hold back break free. "I can't lose him."

"Neither can we, so let's all be strong together," Sean suggests.

They're right. I can't be here, and I can't risk Sebastian learning from someone else. I have to be the one to tell him, and I have to hope that, with everyone around us, we can weather whatever news comes.

thirty-six

Tick, tick, tick.

The clock moves. One hand follows the other in a steady rhythm.

Tick, tick, tick.

I sit, just watching it. It's constant, sure, even when nothing in my life feels that way.

Telling Sebastian was impossible. I couldn't keep it together and kept crying as I tried to say the words. We know nothing. It's been thirty minutes since Catherine called to tell us the plane was not in the immediate search area they thought it was.

And then there's the news.

God, the news. Nonstop images of his face flicker across the screen.

"Jacob Arrowood, star of the Navigator movie series is still missing. His plane is believed to have suffered an engine

issue that forced the flight crew to make an emergency land-ing in Colorado. At this time, we have no confirmation of the plane being found or if there are any survivors. Stay with News Channel Nine for more updates."

Flip the channel. His green eyes stare back at me as yet another channel covers the story.

"We're following the story regarding Jacob Arrowood's missing plane. On Your Side Five is bringing you live cover-age as the search continues." Cuts to a reporter. "I'm here as more search crews are added to the team that are scouring the area for the wreckage of the private aircraft owned by Cole Security Forces. At this time, the company is not available for comment, but we understand that Jacob Arrowood is a friend of the owner, Jackson Cole."

Goes back to the studio. "Are officials concerned that there is any kind of foul play?"

The reporter's face returns and she shakes her head. "No, Katie, at this time they aren't saying anything other than the search is their main concern. If you look behind me, you can see another helicopter is readying. We're told that, at this time, there has been no sign of the aircraft or the missing flight crew."

Katie blinks a few times, keeping her face passive. "Melis-sa, has there been any indication that the search team believes that the crew and Jacob Arrowood are alive at this point?"

Melissa shakes her head. "They aren't saying at this time. We were able to talk to the commander of the search team, and they aren't willing to speculate at this time. However, the high winds tonight don't make things easier and aren't comforting either."

You know what else isn't comforting, Melissa, reporters who don't know anything but speculate themselves.

"Brenna?" Ellie says as she sits beside me and offers me a mug. "I made you some tea."

I've cried so much that my eyes have to strain to see her. "Thank you," I croak.

She pats my leg and turns the television off. "We'll know before them. There's no reason to make yourself watch the coverage of nothing."

"Planes don't just disappear," I say mindlessly. This is the one thing that keeps going around in a loop. Planes have tracking devices. This isn't supposed to be how it happens. "When Luke's plane crashed, they had coordinates immediately."

And then the thought forms, and I regret it: because the plane was in one piece. If Jacob's plane isn't, the GPS system could be in one area and we would have no idea where he ended up.

"I can't imagine how hard this is for you."

"I don't know that I'm processing how hard this is."

Ellie tucks her legs under her. "My parents died when I was young. I struggled so much with reconciling why God could take the only people I loved away from me. They came to visit me at college, and that was the last time I saw them. It was as if I went from feeling safe and as though things were going to be okay to completely alone overnight. I was so afraid of that being the case that I married Kevin without really knowing him that well. It is crazy how we convince ourselves that things like this are our fault in some way."

I glance at where her fingers are fidgeting with the hem of her shirt. "How was the accident your fault?"

"If I hadn't needed them, they would never have been on the road. Then, when Kevin started being abusive, well, I thought that was my penance. A part of me thought I deserved it. Not just because he told me I did or because I was pretty sure I was pregnant with another man's baby, but because I had convinced myself that it was somehow because of the accident."

I reach out, resting my hand on hers. "It's not your fault.

That accident wasn't at all your doing, and you definitely didn't deserve to be abused."

She smiles softly. "I know that now. Connor loving me showed me that. My point is, no matter what lies you're going to tell yourself about this, they are just lies. Loving him didn't make his plane go down any more than it made Luke's. Your fight with Jacob doesn't mean that he doesn't know you love him or that you meant any of the things you said in anger."

I wipe away a tear. "When did you become my shrink?"

"When you looked like you needed one. How did I do?"

The look on her face causes me to laugh, which I didn't think I could do. "You did great."

"It's hard to love someone and have them taken."

I nod. "It's even harder when you have things left unsaid."

Ellie sighs deeply. "I wrote down all the things I wanted to say to my mother once. It was almost like a log of bullet points that let her know how bad things were. If she were alive, I never would've been able to tell her any of it. I think that's part of the issue. We all struggle with our emotions, especially with the people we love most."

"Don't I know it."

I said things to Jacob that I didn't mean. I didn't fix it, which is what I will regret always. I made a vow to myself after Luke died that I would do my best to never leave things unsaid. Here I am, fucking that up.

"Can I ask you something?"

I look to her. "Sure."

"Do you think that Luke or Jacob, if . . . well, do you think that they thought you didn't love them?"

The question stuns me. "I don't know."

"See, that's the thing, I know he knows you do. I don't think Jacob would question your feelings, but he would question his guilt over leaving. You know, deep down, that he loves you. Even if you lose him, you don't have to dwell on that."

She's right. I do know it. I know that Luke loved me, regardless of the decisions he made. He tried, I know he did, but it always felt like we came up short. With Jacob, it isn't that way. We have had such a short time, but it was more intense and heartfelt than I can explain. I know that he loves me—truly loves me. That is why, when he said he was leaving for work, I was so irrational.

I needed that all to be real.

I couldn't handle another half-hearted love that took a back seat to a job which isn't what he was doing, but I couldn't stop the feelings of fear.

Not once in the time Jacob and I spent together did he ever make me feel as if I were second choice.

"That saying about loving and losing is total shit, you know that, right?"

Ellie sips her tea. "Complete bullshit."

Declan and Connor step out onto the porch where the women have congregated. None of us are saying anything but we silently agreed not to leave anyone alone. Hours have passed, and still nothing.

The information is being held very close as the media is relentless. Social media is a shitstorm with "eye-witness" accounts that are false, and after the second false hope scenario, the Arrowood brothers shut it down.

No television.

No social media.

No phones unless it's a call from authorities.

My ringtone blares again, and it's Cybil for the second time. I can't answer, no matter how much I want to. I just . . . can't.

Saying the phrases Jacob is missing, plane crash, and no word from anyone yet would be too exhausting.

The porch door opens and Sebastian steps out. "Mom?"

"Yes, baby?"

"Did they find Jacob yet?"

I shake my head. "Not yet."

"I told Hadley that he's going to be okay. He's the Navigator and he's strong. Watch."

I wish I had his faith, but every minute that goes by is another drop of hope that drains away.

"He is strong," Connor says.

"Yes, he is," I agree.

He's also been missing for five hours . . . somewhere in Colorado. He could be hurt. He could be lying there, dying and in pain, and we just don't know.

"Why don't we get some cookies for you guys?" Ellie suggests.

"Now?" Sebastian's eyes widen.

Ellie leans down. "I think cookies are needed tonight, what do you think?"

He nods, and they head in the house, leaving Declan, Connor, Sydney, and me outside. It's somber, sad, and seems as if this group is sinking into the reality that we may have lost him.

Connor clears his throat. "This waiting . . . it's fucking killing me. I can't fucking handle it."

Declan nods. "The rescue teams are still out, even with the winds, and Catherine has her husband and his team also working on things. We just have to stay optimistic."

"Have you ever been lost in the woods?" Connor asks as he gets to his feet, hands fisting his hair. "I have. It's one thing when you know people have a clue as to where you are, but when you're out there with no supplies . . . Jacob isn't trained to handle this."

"You can't start this shit, Connor," Declan warns.

"The fuck I can't! You can't tell me I'm not the only one thinking this. He's out there right now, and I'm . . ."

"You can't save him," Sydney says as a tear falls down his cheek.

He leans against the wall, head falling back. "I can't fucking save him."

My heart breaks as I hear the pain laced in his words. We're trying, God knows we are, but it's wearing on us all.

Ellie returns and walks over to him, pulling Connor in for a hug. He wraps his arms around her, clutching at her back as he buries his face in the crook of her neck. "It wasn't supposed to be any of us."

His wife soothes him, her hands sliding through his hair as she whispers. "He has something to fight for, Connor. Don't go down this road, not until we know."

All eyes turn to me. Declan stands, walks over, kisses Syd on the cheek, and then jerks his head at me. "Take a walk with me? I think we both could use a break."

I'm exhausted, but I can't just keep sitting here. And I can't handle thinking that I'm the only reason he wants to live, and I can't watch his family fall apart. So, I get to my feet and nod. "Sure."

Declan and I haven't spent a lot of time talking. At the barbeques, he's always a little reserved and more of a watcher. He joins in with banter and is always nice, but he's not like Jacob or Connor, who are talkative. Sean is sweet, but he tends to come off as a bit shy. The fact that Declan's asking me to walk with him definitely has me confused.

The light from his lantern and the moon fill the air around us as we head away from the house, neither of us saying anything, but I don't know what I would say. My words feel like they've been ripped from my throat and scattered around the world, just pieces and nothing whole.

When we go another few minutes, Declan finally speaks. "As much as I've hated this farm, I've always loved it. I became someone here, as did my brothers. Not all of it was good, but the four of us always made each other better."

I imagine the four of them, dirt everywhere as they chased animals, all smiling with bright green eyes and a friendship that no one could break. "I think you're all still that way."

"We are. Even when we weren't close in distance, there wasn't a doubt in my mind that, if we needed each other, we'd be there."

A tear falls. "I wish . . . I wish that we could be there now—for him. He needs help, and none of us can do anything but sit here and wait."

"And it's killing me," Declan confesses.

We approach an area that has a beautiful wooden fence and big trees that blow in the wind. There's a strange sense of calm that settles over me. One that I can't explain.

"Where are we?" I ask.

"This is where my mother is buried. The four of us come out here a lot, which is why there's a ton of flowers."

"Jacob has told me a lot about her."

Declan grabs another lantern that is next to the bench and lights it before sitting. I move to his side, feeling hollow and cold.

"Jacob was always the toughest of us," he begins. "I remember when he was, maybe, six and fell off his horse. My mother was beside herself, worrying that he broke something, but he jumped up with a smile and asked to go again. She wouldn't even entertain that idea."

I laugh once, which sounds more like a breath. "Are you trying to say you think he'll be okay?"

Declan shakes his head. "I'd like to believe it, but I'm also terrified."

"I am too."

"Did Jacob ever tell you about the truths of an arrow?"

"He hasn't." At least, not that I can remember.

He chuckles. "When we were young, our mother thought it would be a special kind of torture to make all of us have this saying about an arrow. If you can imagine four boys who had zero interest in repeating this stupid phrase every single time we pulled into the driveway, I promise, it's worse. We would complain and groan, but Mom wouldn't have it. She'd sit at the end of that driveway, scold us, and still manage to get us to repeat it."

"What's yours?"

"A true second shot will split the first arrow and create a solid path."

I think about that for a minute as I consider what she might have been telling him.

Declan tilts his head toward me. "I think she knew I'd fuck up things pretty good and need to try again."

"I think that's most men."

He shrugs. "Connor's is: you can't take a shot until you break your bow. Because, as a kid, Connor would agonize over every-freaking-thing. So, he needed to take a shot, which meant he had to actually try. Sean's is fitting to him too because he's a perfectionist. But Jacob's has always been a bit of a mystery to me—that is, until you came along."

"Me?" I question.

"Jacob's saying is: removing half the feather will create the curve." My chest feels heavy as I listen to him continue. "For a long time, we thought it was because he followed one path. He thought mapping out his life would give him all the answers. Little did he know that, at the age of seven, he knew nothing about life and how plans work. Honestly, my mother was brilliant because she never really explained it to any of us. She sort of said it and gave us some crap about how it applied to whatever situation she wanted it to, but it wasn't until the last two years that I realized each was about our fatal flaws."

I look over at the gravestone of the woman who knew her children so well she imparted wisdom that would carry them into their adult lives. What a special person she must've been.

"If his isn't what you guys thought it was, then what is it?"

Declan sighs. "He doubts that he's worthy of love, which hasn't allowed him to take chances on love. By removing that doubt that he could get the life he wanted, even if he couldn't protect everyone around him, he was able to give himself a chance with you."

Oh, Jacob. Tears fall again, and I look away, knowing I'll break if I try to speak. He is so worthy of love. He's worthy of everything good in this world, and if he comes back to me, I'll prove it.

I'll give him everything, and I'll fix this mess that I made. These last few hours have reminded me what it's like to really lose someone. The pain that doesn't go away. The fear of a tomorrow in a world that is devoid of that person who makes you whole.

After a few moments, Declan speaks again. "He'll come back, Brenna."

"You don't know that."

"I have to believe it. Jacob is a fighter, and he'll fight to come back to you. You're the path. Sydney is right, you're the woman my brother will live to see again."

I shake my head. "We fought before he left."

His hand rests on my shoulder. "I know what it feels like to think you're going to lose someone you love. I had let Sydney down right before I almost lost her, and I was beside myself, but people assured me that she knew how I felt. And I loved her more than anything."

"How would you have survived losing her if she'd died?"

Declan's eyes cast over, and he looks away. "I don't know, but I truly believe that Jacob will be okay. We have a bond, the four of us, and we'd know. I have to believe that one of us would be sure he was dead, and none of us are. He's alive."

I want to believe that's true, but I know better than anyone that hope can only carry you so far. I start to cry harder, overwhelmed with the pain of not having him here when I need him. Declan pulls me to him, and I soak his shirt.

I'm not sure how much longer I can keep this up. I'm falling apart.

I start to pray.

Please, don't take him. Please don't let this graveyard hold another Arrowood who should still be on this earth. I'm begging you, God, Luke, Mrs. Arrowood, please let Jacob come back to us. I love him. I need him. I can't survive losing him.

Declan rubs my back and then he tenses.

"Hello?"

I sit up, seeing a lantern in the darkness moving toward us. "Declan! Brenna!" Sean yells. "They found the plane!"

thirty-seven

"Just a little bit more, Jessica. Help is coming." I hoist her into my arms a little higher. We have been walking for hours and just spotted two helicopters circling overhead. So, now, we're walking faster to try to meet them. The pilot thinks they are circling there because it's a clear enough space to land.

Her head rolls to the side, and she's paler than before.

"How is she doing?" Elliot asks. He carried her the last hour, and the co-pilot, Jose, is too injured to do it. The two of us swap off, trying to give each other some time to regain whatever strength we can.

"She's okay, right, Jessica?" I ask.

Her eyes open, and she nods. "I'll be fine."

When her lids go down, Elliot starts to talk. "Jess, we need you to keep talking, okay?"

Her injuries aren't too bad, but she suffered a head wound

that has us all worried. At first, she was walking fine, but that went downhill fast. We've been doing everything we can to keep her conscious.

"Talk about what? Do you know I miss Grayson? I loved Grayson, but I was stupid."

"Why were you stupid?"

She sighs. "Because I wanted to see the world, and I gave him up. Like stupid girls from small towns do. Oh, and now I'm with the hottest guy in the world and he smells like oak and whiskey."

I laugh. "There's that."

"Tell me about Brenna," she says as she moves her head to rest on my chest. "She isn't stupid. She probably loves you and would stay."

"She's beautiful," I say with a restless sound. "She has these two kids who I love, and . . . well, I love her. We had a fight, but if we live through this, I swear to God, I'll never piss her off again. I should've called her."

"You mean you didn't forgive each other yet?"

"No."

Jose chuckles. "Stupid man, you never fly angry."

"That's a new one."

"It's like going to bed pissed. You just don't do it."

"You'd think she'd know that since her husband was a pilot."

All three groan. "Big mistake, Jacob," Jessica says.

Jessica's eyes flutter and I shift her, causing her eyes to open again.

"He died."

Her eyes look to mine. "How?"

I glance at the sky and sigh. "A plane crash."

"She must be out of her mind," Elliot says. "I can't imagine how she must feel."

Jose shakes his head. "Here we are, bruised and battered. I have a broken arm, Jessica has a busted head, and we're talking about Jacob's girlfriend."

"Well," Elliot cuts in, "it's better than talking about your broken arm, Jessica's busted head, or my burning plane."

The four of us have bonded together. No one took on more than they could or should. When the door was stuck and Jessica couldn't get it open, the three of us did everything we could to help get her out of the plane. When we realized the GPS transmitter wasn't working and we were literally in the middle of nowhere, no one freaked out. After we formed a plan, we executed it. Together, we helped each other, made sure we had supplies to get through the night if we had to, and did our best to get to a place where we hoped we'd find help.

When the helicopter circled overhead, no one started running, we all remained calm and stayed the course.

"I'm so tired," Jessica says as her eyes stay closed for a lot longer than I'm okay with. "I can't. We should eat . . ."

"Jess, please stay awake. Just for a bit longer."

The exhaustion is becoming too much. I'm tired. She's tired. We're all tired, and I don't know that I can go much farther, but I force my feet to keep moving.

Then there's the very real fear that those helicopters are media and not rescue. If they are, then this will be a frenzy that I'm not ready to deal with.

"Elliot?" I call, and he stops. "When we get to that clearing, I need you to take her."

His face scrunches. "Why?"

I hate this part of my life. "If I'm photographed carrying her, people will write stories and make up their own version of what happened."

He nods quickly. "I understand."

The thing is, it's not about Brenna or anything. She would understand and never jump to conclusions. It's more the optics that would make it seem as if the pilots weren't as heroic as they have been. I don't need or want glory. I just want us all saved.

"I swear, I'm not trying to be a dick."

Jessica touches my face. "No one thinks you are. We've been flying celebrities for years. Just know that if we had to go down, I'm glad it was with you."

I laugh when nothing about this is funny. "Thank you."

And then her head falls back, and she becomes limp in my arms.

The helicopter rescue pilot lifts off the ground, and the EMTs work on Jessica as the three of us try to warm up under the blankets they gave us. "We're glad we found you guys before the storm came in," the helicopter pilot says over the headsets.

I nod, no longer able to speak. I watch as they stick tubes and needles into her. She almost awoke right before the clearing but it was just slurring and then it was back to absolute silence.

"Is she going to be okay?" Jose asks.

The EMT gives him an apprehensive look. "We're close to a hospital, and we'll do our best."

That's not exactly the answer I was hoping for.

"How long was she unconscious for?" the EMT asks.

"About thirty minutes. She was talking and then she passed out. She hit her head hard during the crash." We did everything we could to wake her, but she hasn't stirred at all.

"Have our families been notified?" Elliot questions.

"It's been all over the news, but yes, they know we found the plane and were searching the area. Once we had you on board, another message was sent."

I lean my head back, wondering what the hell everyone has been going through. I wouldn't let myself think of them. My brothers, sisters-in-law, Brenna, and the kids. I just had to pretend none of them existed, which made me more grateful for my skills than I had ever been before. There was pain, and there was the want to throw things and wail, but it wasn't the time.

Now that the last nine hours are behind us, it feels like a fucking movie. It doesn't feel like I just lived it, and all I want is for this to end so I can go home.

To her.

The pilots talk about protocol and what will happen, but I tune it out. My head is a mess, and I can't listen to the next steps. Not now.

The helicopter lands on the top of the hospital, and there's a team of doctors rushing toward us. They take Jessica first, wheeling her inside as a few hang back to help us off.

"Mr. Arrowood, you're with me."

I nod and follow the doctor.

We head into a room, but I see the flashes of cameras from the hallway. Thankfully, there's a partition up, leaving only a very small possibility they saw me. The door closes and the examination begins. He looks me over thoroughly, checking for any signs of physical injuries and asking a ton of questions that I'm honestly too tired to answer.

"Jacob?"

I look up. "Yeah?"

"Everything looks okay, but we're going to run tests. I

need to make sure there's nothing other than the bruises that are covering your side."

"Do you know how far we walked?"

The doctor shakes his head. "I know it was pretty far. You weren't close to the wreckage, but your pilots knew the best way to get rescued with knowing the plane was unstable from the leaking fuel. You're all very lucky."

"Not all of us. The flight attendant, Jessica, she was pretty hurt."

He releases a heavy sigh. "Our team is working on her and are doing everything they can. For now, we need to get you taken care of."

"Right."

A nurse enters with a phone. "Mr. Arrowood, this phone is for your personal use so you can call your family."

I laugh once, and her brow raises. "I don't know their numbers."

She smiles softly. "Is there anyone's number you do know?"

I nod and take the phone. "Thanks." And then I dial Catherine's number and know she'll get everyone in touch with me.

thirty-eight

My body is shaking and not just from the exertion from running all the way back from the gravesite to the house. Nerves are wreaking havoc on my body. Twice now, my cup of tea has been refilled, but I have no recollection of it.

They found the plane about three hours ago, but it was empty.

I've prayed so hard. More than I ever have in my life. I just want him back safely. No matter what happens with us. I need him to be okay. One less loss in my life.

The search party was narrowing down the area they thought they'd go based on what was found in the plane. Not that I have any idea what the hell that means. Did they leave a message? Plans? A diagram? Was there any blood there or a body found?

No one will tell us anything. I'm losing my mind and just want answers.

Catherine arrived just after the news dropped. She was still in the area and is with the brothers, talking about possibilities and how to handle it as well as being a great support to all of us. They're going over what information she was last told, but I can't listen anymore. I understand that they need to strategize for whatever the outcome is, but I know what the reality of him being gone will look like.

Hell.

Alone.

Depression and a never-ending heartache that will destroy my heart for good.

Losing Jacob will be like missing my breath, and I can't live without air.

"Brenna, breathe," Ellie coaxes. "I know you're worried, but you're going to make yourself sick, honey."

I look into her eyes, feeling helpless. "If he's hurt . . ."

"We can't go down that road." Her hand rests on my shoulder. "Just stay on the one we're on. They found the plane, and when they find them, we'll be notified. Why don't you try to rest? The kids are passed out, and you look like you're exhausted."

She must be out of her mind. "Could you sleep if it was Connor?"

Understanding fills her eyes. "I'll get you caffeine."

I smile at my friend. "Thanks."

Ellie starts to walk away, but my hand grips her wrist. "If something happens. If they . . . if they find him . . . I know I'm not his wife or anything . . ."

She shakes her head. "You'll be there, Brenna. The thing about these brothers is that they put the needs of each other first. Connor, Declan, or Sean would give up their seat for you. I know you think that, just because you haven't been around that long, they wouldn't, but they would. Jacob loves you, and they know that. No matter how this turns out, you'll be there because it's what Jacob would want."

A tear falls down my cheek, and I look over at the group of them. Declan is pacing. Sean is sitting back, doing his best to look calm, but there's tension on his face. Connor is talking to Catherine as his leg bounces. All three of them carrying this pain and fear the same as I am. Declan's eyes meet mine, and he smiles softly.

I return the gesture and then get to my feet, making my way over to him.

"Hey," Declan says.

"Hey. Is your family always this exciting?"

He laughs softly. "Pretty much. It's definitely not a good thing."

"I thought moving here was going to be boring and a new normal."

"No one told you to fall in love with an Arrowood," he jokes.

"I guess I couldn't resist."

Catherine's phone rings, which we've learned to just ignore since it's been nonstop since she got here. Her eyes are wide, and she clears her throat. "I understand. Yes." A pause. "Of course. Yes, I'll relay that to the family." She's quiet and starts writing things down. My heart is racing by the time she ends the call.

The four of us stand here, no one moving or breathing as we wait on whatever news she's going to give. "They found him, and he's alive and looks to have nothing life-threatening."

The air that I couldn't find moments ago fills my lungs in a quick whoosh.

Declan pulls me into his arms, and the tears that fall this time are relief.

He's okay.

I don't know what happened, but he's alive, and we can fix anything else.

"Brenna? Brenna, honey, can you wake up?" a voice calls from the edges of my consciousness.

"Brenna, Jacob needs you."

My eyes snap open, and I sit up so quickly that Catherine puts a hand on my shoulder to steady me. "What happened?" I ask.

"Nothing, you passed out, and . . . well, can you take the phone?"

She offers it to me, and when I take it, my hand is trembling. "Hello?" I say tentatively.

"Brenna." Jacob's deep voice fills my ears, and I start to cry. What is with the unending stream of tears? I cry, sniffing and trying to get a grip, but I can't stop. The relief is so overpowering that I can't hold anything in.

He's alive. Truly alive. I can hear his voice, and he said my name.

"Jacob," I hiccup.

"Brenna, beautiful, don't cry."

Oh, God, the sound of his voice. The warm timbre of it makes my heart feel as if it's beating for the first time.

"I was so scared," I admit. "God, I was so scared I would never talk to you again."

"I'm sorry, baby. I'm okay, I promise."

I wipe the tears from my cheeks. "Your plane crashed, why are you sorry?"

"Because you were scared. God, I was so . . . I should've called you. I should've told you I was coming back and I would be there. I'm such an asshole to have done that to you. Please know I regret all of it."

Silly man. He didn't go nuts and act like a total nutcase. "No, it's me who is sorry. You were trying, and I was being stupid. It was just like déjà vu, and I couldn't handle it. I was so stupid, and I knew I was being ridiculous as soon as you drove off."

"We can talk about all this soon, beautiful. Catherine is going to give you a few options." He sounds weary, and I can hear the effort in his breathing. "I'm . . . I'm fading out. They gave me some medicine, but I wanted to call you."

"I love you, Jacob."

"I love you, Brenna. With my entire heart and soul. Put Cat back on please."

I hand her the phone, feeling both better and worse. Hearing his voice was part of the assurance I needed. Now, I just need to see him, touch him, and tell him everything that's in my heart because I won't waste time we're not guaranteed.

thirty-nine

I step off the plane in Pennsylvania, and I could kiss the ground. Catherine got me a flight back on a freight plane that was not equipped with anything fancy or a large crew. However, the plane was large, and that was all that mattered. The trip back was completely uncomfortable and uneventful, which I'll take as a win.

Flying with two fractured ribs and bruises that cover my entire right side was fucking horrible, but I'm almost home. I'm almost to where the people I love are, and I'm desperate to see them.

I have no bags or any personal items. My phone was lost during the crash, and we didn't have time to search for anything as the fuel was leaking.

It was strange leaving the flight crew today. I only spent a sliver of time with them, but it feels like we endured a lifetime together. Jessica is doing much better after her surgery, and I've made sure the team of doctors spares no expense treating her.

She saved my life. I owe her.

"Catherine said you have a limo waiting." The pilot, Luis, exits the plane, pointing to the gate. "There isn't supposed to be any press since they didn't advertise that you left the hospital, but I'm sure they've figured it out by now."

I nod. "Probably. Still, I doubt anyone thinks I'd be flying cargo."

He chuckles. "Doubtful."

"How did this all happen?" I ask.

"Catherine and I went to high school together, and she called and asked if I was still flying. It was really luck, man. I happened to be in the right place at the right time."

"I might have believed that, but Catherine is something of a witch."

"She probably somehow rerouted me without my knowing."

I nod because it's true. She just happened to be able to find a pilot who was able to take me on a freight plane with next to zero notice. I will never doubt her again. "Thanks again," I say with my hand extended.

"Not a problem."

I start to make my way toward the exit where I see a black limo waiting. It blows that I have a little over an hour drive to Sugarloaf, I want to see my girl and this is going to be torture.

Me: I just landed.

Brenna: Thank God.

Me: I feel the same. It's about an hour from the airport to Sugarloaf.

Brenna: I know. I wish they could've dropped you off at the house.

I smile. I wish the same damn thing.

Me: The story about us broke earlier this morning.

Brenna: I saw, it was actually really sweet. The photo was great too.

Me: I agree, but not as sweet as you.

Brenna: What are you doing right this second?

I raise one brow, wondering what the hell she's asking that for.

Me: Walking to the exit so I can get in the car.

Brenna: Are you able to walk and text at the same time?

Me: Yes. I'm able to do two things at once. LOL. I can't wait to see you.

Brenna: Look up.

I do, and there she stands at the car door, her long red hair is blowing in the wind, and then she's running toward me. I'm moving a little faster, but not much, and her smile is wide when she finally reaches me.

"Jacob," she says, stopping just shy of slamming into me.

I take another step, cup her face, and press my lips to hers. Gone is the pain from my ribs or anywhere else. Right now, I have her, and she's healing everything broken in me. Just like she has from the start.

Her hands grip my wrists, and we kiss for God knows how long. It could be hours, and I wouldn't register it. Much sooner than I'd like, she pulls back, her eyes filled with unshed tears.

"I'm here," I tell her.

"I needed to be here. I needed to see you."

I kiss her again, short but sweet. "You weren't alone in that need." My thumb swipes away the tear that falls. "I never should've left you."

She shakes her head. "No, you had to. I never should've tried to make you feel guilty for having to go. You were honest from the start, and I was irrational."

I wish it were that simple. That it was just being irrational, but there was more to it. I knew that my having to leave her and Sebastian after having made promises would be close to what she went through with Luke. I just had no idea that it would end the way it did.

"Brenna, stop. We were both idiots, and . . . I just want to hold you, kiss you, and love you."

Her lips turn up as she releases a soft sigh. "I want that too."

We stand here, kissing, touching, and just staring at each other. I have never felt more grateful than I do right now. "You have no idea how much I thought about you."

"I'm pretty sure I can imagine."

"You're okay?" I ask.

She nods. "I'm okay now that you're here and okay."

"What about you? Are you okay?"

I nod. "Yeah, beautiful. I'm fine now."

"Good. Now let's go home."

She takes my hand, and we walk to the car. When I move to slide in, my side explodes in pain, but I keep it together. After a few minutes, I can breathe normally again and link my fingers through hers. She's sunlight and rainbows after the storms. Being around her, being back together, is everything I hoped for.

"Jacob, what happened? I don't know if you want to talk about it, but . . ."

I don't really, but at the same time, I do. I relay the entire sequence of the crash and the aftermath. I talk about Jessica, the way she passed out, and the fear of her not making it. Brenna listens, holding my hand and wiping tears away silently.

I let the details go, giving her the story that no one else will ever hear. To the press, it won't be quite like that. We'll make it sound much less dramatic, which means they'll make it far more dramatic, and it won't be like the truth being told in this car.

"Is she okay now?" Brenna asks.

"The doctors seem to think she'll be okay, but I don't really have much information. She saved my life, and even after she slammed her head, she was worried about me."

Brenna's thumb rubs the top of my hand. "I'm grateful to her. And I'm sure that, to her, you and the other pilots saved her life."

That's probably true. The group of us, we saved each other. No one got left behind and we kept ourselves together.

"It's over now. I'm here and I want to just be here with you." She smiles softly, and I wipe away the tear she missed. "So, you didn't have opening night?" I ask, needing to change the subject.

"No, you sort of were in a plane crash and the town couldn't go on."

"I really let them down."

"You didn't let anyone down. Not a single person feels that way, Jacob. We were all so worried. All anyone cared about was finding you alive and okay. The play, well, it wasn't even a thought."

I wish I believed that, but I imagine how sad the kids must've been when all their hard work was ruined.

"Did you cancel tomorrow's show?"

Brenna rests her head back on the seat. "No. They had one yesterday once we knew you were alive. Another drama teacher from a neighboring town offered to help because I couldn't do it."

"You didn't go?"

She shakes her head. "I didn't sleep for almost two days. After they found you and the crew, I passed out, but it was only for about an hour. Then, when we spoke, I guess I just couldn't stay awake. My in-laws took the kids after Ellie called them, which is how I was able to be here now."

I push her hair back, so fucking grateful I can just touch her. "How did you get here anyway?"

"Catherine."

She's seriously part witch, I'm convinced.

"I was surprised, but I probably shouldn't have been," I say with a chuckle.

"Good surprise?"

I lean over and kiss her. "Great surprise."

"Catherine was a rock through it all. I don't know that any of us would've known what to do, but she protected the family. We were at your brother's house, and she was there, making sure no one bothered us while she coordinated everything. I was impressed."

I can imagine it. Catherine is that saying about being small but mighty. Nothing scares her during the crisis.

"How did you find out about the crash?" I ask.

She tilts her head to me. "It broke over the internet, and Melanie was the one who told me."

"Jesus Christ."

"I won't lie and tell you that it was easy. Not that I think finding out any way would've been easy, but I don't know, Jacob, it was hard seeing the headlines and learning about it with millions of others."

"I'm so sorry, baby."

And I am. For all of it. One day, I might feel less guilty, but not anytime soon.

"It's over now. You're here and safe, and I can touch you."

I pull her close, needing to comfort her as much as myself. "Yes, you can."

We fall silent, and I try to imagine how she must've felt, hating that she had to go through any of it at all. The limo continues on. We talk here and there, but we don't talk about the crash. Instead, she tells me about how my brothers are holding up and how great they were.

What I imagined to be the longest drive in history passes much too quickly. We've been in our own little world, and I don't want to leave it. When the limo rolls to a stop, I look out the window at Brenna's house, and there is a swarm of people on the porch. My brothers, their wives, and the kids. As much as I'm ready to see them, I wish we could stay just like this.

It was fewer than forty-eight hours, and I feel like I missed everything. Maybe it's because I feel like I aged twenty years in that time.

"You ready?" Brenna asks.

"Can I say no?"

She looks out the window. "It's probably too late to ask the driver to turn around."

"Probably."

Her thumb rubs the top of my hand. "They need to see you too."

"I know."

We exit the car, and Hadley is the first one rushing toward me. Connor's deep voice booms out. "Don't, Hadley!"

She skids to a stop, and I smile down at her. "Hi, Hadley-butt."

"Can I hug you, Uncle Jake?"

"Just be a little careful, okay? I had a stunt go wrong."

She reaches out tentatively, and I pull her as tight as I can before the pain hits. She kisses my cheek and then whispers in my ear. "You're my favorite."

I try not to laugh, but fail. "You're my favorite too."

The other kids come over, giving me hugs and telling me how glad they are. Then Sebastian is here.

"Jacob?"

"Yeah, little dude?"

"I'm really glad you didn't die like my dad."

I hear the intake of Brenna's breath, and I focus on him. "Seb, I'm really glad I didn't either."

"I thought you were—dead."

"I'm sorry you went through that, but as you can see, I'm here."

He looks up at me, lip quivering. "I prayed to my daddy. I asked him to let you live so that Mommy would be happy and I wouldn't have to lose someone again."

I release a breath through my nose. "It seems he was listening."

Declan places his hand on Sebastian's shoulder. "Kids are heading back to the creek to fish. If it's okay with your mom . . ."

Brenna bobs her head, trying to wipe her face without anyone noticing.

He hugs me once more before rushing off.

My stoic and not-very-emotional brother releases a deep breath. "You really know how to be dramatic."

"I learned from you."

"Don't do it again." He doesn't care about my injuries as he gives me a hug. "Seriously."

"Let go, Dec," I say as I wince.

"Sorry."

While Declan pretends he's the rock, we all know he's

nothing but mush. At least, he is when it comes to the people he loves.

"You don't have to worry, I have no plans to repeat any of that."

"Glad you're alive," Sean says as he claps my shoulder.

"Me too."

Connor walks over, shaking his head. "And you all thought I'd be the one to worry about."

"We worried," Declan says with a laugh.

"No one thought it would be Jacob," Connor replies.

"Yeah, because only the good die young, so at this rate, Jacob will outlive us all." As Sean laughs at his own joke, Brenna walks over to me, tenderly puts her arms around me, and we all walk inside.

And just like that, my world is exactly as it should be.

forty

"Jacob, you're being ridiculous!" I yell while he struggles to get his shirt on.

"I'm going, and you can either help me or get out of my way."

I swear, men are a whole other breed of stupid. "You are supposed to be resting!"

It's been two days, and he's the worst patient to ever live. He doesn't do what he's told, his idea of resting is doing laundry or trying to help the kids when he can barely keep his eyes open. Today, I caught him trying to put together a bike that he bought Sebastian.

I might actually be who kills him.

"I am resting. I've been in bed, let you feed me, and watched movies."

I huff. "And you've done things that have made you wince, your bruises are still horrible, and you want to brave the press so you can go to the play."

"The play is a big deal."

"Yes, but you being okay and not hurt yourself more is a bigger one."

Jacob gets his shirt on after quite a bit of exertion. He's huffing and puffing, and I feel zero sympathy for him. Tonight is the last night of the play, and Jacob refuses to miss it, especially because I went to the play last night without him.

Sebastian was fantastic.

Jacob was jealous.

So, when I told him that Devney and Sydney were coming to babysit him while I went to the show tonight, he decided that didn't work for him and that he was going too.

"I worked my ass off on that play, and I'm going to watch those kids. It starts in two hours, and I don't give a shit if the pain is so bad I pass out, just prop me up so I look like I'm awake. I'm going, beautiful, and there's not a damn thing you can do to stop me."

I raise my brow. "Want to bet?"

He grins. "I may be a bit broken, but you won't physically hurt me."

"No, but I am pretty sure there are three Arrowood men who would help make sure you can't escape."

"You wouldn't."

"Wouldn't I?"

He steps toward me, his green eyes focused on me in a way that makes my stomach drop. God, he's sexy. Even bruised and battered, Jacob is all strength and power. "Brenna, I love you, but I didn't live through all that to let Sebastian and the other kids down."

I touch his face. "You're not letting them down."

"It feels like I am. Not being there opening night was fucking torture. I want to go there early and see them on their final night."

He's right. I won't physically hurt him or call his brothers—not that I'm sure his brothers would actually land on my side, but I'm not willing to find out. He's going to find a way there no matter what I say. Stubborn man.

"You shouldn't wear that shirt," I tell him.

Jacob's smile is victorious. "Which one should I wear?"

"One that doesn't match mine."

I'm wearing a green sundress, and we look like we were trying to match. The minute we step near that school, flashes will go crazy. Catherine, who I swear is inhuman, gave me instructions on what to do if we went out. What to wear, how to walk, and how to sit—apparently, posture was everything. She promised the buzz would die down very soon, but until then, I had to endure it all with a smile.

Thankfully, I've stayed home with Jacob the last few days, only fielding calls from Cybil.

"You're so beautiful," Jacob says as I'm laying out the blue shirt from the approved clothing selections. "When I was out there, all I did was picture your face, your smile, your eyes."

I look up at him. Since he's been back, he's barely spoken of the actual crash. He said it was scary, but that was about it. "You know, if you want to talk more about what happened, I'll listen."

"I don't want to talk about the past. I only want my future, Brenna, and that means you."

"At some point, you're going to have to open up more and talk about how you felt, not just the actual event."

He looks crestfallen. "Why? Why do I have to?"

"Because it was traumatic. And this is what I know."

"Please don't be my shrink, not when I'd rather make you something else."

My brows crinkle. "Something else?"

Jacob pulls me into his arms, and I'm careful where I rest my hands. "I want to marry you, Brenna."

"Jacob . . ."

My heart is racing, and a million warning bells are going off in my head. I'm not ready to marry him. We haven't been together that long, and I have two kids to think about. I love him, and there's not a single doubt in my mind that I want to grow old with him, but not like this.

Not because he almost died.

"I saw my life flash before me. I saw the life that we could have. I know we haven't been together long," he says, echoing my thoughts, "but I also know that you're the only woman I've ever loved, and I want to spend my life with you. Marry me?"

Why did he have to say all this? Now I have to answer and pray to God he understands. After a trauma, people often make rash decisions. If this is what he wants, then we need time. "I want to say yes. I want to marry you, grow old with you, raise the kids together, and spend all my days with you, but I want you to propose to me when you're not still reeling from a near-death experience."

"You don't think this is what I want?"

I sigh, running my finger down his strong jawline. "I think that I'm a psychologist. I think that, in my mind, I'd always wonder if this was just some knee-jerk reaction or if I was really the one."

His eyes close, and I see the hurt there. "You have no idea how I feel, do you?"

"That's not it. I know how I feel. I know that I love you in a way I never knew I could again."

He leans in and kisses my nose, my cheeks, and then my lips. "Then believe me when I tell you that I feel the same."

"I do believe you. I'm just asking for a few more months.

Let's get through the craziness of our relationship going public. Let's let the kids settle into this and give ourselves some time to just be us without adding more stress on it."

"Whatever I have to do to keep you, I'm going to. I want you to know that. I may have to leave to go back to Hollywood, but I'll always come back to you."

A tear falls down my cheek, and he leans in and kisses it. "Don't cry, beautiful."

"They're happy tears."

He gives me a soft kiss. "I love you, and I never want to be what causes you pain."

"Then just tell me you'll stay. Promise me that you'll stay for me."

Jacob cups my face, holding me so tenderly that it's as if he thinks I might break. "I'll stay . . . for you. I don't know why you want that because you're perfect and I'm a damn mess."

I take his face in my hands, making sure our gazes are connected when I speak these words. "We're all flawed, Jacob. It's finding someone who sees the beauty in the cracks that makes them perfect for you. You may have tiny imperfections, but that's what makes you who you are. I am not perfect."

He rests his forehead on mine. "There was a time when I didn't think I would ever find someone to love. I accepted it, and then you came into my life. I thought I'd be here for six months and leave while flipping off the Come Back Soon sign. Now, Jesus, I can't imagine leaving you."

"Then don't."

He kisses me softly, yet, it feels deep. It's as though all the emotions that are between us come through this kiss. There's fear, love, happiness, and a sense of comfort all silently mixed together. "I don't think I could."

"Good, because I love you and I want all the things you want. I promise, Jacob. It's not that I don't want to marry you because I swear, I do."

"Shh. I understand it. I should have known better anyway."

I look at him, wondering what the hell he's talking about.

Jacob chuckles. "Sean did this with Devney, and I told him how stupid he was. You deserve a proposal, the flowers, candles, a ring . . . this was . . . you were right, and I'm sorry."

"I don't need all that."

His arms wrap tighter around me. "Maybe you don't *need* it, but you deserve it."

And that is maybe the sweetest thing he could have ever said to me. A sense of calm settles around us as we stand in my bedroom, holding each other. Both of us a little scared, beaten, and whole.

"You know, if we are able to get through things like this, we're going to be a pretty awesome couple."

He smiles down at me. "Why do you say that?"

"Why do you think?"

"Why are we back to you not answering questions?"

I giggle. "Because most of what couples fail to do is communicate. I never want that to be us. If we can just talk, we'll find our way through anything."

"What happened before I left . . . that . . ."

"Was awful."

Jacob nods in agreement. "I won't leave like that again."

"I won't let you."

"Good. Now, we have a date at a middle school play, and I'm not going to be late."

I release a long sigh and give him a peck. "Fine, but you're coming home and going straight to bed."

"And tonight, you and I are going to make love. This is my warning, so get your argument ready."

I take a step back, giving him a coy smile. "Oh, I don't think I'll be arguing."

"Damn right, you won't."

"You're mine, and I'm going to love you for a long time."

He makes a playful growl and kisses me hard. "I like the sound of that. I'm hoping we have forever."

"Me too, Jacob. Me too."

Forever sounds just about perfect to me.

forty-one

I've played a superhero the last two years. I started off as this guy who was average and then found a suit that made him heroic. That was what I loved the most about being the Navigator. I was just a guy who could do extraordinary things. I've never, in my actual life, experienced what he did—until now.

"Jacob! Jacob! You're alive! You're okay!" Clarissa says as she rushes toward Brenna and me. "Are you okay?"

"I am. I'm good."

Clarissa is playing Sandy. For all the crap she gave me in the beginning, she was the best for the part. Even if I wanted to stick her in the chorus line for being a pain during auditions.

"We were so worried," one of the kids in the back says.

Another voice louder. "We thought you were dead."

"Thankfully, I'm not."

"Why did you leave to go to California anyway?" Candi

asks.

Leave it to the kids to bring up the one part of this conversation I was hoping to avoid. I look to Brenna, but there's no anger on her face, just a soft smile. I guess surviving a plane crash really helps with letting go of the original fight.

Not that I plan to use that ever again.

"I had to film and was doing my best to be back. I'm sorry I left you guys and didn't have a chance to say anything. I promise, it wasn't an easy thing to get on that plane."

"We were upset," Candi says without pause.

"I'm sure, and I'm sorry I let you down. Believe me, I care a lot about all of you and I fought with my director about pulling me away. If there had been any way I could've gotten out of it, I would've. Then the plane went down, and . . . unfortunately I missed your two shows anyway."

"Sebastian was a mess," Clarissa says before adding, "when the plane went down."

"I'm sure he was."

Her eyes fill with tears. "We all were. We . . . we were so scared that you were gone and that we didn't get to thank you."

"It's me who needs to thank you guys. Thank you for letting me be your director."

Sebastian steps forward. "I was the most upset. Don't let them fool you."

Leave it to him to inject some levity in the room.

"It's because he's getting it on with your mom." A teenage boy sniggers while ducking down.

As much as I'd like to scold him, he's not lying. And it would be some asshole shit I would've said at fifteen.

Brenna is not as accommodating as to let it slide. "Mr. Neville, I'll see you in my office first thing in the morning to discuss that comment."

He groans. "Yes, Mrs. Allen."

She shrugs subtly, and I smile at her. One day, I want that name not to be hers anymore. I want her to be mine. To be Mrs. Arrowood and then we can flip off the whole world.

I know I was a fool to ask her that way. She was right to say no, as much as I wish she hadn't. The truth is, she's had a lot of half-hearted things in her life. An engagement with Luke that only happened because of her pregnancy. A marriage where he was gone half the time. And even after, nothing was ever how she wanted it.

That all changes now.

She is going to get every part of me, whether she wants it or not.

Clarissa takes a step forward. "We were all a mess, Jacob."

"I'm fine, and I'm just glad I get to be here for your final show."

"Hopefully we make you proud," Sebastian says.

God, these kids just don't even know. "There was never any doubt of that. Never. I knew that you didn't need me to put on a performance this town would never forget. You are all incredibly talented, smart, and funny. It was a privilege to get to work with you all." I turn to Neville. "You, we're still on the fence about. You're a clown."

He laughs and nods. "Jacob Arrowood thinks I'm a clown."

Clarissa rolls her eyes. "And he thinks that's a good thing."

Neville is a great kid and reminds me way too much of myself, which is why I think I like him so damn much. "I was also the clown of the group," I tell them.

Brenna's voice is low, but I hear her. "Still are."

I give her a look and she's unfazed. "But seriously," I say as I turn back to the kids, "is everyone ready?"

David, who is playing Danny, bobs his head. "I'm good. I

got chills."

"Are they multiplying?" Sebastian asks with perfect timing.

They all make varying noises of amusement, and a few clap him on the back. It's good to see this, him bonding with his castmates. He's had a rough time fitting in and finding his people. This was why I agreed to this. To give back to the kids who are often labeled as outcasts and unable to belong somewhere.

"All right everyone, settle down," I say with my fake authority voice. "I'd like to say a few serious things before our last show."

They all quiet down, tossing their arms over each other's shoulders, holding on as if to create a single unit. This is something that Noah forced us to do, and I figured it couldn't hurt to pass it on to the younger generation. When you link together as one, you become one.

Here, on the stage, they're a team. Each one of them needs the other in order to be good at their own part. Their energy feeds the whole, and it serves them to listen as one unit and form that connection prior to their show.

At least that's the bullshit he fed us, and I'm imparting it onto them.

"This play has been one of the best things I've been a part of. You guys have no idea how proud I am of each and every one of you. Not only have you worked harder than anyone I've ever worked with but also you dealt with . . . I don't even know what to call the crash . . . with maturity." I look to Adam Neville with a raised brow. "Except for you, you're still a turd." They chuckle, and he smiles. "My point is, no matter what people say about the play, you should all stand tall. You are all award-winning actors and actresses in my book. Thank you for allowing me to get to know you, work with you, and I can't wait to watch you all show your talent to the world."

"Jacob! Jacob! Jacob!" they all start chanting. I'd be lying if I said I wasn't misting up. These kids wormed their way into my heart. I was afraid I'd let them down and they'd be disappointed, but they were just as confident in my work as I was in theirs.

"All right. I appreciate it. Let's save the acting for the stage. You have ten minutes until curtain call. Break a leg."

They head off in different directions, and Brenna's arms gently wrap around my waist. "Are you okay?"

"I'm fine."

She looks at me with her lips in a thin line. "Don't lie to me. I saw you wince once."

I turned a little too fast, but I thought I covered it quickly. "It's uncomfortable, but it isn't anything I can't handle."

"Are we talking about your injuries?"

"What else would we be talking about?"

She sighs. "What else could you think I'm asking about?"

"The fact that, once again, you're answering questions with questions."

Brenna laughs. "One day I'll stop, but it won't be soon. I'm talking about your heart. Your soul. I know you were worried the kids were upset. You know . . . any of those."

"I'm good now. They mean a lot to me and disappointing them didn't sit well."

"I know, and as much crap as I gave you about coming tonight, I am a smidge happy you didn't listen. I think they needed to see you just as much as you needed to see and be here for them."

I kiss the top of her head. "Anyone ever tell you how amazing you are?"

"A few times."

"Get used to it because I plan to tell you as often as I can."

"Good. I plan to keep you around, so you'll have plenty of opportunities." Brenna lifts up on her toes, softly pressing her lips to mine. "Come on, let's get you to your seat so you can see everyone's hard work."

It takes me a bit longer to get there than it should have, but when I do, there is my entire family in the front row. My brothers, sisters-in-law, nieces, and nephews all passing snacks, talking, and laughing. I make my way to my seat, after all of them stand, hug me, kiss my cheek, or shake my hand, feeling a pride like I have never felt before.

We did this.

We fell in love during this play, and it wouldn't matter if the kids came out on the stage and just stood there making faces. I am proud of what we did here.

The lights go down, and I watch the best rendition of *Grease* ever made.

forty-two

Four Months Later

"**S**top fidgeting, you look beautiful."

Brenna sighs and pulls at her dress again. "I look ridiculous."

I kiss the side of her head. "No, I promise that is not the word anyone will use."

Stunning. Gorgeous. Enchanting. Those are the words that will be printed in the paper about Brenna. She's absolutely breathtaking, and I am somehow lucky enough to be escorting her in public. Catherine had her styled by one of the best designers, who crafted a dress that is elegant without looking as if she's trying too hard. It's long, emerald-green, and has a long slit, giving me the perfect view of her perfect legs. That's not even the best part—no, that's the back.

Or, I should say, the complete lack of it.

Her smooth skin is there for me to touch all night, and I

fully plan to do that and a lot more.

"Can we just say I was sick?" she asks as she looks in the mirror in the foyer of the suite.

I roll my eyes. "No, we can't say you were sick. It's my premiere, and everyone knows you're going to be on my arm tonight."

"But no one wants to see me anyway."

"I want to see you."

"You can see me when you get back."

I love her, but she's killing me. "Look, you're gorgeous, and I want to show you off."

She wraps her arms around my waist, looking up at me. "I like when it's just us."

"Me too, but my movie schedule is grueling, and we talked about this."

"I know, and I'm so proud of you, Jacob. I'm just being insecure."

I shift closer to kiss her, but she leans away with a smile. "No kisses or you'll smudge my makeup."

My hands move down her back, feeling my way down to her ass. "Really?"

"Yes, really!"

"What if I kiss you here?" I ask as my mouth grazes the side of her neck. "Do you have makeup there?"

She giggles softly. "No."

"Interesting . . . and what about here?" I move to her shoulder, pulling the strap as I go.

"No makeup there, but you're going to mess up my dress."

I turn her so she faces the mirror, and I can see that her eyes are filled with lust. While I'm sure Catherine left sex while dressed in formal wear off the list of things we shouldn't do before we leave, it's one I think we both need.

I want her out of her head, feeling as beautiful as I see her. "Lift your skirt," I command. She watches me in the glass, chest rising and falling. "Lift it up so I don't ruin it."

She pulls it up, the slit playing peek-a-boo with her thigh. "Like that?"

I shake my head. "Higher." While she pulls up, my hand slides down the front of her dress. "More, baby. I want to see what you're wearing underneath this dress."

Brenna moans softly as I cup her breast. "Jacob."

"See this woman in front of me? She's a goddess. She makes me fucking crazy with need. There's no one else like her, and she's mine."

"Yours," she says as a breath.

My other hand moves to her thigh, just barely grazing the skin there. "Lift your dress up, beautiful, or I might tear it off."

"Please," she begs softly.

"Please what?"

"Touch me."

I move my hand up, but stop because I still can't see what I want.

Brenna's eyes open, warmth and heat swimming in the depths of blue. "Jacob . . ."

"Lift it. I want you to watch."

She pulls it up just a bit higher, and I see she has nothing on underneath. "All night long, I'm going to sit next to you, knowing you're not wearing anything and thinking about how good you'll taste later. I won't care about the movie or what anyone is saying, I'll think about how good you feel right now." I slide my finger along her seam, parting her. "Look at her," I say when her eyes close. "Look at the woman I love come apart for me. I'm going to show you just how crazy you make me. You, Brenna. Only you."

Brenna's eyes are on us in the mirror. The reflection of us fully dressed, and yet completely exposed. "I love you."

And I know it in every bone in my body. Right now, I want to feel it around my cock. I release her breast and slide my zipper down. "Hold on to the table," I instruct.

Her hands grip the wood, and I have enough sense to hold the back of her dress with my other hand. I slide into her warmth, and we both let out sounds of contentment. "Yes!" she cries out.

"You feel so fucking good," I tell her as I slam into her. "You have nothing to be insecure about. You are the most beautiful woman in the world, and tonight, they're all going to wish they were me." She moans again but not once do her eyes drift from mine in the mirror. "Do you see what I do?"

She nods, her teeth gripping her lower lip.

"Do you see how gorgeous you are?"

"Yes."

"Do you feel how much I want you?"

"Yes!"

I push harder, thrusting with so much force the table is banging against the wall. The sensations are too much. I can't hold back. I rub her clit and feel her tightening around me. "Come on, baby." I coax her, knowing she's close.

I keep at it, kissing her neck, and then her ear. She moans more, and I give more pressure and then slam into her harder. I feel her release as she cries out, and then, I'm done. I can't hold back at the feel of her falling apart and watching her in the mirror.

My head rests on her back as I struggle to catch my breath.

Brenna starts to giggle. "That definitely put some color in my cheeks."

I smile and pull her dress up around her breasts. "Be careful . . . we'll get in trouble if we come out of the hotel looking like we just had sex."

"You should've thought of that before you decided to seduce me."

"It was a calculated risk that was well worth it."

She groans and then heads off to the bathroom. I clean up, thankful that it's a pretty easy fix for me. The clothes look good, hair is fine, and I'm waiting in the front room of the suite where we just fornicated when a text blips on my phone.

Catherine: Your limo will be there in five. Jackson and I will meet you at the start of the red carpet, and I'll direct you from there. Jackson will be there for support for Brenna.

At first, I really wasn't sure of this, but she said the optics of her talking to another person would be much better than of her standing there staring at me.

Me: Got it.

Catherine: Don't be late. There is literally no room for anything outside of the schedule.

Me: You should've been a dictator. Your country would've succeeded.

Catherine: I'll take that as a compliment. And you have three minutes now. Start walking to the lobby.

"Brenna?" I call out. "You okay? Did you fall in?"

"I'll be right out!"

Maybe having sex right before was a bad idea. "Baby, the limo is going to be here, and I'm slightly afraid of Catherine."

"Well, you should be afraid of me. I'm trying to steam out a few wrinkles."

Yeah, definitely was a bad idea. I should make a note to

have Catherine put that on the do-not-do list right before her instruction not to eat after getting dressed.

"Right, but, the limo and . . . we have to go."

The door to the bathroom flies open. "Jacob Arrowood, you fucked me senseless ten minutes ago. I am trying to make sure I don't have a million photos looking like it happened, okay?"

As scared as I am of Catherine, Brenna is formidable right now. "Okay. You know, just . . ."

"If you say hurry, I might choke you with your bow tie or hogtie you with it."

"If you want to tie me up later, I'm okay with that."

She takes a step closer and then steadies herself. "One minute. I just have to fix the back."

"Can I help?" I ask, wanting to help but also wanting to touch her again.

"No, just give me one more minute."

I nod once and then go out to grab our stuff. I can be helpful. Her purse is on the counter, where I'm sure the ten assistants Catherine hired to make sure we didn't do anything stupid put it. My wallet, which I don't need but refuse not to have, and her shoes are waiting by the door.

I start counting, but from this point, if I reach sixty seconds, we are already way over a minute.

Thirty-one.

Thirty-two.

Thirty-three.

I start to shake, not sure which of the women in my life I'd rather have at my throat, when she emerges.

To anyone else, she would look the same as before, but I see the way her face is just slightly flushed and her eyes are liquid. "You look perfect."

"I look late."

"Yeah, and I'm going to blame you if Catherine yells at me."

She rolls her eyes. "Some gentleman you are."

Brenna heads to the door and slips her shoes on. And while I had this elaborate plan for tonight, I don't want to wait another second. Seeing her like this makes me want her to really know how I feel before we step out of this room.

"Ready?" she asks with her hand on the doorknob.

"No."

"No?"

I step to her and then drop down on one knee, pulling the ring from my breast pocket. "I had a plan for us. For you. For tonight. After the premiere, we were going to a rooftop bar that I rented out. There are thousands of roses, candles, and a band is coming to play for us. All of it, every detail was laid out, but looking at you right now, I can't wait another second, Brenna."

Her hand flies to her mouth. "Jacob . . ."

"I love you with every part of my soul. I was so sure that I would never find anyone because I wasn't finding what I needed, until I found you. I don't want to walk that red carpet with my girlfriend who I plan to propose to. I want everyone in the world to see that you're going to be my wife. That I choose you and you choose me. I choose to love you and be with you every day, every minute, every second, because you're the most magnificent woman I've ever met. I love you, Brenna Allen. Will you marry me?"

A tear falls down her cheek, and she nods. "Yes! Yes!"

I place the ring on her finger and kiss her lips, not caring if I smudge her makeup because kissing her is the only thing I want to do.

epilogue

Nine Months Later

"Just a few more pushes, Brenna," the doctor says as she holds my knees apart.

"I hate you, I hate you, I hate you," I chant as I bear down and try to shove this freaking kid out of me.

This pregnancy was never supposed to happen. Yet, here I am, staring up at my husband, cursing him because of that damn .01% chance that came to fruition.

And Jacob was smug.

We hadn't talked about having or not having kids. Honestly, I thought we probably would, but not right away.

I wanted time.

I'd already started a marriage off with a pregnancy, and apparently, I was meant to do it again.

The only difference is that Jacob and I already loved each

other. We didn't get married just because we were pregnant. I guess there's that bonus.

Jacob leans down and kisses my forehead. "I love you, beautiful."

"Please don't tell me that. I look horrible right now."

"Not to me you don't."

"No lies, Jacob."

His eyes dart to the doctor and then back to me. "Okay, you look like hell, but you're bringing forth a baby, and really, no woman looks great during that. However, Catherine has a team ready the minute the baby is out, and in your first photo, you're going to look like you squatted and the baby popped right out without any effort at all."

I glare at him. "Are you trying to make me punch you?"

He at least has the decency to appear sheepish. "I was just telling you that no one other than this team of doctors and nurses, who have all signed NDAs, and me will ever know that you don't feel beautiful. I think you are. Always. You're flawless really."

I'm definitely going to punch him. The doctor taps my leg. "Here comes another contraction. I want you to really push this time. I can see the baby's head."

Not like I have a choice. The pain comes on, and I squeeze Jacob's hand, pushing with all my might.

"A little more," she urges.

I try. I swear I do, but it's so hard, and I'm so damn tired. Every muscle hurts, and I just want them to cut me open because this kid is not coming out on his own. I always thought giving birth was supposed to get easier with each kid, I was wrong.

"I can't!" I yell and fall back.

The doctor tries to smile. "You're doing great. Take a few minutes to breathe."

Jacob's lips are at my temple. "I love you, I'm sorry, I love you, I'll buy you anything you want."

It ends, and I look up at him. "Anything?"

He nods.

"I want you to buy a vasectomy."

"Is that a new car?"

I glare at him. "No, and you know it."

"We'll talk about this soon."

My chest heaves, and I feel the twinges start. "How much more?" I ask, exhausted and sweaty.

"One more big push to get the head out and then the shoulders. The baby is right here."

"Take my hand, Brenna," Jacob says, determination fluttering in those green eyes. "I'm here."

I take a few deep breaths, wanting this to be over. It's been nine hours of labor, and I've been pushing for twenty minutes. I want to sleep, but more than that, I want to hold this little baby that came from the night of his premiere and caused a very, very fast engagement period.

"I'm ready," I tell the doctor.

My jaw clamps tight, and I scream through my teeth as I push with all my strength. My fingers tighten, drawing whatever strength I can from him.

"You're right there, baby. Right there."

"The head is out. On the next contraction, push."

I barely have enough time to catch my breath before the next one hits. I hold Jacob's hand, thinking of all the moments we've had. The time by the creek fishing. The lunch date we shared when I realized I liked him. I think about the dinners at the house, our first kiss, and the Ferris wheel. All of the moments, which are strung together with love, that have brought us to this moment. Where we made a baby. Our baby who symbolizes all the beauty that has come from times of struggle.

I push harder than I did before because a feeling of renewed strength fills my body.

"That's it, baby! You're doing so good!" Jacob's voice is heavy with awe.

My throat is raw, and I cry out again.

And then, I hear him gasp.

The pain is gone, and I lie back, feeling empty and beaten and triumphant.

"You did it." Jacob kisses my cheek. "You did it, beautiful."

The loud cry comes from the tiny baby a second before the doctor places him on my chest.

"Is he okay?" I ask.

She nods. "He's perfect."

Jacob's arm wraps around me as we both stare down at our tiny little boy.

"Jacob," I say, looking up with blurry vision. "He's so tiny. I forgot how tiny they are. We have a son."

"We do. And you have made me the happiest man in the world."

We kiss softly, both our hands touching our son in some way.

The nurse comes back to clean him up a little more and do some tests. Jacob hovers over him, so protective already. They walk back over, placing him back on my chest.

"We need a name," I say for the millionth time.

This has been the great debate at the Arrowood house. Sebastian wants us to go with Mason, which is Jacob's character in the *Navigator*. Melanie wants to name him Eric so that we have a *Little Mermaid* theme or something. I want the name Caleb, but Jacob, he's the one who has me completely freaking baffled. Thankfully, he's not wanting a ridiculous name like Apple or Compass. He doesn't have a name he loves at all.

"I don't have any ideas. Nothing comes to mind that we can agree on."

"That's fine, but we need to come up with something. We have to agree at some point."

He chuckles once and smooths a palm over our baby's peach-fuzz hair. "We need a strong name then."

"Caleb isn't?"

"He's not a Caleb."

I want to groan, but instead, I look at our son and start to try to fit a name to him.

"The one thing we agree on is that we want an Irish name," I say, and he nods.

His mother named all four boys that way, and Sydney sort of followed that. I'd like to as well. Elizabeth Arrowood was a strong and extremely wise woman. Her tradition should be kept alive, even if it's just in this small way.

"Blaine?" I offer.

"No. Maddox?"

I shake my head. "What about Sawyer?"

Jacob snorts. "Sawyer Arrowood? Is he best friends with Huck?"

"It does sound a bit . . . much."

"Mason isn't bad." He was never really against Mason. I love the name, but it feels all wrong because people will automatically think it's tied to his movies.

"We talked about why it's a bad idea."

"I know."

I press my lips to the baby's head, closing my eyes as I inhale the sweet baby scent.

"Owen."

"Owen?"

I look down at him, and it feels so right. As though it were meant for him. "He's Owen. Look at him. He's strong and a fighter. He fought through five years of birth control just to be here. If I remember, it means desire, and he clearly desired to be here . . ."

"It's perfect," Jacob agrees.

"Owen Arrowood."

Jacob gives me a sweet kiss and then kisses Owen's head. "What's one truth about an arrow?" he asks. I fight back the buildup of tears. "No matter how many times you pull that bow back, if you keep focus and keep aiming, your arrow will go exactly where it should." He looks up at me, a smile on his beautiful lips. "I know mine did."

bonus scene

"**Y**ou ready for this? It's a big night," I tell Sebastian as he looks out at the stage.

"I'm ready."

"Break a leg, son."

He smiles and claps me on the arm. "It's nice having a director who actually knows what he's doing."

I roll my eyes and laugh softly. "It's nice that your director has performers who actually know how to act."

He gives me a grin and then goes to his place among the cast. It's crazy that we're here, fifteen years since the first play I was supposed to direct, and Sebastian is at his opening night on Broadway. I don't know that I could be any prouder of him than I am right now. He followed his dream, worked hard, and did it without any help from me.

I head to the front where Brenna, my brothers, and sisters-in-law are all waiting. Brenna and I came in last night. Owen is staying with the Allens as they've basically adopted our son as their grandchild as well and he has a football game tomorrow. Which gives me and my lovely wife a night on the town.

"Did you see him before?" Sean asks.

"Yeah, he looks ready."

Brenna smiles up at me. "You look like *you're* nervous."

"I am. This is a big role to fill."

Connor laughs. "Because it was yours?"

"Damn right."

Sebastian isn't only in a play, he's the lead in a play that is based on a movie that I starred in. When the writers decided to adapt it from film to stage, I should've known that Sebastian would audition.

It's crazy.

Brenna wraps her hand around my arm. "I'm sure he will do it justice."

"Oh, I know he will. He's going to be better than I was, that's what I'm worried about."

Declan snorts. "It's sad when our kids are better at things than we were."

"No shit," Sean agrees. "I swear, Austin is going to blow all of my records. He already did for his rookie year."

Devney shakes her head and looks to Brenna. "If they let women play in the MLB, then he'd really need to be worried."

"For real, Cassandra is better than any of us at sports," Sean agrees. "I guarantee she'll end up in the Olympics or something."

Their daughter is a savant. That's the only word that can accurately describe her talent with sports. It doesn't matter what one she tries, she excels. She's already being scouted for college softball, and she's only in middle school. It's crazy, but she's truly gifted.

"Maybe they'll have professional sports for women by then. You know, real ones that are actually funded."

"Well, if anyone is going to fight for it, it's Hadley," Connor says with pride. "She was in court today with the new law firm she signed on with, fighting a women's rights issue."

Syd smiles. "She's pretty impressive. She's doing well at the law firm."

My nieces and nephews are all pretty impressive if you ask me. Hadley got out of law school with a single goal: to fight for causes that matter. She's not afraid of anyone standing in her way because she'll bowl them over. After everything she saw her mother go through, women's issues and protection was where her heart led her.

She just moved to New York City about a year ago and is already making a name for herself.

"I can't believe she's so new at it too," Ellie says. "I hate her living out here alone."

"She's not really alone," Brenna reminds her. "Melanie is her roommate."

Right on cue. "Mom, Dad." Melanie's voice calls from behind us. "Sorry I'm late!"

And nothing is as impressive as my kids. Nothing. I never knew becoming a stepfather would be like this, but it's incredible. They call me Dad, mostly because it was awkward for them not to when Owen did and because I treated them all the same. No one in our home gets special treatment regardless of bloodline. Once Owen came around, it just became sort of natural to be all of their dad, which has been the greatest blessing in my life.

"Hey, sweetheart," I say as I kiss her cheek.

"You look very handsome."

I grin. "I was dressed by the best."

"Well, I do try."

Brenna hugs her and then fusses with her hair. "You are working too much. When is the last time you got a haircut?"

Melanie shakes her head. "I'm fine. I'm busy with the new line that launches next week. I'll get a haircut when it's over. That color is great on you."

"I love the design and the designer."

Melanie blushes a little. "I wanted you to feel gorgeous and not overdone."

I pull Brenna to my side. "She is always gorgeous."

Her blue eyes look up to mine, and the love I see there is enough to bring me to my knees. "And you're perfect."

"Only for you."

Connor groans. "You'd think after this long they'd be less disgusting in public."

I look to him with one brow raised. "Tell me which one of you loves your wife less than the day you married her? Anyone? Do you not all look at them and wonder what the fuck we ever did in this world to deserve them?"

"Every damn day," Declan replies.

"For real," Sean agrees.

Connor shrugs. "I know I still don't deserve her."

"Exactly. So, yes, I love my wife. I let her know. I don't give a shit if every camera is clicking, in fact, I hope they do." I take her face in my palms and kiss her. After a second, I pull back, staring at her. "I hope they all see how much I love you."

Brenna's hands rest on my chest. "I know I do."

Melanie makes a gagging sound. "You guys are really adorable, but so gross."

I pull both the girls to my side. "It's only because I love you all so much."

That's the thing about our lives now. That will my father made, that sentence to return home that felt like a punishment, ended up being a gift. I'm not forgiving enough to think he did it for our benefit, but it worked out that way, and I think that was my mother. If anyone could've taken the four broken boys and mended them, it was her.

She brought us back home, made us deal with our demons, and guided us to find a way to live the lives we'd been denying ourselves filled with love, good women, and children.

Just then, Hadley arrives. "I'm so sorry I'm late! I had a deposition and . . . anyway, I'm here now." She kisses all of our cheeks and smiles bright. "Everyone is looking all spiffy and not at all like you just came off the farm."

Connor shakes his head. "We aren't all city folk."

"Please, Dad, you are not going to even try that."

Hadley is probably one of the very few New Yorkers who has a horse boarded. She was not even willing to entertain not having access to riding when she needed it.

He pulls her close, kisses her temple. "Yeah, yeah, I know, you can't take the country out of the girl."

"Never."

We chat a bit more, everyone asking about what's new. I am directing my first movie this year. Brenna's private practice is thriving as she found she enjoyed couples counseling for celebrities. We bounce between our house in Sugarloaf during most of the year and Hollywood for the summer. It keeps the kids grounded and remembering their roots as well as granting us a chance to be a normal family.

Not that anyone is normal in this crew.

"Ready to head in?" Declan asks.

As my family walks in and takes up the fourth row, looking up at the stage, I realize just how damn lucky I am.

I have my brothers.

I have my kids.

And I have Brenna.

Everything that I thought I would never have is in this room. A life of happiness. A family I would give my life for. And love. So much fucking love that I could drown in it.

I lean over, taking her hand in mine. "Thank you."

Confusion flares in her eyes. "For?"

"Everything. You gave me everything."

Thank you so much for coming on this journey with me. The Arrowood Brothers have owned my entire heart and soul. I can't begin to tell you how bittersweet this ending is for me. As I was writing Jacob's plane crash, Jessica spoke to me. Very, very loudly. Here was this girl, struggling to be so strong because it was her job, and worrying she would die.

I'm beyond excited to announce the next series will start with Jessica Walker and Grayson Parkerson (you MIGHT know that last name from Sean's book)! I hope you're ready to head to our next small town because Return to Us is coming and it's going to be SO good!

Preorder Return to Us!

acknowledgments

To my husband and children. You sacrifice so much for me to continue to live out my dream. Days and nights of me being absent even when I'm here. I'm working on it. I promise. I love you more than my own life.

My readers. There's no way I can thank you enough. It still blows me away that you read my words. You guys have become a part of my heart and soul.

Bloggers: I don't think you guys understand what you do for the book world. It's not a job you get paid for. It's something you love and you do because of that. Thank you from the bottom of my heart.

My beta reader Melissa Saneholtz: Dear God, I don't know how you still talk to me after all the hell I put you through. Your input and ability to understand my mind when even I don't blows me away. If it weren't for our phone calls, I can't imagine where this book would've been. Thank you for helping me untangle the web of my brain.

My assistant, Christy Peckham: How many times can one person be fired and keep coming back? I think we're running out of times. No, but for real, I couldn't imagine my life without you. You're a pain in my ass but it's because of you that I haven't fallen apart.

Sommer Stein for once again making these covers perfect and still loving me after we fight because I change my mind a bajillion times.

Michele Ficht and Julia Griffis for always finding all the typos and crazy mistakes.

Melanie Harlow, thank you for being the Glinda to my Elphaba or Ethel to my Lucy. Your friendship means the world to me and I love writing with you. I feel so blessed to have you in my life.

Bait, Crew, and Corinne Michaels Books—I love you

more than you'll ever know.

My agent, Kimberly Brower, I am so happy to have you on my team. Thank you for your guidance and support.

Melissa Erickson, you're amazing. I love your face. Thank you for always talking me off the ledge that is mighty high.

To my narrators, Vanessa Edwin and Sebastian York, you are the best and I am so honored to work with you. You bring my story to life and always manage to make the most magical audiobooks.

Andi Arndt, even though you're not narrating this one, I feel like this journey is partially ours. Your friendship over these last few years has only grown and I love your heart so much. Thank you for always having my back. To many more concerts and snowed in sleepovers.

Vi, Claire, Chelle, Mandi, Amy, Kristy, Penelope, Kyla, Rachel, Tijan, Alessandra, Laurelin, Devney, Jessica, Carrie Ann, Kennedy, Lauren, Susan, Sarina, Beth, Julia, and Natasha—Thank you for keeping me striving to be better and loving me unconditionally. There are no better sister authors than you all.

books by corinne

The Salvation Series
Beloved
Beholden
Consolation
Conviction
Defenseless
Evermore: A 1001 Dark Night Novella
Indefinite
Infinite

Return to Me Series
Say You'll Stay
Say You Want Me
Say I'm Yours
Say You Won't Let Go

Second Time Around Series
We Own Tonight
One Last Time
Not Until You
If I Only Knew

The Arrowood Brothers
Come Back for Me
Fight for Me
The One for Me
Stay for Me

Willow Creek Valley Series (Coming 2021)
Return to Us
One Chance for Us
A Moment for Us
Could Have Been Us

Standalone Novels
All I Ask
You Loved Me Once

Co-Write with Melanie Harlow
Hold You Close
Imperfect Match

about the author

Corinne Michaels is a *New York Times*, *USA Today*, *and Wall Street Journal* bestselling author of romance novels. Her stories are chock full of emotion, humor, and unrelenting love, and she enjoys putting her characters through intense heartbreak before finding a way to heal them through their struggles.

Corinne is a former Navy wife and happily married to the man of her dreams. She began her writing career after spending months away from her husband while he was deployed—reading and writing were her escape from the loneliness. Corinne now lives in Virginia with her husband and is the emotional, witty, sarcastic, and fun-loving mom of two beautiful children.

CPSIA information can be obtained
at www.ICGtesting.com
Printed in the USA
LVHW082338151220
674233LV00046B/936

9 781942 834526